PRECIOUS THINGS

PRECIOUS THINGS

GAIL R. DELANEY

PRAISE FOR GAIL R. DELANEY

Whoever the NY publishers were who thought this book shouldn't be published, and that having a hero who's been deaf since birth was a bad idea need to have their heads examined, because Benjamin Prescott Roth is one of the most fascinating characters I've read in a long time

— ESTHER MITCHELL, CRITICALLY ACCLAIMED
AUTHOR OF THE PROJECT PROMETHEUS SERIES

I was intrigued by the hero, who is deaf. I read an excerpt and decided to give the book a try...I savored every page and regretted when it was over. I was left with the heartwarming satisfaction of a well-told story. I've added other titles by Gail R. Delaney to my wish list.

— JUDY, READER POSTED AT AMAZON

If there was a ten star for a book, this would be one. Absolutely one of the best books I've ever read.

— JACLYN DI BONA, AUTHOR

Copyright © 2010, 2018 by Gail R. Delaney

All rights reserved.

No part of this book may be reproduced in any form or by any electronic or mechanical means, including information storage and retrieval systems, without written permission from the author, except for the use of brief quotations in a book review.

This work of fiction is my own creation. I have never, do not currently, and never will use AI/artificial intelligence to write a book. I have never, do not currently, and never will use AI/artificial intelligence to generate artwork to represent my books. When my books are made into audiobooks, I will not use AI to narrate them. I support artists of all kinds whether they be photographers, cover artists, audiobook narrators, or writers. The creation of art in any form should remain a human endeavor.

I deny <u>any</u> and <u>all</u> permission, whether blatant or implied, for my work to be used by any AI program to "learn" or to produce material. I am the copyright owner and deny any attempts to use, replicate, or manipulate my work via any means not initiated by myself as the copyright owner.

Art requires heart.

#SupportArtistsNotAI

www.GailDelaney.com

This book is dedicated first to my husband, Patrick. Without him, I may have given up a long time ago.

And my undying gratitude and friendship goes to Chrystal, Shalon, and Jamie. More than my critique partners, they are my dear friends.

And in special memory of my mother, Jewell Maxine Bingham Hughes, from whom Jewell Kincaid is named. She kept everything I ever wrote in a box. Every poem. Every book report. Every story. Even in death, she proved to me the depth of pride she held in me and she showed me what I was always intended to be. A writer. I know this book would hold a special place of honor. She believed in me, and although she wasn't with me long enough to see my first book released, her love is here and her inspiration will last a lifetime.

BOOK CONTENT EXPECTATIONS

Anyone familiar with me or my work knows that I am hearing impaired, my mother was hearing impaired, and I have written several characters with ranging levels of loss from hard of hearing to fully deaf like Benjamin. Every situation has been different.

A small percentage of readers have said they felt Benjamin's level of ability in a hearing world isn't normal, going so far as to say it's unrealistic and sets an unobtainable standard. That is not my goal; in fact, I wouldn't want anyone to see his life as a goal to obtain. I agree that Benjamin's drive for success isn't the norm. Now should it be. The *reason* he pushes so hard is grounded in trauma, pain, and abuse. In no way is this to be viewed as an expectation and standard.

Through this book, the extent of Benjamin's past trauma and pain will be revealed. Benjamin's drive to be the best in everything isn't because he wants to be a success but to prove someone wrong. I absolutely and wholeheartedly agree Benjamin's apparent "ease" in a hearing world isn't normal…it also isn't healthy. And it's not easy.

My goal was to provide a contrast with Jewell's family, presenting a loving support system and what a difference support and encouragement can make. I hope readers can see his representation is not one I believe is or should be the norm because Benjamin is a troubled man. Benjamin's coping mechanism is his unrelenting and self-damaging need to not be just enough but to be more. To be in control. It is rooted in trauma, not encouragement. Every human being responds to trauma and abuse in different ways; this was Benjamin's way.

However, none of Benjamin's achievements are impossible. He drives, and this is far from unusual. He is hugely successful in his profession, and I actually felt anger when it was suggested that was unattainable. When I originally wrote this book, Marlie Matlin, Nyle DiMarco, and Daniel Durant had not yet appeared on *Dancing with the Stars*, but they showed the world the deaf can dance.

People completely without hearing learn to speak for a variety of reasons. He also reads lips sufficiently in most situations and uses sign language. I specify his language is more like what is sometimes referred to as PSL (or Pidgin Sign Language) or PSE (Pidgin Signed English). In most cases, a child born without hearing would be taught American Sign Language, which is a unique language with unique grammar, structure, and complexities. PSL is a combination of ASL and spoken English. Since Benjamin was on his own to learn this language in his formidable years, his style is closer to spoken English. This wasn't an oversight on my part, but a failure on the part of those who should have provided him support.

Any instances of manual language are presented as dialogue but in italics. The dialogue is written in spoken English format.

Please be aware when reading *Precious Things*, there will be moments of reliving family trauma and emotional and physical abuse but in mention from the past and very real in the moment, anger and anger management issues, unhealthy coping mechanisms, lies, verbal abuse, and revelations. There are also moments of ableism because sadly, people are jerks.

There are also discussions about adoption, the effects of drug abuse, the foster system, and infertility.

Precious Things was my first published novel, and I've updated it since then. When I first shopped it around to the traditional New York houses, I was told more than once that while my writing was engaging and my voice was great, "no romance reader" would read a romance with a deaf hero (or hero with any disability). I refused to switch roles to make it marketable because I believe in Benjamin's story and it's his to tell. I hope you agree.

CHAPTER ONE

"Mr. Burke will be with you shortly, Miss Kincaid."

Jewell nodded and smiled at the woman behind the desk whom Travis Traynor had introduced as LaTrisha Jordan. She took the wait as an opportunity to calm her twisting nerves, pulling in a deep breath as she wiped her palms down her skirt. She'd already been at Bulwark Mutual Funds for nearly two hours, completed preliminary interviews with Human Resources and Mr. Traynor—one of the department heads within the Capital Management division—and had apparently impressed them sufficiently to move on to an interview with Kevin Burke, Mid-Cap Assets Manager.

She turned away from the high paneled, wooden desk to survey the room. Mr. Traynor had called this the bullpen; a twelve hundred square foot open space on the seventeenth floor of the Bulwark building, lined on parallel walls with dark wood doors. There was a desk identical to LaTrisha's for each two doors, six desks on each side of the room, for the administrative support staff assigned to each fund manager team. A brass nameplate on the front of each receptionist-style desk indicated the name of a fund manager and division. Below that, a smaller plate with each manager's executive support staff member.

A low hum of conversation, accompanied by the click of keyboards and the occasional twitter of a phone, skimmed through the room. Someone laughed several desks down.

"I apologize for the delay," LaTrisha said, and Jewell turned. "Mr. Burke has been stuck on a call."

"Not a problem at all."

A door slammed behind her and Jewell jumped, as did everyone within her line of sight. An older woman stood outside one of the many doors along the hall, her cheeks flushed bright red with her hands clenched at her side, her lips bunched up in an angry purse. A young woman with dark brown hair seated at the desk outside the recently slammed door, startled in her chair at the sound. One by one, curious heads disappeared again behind their high desk walls.

The older woman headed for the younger at the desk, cutting her left hand through the air. While Jewell couldn't make out her words, the tone was enough to express anger. Based on the way the younger pushed back, Jewell wondered if she was the recipient of misplaced frustration.

She didn't realize she'd stepped closer until the woman's words came into comprehendible focus.

"I don't know who the hell he thinks he is. Thinks he can get away with talking to me like I don't know what I'm doing. I've been in this industry since before the Dow hit 5K!"

The younger woman looked around, briefly making eye contact with Jewell, her cheeks flushing. "Carol…"

"What? It's not like he *hears* me."

"Carol!" the younger said louder. "He doesn't but everyone else does."

Carol huffed, turned, and stormed away. Once she was away, the younger woman at the desk sighed, her shoulders visibly dropping, and she braced her hand across her forehead. Jewell glanced around and spotted a water bubbler. She crossed the room and filled a cup before going to the desk. The brunette looked up when Jewell set down the cup, looking surprised as she reached for it.

"Thank you."

"Rough day," Jewell stated since it wasn't a question, keeping her voice low. She smiled, trying to keep the conversation light.

The woman shook her head, frowning. "Sometimes I feel like a kid watching my parents argue. Except that would imply that at some point there might have been some sort of affection between them."

"Clashing personalities, huh?"

The woman's laugh was humorless. "That's putting it mildly. Mr. Roth isn't exactly the easiest person to work for. He's demanding and holds everyone to high expectations. Carol is convinced she knows more because she's been *in the industry* longer. She doesn't like—"

"Being questioned?"

April nodded and sighed. Jewell squinted, trying to grab hold of a mental note floating around the edge of her memory.

"Roth. Benjamin Prescott Roth?"

April nodded again, arching her eyebrows in a look of surprise. "Yes. You know him?"

"I know *of* him. My economics professor once used Mr. Roth's profile analysis process as an example in class."

"Mr. Roth is very good at what he does. He's just—" The woman stopped herself, rolled her eyes, and offered a half smile, then extended her hand. "Sorry. I'm April Baker, and the woman who just left is Carol Soldano. Are you applying for the position with Mr. Burke?"

"I am."

"I hope you don't think this is what it's like to work here. Most of the fund managers are very nice, and everyone works great together. And it's not that Mr. Roth isn't nice. It's just Mr. Roth and Carol."

"It's not *me*, it's *him*," Carol snapped, coming back from wherever she'd gone, still scowling. When she spoke again, she said his name with a mocking frown. "*B.P. Roth* is full of himself, obnoxious, arrogant, and demanding. If you don't do what he wants, the way he wants it, when he wants it, he's intolerable."

The office door behind April's desk opened and the commanding presence of B.P. Roth stepped into the hall. Having already formed a mental image of a late-middle-aged, probably barrel-shaped man with a growing bald spot, Jewell was surprised to see a young man, probably mid-thirties, with caramel-blond hair that waved back from his forehead, and a defined, chiseled chin. There was an inherent strength in the set of his jaw. The starched-white shirt and tailored slacks accentuated a tall and athletic build. His distinct profile turned from Jewell, deep brown eyes sought out and found the two women in his employ. April sat straighter, but Carol just sighed deep and long.

He barely glanced at Carol, focusing on April, resting his arm on the ledge of the high desk. "Make an appointment with Rowlings tomorrow. Book a conference room and inform senior management of the incubated Asian fund. Everyone is to attend."

His voice held a softer, somewhat incomplete quality despite its rough huskiness, with a slight rounding of his syllables. Jewell instinctively recognized the inflection, though his voice was perhaps more refined than she was familiar with.

April nodded "Yes, sir."

Only then did Mr. Roth's glare shift to Carol. "Still wasting time, Mrs. Soldano." There was no inflection of question in his voice, but Jewell's intuition said it wasn't for lack of hearing. It was a statement.

"No, Mr. Roth," she said and managed to school her features despite the derisive tone lacing her words. She reached over the side of the high desk to retrieve a pen, and to obscure her face from his view. "See what I mean?" Carol said under her breath. "Barking commands. Wouldn't be anywhere if it wasn't for everyone else doing the work. Entitled son of a bitch."

Jewell might have stayed silent, despite how the situation grated on her if Carol hadn't purposefully dragged her into it. She drew in a slow, balancing breath and released it through her nose as she set her briefcase on the floor to free both her hands. She turned, but only enough that she knew both Carol and Mr. Roth would see her, providing him with the respect Carol Soldano apparently would not.

"What is it you do, Carol?" she asked, keeping her voice level. Carol straightened, the pen she'd used as an excuse in her hand. "What position do you hold?"

Carol scowled but answered. "Executive Support."

"Executive Support," she repeated. "A position of great responsibility." Raising her hands, Jewell signed as she spoke. "I doubt you would be so glib if you were held responsible for your words."

Carol's eyes widened, and she looked from Jewell to Mr. Roth, and back to Jewell. Her jaw worked like a fish gasping in air, and her face flushed bright before she stepped back from the desk and marched toward one of the doors behind the desk.

Mr. Roth turned his glare on Jewell. His eyes were hard, his jaw set, and he squinted slightly as he stared.

Before she lost her nerve, she raised her hands to sign. *"It's hard not to speak up when someone is that rude."* She canted her head and arched an eyebrow when she added, *"Please and thank you might have helped."*

With two long strides, he moved closer to her. A light eyebrow arched high over his eye. "And you are?" he demanded with a jut of his chin.

The momentary disorientation of her senses when he closed the space between them surprised her. His presence was so overpowering, that it acted like a force field around his body pushing against her when he neared. A hint of the masculine scent he wore filled her senses, sandalwood and a subtle oriental spice. Her cheeks warmed.

Not allowing his presence to daunt her, she spoke and signed together, finger-spelling out her name. *"Jewell Kincaid."*

"Do I know you?" he asked.

Jewell shook her head. "No."

"Yet you feel the need to comment on my employee's actions." The sharp movements of his hands expressed his annoyance, but she thought perhaps she caught a glimmer of amusement in his eyes. *"And mine?"*

She noted his method of signing was closer to Pidgin Signed English than American Sign Language, which made sense considering his apparent ability to read lips and use spoken language. The syntax of PSE was closer to the speech pattern of a natural speaker, and to be an effective lip reader he'd be familiar with spoken English's rhythm. His tone and inflection implied he'd been either deaf or profoundly hard of hearing for the majority of his life. It was a strange contrast; one thing implied loss of hearing after learning speech, and the other implied a lifetime without hearing.

Being a child of a deaf adult sometimes gave her more insight than was probably appropriate. But, she couldn't just turn it off when she wanted.

Jewell licked her lips. She felt as flushed as Carol had looked before disappearing into her office. *"I have a difficult time staying silent around ignorance."* She paused, stilling her hands, before adding *"and arrogance."*

His eyebrow arched again, higher this time. *"Are you here for an interview?"*

She nodded.

"Who?"

"Mr. Burke."

Mr. Roth's hand shot out, palm up, in demand. "Give me your résumé."

Jewell met his stare, not willing to yield to his lack of manners. "Please?"

His lopsided smirk told her she wouldn't get the satisfaction of him asking nicely, but he also wasn't angry with her commentary. He wiggled his fingers impatiently, and she thought she caught the instigating glint of a challenge in his eyes. Holding his gaze, Jewell crouched down to retrieve her extra résumé from her attaché case and handed it to him. After he took it and said nothing, she touched her fingertips to her lips and brought her flat hand down.

"You're welcome," she added.

He didn't respond to the sarcasm beyond an almost indiscernible tip of his lips into a smile that disappeared as quickly as it threatened to appear.

"You have your Series Six, Series Eighty-Six, and Series Eighty-Seven licenses," he read. "No Sixty-Three?"

Jewell bit back a snappy response. "No. I haven't decided in what state I want to take the test. I've lived in both New Hampshire and Massachusetts."

Mr. Roth read the whole sheet and handed it back to her. *"What position are you interviewing for?"*

"Administrative support for Mr. Burke."

He shook his head and waved his hand in argument. "You are overqualified."

Jewell conceded with a nod. "Perhaps."

LaTrisha waddled across the space to them, slightly out of breath with one hand resting on her near-ready-to-burst pregnant belly, and touched Jewell's arm. "Ms. Kincaid? Mr. Burke is just about ready to see you now."

"Thank you."

She glanced toward April and smiled. "It was nice to meet you," she said and made eye contact again with Mr. Roth.

His direct stare unnerved her, but she managed a smile and nod in farewell. Jewell followed LaTrisha back to Mr. Burke's office but swore she felt Mr. Roth's stare burning into her back. Just before passing through the office door, Jewell glanced back and confirmed her suspicion. Mr. Roth stood where she'd left him, one hand curled in a relaxed fist against his hip while the other braced against the edge of April's desk. He wasn't smiling, nor was he frowning, and the only acknowledgment she got that he still saw her was the slight lifting of a single brow. Jewel forced herself to look away and focus on the man she hoped would soon be her new boss.

Kevin Burke, a not-quite-middle-aged man with light brown hair and a thick but not heavy build, met her at the door with a smile and ushered her into his office. They sat and talked for the next forty-five minutes about the responsibilities involved in the position. Jewell realized Mr. Roth had been right. This was strictly an administrative position, and with her experience and education, she was severely overqualified. Most likely, she would be bored out of her mind within a week.

But even as administrative support, the position offered $10,000 more a year than her current job at Safeguard Fiduciary. Right now, her concern was money, not job satisfaction. Since her sister had moved in to attend college in the city, her budget had tightened considerably. The whole purpose of Ruby moving in was to save her parents the expense of room and board, and Jewell refused to take any money from them to help. Another ten grand a year would be just the cushion her budget needed. And the benefits were impressive. Jewell resolved the drop in responsibilities would be worth it in the end. Of course, it didn't have to be forever.

As she left the imposing building sometime after one o'clock, Jewell decided she felt good about the entire interview process. She knew she had made a good impression, and felt confident the offer would come. Unless, of course, her impulse to call Mr. Roth to task ended up taking her out of the running.

Jewell shook off her thoughts as she returned to her car in a nearby parking garage. She had enough time to go home and change, maybe get something to eat, before she headed back out to pick up Ruby from the Northeastern University campus. Tonight was family dinner night at the Kincaid house, and Jewell looked forward to getting out of the city for a while.

Jewell's cell phone twittered inside her bag just as she finished dinner at her parents'. She excused herself to the hall and dug it out, wincing as someone banged around pots and pans in the kitchen. A glance at the screen told her it was a number within Bulwark Mutual Funds. Taking a quick, fortifying breath, Jewell answered.

"Hello," she said, hoping she disguised her nervousness.

"Hello, Jewell. This is Travis Traynor at Bulwark. Have I called too late in the evening?"

"Not at all, Mr. Traynor."

"Good. I tend to work late and forget the rest of the world actually has a life," he said with a chuckle. "As you can guess, I'm calling about your interview today."

"Yes?"

Mr. Traynor seemed to struggle for words and Jewell had the sinking feeling this was a different kind of call than she expected. Apparently the interview hadn't gone as well as she thought. Of course, giving attitude to one of their top fund managers before she ever managed to get hired might have been the nail in the coffin. Then again, not many companies bothered to call if you *didn't* get the job.

"There has been a change in staffing needs. That is to say, we no longer need to fill the administrative position. Another individual internally will be taking it."

She dropped her shoulders, but carefully covered up her sigh. "I understand, Mr. Traynor."

"So we were wondering if you would consider a different position at Bulwark."

Jewell stood straighter. "What position?"

"Instead of an administrative position, we would like to offer you one in executive support. It's the next level up and would pay an additional $15,000 a year, with quarterly bonuses and a possible raise after six months."

Jewell's jaw dropped. *Another $15,000 a year would give her $25,000 more a year than she made right now.*

"Do I need to come in for another interview, or is it for Mr. Burke as well?"

"No, you don't need to come in. It's not for Kevin, but the fund manager you will be working with seemed comfortable with your qualifications. Based on your interview today we've already initiated the background check, but I have no concerns. When can you start?"

"I'd like to give a two-week notice to my current employer."

"Well, I understand. But I want to let you know Mr. Roth personally offered an additional $5,000.00 signing bonus if you can begin on Monday."

"Mr. Roth?" The question came out as a rough whisper. A nervous wave tickled over Jewell's skin.

"Yes. You will be working for our best international fund manager, Mr. Benjamin Prescott Roth."

CHAPTER TWO

A different tumbling sensation fluttered around in her stomach the next time Jewell walked the halls of Bulwark Mutual Funds. A niggling edge of guilt at leaving Safeguard Fiduciary so abruptly scraped against the giddy excitement of a new position, all wrapped up in anticipation of seeing Mr. Roth. One single question bounced around in her head, keeping her from sleeping much of the weekend. Did he initiate her employment in his office?

Mr. Traynor met her at the reception desk in the glass and marble lobby of Bulwark, and after setting up her security clearance and giving her a temporary access badge, left her on her own to find her new office. The bullpen hummed with low-key activity as she passed by the first few desks to reach Mr. Roth's—*her*—office.

The desk she originally thought would be hers was empty, but with a flush of recognition, she caught the nameplate now resting on the desk edge. *Carol Soldano*. Well, that explained a few things.

"Good morning, April," Jewell said with what she hoped to be a confident smile as she reached the high-paneled desk. "Good to see you again."

"Good morning, Miss Kincaid," April said with a bright smile. "Welcome to Bulwark."

"Thank you. And please, I'm Jewell."

The young woman nodded. "Mr. Roth said to tell you to wait for him in the office. He has a meeting every Monday morning, but it will be over soon."

"Tell me? Not ask me?"

April smirked. "That's the way Mr. Roth is. You saw that last time you were here." She shrugged. "You get used to it after a while."

"Do you?"

April met her eyes, and her response didn't quite answer the question. "He can also be very generous to his staff," she said with a half-shrug.

With that, Jewell opened the door to Mr. Roth's office and went inside. The room was large and spacious with a bank of windows on the outside wall and looked much like Mr. Burke's office had, with the addition of the windows. The blinds were open and sunlight streamed through to cover his desk in its brightness. The desk itself was huge, being a good six feet across the front, in a rich walnut finish with a left-side return. A laptop in a raised desktop port sat on one corner of the desk, while dual monitors sat in the joined corners of the desk, leaving the space empty when he faced straight on. Several framed degrees and plaques hung on one wall. Curiosity led her to them.

"Harvard School of Business, Masters Degree in World Economics. Bachelor's degrees in both Accounting and Economics. Very impressive, Mr. B. P. Roth," she mumbled to herself as she examined each degree. She moved on to the wood and brass plaques. "Businessman of the Year twice. Top Fund Manager for the last three consecutive years. Mutual Fund Magazine top named fund. Smart Money top named fund twice. You've had yourself some good years." She realized she was talking to herself, and pressed her lips together, turning away from the display.

An open door to her left, near the interior wall leading back to April, led into another office. It had a door leading out to the bullpen, and Jewell assumed it was the other door behind April's desk. The office was a bit smaller than his but offered pretty much the same amount of sunlight. A good-sized desk sat near the door, this one with a right side return against the wall, plus the usual office furniture. A giant bouquet on the desktop greeted her. She couldn't name most of the blossoms expertly arranged in the large vase, but their aroma filled the room. Jewell leaned into the heady scent and let it fill her senses.

Nestled amongst the blooms was a small card with her name neatly written on it. She took it out and opened it to read the single word inside. "Welcome."

"They're from Travis Traynor," said Mr. Roth's subtle voice behind her.

Jewell jumped and turned. He stood in the doorway, his shoulder against the jamb and his arms crossed over his chest. Her stomach tumbled and her pulse skittered at her throat. With her hand pressed against her pounding heart, she fought to calm the flutter beneath her breasts. Mr. Roth straightened and stepped into the office.

"You startled me," she said.

"I see you found your office."

She nodded. His direct stare shifted from her eyes to her mouth. Its powerful effect created a whispered tingle on her skin. Heat rose high in her cheeks and she turned away. Jewell walked to the window before turning back. Unfortunately, it was impossible not to face him.

"*It is very nice,*" she signed, her hand sweeping the room.

He nodded. "Come back into my office. We can cover the basics. There is a meeting this afternoon we both will attend."

Mr. Roth turned and she followed him back into the adjoining room, grabbing a blank notebook and pen from the desk as she passed. He moved behind his desk and sat down in the leather executive chair, indicating she should sit across from him. Jewell was thankful for the wooden barrier between them. At least he couldn't see her hands wringing nervously in her lap.

"I assume Mr. Traynor explained to you what the position entails. We work in tandem on most projects, but you would complete research and compile data for interpretation. April then works on data presentation. You have a strong knowledge of world economics?"

Jewell nodded. "Yes. I'm sure you saw on my résumé I hold a degree in World Macroeconomics. I minored in European Microeconomics."

"From the University of New Hampshire?"

His slight smirk and arched brow irked Jewell. Heat rose in her cheeks. She straightened her spine and squared her shoulders before answering.

"I didn't attend Harvard, Mr. Roth, but I know what I'm talking about if that's your concern."

An amused grin pulled his slight smirk higher. "If I had concerns about your ability you wouldn't be here, Jewell."

His smugness unnerved her. She pulled a deep breath in through her nostrils and cleared the lump in her throat. "Is that the only reason I'm here? My credentials?"

One eyebrow arched. "You're not only a smart woman, but you've got courage. I like that. I don't like working with people who won't stand up and speak."

"Is that why you were so hard on Carol Soldano?" He didn't want her to hold any punches? Fine, she wouldn't.

"Carol Soldano didn't put enough effort into her work because she didn't believe she should be required to do so and I became aware of her tendency to push her work onto April. I don't accommodate for laziness."

"You didn't make it easy for her, from what I saw."

What was it about this man that riled her up so quickly and so easily? He ignited her defenses full force and made her want to come back at every comment with an equal ferocity. If Jewell didn't watch it, she'd talk herself right out of the job.

"I won't make it easy for you either. That doesn't mean I will intentionally make it more difficult. You're getting paid very well to do a hard job. If you're not up for it, we have nothing further to discuss. If you don't think you can handle it, tell me now. But I don't think that's the case."

Jewell smiled slowly and held his eyes without wavering, raising her chin in subtle defiance. "I can handle anything you send my way, Mr. Roth."

"Good." He leaned back in his chair and brought his hands in front of his chest to change to Sign for communication. "*I will require one further responsibility from you. It is obvious you are fluent in Sign.*"

She nodded, matching the form of communication. "*I sign as well, if not better, than I speak. I can adapt from ASL to PSE to SEE as needed.*"

"*Good. From now on, you will attend all meetings I attend. Although I don't generally find it necessary, on occasions it would be helpful if I have an interpreter. Especially in large groups when some are too far away for me to see their faces.*"

"*I understand. Will I be welcome at some of these meetings? I am sure executive assistants do not usually attend many of the same meetings as fund managers.*"

"*You are welcome if I say so,*" was his response.

His statement made her heart skip. Upon being offered the job, Jewell refreshed her memory of B.P. Roth and his business accomplishments. She'd been familiar with some of the funds he managed, but she hadn't connected his name with the handful of funds that still managed to produce a gain during a harsh market. Only a couple of publications made mention of his disability. Mr. Roth was apparently a very powerful man at Bulwark Mutual Funds. More powerful than she originally speculated at their first meeting.

"Do you have any problem with working late on occasion?" he asked, bringing her out of her musings.

"On occasion, no. But I do make plans ahead of time once in a while. If you can give me as much warning as possible, I would appreciate it. Emergencies aside."

Mr. Roth touched his fingers to his mouth and tapped his fingertips against slightly pursed lips. "I understand, Ms. Kincaid. What about company functions? I occasionally attend business dinners, parties, conferences, and such. If you could accompany me on occasion, it would be," he paused and his stare seemed to intensify, "helpful."

"Knowing ahead will help, but I don't see any ongoing issues with attending."

His shoulders bounced in a silent chuckle. "There is a large networking event involving many in the industry two weeks from Thursday evening at the Ritz-Carlton on Boston Common at seven. Are you free?"

Jewell paused before answering and intentionally took the time to unlock her phone and check her painfully blank calendar. She didn't want him to think her calendar was so wide open she didn't need to check. Of course, she didn't have anything planned. Greg might come over, or she might meet up with her friend Kip for lunch, but that was about it. After a sufficient pause, she nodded.

"I'm free."

"Good. It is, of course, a formal dinner. I will pick you up at six. Text me your contact information and address." He took a business card from the holder on his desk and slid it across the blotter to her.

Jewell nodded and took the card. Why did she feel like they'd just set up a date? Of course, it wasn't. So, why did she have a funny twittering sensation around her heart? Her thoughts raced to trivial things, such as what she would wear and how she would do her hair. She pushed them away and brought her thoughts back to the conversation.

Mr. Roth picked up a thin folder from where it sat near his elbow. He leaned forward and passed it to her over the desk. Jewell raised up from the chair enough to take it from his hand. Their eyes met and Jewell's breath caught in her throat. His eyes shifted momentarily from her eyes, then back again. It was so fast, that Jewell wasn't sure she could trust what she saw. Did he have any idea how much power he held with those eyes?

"This is the first project I'd like you to work on. I'm researching a breakout company in Singapore for possible investment in our Pacific Rim Advantages Fund. They just began trading on the Hang Seng Market last week. If they prove to be as promising as I suspect, I want to get in while the stock is young."

"You didn't choose to purchase at IPO?"

Jewell was surprised a man known for his aggressive investment style wouldn't snatch up a company he believed in at the first opportunity. Buying at Initial Offering Price would provide him with the benefit of any gain the company had from that point on.

He shrugged, and in the action, Jewell recognized a kind of concession, like maybe the decision wasn't fully one with which he agreed. Fund Managers held a great deal of power when it came to the buying and selling of securities within a mutual fund, but the guidelines and prospectus were predetermined by the fund trustees. Perhaps the trustees were more conservative than Benjamin Roth.

"The trustees have chosen to avoid IPOs in this particular fund. It isn't provided for in the prospectus."

Jewell nodded and scanned the paperwork he gave her. There were printouts of articles from the Wall Street Journal and some other trade magazines, Internet articles on tech offered by the firm, as well as various figures regarding growth. The first page also listed some technological advancements and devices offered by the company. She was impressed by the profits already achieved in the first quarter of the year.

"You seem to have a great deal of information on Hirotachi already."

"Numbers, yes. I want more than that. I want to understand their philosophy and business plan before I determine their growth potential."

Jewell understood his approach and nodded. "When would you like it by?"

"One week."

She saw the challenge in his eyes. He tested her willingness to jump in with both feet and her confidence to get the job done. Jewell raised her chin slightly and met his gaze. A slow smile tugged at the corner of her lips.

"I'll have it to you by Thursday afternoon."

The corner of his eyes wrinkled when he smiled. It was a full, honest grin. She had just met the challenge. Now all she had to do was carry through with it.

"Good," he answered. "Do you have anything you want to cover now?"

She nodded and closed the folder, putting her full attention on him. "We've spoken verbally for the most part, but is that your preference? Or do you prefer Sign? Here, when it's just us." She cleared her throat and was thankful he couldn't hear the nervous twitter in her voice.

"Manual communication allows us to speak freely, without worrying about being overheard," he answered with a shrug, his hands moving fluidly. *"Not that there is a great deal discussed here of a confidential manner. Unless your hands are otherwise occupied, or speech seems more prudent, we will stay with Sign."*

Jewell bobbed her 'a' hand in affirmation. *"Fine. Outside of us, I'll use my best judgment. Have you used an interpreter before?"*

He shook his head. *"I've never met someone fluent enough and had enough knowledge to be useful. Anything else?"*

"No, Mr. Roth."

"Good. Because I do."

Jewell sat back in her chair. The hardest part about this job, and she could tell it would be ongoing, was having to constantly meet his gaze. He had such an intense face and overpowering stare, that it was hard not to look away and regain her composure. However, the very nature of her position—and her personal experience—dictated that eye contact was not only important but also necessary.

"I believe in formality. Everyone here, except for Mr. Traynor and one or two other fund managers, refers to me as Mr. Roth."

Jewell nodded her understanding. She recognized from the start the formal air he seemed to exude. He was respected and demanded respect by his very nature. A sign of that respect would be how people addressed him. It came as no surprise to her the formality was his expectation.

"Out there," he signed, *"I would prefer you call me Mr. Roth. Especially when speaking at meetings or with others. But in here, when it is just the two of us, feel free to call me by my name."*

A sense of private intimacy crept into the room. The space between them shrank even further. Jewell drew in a slow breath and cursed the heat she felt in her cheeks.

"Do you prefer Ben or Benjamin?"

She felt, more than saw, his gaze fall to her lips as she mouthed the names to accompany the finger spelling. Again, his eyes darkened and his lids slid slightly lower. Concentrated energy spanned the desk to bombard Jewell, its power hitting her chest like a hammer. Dear God! She had to build a resistance to those eyes. He could melt iron with them.

"Call me Benjamin," he said.

"Benjamin," she repeated.

His rich brown eyes closed abruptly and Jewell thought for a moment she heard a soft moan in his throat. Benjamin twisted his chair slightly towards the bookshelf along the wall and didn't open his eyes until his motion stopped. She didn't move as he took a deep breath. He turned back to her.

"That is all I have for now. I have some things to go over before the meeting. Get started on the research."

Jewell nodded and stood. Something just happened but she didn't know what. His face was a plastic mask. He watched her stand and they both nodded in farewell before she walked to the adjoined room. Once outside his vision, Jewell's shoulders dropped and she sighed. She would have to limit herself to short doses of Benjamin Roth until she was able to build up immunity to his effects.

Benjamin watched her walk across the room and into her office. The subtle sway of her hips, and the slight hollow behind her knee just below her skirt's hem, mesmerized him. He swallowed against the dryness in his throat.

What are you doing? Don't go there, Roth!

Benjamin shook his head. What had possessed him to march down the hall last week and bargain with Traynor to let Ms. Kincaid work for him, and not Burke? At the time, he convinced himself it was because of her qualifications. She was tremendously overqualified to work as just a glorified secretary. It was a stroke of good luck for Benjamin to find a woman as qualified as Jewell Kincaid who was also so fluent in Sign. She was a gift from the gods. After an hour of persistence and powerful demands, Travis agreed to give her up for a better position. Now, here she was.

But he was no idiot. She was gorgeous and ten steps beyond sexy. With the simple two-inch heels she wore, Jewell stood close to five-foot-ten. The top of her head would just hit his nose if he embraced her. Her figure screamed all woman with curves in all the right places. Although Jewell wore a professional, tailored suit, it did little to disguise the tempting curves and valleys of her body. Femininity embodied her.

She was dangerous.

He was a fool.

He inhaled and the delicious scent she left behind filled his senses. The top layer was a musky, floral perfume with the slightest hint of oriental jasmine. Benjamin took another breath. Beneath the manufactured scent was her true essence. Mingled with the perfume was a sweet, fruity trail that was probably her shampoo. Peach lotion and the clean aroma of ivory soap completed the layers. Together they were an intoxicating and heady combination. Individually, each was incomplete and hollow.

He shot out of his chair. *Knock it off!* He'd boxed yourself into a corner this time. She was right in front of him, and he couldn't even think about touching her. Not without having a sexual harassment suit thrown in his lap.

Annoyed, Benjamin raked his hair with his fingers. He just had to keep his libido in check. This wasn't her doing, and she certainly hadn't done anything to make him think otherwise. He guessed she wasn't the type of woman who would be involved in an office fling.

Neither was he.

Now he would have to work with her, closely, every day and learn to deal with the consequences of his impulsivity. All because he let the wrong head do his thinking for him. It was like cutting off his nose to spite his face.

Benjamin stalked the room. He was better off with Mrs. Soldano!

He stopped near the door to her office and leaned back to spy on her. Jewell sat at her desk, her back to him, as she familiarized herself with the computer system. She seemed competent as she moved through the custom-designed programs, which piggybacked the basic PC setup. Her hand came up so her fingers touched the small curls at the nape of her neck. Absently, she tucked the auburn escapees back into the tight twist. Benjamin wondered how much hair she hid in the prim style, and how it would look flowing free around her shoulders.

He closed his eyes. Rather than the enticing picture of her flowing hair, his mind filled with the erotic image of her lips as they formed his name.

Benjamin.

Those full, luscious lips pursed ever so slightly when she said his name. They pressed together and slowly separated before drawing together and back in a soft pout. He felt the rumble of a groan in his chest and his eyes snapped open to make sure she didn't notice. Jewell didn't look up. For all he knew, she was playing music or something, and had no idea he watched her.

Frustrated, he turned away and returned to his desk.

CHAPTER THREE

O n Friday of her first week, Jewell opened her desk drawer at 12:22 and scowled at the cold sandwich and bag of chips she'd grabbed that morning. She'd eaten at her desk every day since Monday, when she'd nearly gone bankrupt buying a salad in the company café. She held out until nearly one, when her stomach declared with a loud rumble that it would be fed, and now. The door to both Mr. Roth's office and the main bullpen were open, but the only sound she heard was the mix of keys clicking, phones ringing, and low conversation that prevailed in the big room.

The sandwich still held no appeal, so she shoved back from her desk and went to Mr. Roth's door, glancing inside the empty office. His laptop sat on the desk, open, but with the security password screen showing. She had learned quickly that if he didn't have a lunch meeting, he ate at his desk, if he ate at all. Part of her had hoped he was there and she could convince him to escape for lunch. With a sigh, Jewell turned and left her office through the door leading to the backside of April's desk just as April came down the wide corridor down the center of the bullpen.

"Hey," April said with an open smile, setting her purse on the inside of her desk wall. "Did you need something?"

"Yes, something decent to eat for lunch."

"Have you been down to the cafeteria?"

Jewell snorted a laugh. "Yeah, tried a salad—"

"Ouch," April interrupted, wrinkling her nose. "You don't have to say anything else. I've had one of those salads you need to rob a bank to pay for. Do you want to get out for a while?"

Jewell folded her arms on the high ledge of the desk and looked down at April as she settled in front of her computer. "Is it bad that I've only been here a few days and I'm already going a bit stir crazy?"

April laughed, logging into her system. "No. At least you *can* get out this time of year. A few more months and you'll need a full-body snowsuit just to cross the street."

"Guess I should escape while I can. Any suggestions?"

"Depends. What are you in the mood for?"

Jewell groaned. "Anything but the sandwich in my desk drawer."

"*Bertucci's* is just around the corner and down a block. They have this *amazing* chicken allegro salad."

"Sounds good to me," Jewell said, slapping her hand on the desk. "Point me in the right direction."

Minutes later, Jewell stepped into the bright sunlight of a Boston summer afternoon and slipped on her sunglasses. The humid air hit her in a wave of moist heat, and she swore she felt the hair at the nap of her neck instantly curl into tight ringlets. Unbuttoning her jacket, she shrugged it off and let the sun heat her bare arms. The collar of her shell hugged her throat, but at least she could find some relief from the warmth by carrying the blazer. Another six weeks and autumn would fully hit New England, and she'd need the jacket, but for today it was just too much.

By the time she walked the three blocks, a fine sheen of perspiration dampened her neck and she was thankful to step inside the air-conditioned restaurant. The overpowering smell of garlic, roasted tomatoes, olive oil, and yeasty crust greeted her, and she inhaled. Her stomach immediately growled, rumbling almost painfully, and she weaved through the patrons and tables to the order counter. A dozen or so tables filled the small space, covered with red and white checkerboard tablecloths, with only three occupied at the end of the city's lunch hour.

"What can I get you?" asked a young man of maybe twenty, with slightly stringy hair parted down the middle and a mild case of acne.

"I hear your chicken allegro salad is to die for," Jewell said with a smile.

"Just find a seat. We'll get it right out."

A small table with two chairs sat in front of the large window that looked out on Market Street. Jewell draped her jacket on the back of the chair and sat. A waitress arrived almost immediately with a glass of ice water. "Thank you." Jewell took the glass before the woman could set it down. "It never ceases to amaze me how someone can get so thirsty when you could wring water right out of the air."

The waitress laughed as Jewell drank half the glass of water, the cold making her head ache just a little but not nearly enough to stop. "Do you want anything else to drink?"

"No, just more of this."

She nodded and walked away. The air in the restaurant was at least twenty degrees colder than outside, but Jewell still felt flushed from the short walk. She leaned back in her chair, indulging for a moment by pressing the condensation-coated glass to her cheek.

A sharp rap on the window made her jump, and she nearly spilled the water down her front. Jewell smiled when she saw Benjamin standing outside beneath the green restaurant canopy, his eyes hidden behind dark shades. His straight lip tipped up at one corner for that hint of a smile he teased her with. She motioned him inside and he pulled open the door, letting in a gust of thick air. He slipped off his sunglasses as he sat, dropping them on the tabletop. In practically the same motion, he took her glass of water and turned it to drink from the side she'd drank from. In three deep gulps he drained the ice water and set it down with a deep sigh.

Jewell chuckled, and tried to ignore the slow heat infusing her cheeks. "Are you on your way back to the office?"

He nodded. "I was downtown running errands."

"Have you eaten?"

He nodded again, but his eyes shifted down to her bare arms before he looked her in the eyes again. "Did you just get here?"

The waitress returning with Jewell's lunch interrupted her chance to answer. She set down the plate, followed by two more glasses of water. "Can I get you anything else? Would you like something, sir?"

Benjamin never looked away from Jewell and missed the question. Hoping the dim lighting in the restaurant hid her flush, Jewell quickly signed the question and pointed to the waitress, indicating she had spoken. He finally looked up and shook his head.

"No, thank you."

The waitress smiled again and walked away, but Jewell felt suddenly self-conscious about eating the salad with Benjamin sitting there. The way he watched her was a step beyond what she was used to, even for someone who communicated through body language and lip reading, and the glint in his eyes—barely suppressed—had nothing to do with wanting to know what she said. One part of her knew alarms should have been going off in her head, that bosses shouldn't be looking at her like that. If she didn't enjoy the flutter of awareness that hit her every time he gave her that 'almost smile,' she'd probably listen.

"Do you want some?" she asked, picking up her fork.

"I'm fine, but I'll keep you company if you don't mind. If you're not in the office, no need for me to rush back."

Jewell froze, her lips open and her fork full of gemelli and tomato in front of her mouth. "Did you need me to do something? I can have this boxed up and head back right away."

He held up his hand, then switched to sign. "*No, I just meant that...*" He paused, his hands in front of him, palm up, as he considered. Then his almost grin turned into a full-fledged smile and he leaned forward slightly. "*I mean that there's no rush.*"

Benjamin had plenty to do in the office. His day was filled with reviewing reports, compiling data, and watching various markets as they closed, and opened, depending on the market. But he considered it a stroke of luck that on the one day he wandered outside of Bulwark he would run into Jewell, just sitting in a restaurant, all alone.

She was flushed, bright color blooming in her pale cheeks, and tiny ringlets escaped the french braid that hugged her skull to sprinkle across her brow and along her cheeks. As warm as the day was, he hoped that perhaps he was responsible for the pretty blush and the nervous flutter of her hands. It was wrong, he knew it was wrong, but he couldn't help himself and didn't want to try.

"I feel like I'm holding you up, Benjamin," she said, poking her fork around in the remains of her pasta and chicken. "I peeked in your office before I left to see if you wanted to come with me—"

"You did?"

She nodded, looking at him through her lashes as she created a new bite. He noted how she made sure each bite had at least two pieces of pasta, a piece of chicken, and either a tomato or an olive. Sometimes both, but she was running out of olives. Taking the bite, she set down her fork and wiped her lips with a napkin before signing. *"Don't you go stir-crazy eating at your desk every day?"*

"I've never thought about it."

Jewell sat back, dropping her napkin on the remains of her lunch left on her plate. Her smile made his pulse jump, and he liked it. *"I believe I'm going to need to get you out of the office more often, Mr. Roth,"* she signed, feigning a serious expression as she wagged a finger at him. *"It's my duty as your executive assistant."*

"I don't recall that in your job description."

"I'm taking the initiative."

He was saved from making a completely inappropriate comment, one that was sure to bring a new flush of color to her pale cheeks, by the return of the waitress. Benjamin didn't bother to look up, keeping his attention on Jewell. She looked at the waitress, shook her head, and waved a hand at the empty plate. The waitress took it and set the bill on the counter. Jewell reached for it, but Benjamin was faster. He grinned at the shocked look on her face.

"Hey, now. You didn't even eat."

He just grinned and shifted to take his wallet from his back pocket. Leaving a bill on the table, he stood and offered his hand to help her stand. It pleased him in a way he couldn't qualify when she took it and came to her feet, retrieving her jacket from the back of her seat. He liked her bare arms. They were trim, but just as pale as her face and sprinkled with freckles.

They stepped back into the oppressive humidity of the afternoon, both slipping on their sunglasses against the bright sun. Walking in unison, they turned down Market Street toward the Financial District. The walk was short, but August in New England was as hot and humid as any southern bayou or Florida Everglade, especially here in the city deep in the jungle of massive steel and glass buildings that blocked any cooling breeze that might drift in off the Atlantic Ocean. They reached the light at the corner and joined the mass of people waiting to cross. Benjamin chanced a glance in her direction, catching her huff as she blew wisps of hair off her forehead.

"Perhaps we should save our next lunch outing for a slightly less smothering day."

She smiled and nodded. "Please."

The light changed and they all moved *en masse*. Benjamin cupped her elbow, not realizing until they stepped onto the other curb that he'd once again reached for her. It felt natural, instinctual. And once again, she hadn't moved away. It would be so easy to slide his fingers down the inside of her arm and take her hand, just to see if she'd let him shift his fingers between hers.

They crossed Market and headed down Friend Street toward the tower of steel and glass that housed Bulwark. He dropped his hand from her elbow as they neared the building, and caught the slight tip of her head as she looked down at her bare arm and then up at the gleaming face of the tower. Benjamin stepped forward and pulled open the glass lobby doors.

A refreshing wave of cooler air washed over them. Jewell stopped inside the doors and tipped her head back, a slow smile on her lips. He put his hand against her back to move forward and felt the purr of a groan vibrate through her ribcage.

The reaction in his gut was intense and nearly made him stumble.

She waved to the security guard at the front desk as they crossed the black marble floor to the bank of elevators. He noted that Jewell smiled at every person who passed them, and nearly every one of them returned the smile. She inspired the reaction; he understood that even for himself. When Jewell smiled at him, he couldn't help but smile back.

Benjamin used his security card to call the elevator and let her precede him into the empty car when the doors opened. The interior of the car was polished brass and wood, and each wall acted like a mirror, surrounding Benjamin with images of Jewell. She slipped on her cream-colored jacket and ran her fingers over the twisted curls at the nape of her neck.

"I must look a fright," she said with a tilted smile, trying to get a look at herself in the reflective brass walls.

Benjamin pushed his hands deep into his pockets to keep himself from touching the tendrils along her cheeks. He leaned against the railing that ran along three sides of the elevator car, watching her compose herself.

"You look… fine," he finally said.

Her green eyes shifted to him, then away. The elevator bumped to a stop, and he glanced up to the red numbers indicating the floor levels and saw they had another five floors before they reached their office. The doors opened, and three people stepped on, among them Kevin Burke. Benjamin shifted along the rail to stand closer to Jewell, giving the others more room.

"You two just coming back from lunch?" Burke asked.

"Yes," Jewell answered, turning so she faced both of them and Benjamin could see her face. "Well, I went for lunch and Mr. Roth happened to find me."

Burke looked between them, then his gaze settled on Jewell. Benjamin watched the other fund manager's focus shift from the pretty curls around her face, to the glistening skin at the base of her throat from the heavy humidity outside to her flittering hands as she smoothed and buttoned her jacket.

Benjamin's neck prickled and he slid his hands from his pockets to curl around the handrail. Something about the predatory way the other man looked at Jewell jabbed at Benjamin. He didn't like it. He just wasn't sure *why* he didn't like it.

Jewell touched his arm, drawing his attention. *"I'm going to the break room for a cold drink. Do you want one?"*

He nodded, releasing his grip on the bar to sign. *"Thank you."*

The elevator stopped at their floor and the doors opened. Everyone filed out, and with a final smile in his direction, Jewell headed through the bullpen to the break room on the other side. Benjamin walked slower toward his office door, watching her wave to some and pause at the desk of another for a brief conversation before moving on.

Burke tapped Benjamin's arm with the back of his hand, then pointed after her. "I think you owe me one, Roth."

Benjamin just smirked and turned away, effectively ending the conversation as he went into his office, raising a hand of acknowledgment to April. She held up several pink "While You Were Out" slips that he took as he passed. He didn't bother looking back to see if Burke had walked away, or not.

CHAPTER FOUR

Jewell scanned Benjamin's handwritten notes once again with a frustrated huff. She had learned to decipher in her first week the jaunty, angled hieroglyphics he called penmanship without much problem. Now, well into week two, she barely had to ask for clarification. The difficult part was filling in the "holes" in his notes. He had his own form of making notes where words were left out, phrases were left incomplete, and acronyms were used whenever he felt appropriate.

This was one of those times when it just didn't make sense. She read the scribbles over and over again, each time rendering a different interpretation. Except for this one final point the rest of the report was done. Jewell took off her reading glasses and stuck the end of one bow between her teeth.

She sat back in her chair and crossed her legs, shooting a glance at the clock. It was nearly four o'clock. With clarification on this final issue, she could finish the report and skip out early to get ready for the dinner party.

With a decisive nod, Jewell stood and headed for the door adjoining their offices. Most of the time they left it open so she could hear him come and go. Against the wall by the door leaned an elaborately ornate wooden cane. To most, it looked like a decorative piece, but for Jewell and Benjamin, it served a purpose. She picked up the rod and tapped its tip against the floor three times with a solid impact.

Benjamin looked up. A slow, lazy smile lifted one corner of his lips. It was the same smile he always greeted her with, and despite its repeated appearance, Jewell was still disarmed by it every time. He sat back in his chair, the back reclining slightly.

"Do you have a minute, Benjamin?" she signed with one hand, mouthing the words as well. He nodded and she crossed the room to stand behind his desk. She set the paperwork down on his blotter and pointed out the section she questioned. *"I'm sorry, but I just can't decipher this. Are you referring to the PE ratio or the annual percentage earnings?"*

"Where?" he asked.

Jewell crouched down, trying to keep her balance on the balls of her feet. The new position brought her line of vision just below Benjamin as he sat in the chair. He swiveled to face her better and scooted closer to look at the paper. Feeling precariously balanced on her toes, Jewell hung on to the edge of the desk with one hand.

"This section right here," she said. There was no way she could sign and hang on at the same time. "I understand you're comparing Hiramitsu to Hitachi, Samsung, and Nokia. This chart represents the rate of growth for all four in the last five years. But this number looks like it could be either a rate of growth or a price-to-earnings ratio."

Benjamin leaned closer and touched his fingertip to the paper, his palm partially covering the back of her hand. Immediate heat warmed Jewell's skin and electric sensations raced up her arm, just as it had the week before when he'd touched her elbow when they walked. The revisiting of contact made her breath hitch and she jerked back. The quick movement threw her off balance and she flailed to remain upright.

Benjamin's arm wrapped around her body as she reached for the nearest thing to hold on to—his thigh. He pulled her towards him and Jewell's undignified fight ended as she leaned into his lap. By the time she stopped, one hand clutched desperately to the muscle above his knee and the other grasped the opposite side of his chair. The arm that caught her remained in place and Benjamin's bicep brushed the side of her breast.

Jewell's body tingled and heat rose high in her cheeks. Tentatively, she looked up.

His dark stare was bold and frank in its assessment. Jewell was intensely conscious of his nearness and the masculine scent that surrounded him. A slight late-day beard speckled his strong jaw. With the afternoon sun coming through the window, each whisker appeared as a golden fleck on his skin. Jewell's lungs burned from holding her breath. She slowly released it as she came back on her heels.

The arm behind her slowly pulled back, but his fingertips left a searing trail as they moved across her back to her side. His palm remained against her ribcage, the pad of his thumb painfully close to the bottom side of her breast.

"Thank you," she whispered, thankful once again he couldn't hear the weakness behind the words.

He nodded slightly. His intense gaze remained on her face and one tight muscle jerked along his jaw. Jewell's heart skipped when his eyes diverted for a split second downward to the valley between her breasts exposed by the opening of her blouse. In a reflexive move, she tightened her grip on his thigh. Benjamin's arm shot from her side to cover her hand with his own. His fingers lifted her palm off his leg, but they remained wrapped around her hand.

There was a quick knock at the door before it opened and Kevin Burke stepped in. Jewell shot straight up to a standing position, a hot flush burning her from toes to nose. She tugged down on her skirt, which had worked its way several inches up her thigh in the process.

"Good afternoon," Kevin said, but Jewell didn't miss the momentary expression of shock on his face as he looked from her to Benjamin. "I don't know why I knock, but I always do." His statement was slow, belying the amusement only Jewell heard in his voice.

"In lieu of a knock, you may consider checking with April," Jewell managed to say without snapping, but she doubted she'd hidden anything from Burke.

Benjamin stood slowly and picked up the paperwork from his desk. His leisurely smile and cool demeanor only added to Jewell's heightened embarrassment. How could he be so calm? Did he have any idea what Kevin Burke *thought* he saw? Jewell could only imagine. With a trembling hand, she took the papers Benjamin handed to her.

"I was referring to the price-to-earnings ratio on the stock," Benjamin said in a steady voice. "Did you have any other questions?"

Jewell shook her head and stepped back from the desk. "No, that should be fine, Mr. Roth. I'll have this done in fifteen minutes." She cursed the nervous twinge in her voice.

"No rush. I don't need it until tomorrow."

Jewell nodded and did her best to make a graceful exit from the room. Her face was on fire. Somehow she managed to move around the desk and walk across the room without her legs giving way beneath her. Jewell glanced back at Benjamin and Kevin before closing the door to her office behind her.

They were deep in conversation, Benjamin standing on one side of the desk and Kevin on the other. Kevin's back was to her. Benjamin didn't look her way, but she caught his subtle sign. It meant calm down, but his slight smile eased the message.

She dared another glance at his face, and a slow grin lifted his lips although he didn't look her way. The smile was meant for her. Jewell sighed and shut the door to allow the two fund managers to speak privately.

"So, your head was in his lap when the other guy came in?" Greg chuckled.

Jewell covered her eyes in embarrassment. "It sounds so much worse when you put it like that. My head wasn't *in* his lap, but I'm sure it looked pretty close to that from the door. The desk would've hidden me from view for the most part. Until I stood up."

"What did he do?"

"Who? Benjamin or Mr. Burke?"

"Either one," Greg worked his fingers against her scalp as he styled her hair.

Jewell sighed and enjoyed the gentle pressure. Since she was a little girl, she'd always loved for her mother to comb and style her hair. It was a calming, soothing kind of contact. Now, when Jewell's mother wasn't around to do it, her friend Greg worked his magic.

"Well, needless to say, I saw the shock on Kevin Burke's face. It doesn't take a genius to figure out what he thought."

"What about Benjamin?"

Jewell shook her head and his hands flattened against her hair to silently tell her to sit still.

"He was so incredibly unaffected," Jewell declared as she lifted her hands off her lap. "After the fact, when I had a chance to think about it, I was annoyed. He just stood up, handed me the report, and acted as if nothing unusual at all was going on. He even told me to calm down!"

"With the other guy there?"

"Well, he signed it, kind of down by his leg where Mr. Burke couldn't see."

Greg shook his head and met her eyes in the dresser mirror. Jewell nervously tapped her polished fingertips against the bare hollow at the base of her throat. He had been there for half an hour, and Jewell hadn't stopped talking since he'd arrived. She was so thankful for a friend like Greg she could confide in. Greg listened, comforted, and sometimes lectured, but never judged.

He picked up her hairbrush and pulled it through the thick waves of her auburn hair. Jewell already wore a chocolate brown cocktail dress and some simple costume jewelry. Her makeup was done. All that was left was her hair. Greg twisted the thick mass and held it against her crown. His other hand pulled down stray curls. With a shake of his head, he let the coil drop.

"You want my honest opinion, hon?"

"Of course."

"Wear your hair down. I'll fix it so it will stay off your forehead. It's so thick and alive, it's a shame to hide it. Besides, it'll be sexy as hell."

Jewell diverted her eyes from the mirror. "I'm not trying to be sexy, Greg."

Greg's eyebrows rose with an amused smirk on his lips. "Oh? When you saw yourself in that knockout dress, you didn't think you were sexy?"

Jewell smiled. "Don't you think it would be inappropriate?"

Greg made a dismissive sound with his lips. "Absolutely not. I think it's time you show your boss a different side of you. I mean, you've been in his lap once already."

"Behave!"

He laughed and worked on a new approach to her hair. Half the time Jewell hated the thick, heavy mass of reddish-brown waves. Especially in the hot, humid Boston summer. It had a mind of its own and didn't like to be confined to the prim, businesslike styles she preferred for the office. But the other half of the time she was happy with the deep copper highlights and natural body. Maybe tonight was the kind of night it would be an advantage instead of a burden.

Jewell's mind drifted. Despite her embarrassment over the events of the afternoon, a warm sensation danced over her skin when she remembered it. Jewell recalled the hard definition of his thigh beneath her hand. The muscles of his biceps pressed against her side, creating pleasant ripples through her. He smelled so damn good! Like sandalwood, mountain air, and menthol shaving cream.

She sighed. Greg's laughter broke her reverie. Jewell glanced in the mirror and saw the red flush in her cheeks.

"Oh, leave me alone," she ordered.

"Is he attractive?"

Despite herself, a wide smile spread across her face. Greg tilted his head back and laughed loudly.

"I guess that's my answer," he roared.

"Is this horrible of me?" Jewell asked, and her hands rose in question. "I mean, isn't it completely unprofessional and stupid?"

Greg's mouth opened and he pointed at her in the mirror. But before he could respond, Jewell continued in a hurried voice. Her pulse beat at a furious pace in her throat, fueling her need to talk as quickly as possible and get it all out.

"It's not like I want this. I don't. But he just—I swear, Greg, from the moment I saw him..." She couldn't finish the sentence. It was too hard to describe how she felt the first time. "I am horrible."

"Horrible? No. Just don't let it go past a little flirting if that. Romance in the workplace is not smart, hun. Ever. You'll get burned.

It's inevitable." His hands rested on her shoulders. "You know what happened with Mark and me."

She nodded. The fallout had lingered for months after Greg's five-year relationship with his boss had ended. Although their relationship was great while it lasted, the breakup was nasty and drawn out. Before they'd started seeing each other, Jewell had been the one to warn her friend against business entanglements. Now, the shoe was on the other foot.

Jewell's shoulders slumped. "I know. And I have no intentions to allow anything to happen. Besides, this is all one-sided anyway."

Benjamin watched the cars and buildings slowly move by from the back seat of his limousine. He could have driven to the dinner party himself and usually preferred to do his own driving, but not tonight. If he had to focus on navigating the crowded streets of Boston, he wouldn't be able to keep his attention on Jewell. He could talk as he drove and catch her signs here and there, but that wasn't enough.

He wanted to be able to look at her. It was impossible to take in too much of Jewell Kincaid. She was stunning, sexy, and enticing as all hell. At first, he dreaded the sweet torture of her presence. Now, he avidly looked forward to it.

Jewell certainly added spice and heat to his day. It was now something beyond the bland, sometimes monotonous routine of meetings and research. There was absolutely nothing routine about having her practically fall in his lap that afternoon.

Benjamin took a deep breath and clenched his fists in his lap at the memory. No woman, however wanton and inviting, had ever looked so tantalizing as Jewell while she fought for her balance. It was instinct that shot his arm out to support her, but the incredible feeling of her body kept it there. Her dainty hand on his thigh heated his blood until it threatened to blow unceremoniously out his ears. Despite his usual steel control, Benjamin's eyes were drawn to the deep valley nestled between her breasts. The conservative suits she wore did little to hide her feminine silhouette, and at the angle she leaned into him, the view was unadulterated.

He knew the tension of the moment wasn't one-sided. Jewell's cheeks had flushed, and her glistening eyes looked up at him with hesitation, but no irritation. When his gaze lowered to her beautiful breasts the grip on his thigh was an excruciating torture. Benjamin pulled her fingers away, not because he didn't want the contact, but because if it continued, common sense might not have prevailed.

Benjamin constantly reminded himself of who he was and who she was. They worked together. More than that, he was her superior within the company hierarchy. Bulwark didn't have any firm personnel rules, but *he* had a rule never to become sexually involved with a coworker. It left nasty entanglements and lingering resentments when things ended. Many times over the years he'd witnessed peers who had given in to temptation, and paid later.

He shook his head. Even if Jewell didn't work for him, she probably had a boyfriend, anyway. Some smart guy out there held her heart, and several soft body parts, in his hands.

It was a bad idea to spend time with her outside the control-imposing walls of Bulwark. Benjamin convinced himself this still qualified as work, thus completely above board. The dinner party was to wine and dine some venture capitalists who had expressed interest in developing a working relationship with Bulwark and some of the other large trust firms in the region. If it worked out, this could bring millions of dollars in assets to the firm. Having Jewell with him would just make the evening easier. That was the only reason he'd asked her to come.

Benjamin shook his head. He knew better, but the excuse sounded good. How many countless parties and functions had he attended without someone to act as an interpreter? In the past, he had done just fine. Or at the least, he made damn sure he did just fine.

The limousine pulled parallel to the bumper-to-bumper cars parked along the street and stopped. Stephen turned and signed through the window that this was the address. Stephen would circle the block until Benjamin texted him to pick them up since there were no available spaces, let alone one large enough for a limo. Benjamin nodded and exited the car. Outside, he stood and looked around him. It was a nice neighborhood. The streets were lined with brownstones, most of which were probably converted to apartments decades earlier. He frowned against the heat outside the air-conditioned interior of the car. It was so damn hot in the city, and the humidity was smothering.

Benjamin checked the number on the front of the buildings to find Jewell's. Stephen had done well to drop him directly in front of it. He adjusted his tuxedo's black tie and bounded up the granite steps. A series of locked mailboxes and the control panel of an intercom system greeted him inside the front door.

He found the button with 'Kincaid, J & R' beside it. Benjamin frowned. *J and R? Who was the R? Could Kincaid be a married name?*

Just as quickly as the thought occurred to him, he pushed it aside and pressed the button with his thumb. His other palm covered the speaker. Seconds later, a slight vibration ran across his skin.

"It's Benjamin," he spoke towards the wall speaker. He moved his hand to the door. The handle pulsed in his grip and he pulled back. The door opened.

The halls of the building were stuffy and humid and the elevator was worse. Benjamin wiped away a light sheen of sweat from his upper lip by the time he reached the third floor. He read the numbers on the doors as he walked down the hall. Benjamin fought down the vicious clenching of his gut at the anticipation of seeing Jewell. He mentally scolded himself for such a foolhardy and uncharacteristic reaction. Attraction had never been this debilitating before.

The door opened before his knuckles hit the wood a second time. He tried to hide his surprise at the person standing there. She was maybe nineteen or twenty years old, with outrageously dark makeup, spiked, bright red hair, and an assortment of facial jewelry. Without even attempting to hide the fact, she took him in from head to toe and smiled. Her hand came up in an arched wave.

"She is almost ready," she stated. "I'm Ruby, her sister."

"Nice to meet you, Ruby," he said and extended his hand. "Benjamin Roth."

This was the 'R' on the mailbox. To his own surprise, he felt relieved. It wasn't a secret husband after all. Mentally, he jerked himself back. *What did he care if she was married, or not? Involved, or not.*

He pushed his hands into the front pockets of the tailored tuxedo slacks and stepped into the entry hall of Jewell's apartment. The interior was considerably cooler than the stuffy hallway. Immediately in front of him was the entry to a small kitchen painted in bright yellow and cream. The hall extended to his left and right. On the left, three closed doors lined the way. The end of the hall to his right opened into a roomy space that seemed to serve as both the living room and dining room.

The walls were laden with framed photographs of all sizes. Some hung in clusters, while larger portraits remained on their own. On the section of wall between the kitchen and living room hung one such frame. It was a professionally shot family portrait in a gold-painted frame. Ignoring Ruby's unwavering eyes, Benjamin examined the picture.

He assumed it was Jewell's family. She stood in the back of the clustered group. On one side stood Ruby, dressed only slightly less shocking than right now, but with bright teal hair. On the other side was a man who appeared to be in his early to mid-thirties. His hair was coal black, and his skin was dark in comparison to Jewell's. She was shockingly pale beside him. Her red hair and emerald eyes stood out prominently. Neither Ruby nor the man had such intense eyes.

Jewell stood an inch, maybe two inches, taller than her brother. They weren't lined up by height. If they were lined by age, that would make Jewell the next to oldest. How old did that make her? Her résumé told him the years she attended college and the number of years of work experience she had behind her. Making an educated assumption based on those facts, he put her somewhere between twenty-seven and thirty.

Seated in the picture was an older couple. The man's hair was white, full and thick. He wore thick-framed glasses and an old-fashioned wool jacket. In his hand was a smoking pipe. On his knee sat a small sprite of a girl with white-blonde hair and pale blue eyes. Her skin was even paler than Jewell's, almost appearing translucent. Bright red lips smiled unselfconsciously at the photographer. Finally, seated beside the man was a delicate, frail-looking woman. Her salt-and-pepper hair was wound in a feminine, yet demure, hairstyle. At least one hand of each of her children rested on the matriarchal figure's shoulders.

They were the most diverse and unconnected group Benjamin had ever seen.

A movement down the apartment's hall drew his attention. All air sucked from his lungs as Benjamin caught a glimpse of Jewell as she came down the hall. In a tailored suit and pedantic hairstyle, she emanated sensuality. But now, in a slinky cocktail dress of brown silk that accentuated every feminine curve of her body, Jewell was a goddess.

She stepped towards them, a beautiful smile on her lips and a demure color on her cheeks. One delicate hand reached up to adjust the sparkling stud in her ear, and she wiggled the fingers of her other hand in greeting.

"Hello, Benjamin," he read on her lips and his lungs constricted. *God, those lips!*

She raised her hands to sign as she spoke, and Benjamin caught a glance of bare skin beneath her arm to her waist. He swallowed and pulled his eyes away to focus on what she said.

"This is my sister, Ruby," she told him, indicating the younger girl who answered the door. *"Ruby lives here with me."*

"We met." Ruby had a wide, knowing smile on her face and she raised her hand in another wave. She even winked at him.

Benjamin turned back to Jewell in time to see a man exiting the bedroom at the end of the hall. He was tall and broad-shouldered. Immediate resentment hit Benjamin's chest. When the new man reached Jewell, his hand went to the small of her back, and he leaned down to kiss her cheek.

"Have a good time," Benjamin watched him say. The man turned to him and extended his hand. Ben took it. The grip was firm and direct. "Hi. Greg Jacobs."

"Benjamin Roth."

The newcomer made his farewells and moved past Benjamin to leave the apartment. *Okay, so she might not be married, but she was possibly involved.* Again, for the second time in five minutes, Benjamin cursed himself. Especially for the kinds of things he had in mind.

"I just need to get my evening bag and I'll be ready to leave," she told him and turned to go back to her room.

She walked away and Benjamin's throat constricted. The sight of her nearly took his breath away. Auburn waves of luxuriously thick hair flowed to the middle of her back. She turned her head and the waves undulated like the surface of the ocean with a light wind. From the ends of her hair, until the dress came to a point beneath the small of her back, her skin was bare. The cut of the dress accentuated the indentation of her waist and the soft curve of her hips. Liquid fabric shifted around her calves as she walked. Benjamin thought he caught a glimpse of two small dimples on either side of her spine just within the outline of the dress.

Ruby leaned back against the wall and watched him. Benjamin pulled his eyes away from Jewell's enticing derrière and met her sister's stare. Her grin was huge and expressed some secret knowledge she was unwilling to share. Looking at her, there was no family resemblance between the two sisters. Of course, one or both of them might have colored their hair—no, Jewell's hair was too beautiful to be fabricated where Ruby's red was from a box—but there was no similitude in the facial structures. This girl was willowy with dainty features. Jewell was considerably taller and her body more womanly and curvaceous. A change like that might come with time because Ruby had to be several years younger than Jewell, but he just didn't see it happening. Then again, there was no resemblance between any of the people in the portrait.

"Nice tux," Ruby signed.

Jewell came down the hall again, a small rhinestone evening bag held in one dainty hand. She gave her sister a twenty-dollar bill, and for his sake, signed the conversation.

"Call in for dinner tonight. I'm sorry, but I didn't get a chance to throw anything in the oven."

"Okay. It's too hot to cook, anyway. I'm going out later with some kids from school. We're going back to campus for some research in the library. We might go to the movies."

Benjamin wasn't sure why, but it surprised him both sisters were so competent in Sign. Jewell said once she was very fluent. Who was deaf that both sisters would know it so well? Could they be CODAs?

"Fine. I'll see you when you get home."

Benjamin opened the door and held it for her as she stepped into the hall. He pulled the door shut, and as he did, his arm came in contact with the bare flesh of her back. The intoxicating scent of her hair drifted to him and he inhaled deeply. Her shoes were slightly higher than the ones she wore to the office because the top of her head was closer to eye level with him.

He released the doorknob and rested his palm at her waist. Beneath his touch, he felt her draw up straighter. She turned her head and looked up at him. Her features seemed more glamorous tonight. He didn't know whether it was from the makeup or the hairstyle, but he liked it.

"You're beautiful tonight," he said, not wanting to take his hand from her back to sign. "I think you should wear this to work sometime."

Jewell smiled and color rose in her pale cheeks. She tipped her chin down and looked up at him through her lashes. "Thank you. But I don't think this is appropriate for the office."

Benjamin met her gaze. "Maybe not."

Unable to avoid the purely carnal temptation, he reached up and touched the thick mass of copper hair. It was softer than he imagined. Filaments of fine silk wrapped around his fingers and tickled his palm. He lifted a luxurious tress near his nose and inhaled deeply.

"I had no idea you hid so much hair. It's beautiful."

Jewell's eyes widened and he felt her breath catch. He was dangerously close to making a very big mistake, so with gentle pressure, he urged her towards the stairs.

CHAPTER FIVE

The Ritz-Carlton ballroom was the epitome of elegance in hues of burgundy and golden blonde wood. Open double doors let in the evening air and allowed attendees access to balconies looking out over Boston Common. Champagne flowed freely, and all Jewell had to do was turn around to be offered some new and tantalizing *hors d'oeuvres*. Soft string and piano music drifted through the room packed with the most affluent and successful people in the Boston financial industry.

Phrases and bits of conversation jumped from small group to small group, with words like "bear market", "TRIV", "arbitrage", and "OTC Market" flittering through the jumble of words. As much as Jewell enjoyed the excitement of the industry, she didn't have the desire to spend an entire evening discussing investment strategies and couldn't help grinning at the enthusiasm that some of the individuals around her held for their jobs.

A slight touch against her spine made her jump, and she turned into Benjamin as he laid his palm flat on her back. She smiled when he stepped closer and leaned his other arm on the edge of the bar where she stood. Not for the first time that evening, Jewell felt the slow infusion of heat just below the surface of her skin when he turned his devastating gaze on her and one corner of his mouth ticked up in a small grin.

"I was beginning to wonder where you went," she said softly, relieved that she didn't need to speak any louder to be heard over the din. His attention shifted down to her mouth, and it was all she could do not to lick her lips. Her senses had been on overdrive since they arrived. No, since he picked her up at the apartment. He'd told her on the way that he would prefer to keep the signing to a minimum if possible, which she thought odd since she'd understood her purpose at the event was to interpret. But, if not signing had him standing closer and looking at her the way he did...she was fine with that.

"Drew Kapchik cornered me by the potted ferns," he said with another quick tick of his grin. "He's been trying to get on my team for the last nine months. He wants an excuse to quit Legacy Funds."

"You escaped..." she smiled.

"I told him I had a beautiful woman waiting for me."

Heat bloomed in her cheeks and Benjamin smiled wider. He slid his hand from her back, letting his fingers trace the underside of her arm until he took her hand in his. "Would you like to dance?"

Jewell raised an eyebrow. "Really?"

"I am not without my secret talents."

She tilted her head with a smile and let him lead her to the small area cleared in the center of the room where no more than half a dozen other couples danced to the slow waltz. When they reached a clear space, Benjamin raised her hand above her head and she spun, the chocolate silk of her dress swirling around her legs. When she came around to face him again he drew her against him, his bent right arm angling behind her back so her left hand rested on his shoulder. He took her other hand and pressed it to his chest, holding it in place beneath his warm palm.

"What kind of music are they playing?" he asked, looking down at her as they stood still amongst the dancing couples.

"A waltz."

"Waltz...we dance on the three, right?"

Jewell nodded, but couldn't figure out his intention. More than once, Benjamin had surprised her with his capacity for adaptation. His lip reading was near perfect, and his speech—for someone with total hearing loss—was not only impressively clear but expressive and varied. He understood the concept of whispering, of shouting, and of dropping the tone of his voice to a seductive hum that danced over her skin. He was a perpetual puzzle.

"Give me the beat." Benjamin shifted his hand over hers and tapped his fingers against hers in a steady rhythm. "Understand?"

Jewell nodded and closed her eyes, listening to the lilting music for a few bars. With the next measure, she tapped the rhythm on his shoulder where her hand rested. *One-Two-Three. One-Two-Three.* Then Benjamin stepped, and as simply as that they were dancing.

She opened her eyes, and her breath caught at the warm way he watched her. His lips had only the slightest bow as he turned her around the floor. She almost forgot to keep up with the beat, giving him the taps he needed to stay in step.

"Everyone is watching us," he said low, tipping his head toward her. "They're wondering how I got to be so lucky."

Without missing a step, they danced through the remains of the waltz. As the music neared the end, he arched an eyebrow and she nodded. "It's almost over."

He gave a smirk and his hand shifted on her back. "Ready to be dipped, Ms. Kincaid?"

Before she could answer, he shifted his stance and bent her backward, his strong arm supporting her back. Catching her breath, she laughed and leaned into his chest as he righted her on her feet. Jewell raised her chin to look at him, her cheeks almost hurting from her smile and found herself once again caught in the intensity of his stare. His rich brown eyes shifted over her face, settling for a beat longer on her lips, before looking straight at her again. The hand on her back pressed a fraction firmer, drawing her closer, and Jewell let herself be drawn.

Then movement in her peripheral caught her attention and she looked past Benjamin to see Kevin Burke standing on the edge of the crowd, a grin she could only describe as "smarmy" on his face. He winked and popped up an eyebrow, his gaze blatantly looking both she and Benjamin up and down, assessing their embrace.

"What is it?" Benjamin asked.

Jewell blinked and pulled her attention from Kevin to look up at him. "N-nothing."

Benjamin turned, still holding her against him, and when he did Kevin Burke's entire expression changed—the lecherous glare gone. He raised his hand in a friendly wave and slipped into the crowd. Jewell took the opportunity to step back from Benjamin's hold, her body suddenly so flushed she swore she had to be glowing from embarrassment.

She touched Benjamin's arm to draw his focus, and raised her hands, signing discreetly between them. "*I'm going to get some air. I'll be right back.*"

He watched her with concern pulling at his forehead, but nodded. Jewell turned, nearly slipping on the wood floor, and pushed through the crowd toward the nearest exit from the ballroom. Greg's warnings rang in her head, and she knew she had to get herself under control before she lost focus. There was already enough innuendo and perception stirring around the two of them to cause problems, she didn't need to add to it by actually *being* attracted to Benjamin Prescott Roth.

She snagged a flute of champagne as she passed one of the wait staff and slipped into the wide hallway beyond. A few event attendees mulled in the hall, some seated in small clusters talking, others walking to or from the ballroom. Some of the faces were familiar, but names escaped her. After working in the Boston financial sector from the time she earned her degree, Jewell had been in contact with people from various levels from many of the firms in the city. Unless she worked with them directly, most were just faces in the crowd.

Like tonight.

Except all she could think of was how many of them had just seen her dance with B.P. Roth, and Greg's warnings echoed in her head. The previous fall, one of the higher members of management at Safeguard Fiduciary had been accused of demanding sexual favors from an individual on his staff. The accusations were neither proven nor denied, but the man stepped down and left the company. It didn't matter whether they were true or not, because his name had been sullied and the young woman left the company shortly after because she couldn't take the whispers and gossip.

None of that meant anything when Benjamin looked at her, or when his fingers skimmed her skin, whether intentionally or casually.

Jewell groaned, and two people turned her way as she strode by. She tried to smile but figured it looked more like a grimace, and reached the end of the hall. A cool evening breeze carried in through a partially open balcony door, and Jewell pushed through it to the small ledge beyond. A humid wind blew in off the Charles River but carried enough evening cool to take away the heavy weight of a New England summer.

It only took a couple of minutes for the heat trapped under her skin to turn to a chill in the evening air. She set the champagne flute on the balcony railing and crossed her arms as another breeze kicked up, lifting her hair off her shoulders. Gooseflesh pulled at her skin.

What if all her worrying and musing were for nothing? To worry about the ramifications of a relationship with her boss implied that her boss *wanted* a relationship with her. Okay, so he told her she was beautiful. He often touched her when it wasn't necessary. He looked at her with those eyes that could melt butter. That didn't mean anything more than he was a good flirt.

Jewell sighed and slumped her shoulders, rubbing her hands over her arms to warm her skin. She lowered her head, closed her eyes, and let out a long, frustrated groan.

Benjamin almost missed her standing on the balcony as he moved down the hallway looking for her. Her cascade of auburn hair caught on the breeze that shifted the white gossamer curtains bracketing the french doors, and drew his attention. With a glance up and down the hallway, Benjamin pushed his hands into his tuxedo pockets and moved to the open doorway, watching her.

She was beautiful.

That thought had crossed his mind more than once, but each time the extent of the effect her beauty had on him surprised him. He had met and dated his share of beautiful women, but as much as he appreciated their attractiveness, none that he could remember made his pulse quicken and his breath catch. If he'd been asked his definition of beautiful just a few months before, he probably wouldn't have said rich red hair, green eyes, and the kind of body that made him want to explore every sway and curve.

Jewel rubbed her arms and a small tremor moved through her as another breeze carried off the river. Benjamin unbuttoned his jacket and shrugged it off as he crossed the balcony. She looked up and turned to him with a slight jump as he draped the jacket over her bare shoulders. As she watched him with wide eyes, he ran his fingers beneath her hair and lifted the curly mass from beneath the collar of the jacket. The aroma of her shampoo tingled his senses.

"Thank you," he read on her lips.

He ran his fingers beneath her hair again, all the way to the ends that curled softly around his hand. "*What are you doing out here?*" he signed, regretfully leaving the silk of her hair to drift in the breeze.

"*I needed some air,*" she repeated from the dance floor.

He just nodded, letting her keep the excuse for whatever reason. She reached for the champagne flute and held it to her glossed lips, tipping her head back to drain the remaining golden beverage. Did her hand tremble? Why?

She set down the glass and turned toward him, licking her lips, and he had the sudden urge to know what her lipgloss tasted like tinted with champagne. He raised his hand to touch her cheek, the pink-stained skin cool beneath his touch from the evening breeze. Jewell let out a long breath that warmed the inside of his wrist as she turned into his touch, her eyes closing slightly. When she raised her chin and looked at him, his heart jerked and he had to swallow.

Jewell jumped and stepped back from his touch, her attention swinging to the open door leading back inside. He looked to see who or what made her react so sharply and found Kevin Burke standing in the doorway. His face was cast in shadow with the light behind him, his shoulder against the doorjamb with his hands pushed into his pockets. The movement of his profile indicated he said something.

Benjamin shook his head and looked to Jewell. The interior light hid Kevin's face, but illuminated the deep blush in Jewell's cheek.

"Jewell—"

Before he could finish, she raised her hands. Her lips pressed together in a tight, firm line and her signs lacked their usual fluidity. *"Mr. Burke asked if we're having a good time."*

Benjamin stepped to Jewell and slid his hand to the small of her back beneath the jacket she still wore. Her entire body tensed at his touch and she crossed her arms over her body, immediately dropping them again to clench her fingers in front of her. "Let's step inside for this conversation."

Jewell stepped away from him and walked past Kevin, slipping his jacket off as she crossed the threshold. As soon as he stepped inside behind her, she turned and handed it back, signing a shaky *"Thank you"* before she took another obvious step back. "Do you need me?" she said, shifting her gaze from Benjamin to Kevin and back.

A niggling uneasiness sat on his chest from the way she refused to look at Burke too long, and he wondered just what exactly he was missing. He shook his head and offered her a relaxed smile, hoping it might help. *"I'll survive a few minutes without you. But hurry back."*

The tight press of her lips tipped into a small smile, and for a moment he saw the spark he liked in her green eyes. She nodded and turned away, and he indulged in a few moments of watching the sway of her hips and the swish of her silk skirt around her legs before focusing again on Kevin.

"You really do owe me, Roth," Kevin said with a tick of his head to the side. "I've got to admit I'm jealous. I should have fought harder with Travis to get her."

"She was overqualified to work admin, and you know it."

"You can't tell me her résumé was the only qualification that caught your attention," Kevin said with a wink and a wide grin.

Benjamin refused to react to Kevin's implication; instead, he held his hands out and shrugged. "Ms. Kincaid is a rare find."

"Yeah, I bet she's good with her hands."

Benjamin took a step toward him, focusing on the tension of his throat and the amount of air he released when he spoke. "Kevin, I suggest you keep your theories about Jewell Kincaid's qualifications to yourself unless they are directly related to her job."

Kevin didn't flinch, his jaw tightening as he stared at Benjamin. "Roth, I've worked with you for a while. I respect your performance and your ability. So, as a colleague, I'm just going to remind you that it doesn't take facts to destroy a reputation."

With a shrug, Kevin turned and strode away.

Damn.

The worst thing was that Kevin Burke was right. It didn't take more than innuendo and implication to destroy a career.

Too bad words and convictions didn't stop his body from jolting with awareness and attraction when he looked up and saw Jewell Kincaid walking down the hall toward him.

CHAPTER SIX

"Good morning," April said cheerfully as Jewell reached her desk. "How was your weekend?"

Jewell smiled and shifted her paper-wrapped bouquet of flowers in the crook of her elbow as she set the customary cup of Dunkin' Donuts coffee on April's desk. The two women began a tradition during Jewell's second week at Bulwark. April made a special trip each morning to Bruegger's Bagels for one sesame seed bagel with lite cream cheese and one egg bagel with vegetable cream cheese. They split the bagels so each woman had half. It was Jewell's duty to make it to Dunkin' Donuts for a large "Dunkin' Midnight" for herself and a large french vanilla roast for April. For a month the system went uninterrupted.

"Oh, it was fine. Between doing research for Mr. Roth, I went to a cookout for my little sister's Girl Scout troop and helped my mother do some canning. I'm tired, but I feel like I accomplished something."

April removed the cover of her sweet coffee and inhaled deeply the rousing aroma. "Mmm. Nectar of the Gods."

Jewell looked towards Benjamin's closed door. Anxious tension gripped her insides. "What kind of mood is he in this morning?" she asked hesitantly.

April moaned, closing her eyes. "Black. Very, very black."

Jewell sighed. With steel resolution, she picked up her briefcase and moved to her open door. Despite the lack of necessity to do so, she moved around the office in silence. As she did every Monday morning, Jewell replaced last week's flowers with a fresh bouquet that filled the room with a calming fragrance. She turned on her terminal and opened the blinds on her window. Just as she was about to sit, Benjamin's voice called out loudly from the adjoined office. For someone with no tangible concept of his volume, his voice could be bone-chilling and ear-piercing.

"Ms. Kincaid," he yelled again.

She tugged down the hem of her suit jacket and squared her shoulders in preparation for battle. With resolute steps, she crossed the room and entered his office. Benjamin stood at his desk, one fist planted at his hip. In his other hand he held a bound report Jewell recognized as the one she compiled for him the previous week. A dark scowl distorted his features. As she neared him, he tossed down the report.

"What the hell is this," he demanded.

"*It's the report on England Associated Bank and Trust you wanted.*"

"*I'm talking about these figures. They are completely off and contradict every prediction I formulated for the board.*" His hands moved quickly and abruptly, expressing his anger.

"*They are completely accurate.*"

"Bullshit," he yelled.

Jewell closed her eyes and clenched her fists. When she opened them again, Benjamin stood only feet away, having come around the desk. Now both fists pressed into his trim waist. His forehead furrowed deeply, and his lips formed a thin, straight line. Dark storm clouds rolled behind his stern eyes.

"*You are yelling,*" she signed slowly.

"I don't care."

"*You might not, but I do.*" She accentuated the statement with a sharp jab of her finger into her chest. "*The figures in that report are accurate and up-to-date as of September 15th.*"

"*They don't coincide with the predictions.*"

Jewell threw her hands up in frustration. "*I'm sorry, Mr. Roth, if they didn't live up to your expectations. Perhaps someone should have told the president of the bank what your wishes were. I'm sure he would have worked harder to please you. But those are the facts. The integration of several small chain purchases into their banking system has slowed profits. As far as I know, you didn't hire me to fabricate information. You hired me to research and provide you with truthful and precise numbers."*

"These can't be right."

"Do you want me to pull them out of the air?"

Jewell's frustration got the best of her. She walked to the desk and snatched up the report. Turning to make sure he watched her, she dropped it on the edge near her. As if pulling fruit from a tree, Jewell grabbed at empty air with her fingers. With a scowl, she glared at Benjamin and pretended to drop the imaginary numbers onto the report cover. Report in hand again, she stalked to him and slapped it against Benjamin's chest. Shock registered on his face and he lifted a hand to hold it.

"There," she threw at him. *"Next time I'll pull them from a hat. Or do you have another preferred method of fabrication?"*

Benjamin stared at her for a long time. Jewell stared right back. She was sick and tired of his dark moods and nasty attitude over the last three weeks. Enough was enough! Her chest rose and fell with the exerted effort to calm her nerves. There was no way in hell she was going to put up with him any longer. He might have managed to send other women cowering away with their heads hung low, but damn it if she would!

He looked down at the report and turned it so the title read the right way. Benjamin's stormy eyes snapped up at her. His face was stoic now, almost solemn. The sudden change from his previous rampage disarmed Jewell.

Benjamin walked by her. His shoulder brushed hers as he made no effort to step around her. It wasn't a rough contact, but enough to throw her slightly off balance. The report fell loudly on his desk. Jewell turned and watched his back. Broad shoulders seemed to drop just slightly.

He didn't turn back to her again, but took his suit jacket off its rack and headed to the door. "I'll be gone the rest of the day," she heard him say to April.

Then he was gone.

Moments later, April stood in the doorway with a look of bewilderment on her face, her jaw hanging open. Jewell was pretty sure the same look was on her face. What just happened? After three weeks of snappy comments, dark scowls, and nasty diatribes, had she won an argument with him? Had this ever happened?

"What was that all about?" April asked.

Jewell raised and lowered her shoulders slowly, not even sure in her own mind. "He flipped out over some numbers he didn't like. I guess he just pushed me too far. I got angry, and probably did something I shouldn't have."

As she explained, her voice slowed and a dreadful realization formed. She probably just cost herself a job.

"I think the guys in accounting heard the yelling," April told her. "I've never heard him like that. And I've worked for Mr. Roth for three years." A kind of worshipful awe tinged April's voice.

Jewell figured April had never heard him like that because no one was ever stupid enough to be so belligerent back at him. Jewell crossed her arms over her body and walked to April. She extended her hand, and the woman took it in a kind of farewell shake.

"It's been nice working with you, April, but I have a feeling I won't be here much longer."

April dismissed Jewell's comment with a pass of her hand. "Oh, don't be ridiculous. He wouldn't fire you because you stood up to him. If that were true, you would've been gone weeks ago. Heck, you probably wouldn't have been hired to begin with."

Jewell wished she could believe the affirmation, but right now it was impossible. She turned and went back to her office. Until the ax fell, she figured she would continue with the latest bit of research he wanted.

Two hours later, Jewell pushed back from her desk with a huff and pulled open her desk drawer for the bottle of headache medicine she kept on hand. She'd needed it a lot in the last few weeks, but never as much as today. She grimaced as she swallowed the three tablets with the cold, thick dregs of her flavored coffee. A soft knock at her door drew Jewell's attention as she tossed the now-empty paper cup into her trash. Kevin Burke leaned into the doorjamb with his hands in his trouser pockets. A brand new knot of dread landed next to the first, and unease flittered over her skin. Since the evening event she'd attended with Benjamin—and the snide-but-subtle remarks Burke had made, she'd felt uneasy around him. She could feel his eyes on her when she walked into the hall, and he often smirked when she caught him watching her. Jewell slipped her reading glasses off and set them on the desk.

"Can I help you with something, Mr. Burke?" she asked, keeping her voice level.

"Please, call me Kevin," he insisted as he came into the room. "I think we're beyond formality."

Jewell said nothing to affirm his request, silently waiting for him to continue. He shifted his hip up on the edge of her desk and looked down at her. "I heard the yelling this morning," he stated.

Heat rose in Jewell's cheeks and she rubbed her fingers across her forehead. She leaned back in her chair and crossed her legs. With a subtle push-off, Jewell moved the chair back to create some space between her and Kevin. "I think everyone heard the yelling. I'm very embarrassed over the whole thing."

"Lovers' quarrel?"

Jewell momentarily lost the ability to speak. She realized her jaw had fallen open and looked away from Kevin's smug expression to regain her composure. When she again met Kevin's stare, an all-knowing grin spread across his face.

"I'm sorry?" she managed to ask, her dry throat making it hard to speak.

"It's certainly not a secret, Jewell," he said. "Everyone has noticed the little glances and subtle touches that pass between the two of you. Anyone in attendance at the dinner party a few weeks back had to be blind not to see the chemistry. You looked very hot that night, and Benjamin wasn't the only one taking advantage of the view." One eyebrow bobbed up and down suggestively.

Jewell stood up, no longer feeling comfortable sitting below his line of sight. "You are mistaken, Mr. Burke," she stated, stressing her return to the formal address. "You and everyone else who believes there to be anything but a professional connection between Mr. Roth and myself."

"Everyone there saw the two of you on the dance floor—"

"We weren't the only ones dancing—"

"Have you forgotten how I caught the two of you on the balcony? Looked very cozy to me, Jewell."

"I needed some air," she exclaimed, annoyed at the high-pitched twinge in her voice, and his insinuation.

Kevin smirked. "You arrived together and you left together. Benjamin Roth has never spoken to his EAs outside of work, let alone taken them to formal dinner parties." He leaned forward and winked. "Not that I blame him."

Jewell struggled for words. Why was it she could so easily counter Benjamin's arguments, but when this jerk tossed out lewd and vulgar comments, she had nothing? She was in shock. The man took some very innocent, very meaningless events and made them into something scandalous.

"We both know you two were doing more than reviewing some numbers that afternoon I interrupted you. B.P.'s been around enough. He should know better and lock his door before getting you on your knees."

It was all Jewell could do to keep from slapping the lecherous smile off his face. She bit down hard, focusing on the heat in her cheeks and steadying her breathing again before she spoke. Jewell took a step toward him, and the look on her face had to be enough warning to Mr. Burke because he slid off the edge of the desk and stepped back, giving her plenty of space.

"Mr. Burke," she said, stressing the formal address. "I would like to remind you that sexual harassment in the workplace is an offense that I understand Bulwark takes very seriously."

"We're just having a conversation, sweetheart." Burke shrugged, dismissing her answer before she gave it. "Everyone thinks the two of you are sleeping together already. Do you really think your word will be taken over mine?"

"Do you want to test that theory?"

He didn't move toward her beyond a slight tilt of his upper body. A harsh edge dug into his expression, and when he spoke, it was through tight lips. "Question is, do *you*?

Burke turned on the balls of his feet and left the office. Alone again, Jewell dropped into her chair and held her burning face in her hands.

When the hell did everything go so wrong?

Benjamin threw back another shot of whiskey. It warmed his tongue and burned his throat all the way down. Unfortunately, it did little to clarify anything for him. He stared at the facets of the Waterford Crystal decanter on the lamp table beside him. Artificial light cast from the lamp played on its angles and peaks, momentarily mesmerizing him.

He took a deep breath and set his tumbler beside the vessel. If drinking half the contents hadn't cleared his thinking yet, neither would the other half. One of the few things he had ever learned from Jonathan Roth was the answers to life's problems were never found at the bottom of a bottle of liquor. Benjamin saw his father fail in his search far too many times to leave any doubt.

Today was the first day in all his years at Bulwark he hadn't put in a full day. Not once had he called in sick, left early, or taken a vacation day.

Never before had he run from a fight, either. The fight today was one he could not win and had no business starting in the first place. Jewell was right. He was being an ass. The only thing he could do was walk away.

No, he could have admitted he was wrong. He could have apologized. Benjamin only started the fight in the first place to get her into his office. To see her and maybe catch a hint of her perfume as it drifted in the air. But he was a Roth, right? Roths don't apologize. They don't ask. And they are never, ever wrong! Was that another lesson he'd learned from his father?

Jewell didn't deserve his anger and frustration. The only thing she had ever done was be the most competent EA of any at Bulwark, and be so completely desirable he could think of little else. The last three weeks had been sheer hell.

Since the night of the Bulwark dinner party, Benjamin thought of nothing but Jewell. Never had a woman looked so beautiful as she had been that night, and as cliché as that statement sounded, he believed it. Every set of male eyes in the place was on her, and Benjamin was glad to be the one standing at her side.

But she wasn't just beautiful. Jewell Kincaid was intelligent and witty. He didn't have to pull the conversation along or fill in the gap where her input might have lacked. She was beauty and brains wrapped in one utterly feminine package. Were there any woman in the world compatible enough to devote a relationship to, it would be Jewell.

Compatible enough?

Benjamin shot up off the couch and paced the Oriental rug spread out in front of his fireplace. *Where the hell was that coming from?*

He remembered the infuriated look on her face that morning. Her outburst and the outrageous example she'd made by plucking imaginary numbers from thin air and throwing them in his face, now made him smile. No woman, or man for that matter, had ever dared come back at him like that. Her indomitable courage was highly admirable. Besides, wasn't that the reason he'd fought tooth and nail to get her? Benjamin was sick of cowering, nervous people who backed down whenever he raised his voice to speak or hand to sign. If they expected an ogre, that's what he gave them.

For three weeks he had pushed her hard. In the back of his mind, he realized it was to drive her out. If he pushed hard enough, she would quit. If she quit, she would no longer be an employee of Bulwark and other possibilities would be open to him. That explained only part of his nasty mood. The other, much larger part, was born of pure sexual frustration.

It was obvious now she wouldn't be shoved out. Jewell was too strong-willed and self-confident to let that happen. Leaving would be accepting defeat, and Jewell wouldn't do that. They couldn't go on like this. She was the best executive aid he'd ever had, and could ever hope to find. Benjamin was an idiot to want to get rid of her.

He would just have to get over his pounding libido and idiotic pride and get on with the job at hand. There was only one way to fix things now.

Benjamin went to his bedroom, took a quick detour through the kitchen for a cup of black coffee, and stepped into the giant glass and stone shower stall in his bathroom. Cold water assaulted him, making his heart beat faster and clearing his muted senses. The icy barrage did little to cool his thoughts of Jewell.

He stepped out of the shower onto the Italian marble floors. The elegant and expensively decorated bathroom opened into a carefully decorated bedroom in sage and white. The details of the room went ignored.

Benjamin walked into his bedroom, towel in hand. The darkness outside his window shocked him. How long had he sat on that couch and pondered Jewell? It had to have been hours. Paying little attention to what he grabbed, he dressed and ran a quick comb through his damp hair.

With resolution in his step, Benjamin went downstairs to get the keys to his car. He opened his contacts in his phone as he headed for his garage, and viewed his Maps app to Jewell's address. He'd only partially paid attention the night of the party when he was a passenger. Within minutes, he had his silver Lexus out of the garage and he drove through the quiet streets of Boston.

CHAPTER SEVEN

Jewell curled up in the corner of her couch, a pint of chocolate peanut butter ice cream in one hand and the remote control in the other. Despite the fact midnight quickly approached, sleep eluded her. Too many thoughts raced in her head when the lights went out and the apartment was silent.

How was she going to find another job? How could she explain leaving Bulwark? That was inevitable. Benjamin alone had enough reason to let her go. But there was no doubt in her mind that if Kevin Burke wanted to, he could push for her termination as well. Yes, he made crude sexual comments, but that was beyond the point. The truth was that he had been at Bulwark much longer, and held much more respect, and while it wasn't right it was the way things were.

She tugged at the hem of her cotton shorts as she tried to get comfortable. They were her favorite pair, but she only dared wear them around the house because they were far too short to be worn in public. Some women might have gone out in them, but Jewell couldn't bring herself to do it. She saved short shorts and tank tops for bedtime and midnight television viewing.

With a press of the power button, her countertop-sized television came on in the middle of an old horror flick. She flipped back her loose hair and dug into the ice cream with her spoon. Jewell almost wished Ruby would wake up. At least then she'd have some company.

The knock on the door came at a tense moment in the movie, and Jewell jumped, choking on her mouthful of ice cream. She shook her head and glanced at the clock on the television. Who could be at her door at eleven-thirty at night? And how did they get into the building? A nervous flutter hit her stomach. Her movie gave her lots of possibilities, none of them good.

She set the pint container down on the coffee table and stood up. Moving quietly, Jewell went to the door. Whomever it was knocked again. Jewell jumped despite herself. She didn't answer but looked through the small peephole into the hall. Surprise brought her back. With quick hands, she undid the double locks on the door and opened it.

"Benjamin?" she signed, *"What are you doing here?"*

He stared at her, his eyelids dropping slightly as his gaze lowered a fraction. Right away he met her eyes again. Jewell felt immediately self-conscious. She wanted to cross her arms over her breasts but feared it would only draw attention to the fact she wore nothing under the ribbed cotton of her tank top. Her hair was mussed and haphazard, and she knew she must look a fright. Certainly not anything like she looked in the office.

Benjamin seemed to snap out of his trance. *"I followed another tenant in through the front door. Did I wake you up?"*

Jewell shook her head and opened the door further. *"No, I was watching television. Come in."*

He stepped inside, his arm brushing hers as he moved by her. Jewell nearly gasped at the immediate reaction of her body. Mortified, she finally did cross her arms over her breasts. She watched him walk down the hall to the living room. A small groan worked its way free of her throat.

Benjamin wore a faded pair of jeans that clung to the contours of his backside. His blue long-sleeved tee shirt fit close, but not too tightly. Enough to accentuate the defined muscles of his back and shoulders. Jewell's breath caught and her throat went dry. She had seen Benjamin in professional suits and fancy tuxedos. All in all, she definitely liked him best in this relaxed kind of look. Jeans and tee shirts brought out the sexy shape of his body the other clothing just hid.

She shook her head to clear her mind of such dangerously ridiculous thoughts and followed him down the hall. A depressing realization hit her. Benjamin probably wasn't here on a social call. Most likely, he was here to fire her and tell her not to bother coming in. Jewell wondered if he had heard about the incident with Kevin Burke. If he did, it would have obviously been Kevin's side. A distorted and one-sided version of the truth. Just remembering what he said made Jewell angry all over again.

Benjamin stood in the middle of her living room and looked around him. He stopped and watched the movie playing out on the television. It was a particularly cheesy scene with some buxom blonde running through the woods from some unknown horror. She clutched at her heaving breasts to hold on to the flimsy shirt as it was torn away by tree branches.

He turned to her, a smile on his face. "*High-quality programming.*"

Jewell touched the power button on the set and the screen went black. "*There isn't much on this late at night.*"

Benjamin looked at the clock. Shock registered on his face. "*I didn't realize it was so late.*"

She flipped her hand in dismissal. "*Do you want something to drink? I don't have much, but I have soda and juice.*"

He shook his head.

Jewell sighed. It was going to be a hit-and-run firing. If he had a drink in his hand, it could make the exit awkward. Her heart pounded against her ribs. She looked away to try and calm her nerves, only to have them electrified when she turned back. Benjamin stared at her, an intense seriousness darkening his face. His brown eyes roved quickly over her, and heat touched her exposed skin wherever his gaze fell. When he fixed his eyes again on her face, a small shudder moved through her. One corner of his lips moved up in his offhanded grin.

Jewell couldn't take the stress anymore. "*What did you need, Benjamin? It must be important to bring you out so late.*"

He motioned toward the couch in an unspoken request to sit. Jewell nodded and they both sat down. Benjamin sat at one end, his body turned towards her as far as the furniture would allow with his bent leg on the cushion and sneakered foot dangling over the edge. Jewell did the same, facing him. The couch was small, and despite her best efforts to avoid it, her bare knee brushed the soft denim of his jeans. It might as well have been his hand for the effect it had on her. Jewell wondered what she would do if she didn't have these sweet sensations to contend with daily anymore. She knew nothing would ever happen between the two of them, but the sweet torment was almost worth the endless torture.

"Is your sister here?" he asked.

The question surprised her and Jewell blinked. "Yes. She's in bed."

"Is she a sound sleeper?"

Jewell squinted, staring at him. *Where on earth was he going with this? Or was this just small talk?* "A hurricane won't wake my sister," she answered, almost regretting he couldn't hear the sarcastic lilt in her voice.

His smile was disarming. *"No need for everyone to be awake."* His hands rested on his thighs as he seemed to think about what to say. He drew in a breath as he raised his hand. *"I wanted to talk to you about today."*

Here it comes! Jewell folded her hands together in her lap to hide their shaking. He paused again, his gaze moving over her face and hair. It was as though he searched for what to say. How difficult could it be? You're fired, Jewell. You're fired. Not so tough.

"This isn't something I do very often," he began again. *"My father drilled into my head that men just don't do this. Especially Roth men."*

Jewell was confused. His father told him men don't fire people? That made no sense.

He stared at the melting pint of ice cream before looking back at her. With deliberate slowness, he lifted his hand and made a loose fist. Benjamin pressed his fingers into his chest and made a circle. His tee shirt shifted beneath his hand.

"I'm sorry. I was out of line and had no right to take my bad mood out on you. It had nothing to do with the report or anything else you've done for me. You are doing a great job. I couldn't ask for better work. What happened this morning, and for the last few weeks, is all me."

Jewell was in shock. She knew she stared, but couldn't seem to stop. *He was apologizing?* April had told her never once had she heard the words "I'm sorry" pass his lips. No matter what he had done.

Benjamin's smile widened and he reached out to nudge her knee. *"Hello. Are you still with me?"*

She nodded and laughed at herself. *"Yes. I'm sorry. You just surprised me. I thought you were here to fire me."*

It was Benjamin's turn to look surprised. *"Fire you? I can be stupid sometimes, but not that stupid. Why would you think that?"*

"After this morning, I just thought you wouldn't want to work with me anymore. When you showed up, I assumed you heard what happened with Kevin Burke—"

His hand wrapped around hers to stop her signing. "Kevin Burke? What happened with Kevin Burke?"

Jewell explored his face. She knew by the confused look in his eyes and the way his gaze shifted over her expression that he didn't know what happened. Good lord! Now she would have to explain. How could she tell him what kind of rumors were going through Bulwark? Could she say with a straight face, without bursting into humiliated flames, what Kevin assumed she was doing the day he came in? And what he—and many others at Bulwark—assumed was going on between the two of them.

With a fortifying breath, Jewell lifted her hands and explained. As she detailed the stories and rumors of their affair, his brown eyes darkened. Jewell tried to put a light air to the whole thing, saying how silly everyone was to take such innocent actions and make them into things they weren't. *"He asked if our fight this morning was a lover's quarrel,"* she finished.

His powerful stare held hers, and no matter how hot her cheeks burned, she couldn't look away. *"There is something you aren't telling me,"* he signed slowly.

Jewell had to close her eyes to break the connection, and opened them again to look down at her hands. When she looked back, she had to find a point beyond his shoulder to look toward. She couldn't meet his eyes again.

"Do you remember the day he came in your office and I was..." She

couldn't find the words to explain their positioning that day without sounding like a fool. *"When I nearly fell and you caught me? And Mr. Burke walked in…"* Benjamin nodded. *"He assumed I was…"* She had to stop, her hands shaking. Jewell didn't know the sign for what Kevin thought she was doing. How could you sign oral sex without looking crude, and without dying of embarrassment?

Her stomach clenched and a wave of nausea hit her. This was just too much. Anyone else and this wouldn't be a problem. But Benjamin was different. Just the thought of…oh, God! Hot tears burned her eyes, and she looked away to hide them.

Benjamin touched his fingertip to her chin, gently urging her to face him again. "Jewell, look at me," he said.

Fighting the humiliation of the conversation, coupled with the devastating effects of his slight touch, Jewell looked at him again. His eyes had softened, and the special smile she liked to think of as her very own spread across his face. He caressed her cheek and his thumb brushed away the tear wetting her skin. He seemed reluctant to take his hand away to sign.

"What did he say to you?" She tried to shake her head, but his hand came back to her face, his palm against her cheek. "What did he say to you?"

Jewell swallowed hard, her throat now dry and rough. She couldn't sign anymore and had to rely on him to know what her lips said. When she spoke, his eyes shifted down a slight degree to watch her mouth. "He said you've been around long enough to know you should lock your door before getting me on my knees."

His entire body tensed, his jaw clenching tight. But the touch on her cheek never changed. When he spoke again, it was through clenched teeth. "I'm going to—"

Jewell laid her fingers to his lips, and his eyes immediately jerked back to look straight at her. She shook her head, and let her hand slip away before another warm breath touched her skin. His fingers wrapped around hers and he held them together on the cushion between them. "No. I made it very clear to him that I won't put up with that. If he looks at me crossed-eyed, I'll take it to Human Resources."

"Kevin Burke is an ass and an idiot."

"You won't get any argument from me," she said with a soft chuckle. Her voice barely carried between them, her nerves fluttering with the contact.

"*If he says or does anything, tell me.*" Jewell nodded, thankful he let it go at that. "Now," he said, his entire expression changing as he smiled. "Are we friends again?"

Jewell smiled back, relieved that that conversation had shifted away from her miserable day. "Again? Were we friends to begin with?"

Benjamin grinned and nodded. "Can I get that drink now?"

"*I'm just going to change my clothes,*" she said, quickly indicating her scant shorts and tight top.

His smile took on an amused tilt. "Don't change on my account."

Heat rushed over her entire body. Jewell stood and walked to the kitchen to get a can of cola for him. When she went back into the living room, Benjamin was reclined in a more comfortable position against the assortment of pillows on the couch. He had picked up a small photo album she kept on the coffee table and was looking through it, one ankle balanced on the other knee in a relaxed position with the album open on his lap. Instead of sitting on the cushion, Jewell put her knees on the couch and sat back on her own feet. Benjamin took the cold can from her and pointed at the album.

"You were a cute kid," he commented.

"How do you know which one is me?" she said.

Benjamin set the can down on the side table before pointing toward the hallway. "*I saw your family portrait in the hall. You are the only one with red hair. You don't look anything like the rest of the family. What? Were you adopted?*"

Jewell touched her nose with the finger of one hand and pointed at him with another. "*On the nose.*"

Benjamin's face grew serious. "*I'm sorry. I shouldn't have said anything.*"

Jewell shrugged. "*Why be sorry? We're all adopted. All four of us.*"

His eyebrows arched. "*All of you? That explains why you don't look alike.*"

Jewell laughed. She scooted closer and pointed at the people in the array of pictures. *"You've met my sister Ruby. This is my older brother Garnett. And the blonde-haired angel is our little sister Pearl."*

"Your names are Garnett, Jewell, Ruby, and Pearl?"

Jewell nodded. *"My mother's name is Opal. Daddy figures it was fate that we should all be named after precious gems. Garnett's legal name is just that. Put that with Mom's name and next thing you know, we've got a pattern forming. Daddy says it was providence because they considered us all to be extra precious gifts, so we needed extra special names. They had our names legally changed: myself, Ruby, and Pearl."*

His expression softened and this time when his attention skimmed over her features, she didn't feel the heat of embarrassment. Her cheeks flushed under his gaze, but not from embarrassment, and she held her breath as he touched the feathery ends of her hair where it hung over her shoulder. *"Jewell is a perfect name for you."*

She touched her fingertips to her lips and lowered her hand, palm up. *"Thank you."*

Benjamin went back to the album, smiling at some of the photographs taken more recently. As the pages turned, Jewell explained who everyone was and when each snapshot was taken. One of the last was a picture from her father's sixty-third birthday party just two months earlier. She and her siblings stood around him, each of them kissing some part of his head. The funniest part was her brother, who had to push down Cecil Kincaid's thick hair just to be seen.

"Your parents couldn't have children?" he asked.

Jewell shook her head. *"No. My mother had Reyes Syndrome as an infant. She nearly died. As a result, she couldn't have children. She's also deaf from it."*

Understanding crossed his face and he nodded. *"I wondered where you learned to sign so proficiently."*

Jewell leaned into the back of the couch. It was amazing. The tension and stress of the last three weeks were gone in a matter of ten minutes. Once again, the comfortable camaraderie between them was back.

"I went to live with my parents when I was four. I don't think the actual meaning of deaf hit me until I was eight or nine years old. I was so young and felt so much love from them from the moment I arrived, it just didn't matter."

"You were four?"

Jewell nodded. *"I bounced around in foster homes up until then and wasn't eligible for adoption until I was three. My parents adopted the kids no one else seemed to want. They took on challenges no one expected them to be able to handle. Most of us were older, which in itself is a disadvantage when you're in the system. My brother Garnett was six years old. His parents and four other siblings were killed in a car accident.*

"Ruby was younger. She was two. But she came from an abusive home. She says she doesn't remember any of it, but I wonder sometimes. Pearl was almost two. She was diagnosed as profoundly Deaf at eight months old. Her mother was poor, and there was no father named, so Pearl's mother signed off all parental rights and put Pearl up for adoption. My parents got a call right away, and she was home with us within a week."

"It seems your parents were very open and forward about the whole thing."

She nodded. *"It was never a secret. And really, it didn't matter."*

He laid his warm palm on her bare knee when he finished his sign. She looked down and examined in awe the difference between their skin tones. Benjamin's flesh was darker and warmer, but something less than tan. Her skin was pale and translucent in comparison. Even after a full summer of sun, she remained fair and freckled.

His fingers pressed gently into her thigh. The pad of his thumb ran back and forth across the sensitive skin of her knee. A liquid heat stirred inside her, and spread out to her limbs. The heat worked down her leg as if seeking out the source of the ardor. She fought down the desire to reach out and test the wave of his hair. Was it as soft and thick as it looked?

"What about you?" he asked. "You explained about your brother and sister."

Jewell met his gaze. This wasn't something she spoke about often. Her memories before Cecil and Opal Kincaid loved her were fuzzy, but unpleasant all the same. Years after the fact, she realized how thankful she was to have a new name. The old name seemed foreign and mismatched. For that reason, she didn't tell anyone what it was. It wasn't her. Very few knew Jewell wasn't her birth name. What spurred her into telling Benjamin, she wasn't sure. She swallowed against the dryness in her throat

"My mother was a heroin addict when I was born, and Child Services took me away immediately. I bounced around in foster care until Mama and Daddy took me."

Although the smile never left his face, Jewell caught the slight tensing around his eyes, creating tiny lines fanning from the corners. His thumb stroked across the skin of her knee more rapidly, with just a little more pressure. "You were happy." It wasn't a question as much as a statement, something he'd decided.

Jewell nodded. *"Very happy."*

His hand left her knee so he could set the book down on the coffee table. "Show me another one. I want to find something I can use for blackmail later."

Jewell laughed and stood up to retrieve another album from the bookshelf behind the television. The early morning hours slipped away.

Benjamin's groggy mind acknowledged the stiffness in his back before he ever opened his eyes. When he did, he had to blink against the light coming from the lamp from just behind his head. For several seconds he remained disoriented, glancing around the unfamiliar room.

He looked down and drew in a sharp breath. Jewell curled against his side, sandwiched between himself and the back of the couch they both lay on. Her cheek rested on his chest and her fingers curled against his tee shirt. Waves of auburn hair cascaded over his arm that sat across her shoulders.

Then he remembered. He came here last night to apologize. Somehow the conversation extended late into the night. Benjamin recalled the heavy, dreamy look in Jewell's eyes around three a.m. After the fourth or fifth yawn in as many minutes, she didn't even argue when he touched her shoulder and silently urged her to lean into his side.

She fell asleep almost instantly. Amid a sign, her fingers slowed and rested on his chest. Benjamin remembered the deep breath that pressed her breasts against his ribs as she sank into slumber.

He didn't doze off until after four. Benjamin spent an hour memorizing the facets of color in her hair. Shadows of deep gold, rich red, and burnt copper mingled in a mesmerizing pattern of light. His fingers explored the softness of her skin. The sparse spattering of freckles on her bare arms made him smile. She smelled so sweet, fresh, and feminine.

Benjamin shifted enough to look at the analog clock on the wall over the television. It was nearly half past five. He had only slept about an hour and a half. Yet, somehow, he felt refreshed. The only negative was the catch in his spine from the angle they held against the arm of the couch.

He tried to shift into a more comfortable position. As he did, Jewell stirred and he felt a soft vibration against his ribs. She rubbed her cheek against his chest and drew a bent, bare leg over his thigh.

Benjamin held his breath. *What sweet torture!*

His hands itched to touch her, to stroke her silken hair and learn the fullness of her breasts beneath his fingertips. Benjamin let his head fall back into the pillows and pressed his eyes tightly shut. How many personal rules had he broken so far? Too many to count, that was for sure. They had crossed the "professional" boundary long ago.

Reluctantly, Benjamin slowly worked himself out from beneath her slight weight. With her cheek cupped in his hand, Benjamin crouched beside her and positioned a pillow beneath her head. A slow, soft smile bowed her full lips when Benjamin paused to touch her temple and smooth back her hair.

He pulled a small afghan off the back of the couch, draping it over her bare thighs and exposed midriff. Jewell didn't stir. She had to be deep in sleep. Benjamin contemplated lifting her off the couch and carrying her down to her bedroom. In the end, he decided against it. What if he met Ruby in the hall? How would he explain that? Hell, how would he explain it should Jewell wake up in the process?

Benjamin sat back on his heels and stared at her. She was beautiful in her sleep. Her cheeks held a soft glow and auburn lashes curled gently along her eyelids. How incredible it would be to wake up to that angelic visage every morning.

He shook his head slowly. It did no good to think about Jewell in any way other than his EA. Now that he no longer had her warmth against him, fatigue worked its way into his body. Benjamin's limbs were heavy and his back ached. What he needed to do was go home, take a long, hot shower, and try to get through the day.

Benjamin leaned forward and pressed his lips against her temple. With a rumble in his chest and an ache in his thighs, he stood and looked down at her before he turned and walked to the front door.

CHAPTER EIGHT

J ewell held herself back to keep from sprinting down the hall to her office. Her heels slowed her down and prevented her from taking off at full speed. She looked at phone as she rushed from the elevator.

"Damn. Almost ten o'clock."

She reached the desk outside Benjamin's office, and April looked up with amused surprise on her face.

"Well, good morning," April said, and looked at her desk clock. "Yup, it is still morning."

Jewell took a deep breath and leaned on the high desk. "Very funny."

"What happened?"

Instant heat rushed to Jewell's cheeks. *Oh, I spent the entire night on my couch with Benjamin. We talked. We joked. I fell asleep in his arms. When I woke up this morning, it was after eight and he was gone.* She cleared her throat. "Oh, I just overslept."

"I guess that happens to the best of us once in a while. I missed my coffee this morning, though."

"I'm sorry," Jewell said in earnest.

April laughed. "That's okay. I survived."

She finally caught her breath and tilted her head toward Benjamin's door. "Is he in?"

"Of course. Mr. Roth is *always* here." April rolled her eyes with a grin but quickly shrugged. "Well, except for yesterday, that is."

"What kind of mood is he in?" Jewell asked, pulling her lower lip through her teeth. She wanted to know what she was walking into.

"Seems to be much better, actually."

Jewell smiled and sighed in relief. That was definitely a positive sign. "Good."

"Do you know something I don't know?" April's eyes squinted slightly and her voice carried a curious lilt.

Jewell shook her head, probably a little too adamantly. "No, just wondering."

April still looked at her quizzically as Jewell walked to her office. "Congratulations on not being fired," April called after her, and Jewell laughed softly. Her nerves, frazzled from being late, calmed a bit. She took pride in never being late to work. Then again, last night was not her usual evening at home. A smile pulled at her lips as she thought about it.

The last time she remembered looking at the clock it was almost three in the morning. At the time, she hadn't felt tired at all. They were too busy talking. Other than Greg, she had never felt comfortable enough with a man to talk so freely. Of course, Benjamin was different. It was a strange sensation. Yet, not completely unpleasant.

Benjamin brought her nerves to life. Her senses were finely tuned to every move he made, every word he said, and every nuance of his body. Jewell decided to forego her normal morning routine and go directly into Benjamin's office. Besides, most of the morning was gone anyway. The routine seemed silly at this point. With a smile, she wondered if he was as tired as she. Jewell peeked through the open door.

Benjamin reclined in his chair. His elbow rested on the arm and folded fingers supported his temple. Just as he had on the couch the night before, one ankle rested on the opposite knee in a relaxed position. Jewell giggled when he stifled a yawn behind his hand and blinked his eyes to focus again on the papers in his lap.

Jewell walked in, not bothering with the cane at the door. He looked up and his slow smile sent butterflies fluttering behind her ribcage. There was a faint glimpse of mischief in his eyes. Benjamin sat forward and set down his papers.

"Good morning."

With her hip leaned into the desk edge, Jewell said good morning back. *"Are you as tired as I am?"*

His smile widened. "I'm exhausted."

Jewell felt like the night before was some wonderful secret to be shared between just the two of them. Not a shameful or indecent secret. Just a special, private one for her and Benjamin. He wore a dress shirt and silk tie, but the image of Benjamin in worn jeans and a well-fitting tee shirt stayed prominent in her mind. She knew beneath the loose Van Heusen shirt his arms were muscular and his chest defined.

"I'm sorry I'm late," she said. *"I didn't wake up until well after eight this morning. Ruby didn't even wake me up when she left for school."*

Benjamin came up out of his chair and stood near her, his hands pushed deep into the pockets of his trousers. His gaze moved over her face and hair. She wore the rebellious mass down today, with just a gold clip at her crown to hold back the worst of the curls around her face. The thick underside was still damp from her perfunctory shower, and there hadn't been time to fidget with it enough to get it up in a professional style. As fast as she dressed that morning, it was a miracle she managed to put on matching shoes. Her entire body flushed when he touched some of the long tresses behind her ear.

"You were sound asleep when I left," he said in a slow voice. "I was careful not to wake you."

A small shudder danced up Jewell's spine. She shifted to hide the effect of his nearness. Jewell found it harder to breathe in a steady rhythm. Her pulse throbbed at the base of her throat. A trembling hand reached up to cover the spot. The pounding seemed so violent she thought he must be able to see it. If she were anyone else hearing their conversation, she would assume they had spent the night together. They had, but not in the most carnal of ways.

"What time did you leave?" she asked. She was afraid to sign. He would surely see the tremors in her hands if she did.

Benjamin shook his head slowly. His powerful gaze held hers. "After five."

He stepped closer. Jewell's bottom rested on the edge of the desk, and Benjamin stood so close their bodies nearly touched. But not quite. Her knees felt weak. Before she had the chance to rationalize the stupidity of her actions, Jewell reached out and took his tie between her fingers. She smoothed it down his chest and felt his abdominal muscles tense when her knuckles brushed the buttons of his shirt.

Don't do this, Jewell! Don't let this happen! He's your boss. You're kidding yourself.

Jewell ignored the warnings screaming in her mind. With all the strength she could muster, she lifted her chin and met his stare. The smoldering depths of his brown eyes burned deep into her soul.

Benjamin raised his hands and made small signs in the minimal space left between their bodies. When he spoke to her, his fingertip brushed the lapel of her suit jacket.

"Will your boyfriend be upset when he finds out we spent the night together on your couch?"

"Boyfriend?" she asked. Her hands on the edge of the desk were the only things holding her upright.

"Greg Jacobs. The big guy I met at your apartment."

His finger lingered on the fabric of her clothing. Jewell looked down to watch his touch brush her blouse. She was painfully aware of how close his hands were to her breasts. One curl fell forward over her shoulder, and he let it brush the back of his hand.

Jewell drew in a slow breath to ease the burning in her lungs. She shook her head. Benjamin's fingers pushed up into her hair and wrapped around the column of her neck, her copper curls intertwined amongst them. His thumb pressed against the pulse spot beneath her jaw. Her heartbeat pounded against the pressure.

The shrinking space between them drew her gaze. His hips made contact with hers. Gentle pressure pushed her back into the desk's edge. Jewell drew in a sharp breath.

"He's not my boyfriend," she whispered.

His thumb nudged her chin upward. Slight furrows wrinkled his brow, questioning her, and she realized her foolishness. Benjamin couldn't read her lips when she looked down. The extraordinary blaze and glow of his brown eyes looking down at her forced her heart to skip a beat. Her lips parted, and she struggled to keep her thoughts in order. *Was this really happening?*

"He's not my boyfriend," she managed to say again. The volume of her voice was almost indiscernible.

The space closed further. His body settled against hers, and Jewell was acutely, almost painfully, aware of his hard contours.

"He isn't?" An irresistibly devastating grin tugged at his lips and his eyelids lowered as his gaze fell on her lips.

The effect was as tangible and powerful as a caress. She tried to shake her head, but couldn't stand to move away from his touch. Acting practically on its own accord, Jewell's hand moved from the desk's edge to his trim waist. His breath caught and Jewell smiled at the involuntary reaction her touch created in him. It gave her a heady sense of power over a man who was infamous for his intimidation of others. Riding on the euphoria of her newfound ability, Jewell shifted her body against him and watched the muscle jump along his jaw.

"No," she managed to say. "He's my best friend."

"Is there a boyfriend, Jewell?"

"No."

His open mouth covered hers, and her body reacted intensely and immediately. There was no prelude to the kiss. No slow overture to its intensity. Benjamin's hands held her face, and each time his lips moved over hers, their bodies swayed closer together. Jewell had no option, no choice, but to give in to its power without restraint. Their tongues met as a conduit, and thunder arched her body against him.

Jewell wrapped her arms around him, flattening her fingers against the firm muscles of his shoulders, drawing him closer. Benjamin's hands held her head in place with a gentle massage as his tongue parted her lips and plunged inside. His fingers pressed into her scalp. A low purr reverberated in her throat and her stomach tumbled.

The kiss was hungry. Jewell never realized how desperately she craved this, and there was no doubt in the way he held her, and the way his lips demanded her response, that Benjamin had wanted this just as much as she had. All consequences vanished. All logical thought disappeared. He took a hand from her face to grip her hip and yank her hard against him. She couldn't help the small sound that roughened her throat and felt Benjamin's tight moan against her mouth. Jewell heard the scrape of desktop objects across the wooden top as he tipped her back, reclining onto the desk surface.

A soft tap sounded at the door as Benjamin's mouth moved to her throat, just below her jawline. His mouth tugged gently at her skin, and she gasped. Her eyes fluttered, and she threaded her fingers into his hair, holding him against her skin. Then the knock came again, yanking her hard from the moment. With a groan born of frustration, she ran her hands from his shoulders down his arms, and with over-powering regret, curled her fingers around his wrists and pulled back from his touch. His gaze settled on her mouth, his lips open, his breathing as rapid as her own, and his eyes were an even deeper mahogany. Jewell curled her fingers into his shirt, wanting more than anything to pull him back to her.

The knock came again. Benjamin moved to kiss her, and her hand shot up.

"Someone is knocking on my door," she signed.

Benjamin sighed and closed his eyes, letting his forehead rest against hers. He swallowed hard. The pad of his thumb ran across her lower lip, now swollen by the strength of their kiss.

The knock came a third time. "Jewell?" April's voice called through the wood. She sounded miles away through the blood pounding in Jewell's ears.

"April," Jewell mouthed, and Benjamin laid his thumb on her lip as she spoke. He smiled, which immediately made her smile, too. "I'm in Mr. Roth's office," she called out. Her voice cracked and she quickly cleared it. "Come in."

Benjamin stepped back just in time to avoid April seeing him standing so close as she came in through the other office. Jewell ran a quaking hand over her mouth before turning to face the woman, giving her skirt a firm tug. Not daring to look down, she hoped her clothing wasn't mussed and twisted beyond explanation. He sat down in his chair and moved close to the desk.

"What's up, April?" she asked, thankful that her voice didn't give away the jumbling chaos in her stomach and the twittering sensation under her skin. "Sorry, I didn't hear you."

"You left your phone on my desk and you got a call."

"Thank you."

Jewell took the phone April held out and looked at the notifications on the locked screen. Missed call from Garnett. She took a step away from Benjamin's desk, slid her thumb to unlock the phone, and tapped the notification to call him back. He answered before she heard the ringtone.

"Hey, kiddo," her older brother said, already sounding apologetic. "I'm sorry to call you while you're at work, but Mom asked me to find out if you're coming to that family fun night thing at Pearl's school tonight."

"Is that tonight?" Jewell mumbled, still trying to focus on anything but the way she still felt Benjamin touching her, even though he sat several feet away. April had walked around the other side of Benjamin's desk to show him some paperwork, and she spoke in soft tones to keep from interrupting Jewell's conversation. Didn't matter, her attention was miles away from the family fun night.

"Hey, Juls! You there?"

Jewell jumped when her brother shouted her name, and drew both Benjamin's and April's attention. April arched her eyebrows, but Benjamin looked concerned. She shook her head and focused on the conversation. "I'm sorry. I'm distracted. Yes, tell Mama I'll be there. She wanted us at the house for five-thirty, right?"

He hummed in the affirmative. "Ruby is here already. She asked me to pick her up after class because she figured you'd be staying late at work. Has your boss been working you hard?"

Jewell smirked and slid her gaze to Benjamin again. He focused again on what April had to say, so his attention was on her and not Jewell. She cleared her throat. "No, not really. I'll be there on time."

"Okay, Sis. Love you."

"Love you, too."

A snippet of April's conversation with Benjamin reached her as she disconnected the call. "—Mr. Burke. That's all he said," April ended with a shrug and a smile back to Jewell.

In one stuttered beat of her heart, Jewell's smile slipped, and a cold flush swept up her neck to her cheeks. Logically, she knew she had done nothing wrong when it came to Kevin Burke—but logical thinking didn't prevent the sudden ball of lead in her stomach. Burke had made a single point that voided her logical mind—who would people be more likely to believe? Benjamin's eyes shifted from April to her, and he pushed back from his desk, standing. Stepping around April, he came around to where she stood, his gaze never leaving her.

"Traynor wants to talk with me for a bit. It'll give you a chance to catch up on what you missed this morning," he said with a small smirk she knew he meant to be sexy and dismissive of the lead ball in her stomach. "Emails. Memos," he said, but his hands moved in small motions between them. "*A large coffee with three extra shots.*"

It worked because she couldn't help her smile. His smirk spread into a warm smile and he turned back to April, shoving his hands into his pockets. "Tell Mr. Traynor I'm available when he is."

April nodded and headed for the office door. Before Jewell could step away, Benjamin's long fingers wrapped around her wrist. A warm tingle of awareness danced up her arm, and she drew in a metered breath before raising her chin and looking into his face. He smiled slow, making her heart dance.

"We'll pick this up later."

She returned his smile and pulled from his touch, letting her fingertips skim across his before she stepped away. Following April's route, Jewell went through her office, and out the door April had come in. Mr. Traynor stepped toward Benjamin's office door as Jewell came out behind April's desk, and their eyes met as he reached for the knob. He offered Jewell a cryptic smile that she couldn't interpret, and it chipped away once again at the ease Benjamin had tried to instill before she left the office.

Jewell released a slow breath. "I'm going to the break room to see if there's any coffee left. Can I get you anything?"

"Um, actually, I'll walk with you."

April fell into step with Jewell. They didn't say anything until they reached the common break room for the bullpen, and Jewell had poured a cup from the coffee of undeterminable age and sat at one of the tables. She had managed to ignore her exhaustion while in the office with Benjamin, but now—seated—the exhaustion sat on her shoulders and tensed her neck, making it a challenge just to keep her head upright. She poured extra sugar into the cup to counteract the age of the brew, added some creamer, and braced herself as she took the first sip.

"Oh, that's nasty," she groaned, wincing as she set down the cup. "A long cry from Dunkin'."

April had bought a bottled juice from the vending machine in the corner and twisted off the cap with a pop. "You look wiped out."

"I didn't get to sleep until around three," Jewell said, forcing down another swallow of nasty coffee. "And I fell asleep on the couch." *Curled up against your boss.* "Which is why I never heard my alarm."

"It's funny. Mr. Roth was on time, but he looks more exhausted than you."

Jewell just gave a noncommittal hum against the edge of her coffee cup, forcing down more of the sweet sludge. She couldn't take the burn anymore and pushed the cup away. "What did Mr. Traynor want to speak to Mr. Roth about, do you know?"

"Not specifically, no. He came out of Mr. Burke's office just before he came across and said he wanted to see Mr. Roth when he had free time. That was right after you arrived. He just said he wanted to speak to Mr. Roth privately about some concerns Mr. Burke expressed."

"He didn't say what kinds of concerns?"

April tilted her head, studying Jewell. She hid from April's scrutiny behind her mug. It was either drink the coffee or reveal too much on her face. April twisted the cap back on her bottle of juice and set the bottle down with a thunk. She sat back and crossed her arms, pulling her lips together in a pursed scowl.

"What?" Jewell asked.

"What happened yesterday?"

"I don't know—"

"Yes, you do. You know what I mean. I know about the fight with Mr. Roth, but then what? Then Mr. Burke shows up and leaves minutes later looking *pissed*, excuse my French. And you weren't right the rest of the day, Jewell. Then this morning? Maybe it's none of my business, and you can feel free to tell me so, but a *lot* of rumors are flying around here—"

"What kind of rumors?"

"I asked first."

Jewell set down the now empty coffee mug, already feeling an acidic hole burning through her gut, and matched April's position slumped in the chair with her arms crossed. "Okay, fine. When Mr. Burke showed up, he made some…comments," she paused, clearing her throat as heat rose in her cheeks again. "Comments I didn't appreciate, and I told him so."

"Comments about the rumors?"

"You've got to answer *my* question." Now she'd know if Burke lied about the rumors, or if he hadn't lied and Jewel and Benjamin really were the topic of the company rumor mill.

Of course, ironically, the rumors weren't completely untrue after this morning.

"You sure you want to hear the torrid details?"

"I've already heard some from Mr. Burke. Fill in the details for me." Jewell sat forward, linking her hands together on the tabletop. "April, I don't want anything going around that could jeopardize my career here, or Mr. Roth's."

"Fine, but you won't like it."

CHAPTER NINE

With a twist and a tuck, Jewell managed to tame her hair into a french braid, clipping the plait at the base of her skull with the barrette she'd worn at her crown earlier in the day. It wasn't as formal as she usually wore, but after hearing the litany of stories and rumors April had reluctantly shared, she refused to give the horde of gossipmongers any more fuel for their fires. Her hands shook a little as she smoothed her fingers over her hair, wispy tendrils already falling around her face. That's what she got for improvising.

She huffed out a breath and patted a damp towel against her blotchy cheeks. Her face and neck had been in a constant state of flushed since April started talking, leaving her mottled and looking like she'd spent the last fifteen minutes crying.

That wasn't about to happen. She refused to allow Kevin Burke, or anyone else who wanted to listen and propagate his innuendo, to get to her enough to bring tears. She had done *nothing* wrong, *nothing* to be ashamed of, and nothing she would regret.

"Take that, Burke," she mumbled, tossing the clump of wet paper towels in the trash.

She straightened her spine and squared her shoulders, looking at herself once more in the massive wall of mirrors along one wall in the washroom. With a sharp tug to the hem of her jacket, she straightened her suit and took in a slow, calming breath.

"You've hidden out long enough," she told herself, not even caring that she was talking to herself in an empty washroom. With a firm yank on the door handle, she stepped into the hall and headed back toward the bullpen and her office.

Knowing now what stories and tales actually drifted around the office, Jewell felt each glance her way like a poke with a long stick. She held her head high and marched the distance across the wide space to April's desk. April looked up with a compassionate smile, and Jewell knew April felt as bad about telling her as Jewell felt for hearing it.

"Is Mr. Traynor still in with Mr. Roth?" she asked, passing behind April's desk to set her hand on her own office doorknob. April nodded. "Okay, did you reschedule the meeting from yesterday that Mr. Roth missed?"

"Yes, for this afternoon at three."

"Thank you, April."

"Sure," April said with another smile. It didn't help.

Jewell turned the knob and stepped into her office, keeping her eyes diverted from the door leading to Benjamin's office. It was open a crack, and the low murmur of conversation drifted in, but she figured she would draw more attention by closing it than by leaving it as it was. Instead, she went to her desk and turned on her computer, wincing at the telltale twitter as the operating system engaged.

She managed to do a fine job of ignoring the conversation in the next room and made it halfway through her emails before she heard Benjamin's distinctive and firm "No" come through the crack in the door.

Her fingers stilled over her keyboard. She held her breath, despite herself.

Mr. Traynor's voice drifted to her, but still too low for her to decipher. Jewell released the breath she held and thunked her elbow on her desk, resting her forehead in her hand. She thought herself above eavesdropping, but knowing that Kevin Burke had somehow initiated the conversation in the next room made her stomach flutter, and not in a pleasant way. With a shake of her head, Jewell sat up and checked her emails. There was nothing earth-shattering: a company-wide email regarding an upcoming corporate event, an analysis report on recent fluctuations in the NYSE, and a cartoon that had rotated through the company email system twice already.

"Are you telling me I have to comply to Burke's hissy fit?"

Benjamin's raised voice made her jump, and she bit down hard against her knee-jerk reaction. With a hard tap on her mouse, she opened her preferred music app and set the station to a jazzy, Big Band mix. It was something to fill the silence and block out the teasing bits of conversation she both did and didn't want to hear. She opened a file she'd been working on for the last couple of days and decided to focus on reviewing it before the meeting she'd rescheduled for that afternoon. A meeting she and Benjamin should have attended the previous afternoon. It was busy work, but that's exactly what she needed.

Convinced after a full review that the report was as complete and correct as it could possibly be, Jewell pressed print, swiveled in her chair to stand and gasped, nearly losing her balance. Benjamin stood half way between her desk and the door connecting their offices, silently watching her.

She took a steadying breath, demanding her racing heart to slow down. "You startled me, Benjamin."

His smile was slow and sexy and made her flush from her hairline to the collar of her blouse. He crossed the distance to the end of her desk, his hands pushed into the pockets of his trousers. "I'd like to say I'm sorry, but you're beautiful when you blush."

"Not fair." She shook a scolding finger at him. "Saying things like that just makes me blush more."

He grinned. "I know."

Jewell pushed back from her desk and stood, facing him with the corner of the desk between them. His eyes shifted up and he studied her hair, reaching out to stroke his fingertips along the wisps of hair at her brow.

"You put it up."

"I didn't have time this morning."

"Why put it up at all? It's beautiful loose."

"But not very professional." Drawing a slow breath, she looked down, stepped back, and settled into the corner edge of her desk return. Only when she was a safe distance from his touch did she look up again. "I rescheduled the meeting we missed yesterday for today at three."

"April told me. Thank you." Benjamin came around the corner of the desk and stepped toward her, running his fingertips along the desk as he walked. With each step, her heart fluttered faster and she had to fight to keep herself from hyperventilating. "Did you hear any of what Travis said?"

She shook her head, another wave of heat hitting her cheeks. At this rate, her face would spontaneously combust by lunch. "No, I—" She cleared her throat. "I went with April for coffee, then came in here. I didn't hear Mr. Traynor's words, just…I heard you a couple of times."

Benjamin glanced toward the office door leading out to the bullpen and raised his hands. "*Kevin Burke is trying to throw his weight around. He's making assumptions about you stepping beyond your position here.*"

Jewell scowled, flipping her hand to emphasize her confusion. "*Just how am I doing that?*"

"*On your first day here, you asked me if you would be welcome in all meetings with me. Meetings executive assistants usually didn't attend. I told you that you would be welcome because I said you were welcome. Burke is using your attendance as leverage.*"

Despite the nervous nausea that had haunted her all morning, Jewell laughed and shook her head. "Seriously? That's the best he can do?"

Benjamin shrugged. "*He has no grounds for complaint otherwise.*" One corner of his mouth tipped up in a half smile. "*You bruised his manhood. He's grasping at straws.*"

"*How did I bruise his manhood? Because I didn't fall on my knees in front of him?*"

His smile turned into a teasing grin and he winked. "No, you fell on your knees in front of me."

Jewell gasped and dropped her mouth open in feigned shock, pressing her hand to her chest. "Benjamin Prescott Roth, shame on you."

She tapped the back of her fingers against his chest, but he caught her hand before she could pull away, wrapping his fingers around hers. With a gentle tug, he pulled her toward him. She looked down at his hand and forced her breath to be slow and metered as he stroked her knuckles with his thumb. With his other hand, he touched her chin, urging her to look up. His touch was cool, which only confirmed for Jewell how flushed her face had to be.

A deep 'v' dug into his brow as his gaze studied her, his eyes shifting over her features. Jewell swallowed and curled her lips inward between her teeth. Immediately his eyes slid down, focusing on her mouth, and her heartbeat jumped.

"Something occurred to me when Travis brought up Burke and his assumptions," he finally said, ending the silent study.

"What?" she asked, the act of speaking almost painful.

He took a small step closer to her, but not enough for their bodies to touch other than where his hand held hers. "I want to punch Kevin Burke for what he said to you." Jewell shook her head, but he laid his palm along her jaw, stopping her. "He made assumptions. But, I realize I may have done the same thing."

Jewell tipped her head within his touch. "I don't understand."

"I assumed you wouldn't mind if I kissed you." He had dropped his voice low so it carried only between them, and Jewell mentally noted not for the first time that she was impressed with his understanding of tone and volume even when he didn't know his own sound. "I had no right."

Jewell stared at him, her mouth open because she couldn't find anything to say in response. The thumb that rested against her chin shifted to touch her lower lip, skimming back and forth. She let her eyes close, and summoned up enough courage to purse her lips and press them against the tip. The hand holding hers tightened slightly, and she opened her eyes again.

"What do you think you should have done?" she asked.

Benjamin drew his hands from her, and she immediately felt the loss. "*I should have asked.*" He moved in closer to her, leaving little space for signing just as he had before kissing her against the desk. "*Whatever your answer, I will honor it. Jewell, I want to kiss you again. May I?*"

She smiled and nodded slowly, drawing in a breath before his lips pressed to hers. In comparison to the first kiss they'd shared, this one was sedated, but the effect was the same. Jewell's stomach fluttered and tingling danced over her skin. She raised her arms and combed her fingers into his hair, holding his head as he kissed her slow and deep. Each movement of his lips across hers was meticulous and studied, and when his tongue slid along hers, filling her mouth, she couldn't help the small purr in the back of her throat.

He moved his hands from her face to her back, pulling her closer. The long, slow kiss eased into shorter kisses until finally, he drew back enough to look into her eyes.

"I understand now why office romances aren't recommended," he said with a chuckle. Jewell tipped her head and pulled her brows, saying with her expression that he should explain. He kissed her again, a small peck on her lips, before answering. "How am I supposed to focus on your hands when all I can think of are your lips?"

"I'll just have to kick you under the table when I think your attention is wandering."

Benjamin groaned and stepped back, giving her space to breathe and find her balance again. "Then I have a feeling I'm going to have perpetually bruised shins."

Jewell drew in a deep breath, letting the tension ease from her body. She'd let people like Kevin Burke tie her up in knots long enough. Her life was hers. With a smile she hoped affected him as much as his half-grin affected her, she moved past him to the printer situated near their doors for easy access by both of them. The report had finished printing in triplicate, and with a couple of quick staples, they'd be ready for the meeting.

He stood in his spot as she walked past him again, his hands pushed into his pockets. She felt his gaze on her as she picked up her stapler, tapped the papers, and fastened them. Just having him watch her made her skin tingle and her breath catch enough that she had to take another deep breath before turning and handing a copy of the report to him.

"In case you want to take a look at it before the meeting, to make sure I've got everything right." She smirked, unable to control herself. "I wouldn't want you to be surprised by my report."

He returned the smirk, and she knew her gentle jab wasn't lost on him. "I'm sure everything is fine, Ms. Kincaid," he said with an arch of his eyebrow, jabbing right back. "Your work has been impeccable, even if I haven't liked the results."

"Is there anything you need before the meeting?"

He focused on her lips, and she warmed. His shins might be bruised, but she'd have a perpetual fever if he kept looking at her that way. "Just one thing." Jewell arched her eyebrow. His gaze angled to the door leading out to April, then back to her. "Have dinner with me. Friday night."

Jewell grinned. "Do you want to try *Bertucci's* dinner menu?"

He chuckled and took a step closer, enough that she had to hitch up her chin to hold his gaze but still with space between them. "As appealing as that sounds, I was thinking of something a little different. Come to my home. I'll cook."

Benjamin came through the garage door into his kitchen with a heavy step and a tired yawn. He dropped his keys on the counter and worked the knot out of his tie without conscious thought needed for the actions. Nothing in the refrigerator looked appetizing or sufficient to really satisfy his thirst. Settling for a can of soda, Benjamin popped the top and took a long drink.

He looked around the kitchen, his eyes following the natural flow into the connected dining room. Everything was meticulously clean and tastefully decorated. The scent of lemon cleaner hung in the air, indicating the cleaning service had been there that day. Cream-colored carpets and imported tile covered the floors. Copper pots hung from a rack in the ceiling. The canisters and appliances on his countertops each had their specific place.

This townhouse was too big. What did he need with four bedrooms, five bathrooms, and a half dozen other rooms designated by name for some special purpose. The Den. The Library. The Sitting

Room. The Media Room. What did he need with a media room? On nights like this, when not another soul occupied the huge house with him, his silence seemed too quiet. On nights like this, the silence was something beyond the lack of noise. It was the lack of life.

As Benjamin leaned back against the counter, a folded piece of paper on the center island caught his attention. Feeling tired deep down in his bones, Benjamin leaned forward and picked it up. It was probably a note from the housekeeper. A smile spread across his face when he read it. Leaving the half-empty can of soda on the counter, Benjamin bounded up the stairs. He didn't knock on the spare bedroom door but walked right in.

Victoria sat reclined on the bed, an ice pack pressed to her forehead and a box of tissues beside her. Her eyes were swollen and red. Benjamin's good mood at reading Victoria's note plummeted when he saw her. She'd obviously been here alone, crying.

"What's wrong?" he asked as he crossed the room and sat on the edge of the bed beside her.

What tears had dried up before his arrival returned in a full torrent. His little sister's face distorted in a sob, and she held her arms out, begging to be held. Benjamin wrapped her in his arms. Her small body shuddered against him.

When the trembling stopped, he pushed her back and wiped his thumb across her cheek.

"Vicki, what's wrong?"

Her hands shook violently as she signed, but her chin shook worse and reading her lips would have been difficult. "*Everything is so screwed up, Ben. Can I stay with you?*"

He nodded. "Of course. Tell me what's going on."

"*Daddy is trying to dictate my life again. He's even forcing his way into my love life now.*"

Benjamin smirked and shook his head. "That doesn't surprise me at all. I take it he found out about Dillon Ferguson?"

"*Worse than that. Dillon asked me to marry him and Daddy found out.*"

"*Vicki, did you really think Jon would accept Dillon? What were you thinking?*" he signed, using the jerk of his hands to emphasize his point, doubting his voice could.

Benjamin's sister shrugged her shoulders. Black curls bobbed around her head. *"I told Dillon we had to just run off and elope. I knew Daddy would never give his blessing. But Dillon wanted to do it the right way. He came to the house this afternoon to speak to Daddy."*

"So what happened?"

"Daddy had been drinking all afternoon. I tried to catch Dillon before he went in to see him, but I was too late."

A shudder danced over Benjamin's nerves. Several nasty images and scenarios played in his mind. When Jon Roth, alcohol, and bad news came together the result tended to be explosive. As a boy, Benjamin had spent many of his evenings at home hiding in some remote corner of the house. It seemed the very sight of Jon Roth's eldest child was enough to send him into a tirade.

Until his adolescence, Benjamin was almost thankful for the months he spent at Bridlethorpe School for Boys. While away at school he didn't need to worry about what he might do to trigger his father's rage. But as Victoria grew older, Benjamin's concern turned to her. Would she be another target? Fortunately, Victoria didn't seem to inspire the same outrage as Benjamin.

"What happened?" Benjamin asked, not quite sure he wanted to know, but needing to all the same.

"Daddy went crazy! He locked me in my room and kicked Dillon out. Physically removed him from the house. George tried to calm Daddy down, but you have to know it did no good. I snuck out as soon as I could, but I haven't been able to get in touch with Dillon yet."

Benjamin shifted to face away from her. He knew Dillon Ferguson. Dillon was the grandson of George Ferguson, Jon Roth's butler, chauffeur and whatever else he was told to be. No matter how great Dillon might be to Victoria and no matter how much Victoria loved him, he was still the grandson of a chauffeur. He wasn't a member of the "old money only" country club. His name wasn't synonymous with wealth. For those reasons alone, Dillon would be deemed unacceptable. Jonathan Roth wouldn't allow his progeny to marry so low.

Jon had told Benjamin once "You can sleep with whatever trollop you want, just make sure no one knows it. Don't father any bastard kids who could come back to haunt you later. It happens every day. Trust me."

"*You can stay here as long as you need to,*" Benjamin told his sister as he turned back to her. "*Dillon is welcome here as well.*"

Victoria burst into tears again. Benjamin wrapped his arms around her and held her until she fell asleep.

CHAPTER TEN

"In conclusion, it is Bulwark's goal to continue a steady but conservative rate of growth throughout the bear market. If we need to tone down our aggressive approach to investing, it is what we will do to assuage the fears of our shareholders. Capital retention must be our primary objective over the next quarter to complete the year on a highly positive note."

Jewell signed the speech of their CFO, Barry Westmoreland, to Benjamin. Even as the words came from Barry's mouth, Jewell winced. She knew exactly what Benjamin's reaction would be to Westmoreland's conservative approach. Benjamin's eyes darted from her to their CFO, and back again. He shifted in his chair, the leather upholstery squeaking with the movement.

"*Is he kidding*?" Benjamin asked, one eyebrow arched high and his wrist twisting in question.

She shook her head as subtly as possible.

"Does anyone have anything they want to discuss to close out the meeting?" Barry asked.

Jewell relayed the question and saw the answer formulating in Benjamin's eyes. With slow intent, he sat forward and stood up. They sat on Barry's left, several chairs down from the end along the highly polished oak conference table. Fund managers from the various capital management departments took up all the chairs around the table, everyone from international growth to asset retention.

"I want to clarify something," Benjamin said. "This conservative approach will only apply to those funds where it is most prudent, such as retention or income funds. It can't be an across-the-board tactic."

"Oh, great," Kevin Burke mumbled from his slouched position on the other side of the table. "Here we go."

Jewell didn't even acknowledge Burke's huff by glancing in his direction and didn't bother to translate his comments for Benjamin.

"Ben, the shareholders are worried. The Dow is taking more twists and turns than a thrill-ride rollercoaster. We need to take a step back and assuage their fears."

Benjamin shifted his stance. "Barry, that goes against the general principle of mutual fund investing, and a conservative approach contradicts a good portion of our fund objectives, specifically my team. We can't do that without a shareholder proxy vote.

"Every one of the funds I manage quotes an aggressive approach to international or global investing. It's the investors who have multiple holdings in U.S. companies who are concerned. The individuals invested in my funds are, by their very method of investing, taking an aggressive approach. If they have a diversified portfolio, they fully expect some funds to not perform as well. They expect funds like mine to pull their weight and bring up the average."

"If shareholders are concerned about capital loss, they are going to liquidate. We need to preserve our capital," Mr. Westmoreland pointed out.

"And if we don't perform, our top-tier investors are going to liquidate. Shareholders are going to liquidate one way or another. They'll get bad financial advice, or worse yet, no advice at all. Some will panic and some will exchange into bonds or money markets. Hell, some might just liquidate for a trip to Jamaica or the down payment on a house. But capital is going to leave. If we stay aggressive in the funds where it's called for, and come out at the top of the industry, we will not only retain shareholders, but we will gain new investors who are seeking proven growth histories with well established fund companies. Investors choose my funds exactly because they are aggressive, and if I back off on my investment strategies, they're going to leave because we aren't delivering the goods. Playing safe won't get us to the top."

"We need to reassure our investors—" Westmoreland tried to interject, but Benjamin continued.

"How much money came into Bulwark the first quarter after Smart Money named five of our funds as top performers in the industry? How much above projections?"

"I'm not sure, Ben, I don't have—" Westmoreland answered.

"Four-point-three billion. Two-point-seven billion more than projected. The last half of last year sucked. But we stayed aggressive where we needed to. We won over people who might have otherwise been lining up at the bank for CDs. They came to us because we didn't back down. We stayed honest. Why should we now reverse direction?"

"And B.P. Roth takes all the credit," Burke said louder this time, apparently not drawing enough attention the first time. "Ladies and gentlemen, may I present the biggest badass fund manager in all of Boston."

"Burke, that's enough," Westmoreland snapped, glaring at the other fund manager for a brief moment before turning back to Benjamin. His lips formed a tight line beneath the short mustache. "I think we should continue this discussion offline."

Taking that as their cue, the other managers in attendance stood and gathered their notes to leave. Mr. Burke tried to engage one or two other fund managers in conversation. Jewell fought her smile when she saw each of the other managers scowl and step away from him, avoiding his caustic diatribe.

Benjamin stood in his place, his hands deep in the pockets of his slacks. His face was set and he made no move to exit with everyone else. Jewell didn't stand, but remained in her chair by Benjamin's side. She folded her hands and waited.

The two men faced off over the expanse of the table. The tension in the room was tangible and crackled like electricity. The difference in management views between the two was no secret. Jewell had heard other executive assistants discussing the difference of opinion between the men. That, coupled with the strong wills of each man, made for clashes of ego. Westmoreland knew how to run a company, and Benjamin knew how to run a fund. Both men were good at what they did, but that didn't always mean they saw the same solution to the same problem.

Benjamin reached back and touched her shoulder briefly before signing. *"Jewell, go back to the office. I'll be there in a while."*

Benjamin didn't look down as he signed, his stare holding on Westmoreland. Jewell nodded and stood. The motion brought her body within a breath of his. She wanted to touch his hand or brush his arm as a sign of support but didn't dare. Enough rumors were floating about without adding to them.

As Jewell reached the door, Barry Westmoreland rounded the table and headed for Benjamin. He threw down his presentation folder and planted his fists at his nonexistent waist.

"What the hell was that, Roth? How dare you—"

The closing of the heavy wood door shut Mr. Westmoreland's voice off mid-sentence. Jewell paused, her hand resting on the doorknob. She knew there was nothing she could do to help him. Benjamin didn't need her help, or anyone else's. Nonetheless, her heart ached and she wanted to stand beside him. With a sigh, she dropped her hand and turned down the hall.

April was away from her desk when Jewell reached their office. With a glance at her watch, she realized the woman was probably out for lunch. It quickly approached one o'clock, and Jewell's stomach grumbled in a nasty reminder her lunch sat on the kitchen counter at home. She could just go down to the company cafeteria, but couldn't quite bring herself to pay $15.95 for a tuna melt. Maybe she could convince Benjamin to step out for something before they had to be back for market close. After all, it was Friday.

She smiled as she went into Benjamin's office and sank onto the leather couch near his bookshelf. Tonight was their dinner date, the first time they'd spend some time together that wasn't in the office, near the office, or surrounded by people from the office. The idea made her stomach flutter and her pulse jump. She drew in a deep breath through her nose and blew it out through pursed lips. She looked around the office, eventually focusing on his desk. Memories danced in her thoughts and Jewell's pulse sped up with a jolt. She took a deep breath. Just looking at the desk brought an erotic rush to her bloodstream.

Three days had passed since the kiss. It was the most powerful, arousing, fireworks-going-off-and-melt-your-toes kiss Jewell had ever experienced. Followed by the sweetest, most tender kiss...the kiss he asked permission to give.

Neither had spoken of it since then, and he hadn't kissed her again, but his hand skimmed her arm and his gaze held on her enough for her to know none of it was far from his mind. Benjamin seemed distracted Wednesday morning, distant and not very talkative, but whenever she drew his attention away from his thoughts he smiled, and she pushed aside concerns that she was the cause of his distance. He didn't say what was wrong and Jewell didn't ask. Two kisses certainly didn't give her the freedom to pry into things he might or might not want to share. No matter how much she worried, she kept it to herself.

With a shake of her head, Jewell opened the portfolio she'd brought back from the meeting. Clicking out the lead of her pencil, she made some notes to be integrated into her next report. She still sat on the couch when he returned. The door swung open quickly as he entered. With his hand on the knob, Benjamin quickly searched the room and stopped when his eyes fell on her. She smiled at him and raised her hand in greeting as he shut the door. He walked across the floor, his hands deep in his front pockets, and fell onto the couch beside her. She laughed at the theatrical force of the fall. Benjamin slouched and rested his head on the back of the couch, his arm over his eyes.

She let him relax several minutes, listening to the deep resonance of his breathing, before nudging his knee.

He looked at her from beneath a slightly lifted arm. Benjamin's slow, disarming smile created a sweet flutter in Jewell's chest.

"*Is everything okay?*" she asked.

Benjamin waved his hand in dismissal. "*Fine. Westmoreland blew off some steam, I doused his argument, and he gave in. He left me the freedom to run my funds the way I want. The way they're supposed to be run. We go through this about this time every year, especially when the markets are giving us the worst headaches. You just haven't been here long enough to have the pleasure of seeing it."*

"I wish someone had warned me."

Benjamin's shoulders shook with silent laughter. *"What, and take all the fun out of it?"*

She laughed and looked away. Her pulse pounded at her throat as she struggled to keep her breath at a normal pace, but her skin tingled and her breasts ached from his closeness. His aftershave played on her senses like a potent aphrodisiac of pure male pheromones. As inconspicuously as possible, Jewell took in a deep breath through her nostrils and relished in the heady effect.

She jumped and caught her breath when Benjamin twisted on the couch and reclined, barely getting her portfolio out of the way before he settled his head into her lap. He closed his eyes, giving her no means of argument. A subtle smirk rested on his lips. At first, Jewell sat motionless, her arms held up to keep from touching him. Then he rocked his shoulders and his head settled further against her thighs. One eye opened, looked at her, winked, and closed again. Benjamin sighed deeply in contentment.

Jewell smiled and dropped the portfolio to the floor beside the couch. Unable to resist the temptation, she lowered her hands. One rested on his chest, her palm on the soft silk of his tie. The other fulfilled a fantasy she dreamed about for weeks.

Jewell fought down a gasp when her fingers combed through the softness of his hair. She started at his brow and ran her fingernails along his scalp to his crown. The beautiful golden waves wrapped around her fingers and slid over her skin like satin. It was thick and alive, and amazingly sensual.

Benjamin's chest rose and fell beneath her other hand. She smoothed her palm down his tie and continued to caress his hair.

"This is dangerous," he said softly but didn't open his eyes. "But it feels incredible."

She wanted to whisper, "Why is it dangerous?" but the tactic of keeping his eyes closed prevented any further discussion without forcing the issue. That was something Jewell didn't want to do. They both shifted to get more comfortable. Benjamin swung his legs over the arm of the couch and folded his hands across his flat abdomen, and Jewell wiggled deeper into the soft cushions and tilted her body into him.

This felt nice, very nice. So comfortable and natural. They could be sitting in the living room at home rather than in his office. She stroked his hair and hummed softly to herself. Benjamin's hand moved up and covered hers, holding it firmly against his chest. His heartbeat drummed beneath her fingertips. Soon, the rhythm of his breathing slowed and grew deeper. The features of his face relaxed. All tension in his body fell away. Jewell smiled and almost laughed. He was asleep in her lap. How sweet was that? A low sound in the back of his throat worked its way out and Jewell stifled her giggle behind her hand.

She stroked his forehead with her fingertips and followed the chiseled line of his cheekbone. This was a rare opportunity, to examine him in such a relaxed and natural state. In sleep, his countenance lost the harsh sternness that often furrowed his brow. Jewell stroked her hand over his shoulders and down his arms, as she memorized the contours of his muscles through the crisp cotton of his shirt.

"Oh, Benjamin," she whispered to herself. "What am I going to do about you?" Jewell pressed her fingertips against her lips and transferred the kiss to his mouth with a gentle touch.

His hand snapped up and strong fingers gently wrapped around her wrist. Jewell gasped and looked down into deep brown eyes that glowed with a sheen of purpose. Benjamin sat up, not releasing his hold on her wrist. He held her in his stare as he rose off the couch, turned, and knelt one knee into the cushion beside her. She was vaguely aware of the shifting sound of the leather cushions as he moved.

Jewell couldn't breathe. Her heart pounded an erratic and rapid tempo against her ribs. Benjamin's intense look sent waves of warmth over her skin. With her wrist still held captive, she could do little but look up at him and melt beneath his overpowering presence. He touched her cheek with his other hand. The rough pad of his thumb ran across her lower lip and Jewell's eyes fluttered shut.

The revisiting of his lips against hers was the reliving of a sweet dream. He drew her into the kiss without effort, sipping at her mouth with sensual tenderness. A soft moan escaped from the back of her throat and her free hand moved to his side.

They shifted together on the leather couch, their only communication a physical response to each other. The delicious weight of Benjamin's body pressed her back into the soft upholstery. He released her wrist and moved his hands to her hips. With an open mouth, Benjamin's kiss pummeled her body with sensation. The hot tip of his tongue probed persistently, requesting entry. Jewell parted her lips and met his demand. His tongue made a slow entrance to caress her own, stealing her breath as the circuit sparked between them.

Without breaking the contact of their lips, Benjamin shifted her body and nestled his hips against hers. Jewell gasped. Tingling sensations raced over her body.

His tongue probed deeper, demanding an equal response. She could not deny him. Jewell clung to him, spinning out of control, as the kiss deepened.

Her body arched and Jewell pulled back when his hot palm pressed against the bare flesh of her stomach. Shock and sensibility suddenly overtook the sweet sensations of his kiss from a moment ago. Benjamin responded immediately. He pressed his hands into the cushions of the couch and lifted his weight off her. His deep gaze scanned her face, concern and question as evident in them as their rich color.

A flutter danced around her heart. The grip of a steel fist clenched her gut. She opened her mouth to speak, but nothing would come. Jewell curled her fingers into the fabric of his shirt in a desperate attempt to hang on to the delicious pleasure of his nearness.

Benjamin shifted off one arm, the weight of his body increasing slightly. He caressed her cheek with his fingertips and a smile hinted at his lips. He leaned down and pressed a long kiss against her cheek before shifting and standing to his feet.

She immediately felt the loss of his touch. Hot tears burned her eyes, but she choked back the sentiment and sat up, straightening her skirt with a rough jerk. She covered her eyes with her hand and leaned her elbow into her knee. Mortification burned hot in her cheeks.

Benjamin stood near her. She was painfully aware of his presence without even opening her eyes. A nauseating pain shot through her stomach as she wondered what he might be thinking at that moment. Jewell wrapped her arms around her abdomen to ward off the queasiness. It was one thing to let whatever this was develop between them, it was another thing to be so…she didn't even have words.

He sat back down beside her, his feet set apart with his hands clasped together in the space between his knees. She couldn't look at him, too embarrassed by the way she'd responded, here of all places. His office. His couch. The worst part of it was that she didn't want him to stop. She couldn't remember a time when she'd been so…shameless. Her mother certainly had taught her better.

Benjamin reached out and took her hand. His fingers laced between hers and the other covered their linked hands in a gentle squeeze. She could only bring herself to look at the joined fingers. The simple act of holding his hand calmed her nerves and eased the tumultuous fluttering in her stomach. Jewell took a deep breath and lifted her chin to meet his gaze.

He kissed the back of her hand before releasing it. "*I've wanted to kiss you for three days. I didn't anticipate…*" He smiled his slow, sexy smile and paused in his signing to run his fingertip along her jawline. "*I didn't realize how quickly I am capable of losing control with you.*"

"*I was just thinking the same thing,*" she signed with a nervous grin.

"*I'm sorry.*"

"*I can't say I am. I should be, but I'd be lying.*"

His slow, sexy smile sent short bursts of energy through Jewell's bloodstream. Benjamin slapped his hands on his knees and stood, walked to his desk, and turned to lean against the edge. Jewell relaxed back into the couch cushions. The smile meant only for her remained on his lips. A huge part of her wanted to call him back to sit next to her and continue where they left off.

"You should know something before you come tonight," he finally said. "My sister is staying with me. She'll be at the townhouse when you arrive, but I believe she intends to go out with her fiancé."

Jewell smiled and stood, taking a single step closer to him. "That's great. I'd love to meet your sister."

Benjamin reached for her hand, and she let him take it, drawing her closer to him. He touched her cheek with his other fingers, his gaze shifting as he studied her. Something about the way his features softened when he looked at her made her hold her breath.

A soft rap at the office door made her jump. She pointed towards the door and stepped back. They definitely had to find a better place to be alone than an office with people coming and going. That thought in and of itself was a contradiction in propriety. She quickly moved to the chair opposite Benjamin's at the desk.

"Come on in, April," she called as she sat down.

April came in, a package in one hand and a day planner in the other. She sat down in the chair adjacent to Jewell's and Benjamin moved behind his desk. A small smirk tugged at Jewell's lips when she saw him inconspicuously refasten a button on his shirt that must have come undone. The three of them went over phone calls, scheduled meetings, and upcoming projects. Jewell only dared one or two sideways glances in Benjamin's direction, but each time she found him surreptitiously watching her. His sexy smile was ever-present and always succeeded in warming her blood. It would be a very long day.

Victoria sat on the kitchen island and watched Benjamin move around the large space. He set a variety of fresh vegetables on the counter near her and chopped up a head of iceberg lettuce. With a mischievous grin, she stole a baby carrot and popped it in her mouth.

"This must be some hot chick to have you slaving in the kitchen for her," she signed. *"You don't bring out your culinary skills for just anyone. Chicken Parmigiana, fresh garlic bread, homemade pasta, and salad? I hope you took out a good wine."*

Benjamin smirked. "Of course. A delicious merlot."

He chopped and dumped the vegetables into a large glass bowl. His baby sister continued to steal carrots and olives, and he ignored each theft. He thought it was funny, but hid his amusement by keeping his face down. Once the salad was done, he wrapped it and moved on to breading the boneless chicken breasts. After getting everything combined in a glass pan and in the oven, Benjamin sat down on a tall stool and sipped his cola. Victoria was still on her perch on the counter.

"I thought you didn't date women you work with," she pointed out with a wink.

Benjamin wondered how long it would take for her to get to the question. "For Jewell, I think I might make an exception."

Victoria's jaw dropped.

Benjamin raised the hand that held his soda and shrugged. "Don't act so surprised. I said I might, not that I would."

"You already have. I've never known you to see a woman more than three or four times. Most women can't stand your attitude much longer than that. As far as I know, you didn't care if they liked it or not. Are you telling me this woman is special enough to make you change your bachelor ways?"

He smiled and set down his drink. *"She's very special."*

Victoria made a surprised face. *"Is she the one?"* She emphasized 'the one' with over-dramatic movements of her hands and widened her eyes.

Benjamin shook his head. *"You know me, Vicki. I'm incapable of taking care of another human being. Isn't that what Old Jonny Boy always said?"*

"Since when do you believe anything Daddy ever said about you? You didn't listen when you were a kid, why would you listen now?"

He shrugged. His sister was right. Why he let some things his son of a bitch father said get through, while completely ignoring others, was just as much a mystery to him as to his sister. When his father told him he would be lucky if he ever graduated from high school, he pushed himself harder than anyone else and graduated not only with honors but also early. His father called him a deaf-mute and swore he would never function in the real world. Benjamin couldn't change the deaf part, but he worked for years to master speech and lip reading. Jonathan Roth complained Benjamin would be a financial burden for the rest of his life. So, what did Benjamin do? As soon as he graduated high school, he never accepted another dime from his father. He went to college on a full academic scholarship and worked his way through graduate school. It didn't take many years before Benjamin went from living in a one-room studio over a Chinese laundry to a multi-level townhouse in Cambridge.

"You're ten times the man he is, Ben. Don't let him ruin something for you by not letting it happen. You've never opened your heart to love." Her eyes shined with moisture. *"Love can be a salvation. It can save your life."*

He raised his hands and shoulders in a questioning shrug. *"Who's talking love? I just made her dinner."*

"Have you ever cooked for a woman before?"

He shook his head in answer.

"Then I guess there's a first time for everything," she signed with a smirk.

Victoria hopped down from the counter and came to him. She kissed his cheek and Benjamin put his arm around her. Then she ruffled his hair.

"Benny's got a girlfriend."

He shoved her back playfully. "Cut that out."

She stepped back, a smile on her face. *"Sorry. I wouldn't want to mess up your hair before the big date. Dillon is coming by to get me, so we'll be out of here most of the night."*

"How are things with the two of you?" he asked.

"Good, now that we're here. We're thinking about moving to Boston. Dillon's company has a branch office in Newton. They're willing to transfer him if he wants."

Benjamin stood to check on his garlic bread. "That's great. It would be nice to have you closer all the time."

"Really? You wouldn't get sick of me?"

"Of course not. I miss you when you're not here."

Tears shimmered in her eyes, but her smile was warm. With slow emotion, she signed, *"I love you."*

"I love you, too."

He looked down at his sister. She was beautiful. Victoria didn't look like either of his parents. Her dark hair and eyes came from their grandmother on their mother's side. Then again, he didn't look like either Jonathan or Barbara Roth.

"You're the only person in the entire world I love."

She punched his arm lightly. *"Give this Jewell chick a chance. She might pry the words from your fingers."*

The lights over their heads blinked off and on in a quick progression, indicating someone rang the front doorbell. Victoria's head snapped in the general direction.

"Someone is banging on the door," she told him. *"Hard."*

Benjamin dropped his dishtowel on the counter and headed for the door. Even before he reached the front entrance he knew it wasn't Jewell. She wouldn't knock on the door. He also couldn't picture her pushing the doorbell violently enough to make the lights blink so rapidly. The force of impact on the wood vibrated through the knob when he grasped it. As soon as the door opened, Benjamin stumbled back and into the entrance hall.

Only one man possessed the strength, coupled with the testicular fortitude and stupidity, to physically push Benjamin around, and that was Jonathan Roth. He didn't look in Benjamin's direction and shoved past him into the house, yelling down the hall. His mother followed behind with a tight expression on her face. She grabbed Jon's elbow to pull him back, but he jerked free.

"What is going on?" Benjamin demanded.

Victoria rounded the corner, shock on her face. "Daddy?"

"Victoria, what is going on?" Benjamin demanded again.

His father continued to yell. Benjamin saw the redness rise from his collar into his face. Spittle flew from his lips as he raged in the entranceway. Jonathan wagged his finger in the air, pointing at Victoria as he yelled. Only once his accusatory finger came around to Benjamin's face. Benjamin slapped it away. He still didn't know what his father was shouting, but he didn't really care.

The elder Roth turned back on Victoria. Benjamin moved around and pushed his body between them. Victoria stepped behind him and rested her hands on his arms as she found shelter with her big brother. With his arm wrapped behind him and around Victoria's hips, Benjamin shielded her from their father's rage.

"Either calm yourself right now or get the hell out of my house," Benjamin demanded.

His father's face flamed red and his mouth clamped shut. Large fists doubled at his side.

"Get out of my way. She's my daughter and I intend to bring this stupidity to an end. I'll be dead before I let her whore around with some no-good gold-digger like Dillon Ferguson."

The rancid stench of alcohol assaulted Benjamin's senses as his father shouted just inches from his face. He fought back the initial revulsion and turned away for a split second to recollect his senses. Victoria shouted something over Benjamin's shoulder at her father, but Benjamin couldn't read her lips to know what it was. Without a doubt, it was retaliation to their father's ignorant classification of her fiancé.

"She's a grown woman," Benjamin added.

"How dare you think you can hide her from me. Who the hell do you think you are? You have no right to interfere!"

"I have the right and duty to protect her," Benjamin snapped, the heat of anger pounding in his temples. "She's my sister."

"You are nothing to this family," Jon Roth spit out. "Haven't you figured that out yet? Or are you too stupid?"

Despite the walls he'd built over the years, his father's stinging words hit him harder than Benjamin ever expected. He bit back the rage and clenched his fists at his side. His lungs burned and his ears pounded.

"Get out of my house," he demanded.

"Listen to me, you little asshole. You have done nothing but make this family look bad your entire life. You've defied every rule I've ever put down. You're a disgrace. I will not allow you to drag my daughter down with you."

Victoria stepped around him and pressed her hands into both men's chests. Benjamin breathed deeply through his nose to keep his adrenaline rush in check. His sister looked from their father to him.

"*Stop it.*" She signed and spoke at the same time. "*Daddy, stop it. How can you say such ugly things? About Dillon or Benjamin. He's your son.*"

"Since the day he was born—"

"Since the day I was born I was deaf. Imperfect. Isn't that the real problem?"

In an instant Benjamin was thirteen again, rebelling against his father's iron fist and underlying revulsion for his own son. Even now, despite Benjamin's height and build, his father stood taller than he.

When he was thirteen, his father was a frightening, oppressive force. At thirty-six, Benjamin refused to be intimidated. Despite his resolve, cold memories flashed in his mind like fireworks.

Everything came back to him in a vicious burst. His father refused to learn Sign because he said it was the coward's way out. If Benjamin wanted to function in the real world, he had to get off his ass and not ask anyone to coddle and accommodate him. Even when he learned to speak, and could communicate with those around him, Benjamin was considered less than acceptable by his father.

Benjamin hadn't been allowed to be alone with his infant sister because his father said he was untrustworthy and incompetent to care for a small child. The sickening pain of seeing his mother say he was better off at the boarding school hit him once again, feeling just as horrible as it did nearly thirty years before.

Jonathan Roth continued to yell, his fists waving before Benjamin's face. He only caught some of the words now, his mental state unfocused on the outburst. The hazy edges of the room lost focus and disappeared in a red miasma of anger, rage, and pain. Benjamin shook his head and shot his hands up in a sign of frustration. Chaos happened around him. No matter how he tried, he couldn't keep up with the three fighting people.

"Stop it" he yelled, bringing up his hands in front of his father's face. "I don't know what you're saying."

His father swung around on him, his face inches away. "You worthless, useless waste. Isn't it bad enough you've ruined your life, and mine, that you have to drag Victoria along with you?"

Benjamin looked from his father's red, infuriated face to the ragged, strained face of his mother. Barbara Roth yanked again on her husband's arm.

"Jon, stop this. You said we were coming here to talk. What are you going to accomplish by calling Benjamin names and dragging your daughter out by force?"

Jon Roth shot a vicious, seething look at his wife.

"Shut up, Barbara. Stay out of this."

"I won't. These are my children."

"That's right, Barbara. Your children. You can't deal with them, so leave it to me." He pushed his wife back.

Benjamin forced his father's grip of steel from his mother's arm. He was one man, but he did his best to protect both his sister and mother from Jon's physical abuse. With his shoulder, he pushed his father away. The disgusting odor of the alcohol his father had consumed before coming here wafted in the air to churn his stomach. Victoria's small hands clutched the back of his shirt.

His mother pushed his hands away. Benjamin's first reaction was shock at her rejection of his help. Barbara Roth's eyes flicked up for just a split second to meet his before turning away completely. She crossed her arms over her body and closed her eyes. Heaviness slammed into his chest and shoved him back like an invisible fist.

What had he done, besides being imperfect at birth, to deserve the absolute hatred of the two people who parented him? He covered his face with his hands, attempting to block out the turmoil erupting around him.

Then Jewell was there. Her hands were on him, pushing him back from the melee. Dainty fingers wrapped around his wrists and uncovered his face. Brilliant emerald eyes looked up at him. Concern and shock registered in her delicate features.

"Benjamin?"

His father's arm shot between them and he shoved Jewell. She stumbled back and bumped the hall table. A ceramic vase tumbled and fell to the floor. Pieces shattered in all directions. Jon's forearm slammed into Benjamin's chest and heaved him back against the wall, his arm pressing against Ben's throat.

Enraged, Benjamin pushed back. Hard. His father stumbled and grabbed the still-open door for support to keep from falling down the front stoop. Barbara Roth jumped forward.

"Don't," she shouted with a dramatic flare of her hand.

Benjamin caught what she said, but chose not to respond. He moved past his father's hulking form to Jewell and took her hand to draw her away from the wall. Not looking in his parent's direction, he reached back for his sister. With a woman's hand in each of his own, Benjamin walked away. He didn't care if his parents left or if they stayed. They could continue to yell all they wanted. No longer were they worth his time.

"Get out of my house before I call the police," he said, not even bothering to look back over his shoulder.

The three reached the den. With emotional exhaustion dragging at his limbs, Benjamin shut the door and leaned his forehead into the smooth wood. Gentle hands touched his back, and instinctively he knew it was Jewell. Warmth rested where her hands touched. Benjamin turned and wrapped her in his arms, burying his face into her auburn hair. It smelled of fruit and flowers and Jewell. She held him as tightly as he needed, and he needed her embrace more than anything he had ever needed in his life.

That son of a bitch! His father could have hurt Jewell and he didn't even know who she was. All Jonathan Roth knew was her presence in his son's house, which translated into the demeaning of her value in his eyes. Nothing mattered but appearances outside the walls and in public. But inside…

Benjamin pressed his lips quickly against her cheek and pulled back. Her verdant gaze searched his face, the brightness of her eyes asking a thousand questions in one moment. Two deep lines of concern appeared across her delicate brow.

He cradled her face in his hands, tried to smile, and looked beyond her to Victoria. His sister stood near the window, looking out. Moisture glistened on her cheeks and she held a tissue to her lips. As he watched, she sank into a chair and rested her head against the high back. How much more chaos could Jonathan Roth create? Benjamin looked back to Jewell.

"Are you okay?" he asked. "Did he hurt you?"

Jewell shook her head within his grasp. "No. Benjamin, what is going on? Was that your father?"

He nodded, ashamed to admit a link to the man, though it was only biological. "I'm sorry you had to be here for any of that. I never expected him to show up here."

Victoria stood and walked to them. "*They left. I watched them get in their car.*"

Benjamin pulled his sister against his side and kissed her forehead.

"When there was no one left to fight, it wasn't worth sticking around." He stepped back from both women and sighed. *This isn't the way I wanted it. Jewell, this is my sister Victoria. Victoria, this is Jewell Kincaid.*

Both Victoria and Jewell smiled and exchanged brief greetings between them. Then both snapped their heads around to look towards the door leading to the hall. Victoria turned back.

"There's someone at the door. It might be Dillon."

Benjamin signed for them both to stay put and headed back out. He highly doubted his father would come back to continue the fight, but would rather be safe than sorry. There was no need for either Jewell or Victoria to deal with Jon's arrogance and antagonism again. The light in the hall blinked slowly, indicating a more rational suppression of the button outside.

Benjamin stepped on the broken vase in the hall, feeling it crunch beneath the soles of his shoes, and opened the door. Dillon Ferguson stood outside, a wide smile on his face. As soon as he took in the state of the front hall, and most likely the dark expression on Benjamin's face, his smile faded.

"What's wrong?" Dillon asked.

Benjamin motioned his sister's fiancé into the house. With a glance up and down the street to look for his parent's white BMW, he shut the door. He kicked some of the vase against the wall. Dillon looked down and moved some of the pottery with the toe of his shoe. Confusion pulled his eyebrows together when he looked back at Benjamin.

"Victoria is in the den. Our parents were just here."

"Oh, shit."

Benjamin nodded, agreeing with Dillon's sentiment. Victoria came out the den door and jumped into Dillon's arms. The tall, dark-haired man Benjamin had known since childhood embraced Victoria and kissed her hair. He saw them speaking but didn't attempt to under-stand any of it. Jewell now stood in the doorway of the den and watched. Her face still read of concern and alarm.

"You two go. Get out of this house for a while. Try to enjoy the rest of the night," Benjamin told them.

Victoria wiped again at her cheeks and nodded. "Yes, okay. Ben, I'm sorry for causing so much trouble."

He shook his head and held up his hand. "No. That bastard caused the trouble, Vicki, not you."

Her eyes were sad and angry, but she gave him a watery smile and nodded. Victoria stepped away from Dillon and turned to Jewell, squeezing her hand.

"I'm sorry you walked in on our dysfunctional family. Trouble seems to follow us everywhere. Don't let it discourage you."

Jewell shook her head and touched his sister's arm. Victoria and Dillon joined hands and headed for the door. Benjamin released a long sigh and crossed his arms over his chest as the door shut behind them. The shattered vase shouted out a violent reminder of the hostile pandemonium that followed his father like a plague of pestilence. Deep gouges now scarred the high polish of his hardwood floor. He closed his eyes and leaned into the wall. His fingers pinched the bridge of his nose in an attempt to ward off the growing headache behind his eyes.

This wasn't exactly the way he thought the evening would go. Benjamin hoped for something more along the lines of a short dinner and a quick exit to the living room couch. Holding Jewell in his arms for three, four, or twenty-four, hours would do wonders to elevate his mood.

Thinking of her, he opened his eyes, surprised to see Jewell crouched near the door with a hand broom and dustpan in hand. She balanced on the balls of her feet and swept the bits of broken pottery into the pan.

He stepped forward and stooped down beside her. *"I'll get this,"* he signed and took the half-full dustpan from her.

"I broke it. I'll clean it up."

A jolt of anger pummeled him and he grabbed at the dustpan. "You had nothing to do with it," he said through a clenched jaw.

Her expression darkened and he saw moisture build in her brilliant green eyes. It just fed the anger smoldering inside. His father was such an asshole the effects of his rampages lingered even when he was gone. Anyone and anything that brought tears to those beautiful eyes deserved to be hurt the same way. Whether it was him, his father, or anyone else. For Jewell's sake, he bit back the anger and circled his fist on his chest in apology.

She nodded and gave his hand a quick squeeze. Jewell refused to give him the broom, but brushed it across the floor and added the final remnants to those in the pan as he held it. With all bits off the hardwood, she allowed him to take the small whisk. Benjamin indicated with a tilt of his head for her to follow him into the kitchen. Once there, he dumped the trash into his compactor and hung the items back in the small closet where Jewell had found them.

When he turned back, Jewell stood near the sink, her hand resting on the counter edge. She'd left her hair loose except for two narrow braids she'd pulled back from her temples to clip at her crown. On any other woman, the dark brown of her v-neck sweater might seem plain. On Jewell, it deepened the auburn of her hair and accentuated her pale skin and freckles. He indulged in a few moments of just looking at her.

"Dinner smells wonderful," she signed, rubbing her hand over her stomach.

"It's Chicken Parmigiana. Do you like Italian?"

Jewell nodded. He opened a cupboard door to take down two plates and two wine glasses. She moved to his side and pressed her palm against his shoulder blade. Despite his attempt to hide his immediate physical reaction to her contact, Benjamin sucked in a short breath. The tenderness of her touch was near unbearable. It set him off balance. He dared a look over his shoulder at her.

"Benjamin."

His name on her lips, the way they pursed and wrapped around the word, grabbed his gut like a fist. Benjamin let his gaze wander over the delicate planes of her features. Small, scant freckles danced across the bridge of her dainty nose. Her eyelashes were dark and thick, with the slightest whisper of an auburn tint at the end of each. He laid his palm against her cheek and rubbed the pad of his thumb across the soft skin.

"Benjamin, do you want to tell me about what happened earlier?" she asked. Her face expressed the tentativeness her hands could not. *"The things your father said were horrible."*

"Not tonight," he said, not wanting to take his hand away from her cheek long enough to sign. "I want to spend the evening with you. Is that okay?"

She nodded and smiled. The smile was accepting, reassuring, and sincere. Her palm moved up and down his arm. Needing to hold her, Benjamin turned and pulled her against him. Responsive to his touch, Jewell's arms circled his neck, their bodies aligned from knee to chest.

She tasted so damn sweet!

He pressed his hands against her back and pulled her against him as close as possible. Jewell's body was pliant against him. Benjamin's lips parted hers in a desperate hunger and searching massage. Monday morning he would worry about the consequences. Tonight he needed to hold her and forget.

CHAPTER ELEVEN

"Mom sent me out with a sweater for you," Garnett said as he walked across their parents' backyard.

Jewell sat in the A-frame swing in a corner of the yard. She smiled as her brother approached and scooted to the end of the seat to give him room. A crisp autumn breeze stirred the dry leaves littering the lawn and the scent of earth and rain hung heavy in the air. October was halfway gone and November was just around the corner. It was Jewell's favorite time of the year.

Garnett sat down and wrapped the bulky sweater around her shoulders as she slipped her arms into the big sleeves. Jewell smiled as the comforting scent of pipe tobacco and cologne coming from her father's sweater wrapped around her heart and warmed it as surely as the wool warmed her arms. A hundred wonderful memories came back to her in an instant, all triggered by the smell of Daddy. Sweet emotion tightened her throat and Jewell wrapped the rough wool close to her chin. Her brother's arm moved around her shoulders and squeezed gently, and Jewell let her head fall against him.

"Are you okay?" he asked, a concerned, questioning tone in his voice. "All day you've seemed quiet. Is there something bothering you?"

Jewell sighed. No one in the world knew her like Garnett did. From the first day she walked into the Kincaid home he assumed the position of big brother in full force. The first few months, when she woke during the night crying, he came to her, told her stories, and stroked her hair until she fell asleep again. He told her nothing bad would ever happen to her again because Mama and Daddy loved her. Their love was special, and that made her special. For a long time, it was just Jewell and Garnett.

"Garnett, do you remember much before coming here?"

"You mean before I was adopted?"

She nodded.

"Some. Not much. Just some quick images and feelings more than anything else."

"Do you remember your parents?" It was his turn to nod. "What do you remember about them?"

Garnett looked off across the yard to the tree house they built in the oak tree. Small smile wrinkles formed at the corners of his eyes. "I remember going to a Red Sox game at Fenway Park. My dad bought me a foot-long hot dog and nachos. We were on the third base line and he caught a foul ball for me.

"I remember my mom tucking me into bed at night. She always kissed my forehead, then my cheeks, then my nose. We'd say our prayers together and she'd sing to me before leaving. And she smelled like roses. Just little memories like that. I remember feeling empty and black inside until the social worker brought me to this house." In emphasis, he nodded toward the large farmhouse they all grew up in.

The sway of the swing soothed Jewell like the rocking of a cradle. Her brother's embrace made her feel safe and at ease. Jewell smiled when she saw her mother's face peek through the kitchen curtain to check if she wore her sweater.

"Do you remember anything?" Garnett asked in turn.

"Nothing like you remember, no. I never lived with my mother. I have no memory of her at all. All I remember was moving. Leaving one foster home for another. Lots of faces, but no names. The first really clear memory I have is the day I came here.

"I was scared. I was always scared when I went to a new place. But the lady who brought me told me I wouldn't move again. I don't think I believed her. Then we came into the foyer and I was amazed at the size of the house. It seemed huge to me. And Daddy seemed even bigger. He picked me up and hugged me so tight." Jewell's throat constricted around the powerful emotion the memory created. "He called me Pipsqueak and his beard tickled my cheek. His jacket was rough, but it smelled so good. Then Mama held me, and she was so soft and warm. It was the first time in my life I ever understood what love felt like. I didn't have a name for it then, but it wrapped around me and made me feel safe."

Garnett kissed her temple. "What got you thinking about this? It seems like more than just recalling old memories."

She nodded slowly. "It's Benjamin. I witnessed something at his house Friday night. Ever since, I haven't been able to stop thinking about it."

"What happened?"

"I was walking up the front walk and all I could hear was yelling and screaming. It was Benjamin's parents. His father called him all kinds of horrible names. Said terrible, terrible things. He wasn't signing, just yelling. And Benjamin's mother just stood there, doing very little to stop any of it. Benjamin tried to tell him he didn't understand. His sister was there and the man kept calling her a little whore and as stupid as her brother." Tears choked Jewell's words.

Garnett's arm tightened around her shoulder in comfort. She wiped at the tears as they cooled on her cheeks. With a shaky breath, she continued.

"I have never seen anything in anyone before like the pain I saw in Benjamin's face. He puts up walls. I knew that the moment I met him. Once in a while, I think the real Benjamin sneaks through. But that night..." She couldn't continue, the massive emotions in her throat choked out all speech.

Hot tears burned her eyes and she wiped them away with a vicious hatred for the words that had caused Benjamin pain and hatred for her inability to make it go away. Her heart ached for him. She wanted so much to give him the comfort he needed but didn't know how.

Partially because she somehow knew he wouldn't admit to it in the first place.

"What happened?" Garnett asked in a soft, gentle tone.

Jewell reined in her emotion and took a fortifying breath. As best she could, she described the events of the evening. Everything from the shove that broke the vase, to his father's attempt to choke Benjamin against the wall. Because it was Garnett, and they had always been close, she told him about the desperation and need she felt when he embraced her. He held her until her lungs burned to breathe.

When Benjamin kissed her, there was something in the intimate caress that hadn't been there previously. Jewell sensed need, anguish, and desperation in the way he devoured her mouth with rough intensity. His fingers pressed into her skin so hard, trying to bring her closer to him, the flesh showed slight bruises the next morning. But Jewell didn't begrudge the faint marks. His embrace was so powerful, that she wondered if he would ever let go.

"You never said there was something going on between the two of you," Garnett stated.

Jewell shrugged and sighed. "I don't know if there is or isn't. I'm still trying to figure that part out."

"Sounds like it's more than just working together."

Jewell's cheeks warmed despite the cool evening air, and she avoided meeting her brother's gaze. She'd already told Greg about the kisses in the office and the dinner he made for her, and he'd reminded her of his opinion on work romances.

Don't go there. Ever.

She never *intended* it to happen, it just did.

"Jewell..."

"We've kissed. We've spent some time together. If that constitutes 'something going on', then I guess there is," she finally admitted, glancing sideways at Garnett.

He was silent for a few moments. She studied the fraying edge of her father's sweater sleeve, toying with the worn strings, waiting for him to say something. Finally, he chuckled. "I'll probably get in trouble, but I know a little secret about the two of you."

Jewell looked up at him and arched one eyebrow.

"Ruby told me something she saw," Garnett finally offered.

"Ruby? Something she saw?"

"She said she got up earlier this week and saw you and Benjamin on the couch. Apparently asleep. Looked like you'd been there all night, she said. She hid in the kitchen when she saw him get up."

Jewell slouched down in the swing and crossed her arms over her body. Her face warmed, and she hoped Garnett would attribute the color to the cool wind blowing across the yard.

"He showed up at the apartment around midnight. For weeks he had been acting like a jerk in the office. It kind of came to a head that day and I kinda told him off. Benjamin left the office and was gone the rest of the day. He said he wanted to apologize for the way he acted. It was strange because I assumed he came to fire me."

"So he stayed all night?"

"We just started talking. He saw a photo album on the table and looked at it. Things like that. We fell asleep, or at least, I fell asleep. When I woke up the next morning, very late I might add, he wasn't there."

"Ruby said he kissed you before he left. She saw him fix the pillows, cover you with an afghan, and kiss your cheek before sneaking out."

Jewell's heart nearly burst and new tears rushed to her eyes. They were no longer tears of anger or sadness. What a precious, utterly sweet thing for him to do!

"Really?" she managed to whisper.

Garnett smiled and nodded. "That's what Ruby said. I don't see any reason for her to make it up."

They fell into a comfortable silence as the swing rocked brother and sister back and forth. The dry leaves on the ground swirled up in miniature twisters as the evening breeze swept through the yard. The dry rustle was a soothing song.

"Do you think you love him?"

"That's a hell of a question."

"That's no answer."

She looked at her brother and smiled at the curious twinkle in his dark eyes. Jewell knew she could hide nothing from him. Finally, she nodded. "I think I could."

"How does he feel?"

"We haven't talked about it."

"Have you been intimate?"

Her face burned hotter. Jewell folded her hands together and squeezed them between her knees. "No. Honestly, Garnett, just two or three kisses. He has been a complete gentleman."

"So, what are you going to do about it?"

"You're pushy this evening." Jewell jumped off the swing and stepped away across the lawn. Her leather boots scuffed on the damp grass. "You're not going to lecture me about getting involved with someone at work?"

"You mean your *boss*."

She kept her head down, shuffling her boots in the leaves.

"Kiddo, if the two of you fall in love, then that's it. Nothing is going to make him love you if he doesn't, or make you not love him if you do."

"Oh, that is *so* encouraging. Thank you."

Garnett stood and wrapped her in his arms. Jewell willingly gave in to the embrace and let her head fall on his shoulder. He smoothed and kissed her hair and rocked her gently. The back screen door opened and shut with a loud bang. They both looked to see Pearl running across the yard dressed in a fairy princess costume. Silver gossamer wings flapped behind her and taffeta petals in multiple pastel shades danced around her legs.

"Garnett! Jewell!" she called as she ran, magic wand high in the air. Her speech had improved so much in the last couple of years. She tucked the wand under her arm to sign. "*Look at my costume. Mama just finished it.*"

They pulled their sister into their embrace, and she looked up with glowing cheeks and twinkling eyes. With a smile the size of Texas, Pearl showed them each little detail and nuance their mother lovingly put into the costume. She took Garnett's hands and tugged him toward the house.

"*Come on,*" Pearl begged with a curl of her hand. "*Mama just took some pumpkin chocolate chip cookies out of the oven. Let's get them while they're all hot and gooey."*

They both chuckled and followed the fair-haired fairy into the house where the enticing aroma of cookies and gingerbread met them at the door. With autumn came her mother's need to bake, anything and everything. From now through Christmas, the house would be in a perpetual state of chaos and mouthwatering scents of cookies, pies, breads, and cakes. More than they could eat in a year, and many ended up going to the church for a homeless outreach program. Whether they ate them, or not, she welcomed the memories that came with each inhale.

She looked at her mother, who bent to take another sheet of cookies from the oven. Pearl stood nearby, a wide grin on her face with melted chocolate clumps on each cheek. The soft thud of boots sounded in the hall from the foyer and her father entered the kitchen, his pipe in one hand and a newspaper tucked under his other arm. He smiled and crossed the kitchen first to her mother, kissing her cheek as she slid the cookies off the sheet, and stole a fairly cooled cookie as he turned.

"Hey, Pipsqueak," her father said around the cookie in his mouth and kissed her forehead. The fresh aroma of his pipe wafted around her.

"I wonder what Benjamin's memories are like..." she mumbled, more to herself than anyone else.

Garnett looked at her, his cheek rounded with the pumpkin cookie he'd shoved in his mouth. "You say something?"

Jewell shook her head. "No, I was just thinking."

Her childhood memories were clouded and dark, and the warmth and love of this house—this kitchen—had washed them all away. Benjamin wasn't a child, but she wondered if maybe she could share some of the peace this family had brought to her. She was halfway down the hall to the front door before her father called after her.

Jewell stopped and swiveled back, smiling at her dad. "I'll be back soon."

Benjamin caught sight of his sister in the kitchen as he hit the bottom of the stairs into the front hallway. He was about to say her name when she spoke to someone on the other side of the kitchen, her lips spreading in a wide smile. He assumed Dillon had come by, so walked past the kitchen entryway, letting them have some time to themselves. Two steps from his study, small hands curled around his arm, stopping him.

He looked down at his sister, immediately returning her smile. She tugged on his arm, drawing him back toward the kitchen. "Come on. I was just going to go find you."

"Why?"

She just smiled wider and took his hand, pulling him to the kitchen. He didn't understand why until he rounded the corner and stopped short. Jewell stood on the other side of the kitchen, the center island between them, beautiful with her loose hair windblown and a soft blush in her cheeks.

She raised a hand in a small wave. "*Hi.*"

"*Hi,*" he waved back, rounding the island. "*When did you get here?*"

"*Just a few minutes ago. Victoria and I were talking.*" Her gaze shifted past him to Victoria before looking up at him again.

Benjamin leaned forward to hold her cheeks in his hands and kiss her. Just a brief touch, but a jolt of awareness hit him at the contact, and he immediately wanted more. He realized on one level that in any other relationship he'd had, he'd be more than annoyed at the surprise, uninvited intrusion. But beyond the fact that he was surprised to see her on a Sunday afternoon, he was far from annoyed. He rubbed his lips together as he pulled back, running his tongue across his lower lip.

"Chocolate?"

Jewell grinned and nodded. "My mom has been baking. Pumpkin chocolate chip cookies."

"Did you bring me any?" he teased.

She pulled her lower lip between her teeth and raised her hands. "*Actually…*" She stilled her signs, giving him a smile that made his blood warm beneath his skin. "*That's kind of what I came about.*"

"Cookies?"

"Cookies. And pie. And raw apple brownies," she said, ticking off each item on a fingertip. Benjamin raised an eyebrow and she paused, gifting him with a flirty smile that warmed his insides. *"Every year at the beginning of October my mother starts baking, it's like a compulsion for her, and she's already in full force. I wondered if you'd like to come with me, to Manchester, and help with the sampling of the goods."*

Benjamin took a step back and pushed his hands into his pockets. The warmth that had stirred in his chest instantly went cold and tension pulled across his shoulders. Her smile slipped, and Benjamin looked down to save himself the self-resentment at being the cause. He shifted back to lean on the edge of the center island, his feet in front of him. They were nearly toe to toe, his white sneakers and her brown leather boots. She shifted her feet, adding a few inches between his toes and hers, and touched his arm. Benjamin swallowed and raised his head.

Her smile was back, but it wasn't as open and easy. She took her hand from his arm and signed as she shook her head. *"It was just a thought. You don't have to, especially if you don't want to—"*

He pulled his hand from his pocket and wrapped his fingers around hers, stilling her excuse. "Why did you want me to come?"

Jewell tilted her head, her gaze shifting away a moment before returning to him. "I thought you might enjoy an afternoon of—"

"Family?"

Jewell shrugged. "Among other things." She tilted her head the other way, the smile almost gone. Her expression wasn't angry, wasn't hurt, but almost neutral. She worked hard to mask whatever her true feelings were over his questions. "Benjamin, I'm not trying to push something on you. And I promise I won't be angry if you don't go. I'll be disappointed, but not angry. I'm spending the day with my family, and thought it would be nice if you were there with me." The smile came back, and some of the tension in his chest eased.

His gut reaction was to flinch away from the idea of spending time with a family like Jewell's. Beyond Ruby, he hadn't met any, but he'd heard enough to know they were the polar opposite of the Roths. Before he could form a response—in truth, an excuse—she stepped to him and raised her arms, wrapping them around his shoulders in an embrace. Never even thinking to resist, Benjamin returned the hug. She kissed his cheek and stepped back.

"I'll see you tomorrow."

Benjamin just nodded, hating himself for being thankful that she hadn't forced him to explain or to make up unbelievable reasons. She squeezed his hand and walked past him to leave the kitchen. He crossed his arms and let his chin drop toward his chest, drawing a deep breath. He jumped and jerked when Victoria slapped his arm.

"What?" he snapped, stepping back when she raised her hand to hit him again.

"Why are you being stupid?"

"What are you talking about, Victoria?" She swung at him with a potholder, but he dodged it and moved around behind the island, putting it between them. *"Stop."*

"Why didn't you go with her," she demanded, holding the potholder aloft like a weapon. "She drove here from Manchester to ask you to come with her. Manchester," she repeated, opening her arms wide in an expression of the immeasurable distance she apparently believed it to be between Manchester and Boston. "She cared enough about you to come down here for *you*." She chucked the potholder at him, and he caught it as it bounced off his chest, before it landed on the floor.

"She doesn't want me with her family—" He didn't finish, barely catching the wooden spoon she threw at him. "Vicki, stop." An apple from the basket on the island flew by his head. "Vicki!" he shouted.

"I'll stop when you stop being stupid."

"You know as well as I do that—" An orange bounced off his chest. "Stop throwing things and let me finish."

"I'll stop when you stop being stupid."

"You said that already." She grabbed the last apple from the fruit basket and drew it back by her ear, ready to throw it straight at his head. Benjamin raised his hands, blocking his face. "Okay, okay."

"Will you listen?" He nodded and she lowered the fruit, scowling at him. Just as quickly, the scowl faded to a sad, strained frown. "Ben, please…please don't let him mess this up for you. She saw him, she saw how angry he was, and she still came here today for you. He didn't scare her away, don't you do it."

Benjamin set his hands on the edge of the counter and dropped his head forward, closing his eyes. His knee-jerk reaction had been to pull back, but only because it had been a split second faster than his gut reaction to say yes and go. He felt Victoria's presence beside him just before she covered one of his hands with hers and slid her other hand across his shoulders. She leaned her cheek against his upper arm. He opened his eyes and looked down at his younger sister, and she offered a small smile.

"Please, Ben," she said, her lip quivering with the words. Tears welled in her eyes. She kissed his sleeve. "Go on. Have a good time. Eat a cookie, or twelve, for me."

Part of him wanted to argue more, but he chose instead to let it go. He kissed his sister's forehead and stepped back, taking his phone from his pocket. A minute later, he'd texted Jewell and asked her to come back for him. He still had a niggling sensation of doubt when he walked down the hall and pulled a jacket from the front closet, but he pushed it down and shoved it away before he shut the door.

Benjamin and Jewell came together at the hood of her car and joined hands. "I warn you. Chaos reigns in the Kincaid household," Jewell said, smiling up at him.

"Somehow that sounds strangely appealing."

Jewell's smile widened. She linked her fingers through his and they walked together to the door of the large farmhouse.

The substantial home was painted pale yellow with cream trim and a deep farmer's porch encompassed three sides, with a closed ceiling and large pillars supporting the roof. Along the outside of the porch were the brown skeletons of many shrubs and bushes, now bare with the approach of winter. Benjamin guessed the house to be at least a century old. The home had been well maintained but retained its old-fashioned appeal. Shutters framed each window, and the detail committed to the wood cornices and eaves was a testament to the builders. Benjamin sensed warmth, family, and an invitation to enter. All things he never felt in the Roth mausoleum in Hartford.

They ascended the four wooden steps to the interior of the porch. Beside the door sat two wicker chairs with a wrought iron table between them. Further down the porch, a two-person swing hung from chains anchored in the beams above it. A pink and black soccer ball hid partially beneath one of the chairs. The wood was littered with brown, crisp leaves from the surrounding trees, and a jack-o-lantern in preparation for Halloween sat on the other side of the door.

The interior door was open and Benjamin looked through the screen into the foyer beyond it. Benjamin inhaled the appetizing aroma of vanilla, nutmeg, and cinnamon drifted to them through the mesh.

Jewell pulled open the wood-frame door and cupped her palm around her mouth to call out as they entered the house, and within seconds Jewell's father came down the hall to meet them. Cecil Kincaid was a big man, with broad shoulders and thick, white hair. An old-fashioned cardigan sweater with leather buttons did little to disguise the substantial size of the man. He raised his hand in greeting and pulled Jewell into a devouring hug. After kissing her temple, he extended his hand to Benjamin for a hearty shake.

"Daddy, this is Benjamin Roth."

"Good to meet you, Benjamin," he signed once he withdrew his hand. His signs were fluid and casual, clearly well practiced, but his slightly gnarled fingers showed signs of arthritis and age. *"Jewell has spoken of you. We're happy to have you here."*

Benjamin slid a glance at Jewell, smiling at the blush in her cheeks at her father's confession. *"It's nice to be here, sir."*

Jewell's father waved his hand. *"Please, call me Cecil."* He spelled his name and offered a simple sign to represent it. *"We aren't much for formality in this house."*

"Where is Mama?" Jewell asked.

Cecil Kincaid indicated the room at the end of the hall he had just exited. *"In the kitchen. She's preparing the pumpkin for the pie. I've been instructed to go out to the apple tree and see what I can bring her for apple brownies."*

Jewell took Benjamin's hand and led him towards the source of the aromas making his mouth water and his stomach grumble. *"My mother doesn't speak or read lips. I just wanted you to know."*

Benjamin nodded and followed her down the hall that was wallpapered with an old-fashioned toile print of covered bridge sketches on a pale tan background. He felt like he had stepped back in time. The furnishings were antiques, and the interior itself stayed true to the original style wherever it could. Even the light switches on the wall were push-button rather than toggle. Substantial crown molding hugged the ceiling, and thick baseboards sat along the wall. Half a dozen generations had occupied this house, easily. Benjamin could almost sense the decades of life. It was pleasant and so in contrast to what he understood.

He looked back to Jewell. For a moment, he felt embarrassed that she caught him in his musings. She tugged gently on his hand again and urged him toward the kitchen door. Motion beyond the doorway caught his attention before they stepped inside, a flurry of activity in the form of a little blond girl wearing a fairy costume.

They entered the kitchen to find Jewell's mother and little sister where they stood at the counter. Pearl was busy forming raw crust into a deep stoneware pie plate. The edges were uneven, and probably thicker in some spots, but the six-year-old worked at it in deep concentration, her tiny tongue sticking out one side of her lips. Opal Kincaid stirred a large bowl of pumpkin puree. Pearl looked up from her task and a wide smile lit up her fair face. She jumped down from the stool she stood on, ran to her sister, and threw her arms around Jewell's waist.

Opal turned at Pearl's motion and smiled. Everyone in this house smiled. The notion made Benjamin smile wider. Jewell said chaos ruled here, but that wasn't what Benjamin saw. He saw life, in its most pleasant form, and a family living it. Jewell's mother wiped her hands on a towel before hugging her daughter. The slight woman only reached mid-chest to Jewell. Jewell introduced him to her mother as she had her father.

"Cecil and I were very happy to hear you would be coming back with Jewell," Opal told him as she turned away from her daughters. Her

hands moved with the gracefulness of small birds, fluttering and dancing in the air in delicate choreography.

Nearly every book Benjamin had ever read eventually described the way a person spoke—the timbre and tone of their voice, soft or harsh, grating or soothing. He wondered if the hearing world could understand the subtle intricacies he saw in the motion and play of hands in silent speech. Benjamin took the small woman's hand and kissed the knuckles, having to bend slightly to be able to reach her. She was such a dainty woman. He didn't recall ever seeing such a whimsical lady.

"I'm happy to be here, Mrs. Kincaid."

Opal held his hand and patted it with the other. She stepped back and wiped her hands again before continuing to sign. Like "her husband, Mrs. Kincaid offered her name sign. *"Please call me Opal. I'm sure my husband told you we don't stand on formality in this house. There's too much dust, clutter, and chaos for formality. Come and sit."*

Jewell squeezed his fingers and they went to the table, hand in hand, to sit down. Pearl jumped back on her stool and continued with her crust dough. Cecil came back in with a dozen apples held in the bottom half of his cardigan sweater, followed by a man about Benjamin's age with curly black hair, his arms full of fruit. Jewell touched Benjamin's wrist to draw his attention for a moment and quickly signed that the other man was her brother Garnett. Mr. Kincaid touched his wife's arm as he passed her and she pointed to the table. Both Benjamin and Jewell scurried to keep the freshly picked fruit from rolling to the floor as her father unceremoniously dumped them out.

Benjamin laughed as half a dozen apples escaped their attempts and rolled across the hardwood floor. Ruby showed up in the doorway leading to a part of the house he hadn't seen yet and bent to snag an apple as it rolled past her. In a fluid motion, she stood, waved at Benjamin, and bit into the fresh apple.

Opal set a glass bowl and a small paring knife down in front of Benjamin.

"Have you ever peeled apples before, Benjamin?"
"Yes, ma'am."

She patted his shoulder and smiled. *"Be careful not to cut yourself."*

Jewell smiled and shook her head. *"I'm sorry, I didn't know Mama was going to put you to work."*

Her mother smiled wider and shrugged her shoulders. *"If Benjamin is going to spend the holiday here, he has to work for his meal."* She turned away and went back to her pie filling.

Benjamin looked to Jewell. "My meal?"

Jewell squeezed his hand. *"I think you were just invited to Thanksgiving dinner."*

CHAPTER TWELVE

Jewell nearly choked on her eggs foo yung, and reached for her pinot grigio to wash down the last bite she hadn't quite managed to chew before Dillon finished his story. Dillon and Victoria laughed, and Benjamin chuckled, rubbing his hand across her back. She managed to swallow and waved her hand, trying to say without speaking that she'd live.

Draining the last of the wine, she set the glass down with a thunk. "That was *not* fair," she scolded. "You could have warned me before I put the food in my mouth."

"What's the fun in that?"

Benjamin picked up the wine bottle and poured more in her glass. He leaned over and kissed her cheek, grinning, and went back to his plate of food. She barely had her breath when Dillon launched into another story. This time she learned to make sure and wait until he'd landed the punch line before she took a bite. This was the fifth time the four of them had shared an evening like this in the last three weeks, and she enjoyed each one more than the last. With each day, she'd watched some of the stiffness, some of the edge around Benjamin crumble until his smiles were easy, and he'd even laughed once or twice. It was a wonderful sound, uninhibited and robust.

And each day, she fell more in love with him.

They finished eating, and Jewell helped Benjamin gather the dishes and takeout containers to take into the kitchen. He scraped out the remaining food into the garbage disposal and tossed the containers while she rinsed the dishes and loaded the dishwasher. As she set the last dish inside the washer, Benjamin stepped behind her and set his hands on her hips. Jewell turned within his hold and wrapped her arms around his neck for a kiss that tasted of pinot grigio and chow mein.

"I need to go," she said, breaking the kiss and leaning back enough so he could see her lips.

He wrapped his arms tighter around her waist and pulled her closer. "Why?"

She smiled because it was an old argument. One they had each time she spent the evening at his townhouse, or he spent the evening at the apartment with her and Ruby. "You know why. We both have work in the morning."

He kissed her again, lingering longer than with the first, but still restrained. Every place they were together provided its own form of forced control. Bulwark in itself was an argument for self-restraint, Ruby was at her apartment, and Victoria and Dillon were almost always at the townhouse. She supposed it all could be seen as a blessing or a curse.

The sound of arguing voices carried from the living room and Jewell glanced past Benjamin in the direction of the fight. Benjamin turned his head and looked over his shoulder, following the line of her sight. "They're fighting again."

Jewell nodded when he looked back at her. "What do they fight over? They love each other so much, it's easy to see."

Benjamin stepped away from her, walking around the center island to the other side. He made a show of being busy as he gathered up the remaining packets of soy sauce and disposable chopsticks. Jewell waited until he pulled out his trash drawer and tossed it in the garbage. He closed the drawer with a solid thud and set his hand on the edge of the counter. She leaned her hip against the same edge and crossed her arms over her body. The voices ratcheted up for a moment, then faded again. Benjamin raised his hands.

"I know Victoria loves Dillon. But, I wonder sometimes if she didn't fall in love with him simply to spite our father."

"I don't think I understand."

"Dillon grew up with Victoria. They played together in the yard. They even studied together when they started school. He was always a part of her life, so it's only natural that they love each other."

"That sounds nice. So, how does loving him spite your father?"

"Dillon's grandfather is our butler."

Jewell hesitated mentally when Benjamin said "butler," comprehending perhaps for the first time that his background and childhood were vastly different than her own in more ways than she first understood. She thought she might know what he implied. He must have seen the comprehension on her face, and nodded, tapping his nose.

"No one is good enough for his daughter, especially not the grandson of a servant," Benjamin clarified.

The front door slammed, sending a reverberation through the house that made Benjamin turn. Victoria paused in the doorway to the kitchen as she passed, looked at them both with tears streaking her cheeks, offered a weak and apologetic smile, and disappeared down the hall toward the stairs. With a sad sigh, Jewell turned to Benjamin and took the step needed to kiss his cheek.

"I'm going to head home. You go talk to your sister. She needs you."

He nodded and walked with her to the hall. Jewell turned right and headed for the door, and Benjamin turned left to follow his sister up the stairs.

Benjamin stared up at the ceiling, his hands folded behind his head, as he watched the slow rotation of the ceiling fan. The silver light of the setting moon came through his window and created an eerie semi-illuminated glow in the room. A cool autumn breeze caught the drapes of his french doors and they billowed slowly. The crisp bite of the gentle wind brushed across his exposed torso like the soft touch of a woman.

He sighed. Everything made him think of Jewell. The caress of the wind on his skin was her touch. The heady aroma of fresh-cut flowers was her scent. The gentle flow of his brocade drapes was the feminine curves of her body and the graceful way she moved.

Benjamin turned to his side and glanced at the large numbers on his clock. It was just past five-thirty in the morning. Another forty-five minutes or so and the strong vibrations of his alarm mechanism would shake the bed and tell him it was time to get up. This morning it would not be necessary. Sleep eluded him and wouldn't come before the sun peeked through his window.

His bedroom door opened slightly. Benjamin pushed up onto his elbow and stared through the semi-darkness at the small space. Victoria's head came through the opening.

"*Are you awake?*" she signed.

Benjamin sat up and turned on the small light on his side table. He motioned her into the room.

"*Unfortunately, yes. Are you just coming home?*" After Jewell left, and Benjamin had consoled her for a while, Dillon had returned and asked to take her out. To talk.

Victoria nodded. As she stepped into the light, he saw her eyes were swollen and red from crying. She sat heavily on the end of his bed and wiped at her flushed nose. Benjamin tucked the bed sheet around his waist and swung his legs over the side to sit near her.

"*What's wrong?*" he asked.

Victoria's young face distorted in anguish and new tears poured from her eyes. She hit her thigh with a bunched hand and swiped roughly at the moisture on her cheeks.

"*Vicki, tell me what happened,*" he signed with stern, quick gestures.

"*Dillon and I just kept fighting after we left here. He wants me to give up on Daddy. Wants me to make a choice. Dillon doesn't think it'll work, doesn't think we can be together if I don't.*"

Benjamin saw the pain in her eyes. His first thought was the same as Dillon's. He knew as long as she let Jonathan Roth run any aspect of her life, Victoria would have no peace or happiness with Dillon Ferguson. Many times he had told his sister the same thing, even before she became involved with Dillon. Their father was a manipulator and a controller. For Victoria's sake, Benjamin would not openly agree with her fiancé to try and prevent any further pain to her.

"What did you tell him?"

"What could I tell him? I love Dillon, more than anyone else I've ever known. But how can I leave Hartford?" Victoria's eyes rounded and she leaned toward him. *"Ben, you know how Daddy feels about me leaving. I'm supposed to fulfill some undetermined dream of his, and I don't want to think about what would happen if I defied him."*

Benjamin's mind screamed to tell her Jonathan didn't give a damn about her so she shouldn't give a damn about him. He reined in the snap.

"Did you tell him that? Did you tell Dillon you couldn't choose?"

She nodded and began to cry again.

Benjamin opened the drawer on the table beside him and pulled out a small box of tissues. Victoria took a fresh one and blew her nose. He didn't need to ask Dillon's response. Although he could understand the man's frustration at the situation, Benjamin didn't agree with Dillon's ultimatum.

"What are you going to do?"

Victoria threw up her hands. *"I don't know. Daddy is furious with me for defying him, and Dillon says we are over unless I do what he asks. What do you think I should do?"* she asked. Her hands shook as she signed the question.

Benjamin sighed. *"You know the answer to that question. But it's not my decision to make."*

She nodded, acknowledging her acceptance of his response. Like she did when she was just a child, Victoria turned into him and buried her face against his shoulder. Benjamin wrapped his arms around her and rocked her until the sporadic spasms of her crying jag tapered off and finally stopped.

He still held her when the firm pulsation of his alarm shook the bed. Benjamin eased his sister back onto the mattress, turned off the alarm, and rose on tired legs to move to his bathroom and prepare for another day. Victoria was still asleep, curled into herself in a tight ball, when he finished knotting his tie and left for work.

DATE: NOVEMBER 6 11:19:46AM
TO: BPROTH@BULWARK.MANAGERS.COM (BENJAMIN ROTH)
FROM: LILPRINCESS@AOL.COM (VICTORIA ROTH)
SUBJECT: I'M SORRY...

I COULDN'T TELL YOU THIS FACE TO FACE THIS MORNING, SO IN THIS, I'M BEING A CHICKEN AND SENDING AN EMAIL. I KNEW YOU'D TRY TO TALK ME OUT OF IT.

I'VE GONE BACK TO CONNECTICUT. DON'T BOTHER COMING HOME. MY SUITCASES ARE ALREADY IN MY CAR, AND AS SOON AS I HIT SEND, I'M GOING OUT THE DOOR. I'VE MADE UP MY MIND, I KNOW WHAT I HAVE TO DO, AND IT DOESN'T INCLUDE HIDING BEHIND MY BIG BROTHER. I KNOW YOU'D STAND BETWEEN ME AND ANYONE, BUT IT'S TIME I STAND ON MY OWN AND MAKE MY OWN DECISIONS.

I'LL TALK TO YOU SOON. I PROMISE. I LOVE YOU.

VICKI

Benjamin stared at the computer screen. He ground his teeth together until his jaw hurt and the muscle in his cheek jerked. Hot blood pounded in his ears and the room around him clouded in a red haze as a suffocating tension wrapped around his chest. The pencil he braced through his fingers snapped in two.

A gentle touch on his arm drew Benjamin's attention. Jewell looked across the desk at him. "Is everything all right, Mr. Roth?" she asked.

Benjamin looked from her to the four fund managers occupying the other chairs across the desk from him. All eyes were on him. He sat up straighter, mentally steeling himself, and dropped the broken pencil on his desk.

"What's up, B.P?" Alexi Rouan asked.

With a slap, Benjamin folded his laptop to effectively hide the screen. The source of his frustration disappeared. The lingering effect did not dissipate despite the absence of the confession.

"Nothing," he stated and turned to the desk to show his attention was back on the meeting. "I apologize for that. Where were we?"

"We were going over the projected earnings on our international and global funds," Jewell clarified. "Thus far most have nominal long-term gains, only three have any short-term. All but the America's Fund are without dividends."

Benjamin nodded. "In the Bulwark Family of Funds, it appears our segment shows the strongest performance levels for total growth and the lowest tax implications."

Phillip St. Ormand slapped his hands together and rubbed them vigorously, a huge grin on his face. "Once again. Good job, Roth."

Benjamin looked from one man to the other as they discussed the expected success of their particular funds in a struggling American market. This would be the third consecutive year his international funds finished at the top of Bulwark's list. With the rates of return they projected, he suspected they would finish among the best in the nation. For reasons Benjamin couldn't define, the financial victory didn't hold the same satisfaction as it had in the past. While he knew he succeeded in the objectives set out, the thrill of the 'stock' hunt lacked enthusiasm.

Despite the conversation going on between the four men, and the self-created acclamation party, Benjamin's thoughts drifted again to the email from his sister. If she went back to that mausoleum there would be no chance of reconciliation with Dillon.

The sensation of being watched pulled Benjamin from his contemplations. He looked up and met Jewell's stare. Her gaze was intense with one elegant eyebrow raised in an inquisitive arch. Benjamin locked his eyes with hers, neither of them wavering from the hold. Jewell's eyes asked questions as clearly as if her lips spoke them or her hands signed them. With a deep sigh, he slowly shook his head in a subtle motion. She dipped her chin and looked at the other men in the room.

As soon as the meeting in Benjamin's office wrapped up, Benjamin had a private meeting with Mr. Westmoreland, leaving Jewell to wrap up some research on a Belgian biotechnology firm Benjamin had an interest in for their Global Research and Technology fund. She would have loved to have had just a couple minutes alone with him to ask what could have been in his email to upset him.

She saw the way it hit him, even if the shift was too subtle to be detected by the other fund managers. His entire expression tensed, and she practically felt the emotion rolling off him. She just didn't know what emotion she sensed.

He'd been distant all morning. She'd arrived at the office early, and he was already there, finishing off his second cup of coffee. He told her that Victoria had come home in the early hours of the morning, upset over yet another argument she'd had with Dillon. Whatever news came in the email just added to the tension twisting in him.

"Hey, Jewell. I'm running down to the break room for an iced tea. You want anything?" April said from the doorway.

Jewell looked up and shook her head. "No, thank you. I'm still working on the diet soda I picked up at lunch."

"Okay. Let me know if you need anything."

Jewell's email chimed. She waited until April stepped away from the door before popping open the email window. Several new emails waited to be read, most internal memos and reminders, but the one at the top of the list made Jewell still her hand over her mouse.

FROM: VICTORIA ROTH

Jewell double-clicked on the subject line *You have to understand* and opened the email. It was long, and Jewell blinked several times to focus on the first line.

DATE: NOVEMBER 6 3:32:15PM
TO: JKINCAID@BULWARK.MANAGERS.COM (JEWELL KINCAID)
FROM: LILPRINCESS@AOL.COM (VICTORIA ROTH)
SUBJECT: YOU HAVE TO UNDERSTAND…

Jewell…

I know that by now my brother has told you I've left Boston and gone back to Connecticut.

Jewell paused, blinked, and read the sentence again. With that one statement, Victoria made everything painfully clear. No wonder he had looked so angry when he read the email, especially if that was how he found out. It had to be because if he had known when he arrived at the office that Victoria had gone back, he would have told her.

There had been no time after one meeting and before the next.

She huffed and rubbed her fingertips across her forehead, the low thud of a headache building behind her eyes. Benjamin and Victoria were as close as she and Garnett, and Jewell could only imagine if she had to watch her brother struggle with the choices Victoria felt she had to make. Choose between her parents and two men who loved her—her brother and her lover.

Choices no one should be required to make.

Jewell finished the flat soda left in her can and focused again on the screen.

I know that by now my brother has told you I've left Boston and gone back to Connecticut. I can just imagine how angry he is, and I wish there could have been another way. Maybe there was. Probably there was. But, at the time it was the only course of action I could see.

I like you, Jewell. And I believe that Benjamin loves you, or if he doesn't, he will soon. You're so good for him. I think maybe you love my brother already. You've seen a small fraction of the dysfunction that is our family, but I think you should know more. Jewell, if you're going to be with him you're going to have to deal with everything that comes with him.

Benjamin was eleven years old when I was born. I can only imagine how it was for him when he was young. He has told me so little. My

BROTHER THINKS IT'S A SIGN OF WEAKNESS TO COMPLAIN, OR EVEN TALK ABOUT IT.

BEN WAS BORN DEAF. BY WHAT I UNDERSTAND, THE FULL EXTENT OF HIS IMPAIRMENT WASN'T REALIZED UNTIL HE WAS ABOUT THREE YEARS OLD. ALL THIS INFORMATION I GOT FROM MY AUNT RACHEL, MY MOTHER'S SISTER. SUPPOSEDLY IT'S A RECESSIVE GENETIC BIRTH DEFECT. IT MUST GO WAY, WAY BACK BECAUSE THEY NEVER FIGURED OUT WHERE IT CAME FROM.

FROM WHAT I'VE BEEN TOLD, MOM AND DADDY TOOK THE NEWS FINE AT FIRST. BUT AUNT RACHEL TOLD ME IT WAS LIKE SOMETHING SNAPPED IN MY FATHER. DADDY STARTED DRINKING AND TURNED INTO A JERK OVERNIGHT. HE REFUSED TO HAVE ANYTHING TO DO WITH BENJAMIN. WHEN BEN WAS FIVE, HE WAS ENROLLED IN A BOARDING SCHOOL AND SENT AWAY TO LIVE THERE. AUNT RACHEL TOLD ME IT WAS THE BEST THING FOR HIM, NO MATTER HOW CRUEL THAT SOUNDS. DADDY'S DRINKING MADE HIM VIOLENT, AND MY UNDERSTANDING IS THAT BENJAMIN WAS OFTEN A TARGET FOR HIS ANGER.

Jewell had to stop and swallow hard, blinking against the fury and choking sorrow that gripped her when she read the last sentence. Of all the evils that existed in the world, of all the abuses and the mistreatments—some of which had been the crumbling foundations that had ultimately created the better part of the Kincaid family—Jewell could never fathom the ability of a parent to reap violence on their own child. *Any* child, but especially one's own.

She opened her drawer and took out a tissue, dabbing at her eyes as she tried to tamp down the rawness. The door leading to the bullpen was open, so as much as Jewell wanted to weep, she couldn't. Not without potentially drawing attention she didn't want.

A glance at the clock displayed in the corner of her monitor said it was nearly four. Benjamin would be done soon, and they could get out of here for the weekend. If she already found it hard to read his sister's words, she wondered what else the lengthy email held, and hoped she wouldn't be in tears when he came back. A quick passing thought told her to stop, but she knew she couldn't. She needed to continue.

My father refused to learn sign language and forbade my mother from learning. I can remember my father stating it would do Benjamin no good to be coddled. He had to learn to live in a world that didn't give a damn he wasn't normal. He was expected to conform to us, not us to him. It took years to do it, but Benjamin learned to speak and read lips. Of course, not with any help from them. He found people to teach him all on his own.

Benjamin tried to shield me from the worst of it, even before I knew what all the tension and yelling was about whenever he was home. But my parents did nothing to hide anything from me. In fact, when I was nine or ten, my father told me I should steer clear of my brother when he came home because he brought nothing but disgrace and hostility with him. My father told me he was a strain on the family and a burden I would have to carry when they were gone, because he would never amount to anything.

Even at that age, I couldn't believe how blind my father was to the truth. Ben was twenty-one years old, had graduated from high school at sixteen, finished college, and was working on his Master's Degree. All on full academic scholarship. But according to my father, Ben would never amount to anything. How ignorant is that?

The highlight of my life was when my big brother came home for brief visits. My earliest memories are of sneaking into his bedroom in the middle of the night. We'd hide under the covers of his bed and he would let me talk for hours about dolls and storybooks until I would finally fall asleep. I was probably four or five, so he was already a teenager. He looked so big, handsome, and wonderful to me. And he always smiled at me. Benjamin was the only one who ever smiled...

He spent all his time with me when he came home. Or at least as much as Mother and Father would allow. Daddy said he was incompetent and couldn't be trusted alone with me. But when I got older,

BENJAMIN SNUCK IN AND PLAYED WITH ME FOR HOURS ON END. HE TAUGHT ME SIGN LANGUAGE. IT WAS AS NATURAL FOR ME TO LEARN AS ENGLISH. WE WEREN'T ALLOWED TO USE IT AROUND GROWN-UPS, SO IT WAS OUR PRIVATE LITTLE LANGUAGE. WE COULD SPEAK ACROSS A ROOM WITHOUT ANYONE KNOWING IT. BUT BEYOND EVERYTHING ELSE, I REMEMBER LOVING HIM. I ADORE HIM.

WHICH IS WHY I'M TELLING YOU ALL THIS. I LOVE MY BROTHER. I WANT HIM TO BE HAPPY. I HAVE NEVER SEEN HIM AS HAPPY AS HE IS WITH YOU. YOU ARE HIS HAPPINESS, JEWELL. I DON'T WANT TO PUT PRESSURE ON YOU, BUT I WANTED YOU TO UNDERSTAND.

LOVING HIM WON'T BE EASY, JEWELL. HE'S STUBBORN, HE'S SHIELDED, HE'S OPINIONATED, AND HE CAN BE A REAL BUTTHEAD. BUT, IF YOU GAIN HIS LOVE, JEWELL...HE WILL LOVE YOU WITH EVERYTHING HE HAS.

JUST PROMISE ME YOU'LL DO THE SAME.

VICTORIA

The words were a blur by the time she finished. Jewell blinked, and tears rolled down her cheeks. She turned her back to the open office door and bowed her head, clenching her hands in her lap. She wasn't sure what affected her more deeply—the trauma of his life, or the beauty of his love for his sister. And her love for him.

Her chest ached, her throat ached, and her whole body ached for them both. Not for the harsh, accusatory, loveless man who had intruded into Benjamin's home. Not for the meek woman who had done nothing to protect her son. For Benjamin and Victoria.

She drew in a shaky breath and raised her head, looking toward the large window along her back office wall that looked down onto Friend Street. The sun was bright today, but she knew the air held a fall chill. The cold could easily be forgotten with the sunlight streaming in to warm the small office. Jewell stood and went to the window, looking through the jungle of steel, glass, and brick that made up the Financial District. Orange construction cones blocked off some areas of the street, and people moved up and down the sidewalks, avoiding obstacles and each other. No one walked with anyone, everyone moved independently. Alone. Cell phones to their ears and briefcases in their hands.

She leaned her forehead against the warm glass, closing her eyes.

Warmth and light seeped into her, pushing away the cold in the center of her chest.

Benjamin's touch on her shoulder pulled her from her impromptu meditation, and she turned before she even opened her eyes, raising her arms to wrap them around him. For that moment, she didn't care if he'd left the door open. She just needed to hold him.

He wrapped her in his arms, his hands pressing firmly into her back, and he turned his face into her neck. Neither said anything for a long time, but even then, when he pulled back Jewell wanted to tell him it was too soon.

"Come on," he said, sliding his hand from her back to her arm and down to lace her fingers with his. "I need to get out of here." He paused, smiled, and touched her cheek with his other hand. "I need some time with you."

Jewell smiled and stepped away from him to retrieve her purse from her desk drawer. He left her to close up his office, and Jewell leaned over to shut down her system. Her attention shifted for a moment to the open email, and she wondered if he'd noticed when he walked past. With the computer turned off, she moved through her usual routine of shutting the door between their offices, smiling at him before shutting the door, and exiting her office into the space behind April's desk.

"Any plans for the weekend?" she asked as she shut and locked her office door. Only then did she send up a silent thank you that Benjamin had thought to shut it when he came in.

"I have a date tonight," April said with a wide grin, spinning around in her chair.

"Oooh." Jewell set her purse down on April's desk, leaning against the edge. She glanced up as Benjamin came out of his office and likewise locked his door. "Tell me about him."

Benjamin set his hand on the high wall of April's desk, looking at them both. "Good night, ladies," he said simply and stepped away, raising the same hand in a short wave.

April waved back but turned her attention immediately back to Jewell. "His name is William Morgan, and I met him in my night course over at BC. We're going to dinner tonight."

"Is he cute?"

Benjamin reached the elevator and pushed the call button, never looking back. This was the game they played. It wasn't against corporate policy for Bulwark employees to date as long as they kept things professional in the workplace, but they agreed there was no need to add grist to the rumor mill, and besides that, it was no one's business but their own. No need to advertise it to the likes of Kevin Burke, who loved to stir the pot.

"He's *gorgeous*," April went on, fanning herself with her flat hand. "Dark hair, dark eyes, arms the size of torpedoes…"

Jewell laughed, and in the distance, the elevator dinged as it descended.

She spent another five minutes listening to April describe her new man as April shut down her own equipment for the weekend. They walked together to the elevator and rode it to the street. April drove since she lived in Chelsea and said the train was too much hassle for such a short distance, so she headed across the street to a parking garage used widely by Bulwark employees. With a wave, Jewell started down Friend Street, rounded the corner, and climbed into Benjamin's waiting car.

"She gave you no hint she was planning to leave?" Jewell asked from her perch at his counter bar. She had to wait for an opportune moment to sign her question as he bustled around his kitchen.

"She wanted to be with Dillon, so I can't understand why she'd choose to go back to Connecticut. It makes no sense," he answered over his shoulder as he sautéed asparagus in a hot skillet.

The aromas of garlic, baking rolls, and broiling steak mingled in the air making her mouth water. He'd driven her to the townhouse without asking what she'd like to do for dinner and had wasted no time in cooking their meal. He was a great cook. Just one more thing in a long list of accomplishments Benjamin Roth could claim.

She hadn't failed to notice that four steaks had been set out to thaw, so he had planned—or perhaps hoped was a better word—that Victoria and Dillon would be with them for dinner. He'd put the steaks away without a word and ordered her to sit at the counter bar while he prepared the meal.

She couldn't ask him anything else for the next several minutes as he made the final preparations for the meal. By then, all they had to do was wait a few minutes until everything was done. He wiped his fingers off with a small towel and turned to her. "Wine?"

Jewell nodded, and he grabbed two goblets from his hanging rack and took a bottle of merlot from his wine cabinet. When he motioned with his head toward the adjoining dining room she patted the counter. "Why don't we eat right here?"

He was a bundle of energy, keeping himself moving constantly. She wasn't sure, but she figured it was probably all avoidance. Benjamin set down the glasses, and poured the wine, but before she could say anything more, he tried to take off again. Jewell hopped down from her high stool and gripped the fabric of his sleeve, stopping him short. He pointed toward the oven to offer an argument, but she took his face in her hands and pulled him to her for a kiss. It took all of two seconds before he turned fully into her and his fingers pressed into her hips, drawing her closer to him. His mouth tasted of the garlic and butter he'd sampled off his fingers while cooking. Jewell opened her mouth and his groan whispered between them.

She kissed him until his hold felt less intense and more impassioned, and then she stepped back, offering a wink. "Check on dinner, Benjamin."

He pulled a face that was somewhere between "Oh, you're evil" and "I'll get you for that later" before opening the oven to take out their filet mignon steaks.

Reminding him that there were other things to focus on seemed to ease a little bit more of the tension that pulled at him. They talked and signed all through dinner to the point that her final bites of steak were cold, if not still delicious.

With a chuckle at her story about Pearl's first attempt at making fudge, Benjamin stood and picked up her plate, taking it to the sink. "How does one get exploding chocolate out of the curtains?"

Jewell laughed, standing with him. *"You don't. You buy new curtains."*

Benjamin set the dishes in the sink and turned to the refrigerator, taking out a four-layer chocolate torte with raspberries and crystallized sugar decorating the top. It was huge, clearly intended to serve more than two, and packaged inside a clear container bearing the logo of a local bakery. As soon as he removed the lid, the mouthwatering aroma of chocolate and raspberries hit Jewell. She laid her hand against her stomach.

"Goodness, Benjamin. You keep feeding me like this, nothing is going to fit me anymore."

His gaze shifted from her hands, down her body, and back to her face as a lecherous grin curled his lips. "Is that a bad thing?"

She wasn't sure who moved first, or who reached first, but she was in his arms. His kiss poured molten honey through her, pooling in her limbs and her stomach, and in an instant she wanted 'more'. More of his touch. More of his kiss. More of his taste. More of his skin.

Just more.

Benjamin turned them, edging her toward the hallway...and the possibilities beyond sitting rooms with comfortable couches, plush carpeted floors in front of fireplaces, and stairs that led to...his bedroom.

If they made it that far.

Benjamin put her against the wall, his mouth magic on her throat. Jewell couldn't stop the bombardment of sensations. His hips pressed against her, declaring without any doubt the physical evidence that he felt the same. His tongue smoothed beneath her jaw, his lips sucked at her throat, and his hands tugged her blouse free from the waistband of her work trousers.

Jewell groaned when his hot palm pressed to her side.

He held her so close that she felt the vibration from his smartphone in his pocket when it went off. He never moved to answer it. If anything, he pressed his body harder against her, the shift of his hips eliciting another flush of sensation through her.

Benjamin bent at the knees, aligning his body lower with hers, his mouth finding the exposed skin at the collar of her blouse to kiss the valley between her breasts. With his breath hot on her skin, he rubbed his body against hers from thigh to chest. Jewell threw her head back, exposing her throat. His fingers laced with hers and he pushed her hands above her head, holding her against the wall.

The phone vibrated again and he released her hand long enough to flail blindly to his pocket, tossing the phone on the floor where it rattled and shook.

Go away! Leave us alone! God, Benjamin, touch me again!

Her thoughts splintered in thousands of directions but nothing mattered.

His open mouth found hers again, his tongue plunging in to devour the sounds she couldn't stop any more than her next breath. He stopped the kiss, releasing her hands to hold her face between his palms. Their rapid breath mingled in the space between them. Benjamin stared down at her with dark eyes, and a smile ticked his lips. Jewell almost wanted to giggle with the giddy sensation his aroused smile inspired.

Without needing to speak, Benjamin took her hand and stepped back, leading her toward the stairs. Her heart pounded in her chest like a caged bird, desperate for escape. The phone rattled again on the floor and the screen lit up. Benjamin stepped over it, intending to leave it where it lay, but the screen caught Jewell's attention and she had to stop.

Victoria Calling.

Jewell tugged at Benjamin's hand to stop him and crouched to pick up the phone. He turned, the smile still on his face, but confusion tugged at his brow. She held up the phone so he could see what the screen said.

"She wouldn't call," he said simply.

The champagne warmth under her skin almost instantly dissipated.

He jerked his chin toward the phone, his smile completely gone. The phone vibrated in her hand. Swallowing, Jewell pressed the green icon to answer and pressed the phone to her ear.

"Hello."

A shuffling sound carried through the phone and she heard an elderly man's voice. "I don't know if I did this right. Take a look, Bea." The voice was distant but close enough that Jewell knew he held the phone.

"Hello," Jewell said louder, hoping he'd hear.

"You've called them, George. Someone is on the line."

"Oh, goodness." There were more shuffling sounds. "H-hello?"

"Yes," Jewell said, looking at Benjamin as she spoke. He gave a jerky sign to ask who it was, and she shrugged. "Hello. Who is this?"

"Uh, um, this is George Ferguson. I'm hoping to reach Benjamin Roth. Have—have I done that? Who is this?"

"I'm Jewell Kincaid, a friend of Benjamin's. Can I help you?" With her free hand, she finger-spelled the caller's name.

"He's Dillon's grandfather," he told her.

"Oh, Miss Kincaid," the older man declared with such enthusiasm Jewell had to take the phone away from her ear. "Oh, thank goodness. Victoria and Dillon speak so highly—I—Miss Kincaid, I'm sorry. I have been trying all day to find a way to reach Ben, but no one here —and then I found Victoria's phone. I don't even know what I did to—"

"Sir, is there something wrong?" Jewell interrupted. His sentences were so broken, his thought chains scattered, she couldn't figure out the point of the call.

"Wrong?" His voice nearly broke, and he cleared his throat. "Yes, terribly wrong. Victoria…Victoria has been shot. She—"

"Shot?" Jewell swayed and reached out with her free hand, and Benjamin caught her, his attention never leaving her face. She knew he'd read the word on her lips.

"Yes. They—uh—the police arrested my grandson, but he didn't— that's not—"

Jewell wanted to scream at him to just *say it*. She closed her eyes and pressed her fingers to her forehead. *"Please,* sir, please tell me. Is she alright?" Benjamin's grip on her arm tightened and she opened her eyes to look at him.

"She survived surgery, but they don't know if..."

"If what, Mr. Ferguson," Jewell snapped.

"They don't know if she'll make it through the night. I thought—I knew—I knew Ben would need to know, but—"

Jewell's heart froze and her knees buckled. "Dear God," she managed to whisper.

"You've got to tell Ben, Miss Kincaid. He needs to come. He needs to help fix this. It's—they say Dillon did it, but he wouldn't—he could never..."

"We'll be there in a few hours," she choked out and managed to end the call without the phone falling out of her trembling hand.

Jewell hung up the phone and swallowed hard against the hot lump in her throat. She forced herself to look up, slipping the phone into her pocket. There was no way she could speak, and if she tried to sign and hold the phone it would end up a shattered mass of bits and pieces on the tile. Deep lines furrowed his forehead and his eyes searched her face. With Herculean effort, Jewell raised her hands and told him.

Benjamin shoved her hands away as she signed, as if in an attempt to silence her. "No."

"*I'm so sorry.*" Jewell couldn't speak, the words caught in her throat. "*Benjamin, I'm so sorry.*"

He turned away before she finished the sign, and took the staircase two steps at a time. Jewell tried to keep up, but he reached his bedroom before her and came out of the closet with a suitcase when she came through the door. She stood helpless, watching him make two trips between the open suitcase on the bed and his closet. It wasn't until he came out of the attached bathroom with his sachet that he faltered in his frenzied attack on his wardrobe. He hunched over the suitcase, his hands braced on the open edge of the luggage, his head down. Jewell took a step toward him, her heart aching in her chest.

When his shoulders shook and a strangled cry ripped through him, Jewell rushed to him and wrapped her arms across his back. He tried to shrug her off, but she held on and the attempt was only halfhearted.

His knees hit the floor with a loud thud, Jewell moving with him. A heart-wrenching sob shook his shoulders. Jewell leaned over him and wrapped her arms around him as best she could. His arms circled her waist and he buried his face in her lap. Silent cries rocked his body and his tears soaked through her blouse. She could do nothing but hold on and pray.

CHAPTER THIRTEEN

Jewell drove Benjamin's car the near-two hour drive to Hartford, Connecticut. He didn't speak a word from the time they left his house until they reached the Hartford city limits. His silence worried her and made Jewell's heart ache. She wanted to ease his pain somehow, but didn't know what to do. The only thing she could do, that he would allow, was to hold his hand across the center console. But his fingers were flaccid in hers.

Benjamin provided only enough instruction as was necessary as they came into Hartford. Turn here. Next exit. Stay on this road. They moved through downtown and headed into the suburbs. The buildings changed from brick apartments to small cottages and colonials, to larger colonials and Victorians, finally growing in size to huge homes and mansions. The lawns grew in size in proportion to the size of the houses. Benjamin indicated an upcoming right turn onto what looked like a side street.

"It's right here," he said quietly. His voice cracked as he spoke.

Jewell slowed and turned the car. When she did, she realized it wasn't a side street but a driveway entrance. White granite pillars stood on either side of the drive with an iron banner bridging them.

Within the arch, she read the name Willow Wood Manor. The wrought-iron gate stood closed and foreboding.

She stopped the car. Like a speaker at a fast food drive-thru, a small box protruded from the ground on the right side of the car. Jewell looked to Benjamin.

"*Just tell them it's me,*" he signed in a tired, slow action.

Jewell nodded and rolled down the window.

"State your name and business," said a dull, deep voice through the static of the speaker.

"Jewell Kincaid and Benjamin Roth." The words stuck in her throat. What else should she say? How could she say it?

She heard a click and the gate slowly opened. An ominous sense of dread settled into her bones. As they pulled through, Jewell felt like an inmate on death row walking the green mile. Silver moonlight bathed the expansive piece of property. She drove slowly up the winding drive of paved cobblestone. Giant, ancient willow trees lined them on both sides with their long branches drooping down to nearly touch the ground. Green-silver leaves covered the grass and stone.

"Oh, my God," Jewell mumbled as the house came into view.

It was huge. Jewell had only seen houses like this on *Lifestyles of the Rich and Famous*. Or maybe *Gone With The Wind*. Four marble columns, three stories high, framed the front entrance that was reached by a dozen marble steps fifteen feet wide. The entire house glimmered a pristine white in the moonlight. Rows and rows of oversized windows created the front façade of the house, and light streamed onto the ground through half a dozen of them. The drive opened up in front of the house to create a large parking area. She pulled the car to an open spot on the left side of the space and turned off the ignition.

Jewell looked across the small space to watch Benjamin's profile. The fingers of his right hand drummed on his thigh as he stared at the lights of the house. Tears burned in Jewell's eyes and the ache that had wrapped around her heart since the call came grew to an almost unbearable weight. More than anything in the world, Jewell wanted to take a portion of the darkness from his eyes and carry some of the weight for him. She laid her hand on his shoulder, kneading gently the tense muscles beneath her fingers.

He didn't take his eyes off the house. With a weary slowness, Benjamin lifted his hands just far enough off his lap to sign.

"I want to apologize now for what will probably happen in the next few days. You shouldn't have come here."

Jewell leaned across the console between them and laid her cheek against his arm. She signed in front of them.

"I'm here for you. Don't worry about me at all. You do what you need to do, and I'll be beside you when you need me."

He reached up to wrap his fingers around her hand and press her knuckles against his lips. Still, Benjamin didn't look at her. Jewell wished he would show some sign of emotion beyond the detached and stoic expression. Since his initial and intense reaction to the news of the shooting, Benjamin had shown no other emotional sign. Only a matter of hours had passed since George's telephone call, but it worried her.

Benjamin sighed heavily. He released her hand to sign. *"You've seen a small glimpse of what my father is like. You have no idea the extent of contempt he holds for me. Because you are with me that contempt will also fall on you."* He shook his head. *"What the hell was I thinking? Take the car and go back to Boston."* The firm jerk of his hand indicated it was an order, not a request.

Jewell shook her head. *"No, I'm here for the duration. For you. I can handle whatever comes."*

He finally turned his head to meet her eyes. "I believe you can handle it, Jewell. I don't think you should have to."

She gave him a small smile and touched his cheek with her fingertips. Her heart reached out to him, and Jewell wished more than anything in the world that Benjamin knew how much she loved him. How far she would go and how much she would do for him.

With a deep sigh, Benjamin opened his door and pushed himself out of the car. They each took a suitcase from the trunk, and Benjamin held her hand as they moved toward the house.

He opened the substantial front door, shedding light across their bodies and over the top step. Jewell heard voices coming from somewhere in the house, but couldn't determine from what direction. It was nearly one in the morning, but the house was lit up like it was mid-evening. The front hall was huge and seemed to gleam. White marble made up the floor, and the crystal chandelier that hung two stories over their head bathed the pristine marble in a warm glow.

Benjamin set their suitcases at the foot of an open, winding staircase and held out his hand. Jewell took it and allowed him to pull her forward. His grip was firm, almost too firm. If he had to hang on a little tighter than usual, Jewell wouldn't refuse him. If he hung on so tight it took her breath away, she wouldn't say no.

A man dressed in a dark suit came out of a door down the hall that branched off the foyer. Even though it had been years since he had set foot inside this cold mausoleum, Benjamin recognized him as the head of security for his parent's estate, Tom Declan.

"Jimmy informed me you came through the front gate," the man said, his expression flat and unfriendly. Benjamin couldn't recall ever seeing a smile on Tom's face.

"Where is everyone?" Benjamin asked.

"They're in the sitting room." Benjamin took a step around him. Tom raised his hand. "I don't think that's wise, Mr. Roth. Tensions are high right now."

Anger momentarily filled the black hole in his chest, and he clenched his jaw. Benjamin shook his head. "Not your decision."

"Mr. Roth."

"This is not up for debate, Declan."

The security guard nodded his head only slightly. He motioned with his hand down the hall, a half-hearted concession to Benjamin's statement.

He turned to Jewell, who still stood at his side, her small hand engulfed in his. She looked up at him and her gaze was a cooling salve to his fury. For her benefit, he tried to smile. "Jewell, why don't you go get some sleep? It's been a long night for you. I can have someone show you to a room."

Jewell shook her head and put her hand in the bend of his elbow. "No. This is where I'm staying. The sooner you accept that fact, the easier it will be."

Benjamin laid his palm against her cheek and stroked her lips before he kissed them. His kiss was nothing more than a brief touch, but it was enough to make his feet move down the hall. She wrapped her arms around his body and squeezed him tightly. With her arm behind his back and his across her shoulders, they walked past Tom Declan and down the hall. He saw her take in the silver accents and crystal chandeliers and overly opulent décor but avoided looking around himself. For Benjamin, this wasn't a homecoming. This place held no positive memories for him except for the ones with his little sister.

Something in him seized. It nearly knocked him to his knees. Pain shot through Benjamin's chest as if his heart were truly breaking into thousands of pieces. His steps faltered. If it weren't for Jewell's arm around him, Benjamin wasn't sure he would've remained standing. He turned and leaned back against the wall, Jewell moving with him. Her hands held his side and Benjamin wrapped his arms around her.

Jewell's lips formed his name and moisture glistened in her bright eyes.

He looked to the ceiling. How tight could he hold Jewell before she pushed away? She wrapped her arms around his neck and he bent to bury his face in her hair. Viciously, he swallowed the lump that choked him. Somehow, when he felt the most out of control and overrun, holding Jewell in his arms gave him a raft in the chaos. Never in his thirty-three years did he believe one person could be so much to him. Didn't ever think he needed someone this much. But now that he had her, he wondered what he would do without her.

She stroked his face, and Benjamin straightened to look down at her. The verdant green of Jewell's eyes sparkled with unshed tears. Jewell ran her thumb across his cheek to dry moisture he didn't realize was there.

"I can't lose her," he signed. He didn't want to risk being heard by anyone but Jewell. *"I can't. If I do, I'll go crazy. Crazy."*

She stroked his face and chest and held his hands still. Jewell kissed his knuckles, palms, and fingertips. She stood on her toes to kiss his cheek.

"You won't go crazy," she told him. *"I won't let you."*

Benjamin took a deep breath into shaking lungs. He fought the chaos inside and held her cheek against his chest. The fragrant scent of her hair drifted up to him and he kissed the softness. With a quick touch of his lips to hers, Benjamin pushed off the wall and took her hand.

They reached the closed parlor door, and Benjamin hesitated with his hand resting on the brass latch. With a quick look into Jewell's eyes, he pushed it down and the door opened. People—family members he hadn't seen or spoken to in years—sat or stood around the room in small clusters. As soon as he stepped inside, all heads turned in his direction.

The next several minutes were a blur, partially because everyone tried to speak to him at once. Aunts, cousins, and a variety of other relatives surrounded them. A glance over everyone's head told him neither of his parents was in the room. Benjamin raised his hands in a silent request for everyone to be still.

None of them understood. None of them even considered that he might not be able to absorb at once a dozen people waving their hands and speaking at the same time. Why would they? They never had to deal with the deaf boy Jon Roth had hidden and pushed aside.

He looked to Jewell. What he had to do grated on every nerve and fought every resolve Benjamin held since being sent to boarding school at five years old. Benjamin hated doing it, hated admitting it, but he needed help. Needed her help. There were too many faces and too many questions. Too many people who didn't know how to let him understand and ignorant as to why he couldn't.

Jewell stood waiting. Near enough he could touch her, but far enough away to not suffocate. Benjamin held her gaze for a split moment before raising his hands.

"I need your help."

She smiled a slow and warm smile that immediately calmed Benjamin's frazzled nerves. Not completely, but enough to clear his mind. Jewell nodded and stepped closer to face him.

Benjamin turned to his Aunt Frances, sister to his son of a bitch father. "Where are my parents?"

"Your father and Dr. Khalil just took your mother upstairs to her bedroom.

Dr. Khalil prescribed some tranquilizers and sleeping pills. She was hysterical, near out of her mind," Jewell signed for him his aunt's words.

Benjamin nodded. Jewell pointed to his Aunt Margaret, another Roth sister, to indicate she now spoke.

"It's been horrible, Ben. We all have been here since yesterday afternoon, and she hasn't calmed down since it happened."

Benjamin straightened and looked at Aunt Margaret. Heat rushed over his entire body and an immediate fury fired his blood in a split second.

"Friday afternoon?"

"Yes. Your father called from the hospital to say they were taking Victoria into surgery. We all came straight here."

"Why wasn't I contacted sooner?"

"We assumed you had been."

"And what...I didn't come?" Benjamin could barely see Jewell's hands anymore. Anger blurred his vision. That son of a bitch! Victoria had been in surgery for hours—she could have *died*—before anyone had bothered to call him. Even then, it was a member of the staff and not even family who had contacted him. A vicious rage choked him.

Jonathan Roth picked that inopportune moment to come back into the parlor. Benjamin saw his father come in out of the corner of his eye and turned sharply on him.

Two deep strides closed the space between father and son. Benjamin clenched his fists at his side to keep from raising them in violence. He ground his jaw together. Jonathan Roth seemed surprised to see him, and Benjamin realized the man probably had no intention of calling him at all. His father probably didn't know anyone had.

"Who the hell do you think you are?" Benjamin said, projecting his voice until his throat hurt. "I should have been called as soon as— soon as—"

As soon as what? As soon as she was taken to the hospital? Damn! He didn't even know what happened yet, only that Victoria could die.

"I could lose my daughter!"

"She's my sister." Benjamin felt a catch in his throat. "She's my sister!" Damn it! His eyes burned. He clenched and released his fists to try and maintain his slipping control.

The other people in the room intervened, moving between the two men to put space between them. Jewell's hand pressed against his chest. Benjamin spun on the balls of his feet and stormed through the mass of people, the heels of his hands pressed against his eyes. When Benjamin reached the far wall, he looked back over his shoulder. Everyone moved and talked in a frenzy.

Jewell moved towards him, and his father lifted his hand to point at Benjamin. Jon Roth's ugly face twisted in a nasty grimace as he said something Benjamin could not read. Benjamin was surprised when Jewell turned on his father and shot her hand up to block his face. Her brow furrowed as she said something back. Jonathan's face registered shock and his agape jaw snapped shut.

She reached him and her calming hands touched his back and arm. Benjamin stared out the window into the dark night. He fought down the emotion raging through him. His loss of control was infuriating. It was a weakness he hated and couldn't allow.

Jewell touched his cheek and gently urged him to look at her. Her eyes were distraught and she took in the details of his face.

"Benjamin," she said.

No matter how many times he watched those lips speak his name, it always had the same powerful effect. Jewell instantly had his full and undivided attention. She took her hands off him to sign and he immediately felt the loss.

"Let's just go get some sleep. You need rest."

He didn't look in his father's direction and did his best to avoid the condescending eyes of his family. Benjamin took Jewell's hand and quickly left the parlor. Without pausing, he grabbed their luggage and led Jewell up the giant staircase to the second floor. At the top, he turned left and took her to the furthest corner of the family living space. His old bedroom was in this wing, separate and distanced from the family suites, but he didn't want to go there. Too many memories.

They reached the last few doors of guest rooms. Benjamin opened the last one and led Jewell inside. A large brass canopy bed sat against the opposite wall with an assortment of furniture scattered throughout the room. He turned on a small lamp beside the bed and it shed a soft light over everything.

"The bathroom is through that door there," he said, pointing to the partially open door. *"One of the housekeepers can get you whatever you need."* He took Jewell's bag and set it on the bed. *"Try to get some sleep."*

Jewell touched his arm. *"You sound like you're not going to be here."*

"I'm taking the room across the hall. No one else will come down this far. These are the smaller, less used rooms."

Jewell shook her head and took his hand in a firm grip. *"No, Benjamin. Don't."*

"Don't what?"

Jewell slipped between him and the edge of the bed. She laid her hands on his arms and looked up at him. The softness of her eyes warmed him and he wanted to wrap her in his arms to forget the entire night.

"Don't sleep in the other room. Stay with me."

He tried to read her eyes, but what Benjamin saw confused him. Was it concern or pity? Since when did he want either one? Certainly not pity. In his entire life, he neither sought nor received affection or consolation from another person, with the exclusion of his sister. Even then, while he would willingly and happily accept her love, he refused any attempt by her to comfort him. When did he become so weak and needy?

Benjamin stepped back and stalked across the room to the french doors that opened onto a balcony outside. He raked his fingers roughly through his hair and turned back to face her.

"Don't coddle me, Jewell. I've never been coddled and I don't intend to let it happen now."

She crossed her arms over her body and took a step towards him. The slight shake of her head tossed her hair gently around her shoulders. "Benjamin, coddling and caring are two different things. I care. Very much. I don't want to be alone tonight any more than you do."

He stared at her and wondered what this beautiful woman was doing here with him. What made her give a damn about him? Could two people be any more opposite? Jewell moved to him and took his hands. The dim light from the lamp lit her hair like a halo. She looked like an angel.

"Sleep here. With me. I won't be able to rest at all if you don't."

He grinned. "*Do you think you'd rest if I stayed?*"

Jewell smiled and wagged a scolding finger against his chest. "Yes, I do. We are both very tired and I think that once our heads hit those pillows, we are going to be out until morning."

Benjamin nodded and conceded with a smile. He knew she was right. Sleep already pulled at his eyelids and weighed down his limbs. A deep sigh filled his lungs and pushed Benjamin's shoulders down with its release.

"Stay with me, Benjamin," she said again.

He touched his fingertips to her cheek, and she turned slightly into his touch. "Can I deny you anything?"

She smiled and stepped into him, her hands sliding along his sides to his back. "We'll have to test that theory sometime."

When Benjamin kissed her, he half expected every sensation of need and desire he'd shoved aside hours before to slam into him, but Jewell was right. Yes, his nerves sparked and his skin warmed at the kiss, but the exhaustion that dragged at his limbs and made his head weigh twenty pounds smothered any desire he might have mustered. Her mouth hummed against his as she drew her body away from him first, then her hands, and finally her lips. She smiled at him as she picked up her travel bag and disappeared into the bathroom, shutting the door.

Benjamin sighed and set his hands at his waist, dropping his head back to look at the ceiling. As soon as she left him, Ben felt the loss. When had he become dependent on her? When had she become so integral to his life that he—could he admit it?—needed her.

With each moment, the exhaustion sat heavier on his shoulders. He raised his arms and gripped the collar of his shirt behind his neck to pull it over his head. Tossing it aside, he toed off his sneakers and dropped his jeans in a pile on top of them. In just his boxers, Benjamin slid into the bed as Jewell came out of the bathroom dressed in flannel shorts covered with images of Jessica Rabbit and a black ribbed tank top.

Benjamin reclined on the stack of pillows at the head of the bed, folding one arm behind his head. He smirked as he looked her up and down. Jewell shrugged, deep color creeping up her throat to her face.

"*I packed quickly,*" she explained after setting her luggage against the wall.

"I'm not complaining."

Benjamin never maintained a relationship with a woman that allowed for the intimacy of a bedtime ritual. Women came, they enjoyed themselves, and then they went home. Or, he went home. Whatever the case may be. He had never reclined in a bed and watched a woman perform a bedtime regime, and realized as he watched Jewell, that it was both fascinating and appealing. Jewell crouched beside her bag and removed a hairbrush, running it through her thick waves several times until they fell across her shoulders and back. She disappeared into the bathroom again for just a couple of seconds, running her hands over her bare arms when she came out as she rubbed lotion into her skin. Her skin glowed like she'd scrubbed her face clean, all signs of makeup gone.

As she climbed into the bed, pulling the blankets over her bare legs, the scent of citrus and spicy floral from the lotion wafted around him. Benjamin watched every movement through heavy eyelids, sleep slipping over him even though he wanted to watch her. She shifted to the space beside him, leaning up on her elbow to look down at him. Her hair fell forward from behind her shoulder, the curled ends brushing his chest.

"Thank you."

"For what?" he asked.

"For staying." She kissed his cheek, flipped over to turn off the light, and in the dark rolled back to curl against him, her cheek on his chest.

Benjamin shifted further into the bed and drew her closer to him. Sleep hit him almost immediately, and he slipped into the darkness with the scent of citrus and spice around him and the feel of a woman's warm body in his arms.

A soft knock at the door stirred Jewell from sleep a few short hours later. Somewhere on the outskirts of her conscious mind, the low but steady rapping worked its way into her senses. She pushed back her hair and lifted her head from the pillow.

The pleasant weight across her waist didn't register until she moved to sit up. Benjamin's arm draped over her hips and his body pressed against hers in sleep. Jewell edged her way from beneath his hold, trying not to wake him, and slipped from the covers. She hated leaving the warmth and sensation of Benjamin's sleeping body beside her.

As she edged away, his fingers curled and hung onto the edge of her tank top. A smile edged up her lips and Jewell slowly freed her shirt from his sleeping grasp. He moaned softly and shifted. The knocking continued and, with a groan, she extracted herself completely from the bed.

Jewell wished she'd packed a robe, but hadn't anticipated early morning visitors. She flipped her hair over her shoulder, crossed an arm over her chest, and opened the door.

"Yes?" she said as she peeked through the crack.

An older gentleman stood in the hall, his gray hair mussed and dark bags beneath his eyes. He looked as tired as Jewell felt.

"Miss Kincaid?" he asked, his voice sounding weathered.

"Yes?" she said, stifling a yawn.

"I'm sorry to wake you so early, Miss Kincaid," said the elderly man. "My name is George Ferguson. We spoke on the phone."

Jewell opened the door a little further to take in the man. He wore black trousers and a black jacket with a vest, all impeccably pressed and wrinkle-free. Reality worked its way through her sleep-muddled brain, and all the dots connected. George Ferguson was a member of the staff in the Roth household, by his clothing probably staff management, and Victoria Roth had fallen in love with his grandson. Knowing what she knew about the family, coupled with what she could surmise, she saw clearly why Jon Roth would be so enraged at his daughter's choice. A man like John Roth wouldn't accept anyone so mundane as the grandson of the head of staff.

"I'm looking for Benjamin. I tried his old room, but he wasn't there. One of the other members of the household staff said she thought this was your room, and I hoped you might know where he is."

Jewell swung the door wide open. "Please, come in."

"I'm sure both you and Benjamin were told that Dillon shot Victoria. It's just not true."

"We haven't heard much of anything," Jewell explained, motioning him into the room. "All we know is what you told me on the phone. Some of it was confirmed when we got here, but no one said Dillon was a suspect." She shut the door behind the older man.

Benjamin stirred again in the bed and reached across the mattress to where she had been. "Jewell?" he mumbled in a sleepy voice.

She walked back to the bed so he could see her. When Jewell stepped into view, Benjamin smiled and reached out to her. Never had she imagined anything so sexy as Benjamin, naked from the waist up and looking slightly rumpled from sleep, beckoning her to join him again beneath the covers. Jewell took his hand and he tried to pull her back into bed.

"What're you doing out of bed?"

Jewell smiled back and glanced towards where George Ferguson stood. He looked away, not meeting her eyes, and Jewell realized what he must assume. He came here thinking she might know where Benjamin was, and there he lay in her bed. She didn't know whether she should be ashamed or pleased with her lack of embarrassment in the discovery.

Reluctantly, she released his hand. *"George Ferguson is here, Benjamin. He needs to speak with you."*

Benjamin sat up and looked around the canopy of the bed to see the man. He nodded and the shadows returned to his face. Obviously, for a few minutes, he had been able to forget why they were there. George's presence brought it back. Slowly, he forced himself from the bed and pulled on his jeans as he stood.

"Come sit down, George."

George sat in an upholstered chair adjacent to the bed. Benjamin raked his wavy hair with his fingers and rubbed his palm over his face. His glance fell on her briefly and one eyebrow arched. She nodded slightly, letting him know she was fine.

Jewell stood off to the side. She felt this was something of which she wasn't quite part. Even though she knew Victoria, and was devastated herself by the young woman's attack, Jewell still wasn't quite part of it all. Self-conscious, she slipped back and went into the bathroom, grabbing her case along the way.

With the door closed behind her, Jewell hesitantly looked in the mirror. The fatigue on her face was clear as day. She glanced at her wristwatch. It was six o'clock in the morning. Good Lord! They slept maybe four hours if that much. Wanting to give Benjamin his space, yet wanting to be close if he needed her, Jewell set her bag on the counter and crossed the bathroom that was bigger than her living room to turn on the shower. She washed her hair quickly and dried off just as quickly. After putting on a pair of wool blend slacks and a sweater, she worked her damp chaotic curls into a neat french braid. A cool washcloth and a touch of makeup took some of the weariness from her face. After slipping on a pair of shoes, Jewell opened the door and went back into the bedroom.

George had moved the chair closer to the side of the bed. The two men sat close together, their stances angled into the small circle formed by the chairs and bed. Even as she came around the end of the bed, Jewell saw dampness on George's cheeks. For the moment, none of them spoke. Benjamin sat forward with his right elbow braced on his thigh and his brow in the palm of his hand.

Jewell swallowed back emotion and moved to Benjamin's side. She touched his shoulder gently. Not looking up, he took her hand and pulled her down to sit beside him. The grip on her hand was almost painful, but she didn't pull away. She looked to George.

"Mr. Ferguson?"

He sighed and shook his head. "I don't know who else to turn to."

"George has asked me to post bail for Dillon and help him find a lawyer."

Shock forced Jewell to look from Benjamin to Mr. Ferguson. Dillon's grandfather wiped a line of moisture from his wrinkled cheek.

"Dillon did not shoot Victoria. Please, Benjamin, please. Go and talk to him. He'll tell you what happened. Benjamin, you know Dillon loves your sister more than his own life."

Benjamin watched George speak, and the more George explained the tighter the grip on her hand grew. Jewell covered their joined hands with her other.

George continued. "Dillon swore to me, before they took him away, that your father had threatened him with the gun. They struggled, and Victoria tried to intervene. The gun went off, and Victoria was hit."

A cold shudder moved down Jewell's spine.

Benjamin stood abruptly. "What evidence did they have to arrest Dillon other than my father's word? There had to be something else."

George shook his head. "Your father's word, mostly. When he made the accusation, they tested Dillon for..." He paused, stuttered as if trying to find the right word. "Gun shot residue. They found traces of it on his hands. There is a hearing Monday morning for bail."

"Was my father tested?"

Mr. Ferguson shook his head and shrugged, a strangled sob catching in his throat. "I can't be sure, but I think so. He was...he was covered in blood. He kept saying Dillon did it."

Benjamin jumped to his feet and moved to the window, leaning his arm against the frame. His thumb pressed against the bridge of his nose and he closed his eyes. The muscle along his jaw clenched and a vein along his neck bulged. Tension pulled his body tighter than a bowstring, and Jewell was afraid he would soon snap from the strain.

George stood and touched Jewell's shoulder. "I'll be here when he needs me. Tell him that for me."

Jewell nodded and he left. She was lost and didn't know what to do or what to say. Sitting on the edge of the bed, she watched the man she loved fight a battle deep in his soul.

CHAPTER FOURTEEN

"You're where?"

"Hartford, Connecticut."

"What are you doing in Hartford?" Garnett asked. His voice carried his surprise through the phone line as it raised several octaves.

Jewell rested her elbow on the bedside table and covered her eyes with her hand. She was so tired. Her head pounded and her eyelids felt as if they were lined with lead. It would be so easy to just shift from the chair to the bed and snuggle down into the softness.

"Something pretty terrible happened, Garnett. Benjamin's sister, Victoria, is in a coma and they don't know if she'll survive."

"What? What happened?"

"She was shot, supposedly by the man she was engaged to. It happened yesterday morning. We got the call late yesterday and arrived here early this morning. I'm going to stay here until..." She shrugged, not knowing what defined *until*. "I need to be here with Benjamin."

Garnett mumbled a curse under his breath. She barely heard through the earpiece. Jewell knew it wasn't an expletive spawned from anger, but more from shock and empathy.

"Okay. I'll tell Mom and Dad. Do you think Ruby will be okay at the apartment alone?"

Jewell nodded against her hand in a subconscious answer. Her eyelids slipped down and weights pulled at her limbs. "She'll be fine. It'll only be for a few days. I asked Greg to stop by a couple of times to check on her." She heard the shower turn off in the bathroom. "Things are horrible here, Garnett. Keep us in your prayers."

"Take care of you."

"I will. I love you. Give everyone my love."

She tapped the screen of her phone to end the call and stifled a yawn behind her hand. Jewell didn't know what she needed more, breakfast or sleep. Her stomach grumbled loudly and painfully in the argument for the top position.

It all still seemed unreal to her.

Jewell sat up and forced her eyes open. With an exhausted moan, she looked around the posh bedroom. Benjamin told her these bedrooms were never used because they were smaller and not as lavish as the others. Smaller? Less luxurious? Good Lord! This one suite was nearly as big as Jewell's entire apartment. She could fit her whole bathroom in the shower.

The house was more extravagant than Jewell ever imagined any house being. It wasn't a house. It was a mansion. Everywhere she looked was silver, crystal, and gold accents to the point of being gaudy. The floors were marble or hardwood and rich brocade or velvet draperies covered the windows. Jewell couldn't imagine living in a place like this all the time. It was opulent and occasionally beautiful, but also sterile and cold. She would much rather live in a small, warm home where the people in it were more important than the materials that constructed it.

Jewell looked at the bed. The covers were still rumpled from their few short hours of sleep. A warm glow flowed over her body.

"*What are you smiling about?*" he asked, sitting on the edge of the bed to face her.

Jewell smiled wider and leaned back in her chair. "*Some pleasant memories.*"

Benjamin looked away and rubbed a small towel over his damp

hair. She studied the multiple facets of his expression. On the surface, he had a smile on his face and seemed calm and composed. But Jewell saw something behind his eyes. They lacked their usual lively spark, replaced by a smoldering fire. The rich brown color seemed muted and dulled by the events of the last few hours.

He raked his fingers over his scalp and sighed. Jewell reached out to take his hand. After a small, and all too short, squeeze he let go. A twinge of disappointment raced up her spine.

"Are you hungry? If nothing has changed, my parents eat breakfast in their bedrooms so we should be okay to go downstairs and eat."

Jewell nodded and they stood.

"I want to talk to you about something while we eat," Benjamin signed as they walked.

The house was quiet, almost too quiet. Not a single sound, except for the soft click of her shoes on the stairs, echoed through the tomb-like halls. Jewell followed Benjamin down the steps and to the back of the house. A room built of glass and steel opened up beyond a double set of french doors. She looked out onto a vast lawn elaborately decorated with large hedges, flowering bushes, and Grecian-style pottery. The landscaping bordered on pretentious.

"Sit down here. I'll see what I can find in the kitchen. Do you want anything in particular? Eggs? Bacon?"

Jewell shook her head. *"Anything you find. Don't make anything."*

Benjamin disappeared through the doors again, leaving Jewell alone in the huge room. She sat down at a small, round table and fought the desire to put her head down on the beveled glass top and close her eyes. The sound of the door opening again brought her attention around toward it. A man came in and seemed surprised to see her sitting there. He looked to be in his late fifties, perhaps early sixties, with thinning hair that might have once been blond, now speckled with gray. Jewell immediately recognized a family resemblance between this man and Benjamin. The brown of their eyes was the same, and this man had the same strong facial features.

"Oh, I'm sorry to disturb you," he said and turned to leave again.

"No, please. Come in. You're not disturbing me."

He smiled and came further into the room. There was a pipe in his right hand and he lifted it, silently asking if she minded.

"Go ahead. My father smokes a pipe. I love the smell," Jewell told him with a nod.

The comforting aroma of applewood, cherry, and tobacco filled the room once the tobacco was lit. He sat down in a chair nearby and puffed on the wooden pipe. The scent was the first comforting thing Jewell found, except for Benjamin, since coming into this mausoleum house.

"Did I see you come in with Benjamin?" he asked.

Jewell nodded. "Yes. I'm Jewell Kincaid."

He stood and leaned forward enough to shake her hand before sitting again. "Ben Prescott." Jewell arched her brow. "Yes, the original. I'm Ben's godfather. Most just call me Prescott."

Jewell cocked her head slightly and looked again into Prescott's face. "Oh, I thought you were perhaps an uncle. There seemed to be a family resemblance."

This new Benjamin smiled, though it seemed tentative. "I'll take that as a compliment, seeing what a fine-looking young man my godson is."

Jewell chuckled. She took an instant liking to this man. There was warmth in his eyes she hadn't seen in anyone else here. Except for Benjamin, her Benjamin. What a nice thought. *Her Benjamin*. Mr. Prescott reclined and released an aromatic puff of smoke into the air.

"How did you and my godson meet?" Prescott asked.

"I work for him."

One eyebrow arched when he looked at her. "Excuse my surprise, Miss Kincaid, but what I saw last night didn't seem like an employer-employee relationship. The two of you appeared to be close."

Jewell felt heat rush to her cheeks and she looked down at her folded hands. "Well, it is more than that. He's a friend. I care very much for him."

Familiar brown eyes looked at her from beneath gray-speckled brows. A smile creased the wrinkles at their corners. "Good. Benjamin needs someone to care for him."

A comfortable silence settled between them as Benjamin's godfather enjoyed his pipe. The fragrance calmed Jewell and she felt her eyelids grow heavy. Morning sunlight came in through the glass ceiling and bathed her in natural warmth. It seeped into her bones and increased the heavy sensation of lethargy. A long, deep sigh filled Jewell's chest and drained her limbs with its release. Prescott spoke and brought her back to attention.

"You sign very well. Where did you learn?"

Jewell forced herself to sit up straighter and open her eyes. "At home. My mother is deaf."

He nodded. "Benjamin is very successful in what he does."

Jewell struggled to find a connection in his line of conversation. "Yes, he is."

The man examined his pipe and his forehead furrowed in thought. "He did it all on his own. From day one. Never got an ounce of support from Jon. I'm ashamed of all the years I stood by and let it happen." He looked at her and Jewell saw sadness in his eyes. "I didn't want to, but I didn't have much say or influence in the matter. It's about time someone came along to give Benjamin what he needs."

Jewell sighed and sat forward. "Can I ask you something, Mr. Prescott?"

"Of course."

"You aren't the first person in Benjamin's family who has told me he needs love and support and just plain *someone*. I've been told things about his childhood—not from him—that makes me want to cry. Why is it if everyone knows he needs this, Benjamin had to wait until he was thirty-six years old and hired me as his executive assistant before he got it? I don't mean to sound judgmental, but I don't understand."

He nodded. "You're a very perceptive young woman, Jewell. I think if you were to choose one word to describe this family, that word would be denial. Deny the pain and it won't hurt. Deny the problem and it'll go away. Better yet, someone else will come along and fix it for you."

The door opened again and Benjamin came into the room. "I found some bagels, muffins, fruit, and juice. Do you want some coffee? I brought that, too." He set an overflowing tray of food down on the table.

Jewell looked up and smiled. "Thank you. I was just having a nice talk with your godfather."

Benjamin turned and saw Mr. Prescott for the first time. He nodded in greeting. "Ben. How is Abigail? Last I heard from her, she was about to graduate from Emerson College."

Ben Prescott nodded. "She's upset over Victoria, of course. We all are. But other than that, she's well. I'll tell her you asked about her. Abigail always looked up to you."

Jewell looked into Prescott's face. She thought she heard a slight waver in his voice when he spoke of Abigail. Just from the drift of the conversation, Jewell assumed Abigail might be Prescott's daughter, and probably several years younger than Benjamin.

Benjamin nodded. The small talk ended and an uncomfortable silence settled into the room. In Benjamin's face, there was little expression, but the other man's features struggled to hide a wealth of emotion. Prescott pressed his lips together and he finally looked away. That was the extent of the conversation between the two men and Benjamin sat down across from her. Within moments the older man stood and left the room. Jewell watched him go, then turned her attention back to Benjamin.

"Everything looks delicious. I'm starving."

Benjamin set a steaming cup of coffee in front of her along with a gigantic blueberry muffin. Jewell took a small cup of melons and strawberries from the tray. After taking several bites of each, she realized Benjamin wasn't eating. Self-conscious, Jewell set her fork down.

"You aren't eating?"

Benjamin lifted his cup of coffee. "This is enough for me. I'm not hungry."

Jewell pushed aside the remains of the muffin. *"You said you wanted to talk to me about something."*

Benjamin held her gaze and his eyes seemed to grow darker in intensity. A small 'V' formed above the bridge of his nose. He reached across the table and took her hand. His thumb rubbed in a gentle caress across Jewell's skin. But Benjamin didn't speak, didn't sign. It was a strange silence. The silence of anticipation. A quivering tension fluttered in her stomach.

"Benjamin, what's wrong?"

He stood abruptly and brought her to her feet. Before Jewell could react or wonder what he was doing, Benjamin pulled her into a firm embrace. His lips covered hers as his fingers tilted her head back to deepen the kiss. Without a moment's thought to resist him, Jewell returned fully every ounce he gave. The kiss surprised her, but the tumbling butterflies in her stomach rewarded her shock.

Their lips parted, but Benjamin didn't loosen his hold. Jewell tilted her head to look up into his face. A smile tugged up at the corner of her mouth.

"Was that what you wanted to talk to me about?" she asked with a chuckle in her voice.

One corner of his lips curved up and his eyes fixed on her mouth. "Close enough. Thank you for coming here with me."

"You're welcome, but you don't need to thank me. I never thought of doing anything else."

Benjamin kissed her again quickly before freeing Jewell from his hold. "You look tired."

As if spurred by his statement, Jewell stifled a yawn behind her fingers. "I guess so."

Benjamin's fingers touched her cheek. "I have some people I want to see and some things I need to look into. No need for you to come. Why don't you go back upstairs and lie down?"

"Are you sure?"

He nodded. "Go on back up and get some rest. I want you bright and chipper this afternoon."

"Oh? Why?"

His smile was wide but lacked its usual depth. Even when they first met, and Jewell hadn't gotten through his abrasive exterior yet, she saw more animation and personality behind his eyes than she did now. The walls that Benjamin had built in the few short hours since learning of his sister's shooting were now high and thick. Jewell wondered what it would take to get them down.

"I want to go to the hospital this afternoon."

Jewell nodded, her throat squeezing at the thought of seeing Victoria. If she felt it this deep, it must be nearly smothering for Benjamin. "All right. I'll go take a small nap. Where can I find you later?"

He kissed her again. *"I'll find you."*

Dillon sat across from Benjamin without speaking. His fingers laced behind his neck, his forehead resting on the green metal table in the tiny interrogation room. The air smelled of stale cigarette smoke and body odor. Benjamin wrinkled his nose at the stench and drummed his fingertips on the cold steel. Dillon's shoulders rose and fell.

"Talk to me, Dillon," Benjamin said.

Dillon slowly raised his head, his bloodshot gaze meeting Benjamin's. His upper lip was pulled tight over his teeth, but his chin quivered as tears ran unabated down his cheeks. His hands curled and opened in tight fists.

"Why are you here, Ben?" he asked. "Do you want me to confess? To say I shot her? Your father's lawyer has already been here, and I wouldn't admit it to him. Why should I to you?"

Benjamin shook his head. "I'm here because George asked me to come. He wants you to tell me what happened."

Dillon slammed his fist on the table, the shock vibrating through Benjamin's hands, and he jumped to his feet. "I didn't shoot her. God, she's my life!" The force of his shouting reverberated in the air.

Benjamin fought fiercely against the hard, unforgiving lump in his throat. There was no way he would let the raw ferociousness of his emotions get to him here. Not now. Not until he knew Dillon's version of the truth.

"Dillon, you know me well enough to know that I would not be here on my father's behalf. I need to know what happened."

Dillon shoved his fingers through his hair before sitting down again. Perspiration glistened on his forehead and he wrung his hands together as if trying to remove a smudge or stain.

"Victoria called me Friday morning from the road. She told me she'd decided to leave your father's house for good. She wanted to be with me, no matter what, and prayed your father would eventually accept it. She told me to come to the house and pick her up.

"But when I got there, your father was in a rage. I heard him screaming from his den, then I heard Victoria's voice. I ran in and they were arguing. He had her arm and she was fighting to get away from him. I jumped in."

"Had he been drinking?" Benjamin asked.

Dillon nodded. "I would say yes. There was a broken bottle of scotch on the rug, so the room reeked of it. His speech was slurred and his eyes were bloodshot."

"What was he saying?"

"That he wouldn't let her leave. Wouldn't let her destroy her life by marrying me."

Benjamin ran his palm over his face. He could almost see the scene play out in his mind. It all sounded so typical of Jon Roth. Memories of his adolescence and teen years flashed in his mind.

"I stepped in—fought him to release her. He let go and we started to leave. Then your father yelled out and I heard the click of a gun."

Dillon pressed his eyes closed, tears pressing out. His face twisted with anguish. Benjamin's chest squeezed tight and it was hard to take in a deep breath. His throat burned.

"Did you fight him with the gun? Is that how it went off?"

Dillon slowly nodded his head. The pained expression that twisted his face made it hard for Benjamin to read his lips. He had to ask Dillon to say it again. The man who could have been his brother-in-law wiped his hand over his face, attempting to dry his cheeks. He took a deep breath and shoved his fingers through his hair.

"I shoved Victoria behind me and told her to get out. Jon was waving the gun around. I don't remember most of what he said, but I tried to reason with him. The gun went off once and hit the wall behind our heads.

"Jon was crazy," he continued to explain, his head moving slowly side to side and his eyes distant. "I had seen him angry before. Like the day he found out about us. But I never imagined anything like this."

Dillon took a moment to sip at the cup of coffee Benjamin had brought him. It had to be only lukewarm at best and was from the stained pot in the officer's bullpen, so Benjamin imagined it was bitter and tasted like something akin to tar. The grimace on Dillon's face confirmed it.

"My father can be a violent man. But Dillon—"

"Violent doesn't begin to describe him," Dillon insisted, raising his hand to stop Benjamin mid-sentence. "I tried to get Victoria out of the room. I was pushing her toward the door. That was when Jon said he'd see me dead before he allowed her to be with me.

"He lunged at me and grabbed my arm, trying to keep me from leaving. I grabbed his wrist and tried to push his arm down. Victoria tried to push us apart—then the gun fired."

Dillon stopped, covering his face with his hands.

"Dillon," Benjamin snapped.

Dillon dropped his shaking hands, his lips trembling so hard Benjamin had to stare at him to make out the words. Tears dripped from the man's nose. "I didn't know she was hit until she…she…she fell."

Benjamin only caught bits and pieces of the rest of the story. Unshed tears blurred his vision. Dillon was so distraught he often looked away and Benjamin couldn't see his lips. What he caught was horrible. Victoria fell to the floor. He held her while her blood seeped into his clothing and the rug beneath them. Jon tried to push him away until they were both covered in her blood. People came in, but Dillon didn't know who. Didn't care. He just held Victoria until the paramedics pried her body from his arms. Then the police took him into custody and later read him his rights and put him under arrest.

Benjamin swallowed against the lump that filled his throat. He almost wished for a cup of bitter coffee.

Now that he knew the truth, how could he go back to that house? Face his father. He had no doubt this was the truth. Everything Dillon described sounded like actions Jon Roth would be fully capable of doing. But how could Benjamin face the man without wanting to squeeze the life from his murderous heart? How could he look into the face of the man who fathered him, and not see a demon? A greater beast than he had ever known?

Somehow, he would find a way. Until he could prove his father as the violent bastard he was.

CHAPTER FIFTEEN

"Good morning! Thank you for calling Bulwark Mutual Funds, office of Benjamin Prescott Roth and Jewell Kincaid. April speaking. How may I help you?"

Jewell chuckled softly into the phone mouthpiece. "Do you take a breath when you say that?" she teased.

"Jewell? Where are you? This is bizarre. Mr. Roth hasn't come in yet this morning either," their assistant said quickly.

"That's why I'm calling. We won't be in until Thursday at the absolute earliest, perhaps not at all this week. I need you to cancel all meetings we've got set up between now and Friday and reschedule until next week. Anything we're supposed to attend, please pass the word on we won't be there."

"We? Why? Jewell, what's going on?" Then Jewell heard April gasp sharply. "Are you with Mr. Roth?"

Jewell rolled her eyes and shook her head. "April, don't get nuts on me. I need you—"

"Oh, my God," April blurted, accentuating each word. "Where are you? I can only imagine where Mr. Roth would take you. I knew something was going on between you two. I just knew it!"

"April," Jewell said loud enough to get through the other woman's ravings. She heard a small hiccup sound as April reined in her enthusiasm. "Are you done?"

"Sorry. What should I give as a reason?"

Jewell looked to her left and right down the wainscoted and fabric-paneled hall to see if anyone might be within earshot. She saw no need to aggravate things with Benjamin's family any more than she had to right now. This was the morning of day three in Hartford and things were as tense as when they arrived, if not more so.

She sighed heavily. "Mr. Roth's sister was..." she stuttered over the words. "His sister was seriously hurt on Friday, and I came to Hartford with him. To help interpret," she tagged on.

April groaned. "Oh, how terrible."

Jewell blinked back the tears that burned her eyes. She cleared her throat. "Yes, it is. All you need to say is there is a serious family situation. Mr. Roth will return when his family obligations are done."

"That's Mr. Roth. What about you?"

Jewell sighed and swallowed against the lump in her throat. Her nerves were raw and her stomach had been in knots for three days. The worst part was the growing distance between her and Benjamin. The first night here, if the three hours they slept counted, he stayed with her. She slept in Benjamin's arms the entire night and awoke warm and content beside him.

The second night, Benjamin was physically in the room with her, but Jewell knew his mind was somewhere else. He didn't lie in bed with her, but sat in a chair and stared into space. Jewell asked him to join her, and told him he needed the rest, but most of her signs went unanswered. When she woke up the next morning, the chair was empty and his side of the bed had gone undisturbed.

Last night he never came to the room. At three in the morning, Jewell went looking for him and found Benjamin asleep on a down-stairs couch. She knelt beside him and watched him sleep for several minutes. Even at rest, his brow furrowed in deep lines and his eyelids shifted impatiently. Jewell didn't wake him. He needed rest, and if he got it best away from her then so be it.

The little things Jewell observed bothered her most. Benjamin's aversion to meeting her gaze and his avoidance of physical contact, no matter how slight or inconsequential, didn't go unnoticed. He kept his hands buried deep in his pockets most of the time and made sure to stay at least an arm's length from her when they were near each other. The constant expression of frustration and annoyance weighed heavily on her heart.

"Jewell?" April probed, snapping Jewell back from her silent musings.

She chuckled wryly. "Tell them we ran off and got married." Jewell heard no response and assumed April was at a loss against her uncharacteristic attitude. "I'm sorry, April. Quite honestly, I don't have the patience to think of any excuse other than the truth. I'm here assisting him, that's my job. I assist."

"Okay, Jewell. I'll take care of it."

Jewell ended the call, letting her hands drop heavy into her lap, and rested her head against the wall. She felt so out of place here. So foreign, backward, and uncultured. Many times in the last two days certain things Victoria told her came back to her as she witnessed the dynamics of Benjamin's family. His godfather was right about the denial aspect. Denial and avoidance.

"Did you marry my son?" asked a small, slightly slurred female voice somewhere nearby.

It startled Jewell in the tomblike silence of the upstairs hall. She stood and looked around, but didn't see the source of the question. With slow, cautious steps Jewell moved down the wide hall. A quick glance through the first open door on her right confirmed it was empty. The voice hadn't come from there. The sitting room was empty. The next door down was closed, but the door across the hall was open.

Benjamin's mother sat on an elaborate Victorian settee near a gigantic window draped in mauve velvet panels. Barbara Roth sat so still and motionless that Jewell almost didn't see her. Her eyes were distant and she looked pale, her hands and cheeks seemed transparent. A shallow stare met Jewell as she stepped inside. Silence stood between them like a wall.

Jewell stepped forward and crouched down near Mrs. Roth's knee. She tried not to remember the way this small woman had stood to the side and watched her husband verbally and physically abuse their son.

Barbara Roth might very well lose one of her children. Anyone in her position deserved a sympathetic turn.

"Can I get anything for you, Mrs. Roth?" Jewell asked.

Barbara turned her shallow gaze from the doorway where Jewell had stood to where she was now. She stared at Jewell for several seconds before a mild sign of recognition turned up her lips. It was obvious the woman was heavily medicated. Her dark hazel eyes were muted and glassy, and her attention focused too long on unimportant pieces of furniture or empty spaces across the room.

"You're Benjamin's wife?"

Jewell shook her head and tried not to smile. "No, we're not married. I was just trying to think of something to say to someone on the phone." Right now, it sounded like a very lame excuse.

"You didn't marry him?"

"No."

"But you're here with him?"

"Yes."

Jewell felt self-conscious beneath the quiet woman's long and shallow gaze. The corner of Barbara's mouth edged up in a small smile and her eyes brightened slightly.

"I remember you. I saw you at my son's house once."

Jewell didn't know how to answer without dredging up unpleasant memories, or confusing Mrs. Roth any more than she was right now. She leaned back on her heels and looked around the room for a glass of water, or perhaps something else she could offer the woman.

Mrs. Roth nodded slowly and her brow wrinkled in deep thought. She seemed to have difficulty keeping up with the most basic of conversations. "Are you that wonderful girl who works with Benjamin?"

Wonderful? It surprised Jewell to hear Benjamin's mother describe her as wonderful. This was the first time they'd ever actually spoken. The woman had barely opened her mouth that night at Benjamin's house, and nothing she'd said had been directed at Jewell.

"I work with Benjamin, yes."

The older woman nodded. "Victoria told me all about you. She likes you very much. Said you're good for Benjamin. Are you going to marry him?"

"Do you need anything, Mrs. Roth? A cold drink? Something to eat?"

The simple question was enough to distract her from the original subject. "No, thank you."

With a nod, Jewell stood again and headed for the door. She would take the opportunity to leave the woman alone. Jewell was nearly out when Benjamin's mother spoke again.

"Benjamin is a good boy. I'm so proud of him. His father always wanted to do so much for him, but Jon's pride always got in the way."

"What are you doing in here?" an angry male voice boomed from the doorway.

Jewell jumped and turned to see the ominous form of Benjamin's father filling the open space. His fists were planted firmly at his waist and an ugly scowl twisted his features. Her breath caught in her throat and her pulse quickened for several seconds before Jewell calmed herself.

"Hello, Jon," his wife said with falsetto cheer.

"My wife is not to be disturbed." Mr. Roth's stern voice ground out through his clenched teeth.

"I—I'm sorry," Jewell mumbled and moved quickly past him into the hall.

She collided immediately with a solid force. Arms circled her and kept her from falling. Jewell looked up into Benjamin's surprised face and his hold momentarily tightened around her. He dropped his arms away as soon as she had her balance.

"What's got you running so fast?" he signed.

Jewell looked over her shoulder in an impulsive reaction. Benjamin followed her gaze and his face hardened when he saw his father. His rock-solid stare came back to her and his hands gripped her upper arms.

"What did he say to you?"

She shook her head, hoping her lack of explanation would let the situation die without incident. Mr. Roth reached past Jewell to grab Benjamin's arm. His action shoved Jewell forward into Benjamin's chest again. Her chin bumped his shoulder and she bit her lip, the coppery taste of blood assaulting her tongue. Jewell felt like a ball in an arcade game. When her hands touched Benjamin's torso in an attempt to stay upright, he flinched away. The knee-jerk action grabbed and squeezed Jewell's heart in a painful thrust.

Benjamin immediately yanked his arm away from his father's grip, and in the same motion, put himself between Jewell and his father, shoving her behind his back. His father pointed his finger in Benjamin's face, only an inch from his nose.

"Keep your little whore away from your mother. She isn't to be upset."

"She didn't upset me, Jon. The girl is very—"

"Be quiet, Barbara," Jon shouted as he turned back abruptly to the doorway.

Jewell flinched at the harshness and loudness of Jon Roth's voice. The older man turned to them again and was met by Benjamin's fist. He stumbled back and hit the wall. Before Mr. Roth could recover and possibly retaliate, Jewell pushed back on Benjamin's chest and urged him to move away down the hall. She glanced back to see Mr. Roth touch the bloodied corner of his lips with his knuckle.

She couldn't look at Benjamin until they reached her bedroom. He pulled her along and propelled her forward when they reached the room. Jewell went through the door first and Benjamin slammed it shut behind him. The sound made Jewell jump. The raw ends of her nerves sparked and her stomach tumbled. Where did her intentions to be helpful go wrong? What happened? Her thoughts raced and Jewell fought tears of panic as she moved to the window.

A gentle wind stirred the tree branches outside. The bright oranges and reds and lush green lawn belied the chaos within the house walls. She drew a deep, long breath in through her nose and released it with a huff.

Benjamin came to her side and pulled her around to face him. His face was angry and deep furrows marked his brow. Darkened eyes skimmed her face and Jewell tried to look away before tears ran down her cheek. His thumb skimmed the corner of her mouth, coming away with a tinge of blood on his skin.

"What happened?" he demanded.

"I'm sorry. I don't know what I did."

The stress of the last few days, and the restraint she forced on herself, was suddenly too much for Jewell's frazzled nerves. She had no comprehension of this family's workings or what the rules of the game were. This opulent house and cruel family dynamic were so far removed from her understanding that she knew it would take a lifetime to even begin to make sense of it all. But right now, it was too much. The violence, the anger, and the resentment that all seemed without instigation by those receiving the brunt of the backlash, finally hit her with the force of a punch in the gut.

Benjamin grabbed her arms near the shoulder and forced her to meet his gaze with a quick jerk. She caught her breath and looked into his sharp face.

"Jewell," he snapped.

Jewell took a breath and nodded her head. "I'm okay now."

He released her arms, and Jewell immediately felt the loss of his touch. Her body swayed towards him, the magnetic pull of his body tugging her off balance. Jewell steadied herself and crossed her arms over her stomach. Physical contact between them had lessened to a bare existence in the last two days. She hungered for even the briefest comfort, whether a touch of his hand or a kiss of his lips on her hair. Passionate glances and desperate embraces weren't appropriate, or even really wanted, at a time like this. But a reassuring moment in each other's arms would mean the world to her right now. Benjamin took one step back and shoved his hands into his pockets.

"Tell me what happened."

Jewell leaned her back against the frame of the window behind her. She flipped her hair back behind her shoulder and sighed.

"I was sitting in the hall to call April and tell her we won't be in until the end of the week. When I hung up, I heard your mother say something from one of the rooms. I just went in to speak with her for a minute or two. She seemed tired and overly medicated. When I went to leave, your father was at the door. He was furious I was there and told me I wasn't to bother her, so I tried to leave."

His frown was deep and overpowered his face. Benjamin started to turn away, but Jewell grabbed his arm. She gently urged his hand from his pocket and laced her fingers with his. He stared down at their joined hands for several moments before looking up.

"I'm sorry, Benjamin," she said in apology for all the pain, memories, and whatever she might have done to fuel the fire.

He pulled his hand free of hers and turned to walk away. Jewell quickly stepped forward and got in front of him, planting her palms against his chest to stop him. His eyes rounded with surprise. Before Benjamin could pull away again, she closed the small space between them and curled her fingers into his shirt. A deep, long breath filled his chest and one warm palm covered the back of her hand.

"Benjamin, please stay here and talk to me."

He shook his head. "Not now, Jewell."

"You're pulling away from me."

Benjamin stared down at her. Jewell saw a slight softening of the worry lines around his eyes, and his frown straightened. It wasn't a smile, but no longer a scowl. He laid his palm against her cheek and Jewell turned into its warmth. She wrapped her fingers around his wrist and looked up at him. Jewell held her breath as he leaned forward. His lips pressed against her opposite cheek, then both hand and lips left and he moved away.

Jewell watched his retreating back. Benjamin paused at the door and leaned his hand into the jamb. Her lungs burned as Jewell held her breath and waited for him to come back. But he didn't. After several moments, Benjamin dropped his hand and disappeared down the hall.

Her vision blurred with hot moisture. Jewell lifted two fingers to her lips, kissed them, and turned her hand out to him as he disappeared. A deep shudder shook her body.

"Just know I love you, Benjamin Roth."

Benjamin sat in the humid warmth of the solarium and watched the sun slowly fall behind the horizon of treetops. He closed his eyes against the momentary intensification of light just before it vanished completely. A deep breath through his nostrils filled his head with the earthy aroma of soil and fertilizer from the potted plants along the wall. Dusk settled over the landscaped yard as he took another sip of his iced tea. After the headache he woke up with, Benjamin decided to steer away from liquor this evening.

Despite his avoidance of any firewater, his head pounded. Were this house a pressure cooker, the lid would've blown off and taken a chunk out of the moon by now. Benjamin felt like two people—or one being torn down the middle. Each inner person was equal in their resolve to rend him to pieces.

Part of him wanted to just pack his suitcase and go back to Boston. Leave all of this behind him once and for all. Be done with the crap.

In equal part, he wanted to stay in this house and be the thorn in his father's side until he could take Jon Roth down, and destroy him for destroying their family.

The part that wanted to see his father destroyed was the part that pushed Jewell away this morning. She forced him to recognize and acknowledge things about himself he never realized or cared about previously. Jewell taught him he needed someone to be here with him, whether he wanted to need her or not. He didn't like needing her. Benjamin hated it, or at the least reminded himself that he should. If he pushed away hard enough, he'd eventually not need the comfort she willingly gave. At least, that was what the cowardly side of his inner self tried to believe.

The other part of him wanted to hang on to her with desperation. He wanted to draw strength from her. She could give him strength enough to get through the next few days, and strength enough to get through all the days to come. The part of his heart she brought to life knew all this and wanted to accept it for what it was and what it could be. But the part of his heart that had run his life since the first time he understood rejection didn't want to give in.

It would be different once they were back in Boston. He would be back in his own world. Back where they both could relax and pick things up where they left off.

Benjamin shook his head. Who was he kidding? Nothing would be the same again. His sister was in a coma, put there by their own father. And just where was it they were going to pick up from? He didn't know where that was because they never talked about it. It was a topic avoided with stealth and cunning on his part.

Someone tapped the small table where Benjamin's hand rested and he looked up. His godfather stood beside the chair with a pipe in his hand. A slow smile spread Ben Prescott's lips and he nodded.

"Good evening, Benjamin."

"If you say so," he said with a shrug and took another sip of his drink.

The elder man sat down in a chair adjacent to Benjamin's so they faced each other. Prescott struck a wooden match and puffed on his pipe until fragrant smoke billowed from its open end. With a flick of his wrist, he extinguished the match and dropped it on the tile-topped table.

"Your girlfriend is quite a catch," his godfather said as he put the pipe down far enough for Benjamin to see his face. "She's very sweet, absolutely beautiful, and cares for you quite a bit. Can't ask for more than that."

Benjamin examined Ben Prescott's face. He looked sincere enough, but with the people in this house, there could always be an ulterior motive. As soon as the thought crossed his mind, Benjamin cursed it. His internal cynic reared up and fed on the negative energy in this house. Prescott had always been straightforward with Benjamin and didn't seem to play the kinds of games for which the Roths were famous. Until shown otherwise, Benjamin decided to accept Prescott's comments at face value.

"She is beautiful," Benjamin responded.

Prescott nodded and leaned back to bring his leg up. He rested his ankle on the opposite knee and puffed lazily on the pipe.

"I came by this afternoon to see how Barbara was doing. It's hard to tell what's going on in her head, no thanks to the pills that quack doctor is feeding her. She said, as best she could through the medication, Ms. Kincaid stepped in to talk to her this morning."

"I heard," Benjamin said.

"According to your mother, you and your lady friend are getting married. Or maybe she said you already were. I'm not sure now. But it had something to do with you, Ms. Kincaid, and marriage."

Benjamin set his glass down and stared hard at his godfather. He swallowed the liquid still in his mouth. "Where would she get an idea like that?"

Ben shrugged. "Wishful thinking, maybe? Perhaps a premonition?"

Benjamin shook his head. "The only thing my parents wish for me is that I leave, as soon as possible."

The other man's face grew stern and he leaned forward to point his pipe in Ben's direction. "It wasn't always like that, Benjamin. When you were born you were the most precious thing in the world to them."

"Until they found out I was deaf."

"That's not what happened." Benjamin read the strength of Prescott's exclamation on his face. Then the man's shoulders slumped and he sat back. "It wasn't like that."

"Then what was it? All I've ever heard from Jon is the disgrace I've been to this family since the day I was born. I've been buried, hidden, denied, and ignored. If it wasn't because of my deafness, then what was it?"

The only answer was a shake of the other man's head as he dropped his chin towards his chest. He didn't expound on his beliefs and turned away to look out the solarium windows. Benjamin took a deep breath against the empty hole between his lungs. It varied in size from hour to hour. Right now it was livable, even after the brief conversation with his godfather.

"I'll see you tomorrow, Prescott," he said and stood up.

Benjamin walked slowly from the solarium with his thumbs hooked through his two front belt loops. George met him in the front hall, a distressed look on his face. He waved Benjamin over to him with a fervent hand.

"Benjamin, I've been looking for you for half an hour."

"I was in the solarium. What's wrong, George?"

"It's Ms. Kincaid."

"What about her?" The hairs on the back of Benjamin's neck bristled and his insides clenched in immediate dread. "Did something else happen with her and Jon?"

George shook his head. "I called a cab for her twenty-five minutes ago. She's going to the airport to rent a car. I believe she's returning to Boston."

"What? Where is she now?"

"She just came down with her bag," George clarified.

"Shit," Benjamin cursed and sprinted to the front door.

Jewell sat near the bottom of the front stairs. Her knees were drawn up to her chest and the autumn breeze shifted her loose hair around her shoulders. Benjamin slowed his stride to walk to the end of the landing and took a deep breath before he took the first step. From his position behind her, he saw her wipe her fingers across her cheek.

Benjamin knew her reason for leaving. He had made a royal ass of himself. Again. Could he blame her? Absolutely not.

She turned and looked up at him just before he reached her. Her smile was small and hesitant, but there nonetheless. Jewell took one hand from her coat pocket to give him a small wave and mouthed, "hi." Benjamin sat down on the cold marble step beside her. He tried to read her face, to judge her level of anger, but saw none in her soft expression. Her appearance wasn't one of sadness or melancholy, but more like defeat. The loss of spark in her usually bright eyes made Benjamin feel about an inch tall.

"*Were you going to leave without telling me?*" he signed.

Jewell shook her head. "*I left you a note. Just to let you know I'd see you when you got back to Boston.*"

Benjamin took in the details of her beautiful face. Jewell's cheeks were milky white with the slightest shade of pink from the November wind. A smattering of freckles bridged her nose. As always when he looked into her eyes, the dazzling depth of them amazed him. The color itself was alive, despite the diminished glint, as alive as the burnished copper of her hair. He took in a deep, tired breath.

"*Why are you leaving?*"

Jewell seemed to focus on the movements of his hands more than what was necessary to understand his question. He caught a slight quiver of her chin before she shifted her gaze past him. His gut sank like a lead weight.

"*I came here to be a help. Something tells me I'm more of a hindrance.*"

"*Why would you think that?*"

She waved her hands in frustration. "*I don't know what to do for you. Or what to say.*"

"*I don't expect you to do or say anything.*"

She tucked her chin into her chest and covered her eyes with her hands for a moment before looking at him again. "*I've caused more friction between you and your parents. Just look at this morning.*"

Benjamin adamantly shook his head. "*No. No. This morning had nothing to do with you. It's my fault. I knew the animosity against me would carry over to you. You could be Mother Theresa and he wouldn't respect you, just because you're with me. For that I apologize.*"

A yellow cab came through the open front gate and pulled up the drive, and Benjamin read the name Hartford Cab Company on the side of the sedan as it stopped. Jewell stood up and reached for her suitcase. He jumped to his feet and stopped her hand before she picked it up.

"Don't leave."

Jewell's chin lifted slowly to meet his stare, and moisture glistened in her eyes. "Benjamin, I'm not trying to be a drama queen or to get your attention. In fact, I think you need as little drama in your life as possible right now. I had wanted to be gone by the time you found out. From the moment we heard the news, I've wanted to do whatever I thought was best for you. Right now, this is what I think is best."

She took the last couple of steps to reach the cab and opened the back door. The old Benjamin would have let her climb in and ride away. The choice was hers to make, and he wouldn't have thought twice about letting her decide. But he was a different Benjamin now. Different because of her and now he couldn't let her leave.

He took the one step needed to get between her and the cab. Her eyes rounded in shock.

"Don't leave," he said again.

She set her suitcase on the floor in the back of the cab before facing him. "*Benjamin, deep down I don't think you want me here. We'll have time later. When you get back to Boston. I swear, I'm just giving you space here. I'll be waiting when you come home.*"

He shook his head and cupped her face in his hands. "Jewell, sweetheart, it isn't a matter of wanting you here or not. If you don't want to stay, I won't make you. I can't. But you are the only sanity I have right now."

She pulled her lower lip through her teeth and met his gaze. "I don't think so, Benjamin. I'm just something else you have to deal with. You need to focus and get through what you need to get through." She touched his cheek and stood on her toes to kiss the corner of his mouth. "I'll be waiting for you. I promise."

Jewell pulled away and slid into the back seat of the cab. She wiped a tear from her cheek before she looked up at him again. Benjamin's insides were in knots and his pulse pounded in his temples. What was he doing! Why was he letting her leave? She blew him a kiss from her fingertips.

"Goodbye," he read on her lips.

She spoke to the cab driver and pulled the door shut. Benjamin stepped back as the car slowly pulled away. Jewell said something through the window he didn't catch. Something suddenly burst in his chest and he made the decision. With a quick sprint, Benjamin caught up with the cab and banged on the trunk to get the driver's attention. The car stopped.

Benjamin pulled open Jewell's door and crouched down to see her face. Tears streaked her tender cheeks and her lips parted in the unasked question.

"*I need you*," he told her, hoping he could somehow express just how much he didn't want her to go. "*Jewell, I need you.*"

She held his gaze for an eternity and several new tears rolled down her moisture-spiked lashes. An almost indiscernible quiver shook her chin and she brushed back a wave of hair from his temple. The touch of her fingertips warmed his cheek. Benjamin held her palm against his lips and kissed the soft flesh.

"Please," he asked. She shook her head, but he squeezed her hands tighter. "Please."

Jewell's lip trembled when she attempted a smile. "Okay."

A soothing rush spread through Benjamin's chest and he released a long breath, pressing into lips into the palms of her cool hands. She turned to the driver and apologized for making him come out for nothing. The middle-aged man smiled earnestly at them and said it was no problem at all. Benjamin gave the man two twenties for his trouble. Then he stood and offered his hand to Jewell to help her from the car.

When they stood alone at the foot of the front steps, Benjamin turned to her and pulled Jewell in a hard embrace. He pressed his face into her fragrant hair and felt the softness of her skin against his cheek. Her arms wrapped around his neck, and he cursed the jacket she wore and cursed his reluctance for the last two days to hold her like this. Benjamin tightened his hold and felt a surge of energy in his blood as Jewell fed him with her touch.

She pulled back, looked up at him, her eyes bright, and touched his face and neck with her fingers. "You're cold. Let's go inside."

Benjamin shook his head. "Why do you worry so much about me?"

She smiled and slipped her hand into the bend of his arm. "Because you need me."

Jewell sat on the bed with the day's *Wall Street Journal* spread out on the duvet. She glanced over a variety of stock quotes and market closings with marginal interest. Her true interest was the sound of the shower running in the bathroom. Without question or reservation, Benjamin came up to the bedroom with her after dinner. As he showered and shaved, she waited with intense anticipation.

The bathroom door opened and she looked up. Jewell's heart leaped to her throat and a hot flush ran over her entire body. Benjamin stood in the doorway with a bath sheet wrapped around his narrow waist and a smaller towel around his shoulders. He rubbed the smaller towel vigorously over his damp hair.

Jewell tried to remember why they were there, and the solemnity of the whole thing, but the sculpted beauty of Benjamin's torso was undeniable. Moisture glistened in droplets on his arms and chest. He turned his back to her and bent over to retrieve something from his suitcase. The way the damp towel clung to his backside made Jewell's stomach flutter and she groaned loudly. She ran her hand over her face and forced herself to look away. With a sharp rustle, Jewell folded the newspaper and stood to toss it in a nearby chair. She took off her reading glasses and set them on the bedside table.

Benjamin turned and ran his fingers through the damp waves of his hair. That intoxicating, seductively slow grin of his made Jewell's knees weak and it was all she could do to smile back. Suddenly, the short pajamas she wore seemed highly inadequate and overly revealing. They were not intended for seduction, but with the heat and electricity that rushed over her skin, a turtleneck sweater and thermal ski pants wouldn't have been sufficient. She crossed her arms over her body and walked back to the bed.

"*Are you okay?*" Benjamin signed with arched brows and a smirk on his face.

Jewell nodded and put one knee up on the mattress to sit down again near the pillows. "*I'm fine. Did your shower help with your headache?*"

"*It did. I think I just needed to come up here and get away from everything else.*" His brown eyes held her gaze and his lips pursed ever so slightly. "*I needed to come be with you.*"

Jewell lifted one shoulder in a nonchalant gesture. "*I've been here for three days.*"

He sighed and picked up a pair of silk boxer shorts in navy blue paisley from the bed. "I know…now."

Jewell gasped as he dropped the towel and pulled on the boxers. The nonchalant expression on his face was a sharp contrast to the unsettling shock that coursed in Jewell's veins. The mattress was high enough that she didn't actually catch a glimpse of Benjamin in his fully naked state, but enough was revealed to set off butterflies in Jewell's stomach and turn her blood to liquid heat. The enticing angle where his thigh met his hip teased her with what hid only scant inches away. She swallowed against the giggle in her throat and the grin stretching her lips.

The elastic waistband snapped against his skin and he tossed the towel through the open door of the bathroom. Benjamin took the edge of the duvet and pulled it back to slip beneath the covers.

"Anything in the *Journal* I need to know?" he asked.

How could a man with no understanding of adjectives like "husky" and "throaty" make his voice sound so sexy? Even when asking a far-from-sexy question? Jewell shook her head and built up enough nerve to move beneath the covers. She reclined back on the pillow and Benjamin moved closer so he looked down at her.

"The NYSE closed up about fourteen points. The California software firm you wanted to watch is up a dollar twenty-five a share. Bernanke is threatening to lower the interest rates again. Nothing too earth-shattering."

Benjamin leaned closer and touched the base of her throat through the open collar of her pajama top. Despite the restraint she tried to maintain, Jewell closed her eyes and a low moan shuddered up from her chest. Hungry for the simplest touch for the past two days, this sensual contact amplified her senses two-fold. His fingertips ran the edge of the shirt to the valley between her breasts, then back up to her collarbone. With tremendous effort, Jewell opened her eyes and looked up at him.

Benjamin's eyes were dark with arousal. She couldn't move, couldn't breathe. Her body ached. She'd come close to making love to him once, and her body already hummed from his nearness. Her mind screamed for sanity, warning her that this was neither the time nor the place. But for now, she could not deny his touch.

"Thank you for putting up with me," he said and continued to caress her skin.

She nodded, the only answer she could give. In a purely reactive response, Jewell drew up one knee and turned more in his direction. More than anything, she wanted to wrap her arms around his body and pull him down to her.

Benjamin shifted and moved his entire body closer to hers. The crisp hairs on his thighs brushed her legs and she ran her ankle up the side of his calf. His lips covered hers in a slow, drugging kiss that left her short of breath and hungry for more. The heat of his mouth led a path down her throat to her shoulder and along the base of her collarbone. Jewell moved her hands to his side and the muscles of his back flexed and relaxed beneath her palms.

It was so easy to melt into him.

Neither had to explain why Benjamin stopped before it went too far, or why he shifted to stretch out beside her, tucking her head beneath his chin. This place, this house of tension and anger, was not the place she wanted to remember as the place she made love to Benjamin the first time. Or, maybe any time. And if she felt that way, his opinion on the matter was probably much stronger. Jewell closed her eyes, letting out a long sigh as Benjamin turned off the light. He circled his arm around her shoulders, bringing her closer, and kissed her forehead.

"You just wait until I get you back to Boston," he said in the darkness, and she smiled against his bare skin.

CHAPTER SIXTEEN

"Staying here isn't good for you, Ben."

Benjamin dragged a bite of his prime ribeye through his mashed potatoes, avoiding the response he knew Logan expected. Jewell sat to his left, and Abigail Prescott to his right with the rest of the Prescott family wrapping the round table at one of the finer steakhouses in Hartford. He'd made a comment when he sat that he was the thorn between two roses, and it had garnered a smile from Abigail. She wasn't family, but she was almost as important to him as Victoria, just like another younger sister.

Logan and his wife Patricia sat across the table, with Prescott between Patricia and Jewell. This was the first time Ben had been home since Prescott's wife Gladys died six years before. It seemed strange to sit with the Prescott family and not have Gladys with them.

Benjamin took his time chewing the steak. The only person at the table who signed was Jewell, so they all would just have to wait while he ate. He swallowed, wiped his mouth, and took a sip of merlot before meeting Logan's eyes across the table. "I'm not leaving her. Not until I know what happened."

"We have no idea when that's going to be," Logan emphasized with a wave of his fork through the air. Patricia raised a subtle hand and guided his fork back to his plate before *au jus* dripped on the white tablecloth. "The doctors won't even say when they're going to bring her out of the medical coma. Are you going to stay in that house of misery until she does?"

"No," he answered quickly, glancing toward Jewell. Her face was down, her attention riveted to her seared scallops. "I've registered a suite at the Crowne Plaza until this is resolved."

Jewell raised her chin enough to look at him and offer a smile. He'd told her his plans that morning over breakfast, and she had neither agreed nor disagreed. She simply nodded her head and squeezed his hand. Even now, she avoided giving an actual opinion.

He wasn't sure if he was happy she hadn't disagreed, or frustrated that she left the decision completely on him.

"For how long?" Logan asked, now emphasizing his point with a wave of his buttered roll. Benjamin had a passing thought that Logan would do well to learn ASL since he already spoke so much with his hands. Logan pointed the roll at him. "Just how long do you think Bulwark is going to let one of their best managers just disappear for weeks at a time? I mean, I'm sure you can do some of whatever it is you do," he said with a flip of his hand, making it clear he didn't know, "from your laptop, but for how long?"

"Do you think my job is more important to me than my sister?"

"No, of course not," Prescott interrupted. "But, other than Victoria, your life is not here in Hartford. It never has been. Victoria is going to be fine, and just how do you think she'll feel if you lose everything you've worked to gain because of her?"

Benjamin sat back and tossed his napkin on his plate. "Don't try to motivate me with guilt, Prescott. I won't have it."

Prescott raised his hands in surrender. "Okay, I'm sorry. I didn't intend it to come off that way."

Jewell reached beneath the table and laced her fingers through his, drawing his hand to her lap beneath the tablecloth. Benjamin drew in a deep breath through his nose, and released it slowly, letting go of the anger Prescott's question had inspired. He knew his godfather was probably trying to help, but Ben Prescott and his children couldn't begin to understand the reasons Benjamin didn't want to leave Victoria without protection of some kind. Even if it was only his presence when she woke up and told the world the truth.

"I apologize, Prescott. I know you have Victoria's interest at heart, but there is more here than you understand."

"That you suspect Jon shot Victoria? I understand that." Prescott shifted, setting his elbow on the table to rub his finger across his upper lip. He had had a mustache for years, and the action was probably habitual. "Ben, we all want to find out the truth as much as you do."

"I don't need to find out the truth, I just need her to tell it. I know what happened. There's no doubt in my mind, Prescott."

"The only person still convinced that Dillon Ferguson shot your sister is Jon himself. And that's only because he's declared it so many times he's started to believe it."

"You don't think Dillon Ferguson shot Victoria." It was no longer a question.

Prescott shook his head. "I've talked to a contact I have at the police department. They held Dillon based on the evidence and testimony they've got, but their evidence is in conflict. Depending on the angle you take, both Jon and Dillon look guilty. They're just waiting for Victoria to wake up to hear what she has to say."

"Is that the only reason you're entertaining the thought? Because of the evidence?"

"No."

"Say it for me, Prescott," Benjamin demanded, leaning forward. "Say you believe my father is responsible. Say you believe my father shot my sister."

Prescott flinched at the words, but he didn't look away. "Benjamin, I believe Jon drew a weapon with the intent of making Dillon Ferguson leave, and when they struggled over it, the weapon went off. He may not have pointed a gun *at* Victoria," he emphasized with a jab of his finger, "but he is responsible."

Benjamin looked quickly between all the Prescotts at the table, including Logan's wife Patricia. Every one of them looked at him with the same conviction. Jewell's hand tightened on his under the table. He shifted and cleared his throat, holding his gaze on Prescott, watching for the slightest flinch. But his godfather didn't waver.

"That's your business partner of nearly forty years you're calling an attempted murderer, Prescott," he finally said, waiting for the reaction.

Prescott simply nodded, a slow and deliberate movement of his head.

"We're going to watch out for her," Logan said, leaning slightly toward his father to draw Benjamin's attention away from Prescott. What had been a light, casual expression on his face when the conversation began was now serious, unwavering. "We'll watch out for her, and when the doctors are ready to let her wake up, we'll let you know. We'll make sure she's never alone until she comes around and tells the police what happened. Dad has already worked it out to have someone there. He told Jon it was to protect Victoria since Dillon has been released on bail."

Benjamin gritted his teeth and released Jewell's hand under the table, bringing his hands together in front of him with his elbows on either side of his plate. The idea of leaving Hartford twisted in his gut like an angry snake.

The subject was dropped for the rest of dinner, and Benjamin focused on catching up with the people who had been more like a family to him than his own. Logan was only slightly younger than him, and they had attended Bridlethorpe together until Benjamin accelerated his education and graduated early. They had roomed together, and while Logan hadn't learned to sign, he had assisted Benjamin with his speech therapy and lesson notes. Every year, the Prescotts invited Benjamin to their home for the holidays. The only reason he turned them down was because he wanted to go home to Victoria.

Abigail was younger, just a fraction older than Victoria, so the two Prescott children fell between the Roth children in age. It was difficult for Benjamin to look at the beautiful young girl sitting beside him, and reconcile her with the little girl who followed him and Logan around, constantly asking them to play dolls or come to her tea parties. He wished now he'd agreed more often than he did. She was a college graduate and working as a paralegal at the Law Firm of Roth, Prescott, and Heinlein. She was engaged, and Logan and Patricia were expecting their first child.

Life moved on.

He just wondered if life had left him behind.

The hospital was still and quiet, the only sound of the occasional nurse speaking to another or the distant beep of a life monitor. The lights were dimmed in the ward, giving the illusion of rest. The sound of the bottle of juice dropping through the vending machine seemed intrusive, and Jewell looked down the hall to see if anyone had been disturbed. The hallway was vacant save for the one nurse at the main desk who stood on the hall side, writing on a clipboard.

Visiting hours had ended long ago, but the nurses didn't say anything when Jewell and Benjamin arrived at nearly ten o'clock. They just smiled and nodded and motioned toward Victoria's room. Comparatively speaking to Jon Roth and the rest of the family, Benjamin had to be easy to deal with.

Jewell walked back down the hall toward Victoria's room, offering a smile to the nurse on duty as she passed. She paused outside the door, bracing herself before she went inside.

Victoria's doctors had moved her from the ICU to a private room with pale green walls, intended to soothe, with watercolor landscapes framed on the walls and carpeting on the floor instead of cold linoleum. A heavy stillness filled the room, and the burn of antiseptic tingled her nose down the back of her throat. The air was thick, humidified, but cool.

The narrow hospital bed engulfed her. White sheets and pale blue blankets blended with her too-pale skin, her dark brown hair a sharp contrast to the lack of color and life. While the image of her newest friend lying so still and pale always made Jewell's chest tighten, it was the tableau of the man seated beside the bed that gripped hardest at her.

He had pulled one of the two visitor chairs to the side of the bed, as close as he could get. His head was down, his arms folded on the edge of the mattress beside Victoria's hip, his hand covering hers. Benjamin looked broken and tired, hunched in supplication to something greater than himself that Jewell doubted he even understood.

They'd been given the medical rundown. The bullet had punctured Victoria's liver and perforated her intestines. It had ripped straight through her thin body from back to front, leaving vicious gashes in her abdomen. The skin would heal, and the scarring could be reduced with proper plastic surgery, the liver would repair itself. It had been the perforation of her intestines that had caused the most concern.

The doctor told them any injury to the digestive tract could be deadly. Sepsis and infection could run rampant through her body and kill her within a couple of hours of an injury like this, but the doctors had hit her with massive doses of antibiotics before she even went into surgery. The first few days everyone had held their breath, waiting for signs that infection had taken over her body or that it had been beaten back in time. After only a mild fever, all signs indicated she'd gotten past the worst threat.

Now, she rested in a drug-induced coma while her body healed. The doctors told them that the pain would be very bad, and she could recuperate faster if she just slept through the worst of it until she could better cope with the pain of healing.

But, her recovery would be complete.

Now, they waited…and Benjamin watched.

Jewell set the bottle of juice on the rolling bedside table and walked around the foot of the bed to his side. She laid her hand on the back of his head, combing her nails through the soft waves of his hair. With a heavy sigh, she looked up to Victoria's surreal, serene face.

"He's trying to decide if he can leave you, or not," she said softly, knowing that perhaps her words would carry through the silence in Victoria's sleeping mind. "He's afraid to leave you alone but knows he can't do anything here until you're awake. I know you won't hold against him whatever he does, he just doesn't know that."

Benjamin shifted his arms so his forehead rested in the crux of his elbow and reached around his head to take her hand from his hair, folding his fingers around hers. His lips brushed her knuckles and he pulled her closer. When her legs hit the side of the chair, he sat up and turned into her, resting his temple against her stomach. He wrapped his arm around the back of her legs, pulling her as close as he could with the chair arm as a barrier between them.

"We'll go back to Boston tomorrow morning," he said after several minutes in that position.

Jewell held out her free hand so it was within his line of vision and spelled "O.K."

"I'm going to come back this weekend, and every weekend, until she's awake."

She repeated the action of stroking his hair with one hand and affirming his choice with the other. Benjamin tipped his head back, looking up at her. "Am I doing the right thing?"

Jewell smiled and laid her hand against his jaw. "You don't need me to tell you."

He smiled, but it didn't quite reach his eyes. "I could choose to sell my townhouse and live in a double-wide trailer to be closer to her, and you'd support me, wouldn't you."

She stepped back enough to hold his face in both her hands and leaned over to press a long kiss to his forehead. Then she kissed each cheek before kissing his lips. "Maybe not the double-wide," she said with a smirk once she drew back enough for him she her lips.

Benjamin chuckled and stood, kissing her cheek before he turned to the bed. He squeezed his sister's hand and leaned over to kiss her forehead. Then he stepped back, took Jewell's hand, and they walked out together.

CHAPTER SEVENTEEN

The offensive buzz of Jewell's alarm clock shot her from the fringe of her unproductive sleep. She flung her arm out and hit the clock with deadly aim. All went silent. Jewell pushed her hair out of her eyes and tossed back the quilt, taking out her annoyance on the hapless covering.

Last night was one of the worst nights of sleep she'd had in her entire life, just barely beating out the night before that. She hadn't had any type of real rest in the past two weeks. Her nights were spent tossing and turning, seeking whatever it was that would gift her with refreshing sleep. It was never a good sign to wake up with a headache when drinking the night before wasn't involved. It wasn't natural. Jewell sat up and drew her knees to her chest where she could rest her elbows.

She knew the reason sound sleep escaped her. After only a few nights of sharing a bed, Jewell was addicted to sleeping in Benjamin's arms. They'd barely had time alone together, unless the time between meetings counted, in the last two weeks. He'd spend the weekends in Hartford, leaving mid-afternoon on Friday and coming home late on Sunday. He was exhausted from the travel and from struggling to catch up and keep up after being away. They were both tired and needed some time to decompress.

Thankfully, it was Wednesday and tomorrow was Thanksgiving. Benjamin didn't plan on leaving for Hartford until Friday afternoon, so they might have a solid day and a half to spend together.

With that encouraging thought in mind, Jewell forced herself from the hollow warmth of her bed and stumbled down the hall to the kitchen. Within minutes, the reviving aroma of hazelnut coffee filled the small apartment. She inhaled the heavenly scent as she stepped out of the bathroom, her wet hair bundled in a towel.

Ruby's door opened and Jewell called a morning greeting to her sister. The response was a grumpy grumble as the bathroom door closed with a hard thud. Jewell smiled. Despite the lack of sleep and the feeling of something missing in her bed, a good mood stirred.

Victoria's condition improved every day, and with each affirmation from her physicians that she was getting better, Jewell saw some of the tension ease from Benjamin's face. He'd gone back to Connecticut twice and Jewell had stayed in Boston.

By the time she reached Bulwark, Jewell's bad mood was completely gone and she hummed as she pushed through the giant glass doors. She greeted everyone she met in the lobby, the elevator, and on the walk to her office. Cheerfully, she set April's cup of coffee on her desk. April looked up and smiled.

"Someone took a happy pill this morning," April joked.

"It's a beautiful fall day, it's the last day before a long weekend, and —and—isn't that enough?" Jewell answered with a shrug.

April shook her head and sipped from the cup of coffee. "Whatever you say, Jewell."

The door to Benjamin's office opened and he stuck his head out. "April, has Ms. Kincaid come in yet?"

April nodded and pointed, unable to speak around the hot liquid in her mouth. Benjamin turned and met Jewell's gaze. A sweet, warm rush flowed into Jewell's limbs like hot buttered rum. She knew she grinned like a fool but was unable to control the reaction. His lips spread in the signature grin that set Jewell's nerves to sparking.

"Good morning, Ms. Kincaid. I'm glad you're here. I need your assistance with something." She nodded and stepped towards his door. "We're not to be disturbed for the next hour."

April mumbled something under her breath as they went through the door. Jewell cast a glance over her shoulder to see April grinning from ear to ear.

"Behave yourself," Jewell said in a theatrical whisper.

April flattened her palm against her chest and feigned shock. "Me? I can behave perfectly well. It's you I'm worried about."

Jewell chuckled and shook her head as she entered Benjamin's office. April hadn't come out and asked, and Jewell certainly hadn't outright confirmed anything, but she was pretty sure April wasn't blind or dumb to what might or might not be happening between her two superiors. She slipped off her light coat as he shut the door. The discernible click of the lock brought her attention back around, and Benjamin met her with a wicked grin. A small giggle escaped her throat before he pulled her into his arms and covered her mouth in a deliciously decadent morning kiss.

Jewell stepped back enough to sign, although his hands stayed at her waist. "*I thought you said you needed my assistance with something?*"

He went back to her throat without pause. "I do," Benjamin said against her skin. His baritone voice vibrated against the sensitive flesh. Jewell's eyelids fluttered and she fought to breathe. "I've got this terrible ache and I need your assistance in relieving it." He shifted again and his hips settled seductively against hers.

Jewell's nerves sparked with electricity. Every hair, every cell, every inch of her body was immediately attuned to each move and each touch. But just as dozens of times before, they both knew now was not the time and the office was never the place. The kisses slowed until the initial fire eased to glowing embers.

"So, Roth, how is your executive assistant working out for you?" Travis Traynor asked as he matched Benjamin's step down the hallway.

Several comments came immediately to mind, but Benjamin

suppressed his inner amusement behind a wide smile. "Just great, Travis. I'm glad I convinced you to let me have her."

"Good. I'm glad she's working out. I had a nagging feeling when I interviewed her she had too much background to be in administration. I wish you'd mentioned your difficulty with Carol's shortcomings before you did. We could have dealt with it sooner."

More illicit thoughts he had to keep to himself. "Timing is everything. Carol is far better suited where she is now."

"Well, Jewell must be good because you certainly seem more relaxed."

Benjamin did his best to hide his lurid grin. He wasn't sure what he felt around Jewell constituted as *relaxed*, but he knew he was happier.

Not happier.

Happy. Something he wasn't sure he'd ever been.

He just shrugged and nodded and let the comment lie between them without expounding on it and possibly losing his composure altogether.

They continued down the hall together to the door of Benjamin's office. Once there, Mr. Traynor extended his hand in a hearty shake.

"We were all very sorry to hear about your sister. How is she doing?"

Benjamin nodded. "Her recovery will be slow, but she'll be just fine. I wanted to thank you for the flowers you sent. They were thoughtful."

Traynor nodded. "It was the least we could do. If you need to take more personal time just say the word. You've certainly earned it."

"I appreciate that, Travis. But we're coming to the end of the year. Things get crazy for us the last quarter with tax reporting and earnings calculations. I've been going on the weekends, and if I need the time, I'll let you know."

Travis nodded his understanding and patted Benjamin's shoulder before he walked away. Benjamin turned on his heels and smiled down at April. Unlike the first several months she worked for him, she greeted him with a smile back instead of a panicked expression.

"Has Ms. Kincaid returned from her meeting yet?"

April shook her head and tapped the end of her pencil against her cheek. Benjamin recognized the devious twinkle in the young woman's eyes and wondered what put it there.

"No. I heard the meeting is running long. Might be another hour. Do you want me to let her know you're looking for her when she gets back?"

"I'm sure she'll stop by my office."

He turned, but a motion of April's hand brought his attention back.

"A gentleman is waiting to see you in your office, Mr. Roth. He said he was your godfather and wanted to wait until you got back."

Benjamin arched his eyebrow. "Thank you," he said before opening the door.

"Do you want a drink?" Jewell asked as she let Benjamin into the apartment shortly after seven that evening. By the look on his face, she thought he needed it.

Benjamin nodded his head and draped his coat on a chair in the living room, dropping heavily into the cushions of the couch. His fingers flicked across his lips and he stared at some indiscernible point on the floor. With a sharp tug, he loosened his tie and yanked it out of his shirt collar.

He had been gone when she returned to the office after her meeting. April filled her in with sparse details only. Ben Prescott had been there, and after he left Benjamin said he'd be gone the rest of the day. It was mid-afternoon, and he never returned. By the looks of it, he had a hell of a day.

Jewell came out of the kitchen and joined him, carrying a chilled glass of wine in each hand. She sat beside him and slipped into the circle of his arm. He drank nearly the entire glass before setting it on the coffee table. Jewell waited patiently for him to explain. When the lack of clarification continued on for several more minutes, Jewell pressed her hand against his chest and drummed her fingers to draw his attention. Benjamin turned a slow gaze her way.

"What happened today?" she asked.

He stared at her for several long moments, his brown eyes skimming over her face. Benjamin's fingertips brushed her cheek and smoothed over her mouth. She enjoyed his gentle touch and parted her lips slightly. Jewell looked up into his face, and her stomach tumbled with a sweet, aroused sensation. She curled her fingers into the fabric of his shirt.

Benjamin shook his head, and Jewell struggled to remember the original question. "Not tonight. Don't worry about it."

"*Are you sure?*"

A storm stirred behind his eyes. "Not now, Jewell," he snapped.

His was not a mood to be trifled with this evening. The fire in his gaze caught her off guard, and Jewell's jaw fell open as she struggled for an appropriate answer. Before she could speak, the smoldering challenge in his eyes died and he looked away. Benjamin sighed heavily.

"I'm sorry," he said in a deep baritone. "I didn't mean that. Bad day."

Jewell touched his temple and smoothed back a light caramel-hued wave of hair. Several strands fell over her fingers and she pushed her nails further into the luxurious softness. When she thought of men's hair, she never thought "soft" or "silky." Women spent hundreds of dollars to pamper, coddle, and moisturize their hair and give it that "touchable" feel. He probably didn't even know the name of the shampoo he used. The thought made Jewell smile.

"*We all have bad days. Let's just forget about it.*"

He shook his head and pressed one of her hands between his, rubbing both the palm and back in a slow caress. "I keep forgetting there is someone who cares."

She curled her fingers around his hand. "And I do care. Very much."

Benjamin lifted her hand and kissed her fingertips, a wry smile on his lips. "I'm learning." He sighed deeply before continuing. "Prescott came to the office today to tell me my father was arrested last night."

"Oh," Jewell said softly. "I thought the investigating officers didn't want to move on arresting him until Victoria came out of the coma. She hasn't, has she?"

A pained expression pinched around Benjamin's eyes, and he

nodded his head. "They planned on bringing her out on Friday, but the doctors felt she was regressing because of the heavy sedatives and stopped the IV during the night. My mother told Prescott, who made sure an officer was present when she came around. She confirmed to the officer that my father drew the weapon and threatened them." He continued the massage of her hand between his. "How do you feel about going to Hartford with me tomorrow night? We can still have dinner with your family, but I want to see her as soon as—"

She leaned over and kissed him, stopping his explanation. When she leaned back, his gaze remained on her lips. "Of course. How is she doing? Have you heard?"

"Prescott said she's uncomfortable, but the pain is manageable." His lips pulled tight over his teeth, and his voice caught. He focused on their hands.

Jewell touched his chin to get him to look at her. "She's going to be okay, Benjamin."

He kissed her, but the contact felt more despondent than sensual. Jewell stroked his cheek and ran her thumb along his lower lip. "Does that mean they've ruled out Dillon as a suspect?"

Benjamin nodded, folding her hand between his again. He seemed fascinated with smoothing his palms over hers, turning their hands over and back. "Their focus now is on my father, and he is furious by what Prescott told me. He's claiming Victoria is incompetent and her judgment is compromised. He found out at the booking that I hired a lawyer for Dillon and I was the one who paid his bail."

"Is your father still in jail?"

Benjamin's nod was slow and tired, and he lifted one hand to rub the back of his neck. Jewell shifted to take over the massage, kneading her fingers into the tight muscles of his shoulder. A moan rumbled in his chest as she worked her thumbs along his spine.

"Bail won't be set until Friday because of the holiday. So, he's got at least a good thirty-six hours to stew in his juices."

She took her hands away from the massage just long enough to sign. "*Where did you go after Prescott left?*"

He twirled his finger in the air. "*Here and there. I drove mostly. Trying to think.*"

Jewell shifted again on the couch to kneel beside him, resting her elbow on the back and her cheek against her fist. "Well, you're here now."

Benjamin nodded, his eyelids lowering over his dark brown eyes, and pressed his lips against hers. His fingertips applied a slight pressure to urge her closer to him. A sweet commotion immediately flooded her veins and Jewell rested her head in the bend of his elbow as he kissed her deeply and soundly.

"Get a room, huh?" Ruby called from the hallway.

Jewell pulled back and scowled at her younger sister. Benjamin turned to look towards the hall. His arm tightened around her and pulled her closer to his side. For his benefit, Jewell signed Ruby's comment. He smiled.

"Hello, Ruby," he said. There was no indication of awkwardness in his face or voice at "being caught" by the younger girl.

She waved her hand and smacked her gum. Tonight she'd chosen one of her more subdued outfits—torn jeans over black leggings, a wide leather belt hanging off her hip, and a black and red oversized sweater over a black turtleneck. She'd changed the stud in her nose for a tiny turkey. At least she was in the holiday spirit. "Hey, Benji. How's it hangin'?"

"Ruby," Jewell said with shock. "Good Lord, have some manners."

"Whatever. Mom told me you're coming to the house for dinner tomorrow." She indicated the statement was for Benjamin with a forward jut of her dainty chin.

Benjamin nodded. "I can't wait. If your mother's cooking tastes as good as it smelled I'm going to eat myself into a coma."

"*Speaking of which, do you want to help me make Watergate Salad?*" Jewell asked him, spelling out the recipe name.

Amusement twinkled in his eyes. He chuckled softly. "*What is Watergate Salad?*"

Jewell stood up and held her hand out to him. Ruby mumbled something about seeing them the next day. Since Benjamin had accepted their mother's invitation to dinner, they planned on driving up together, so Ruby was taking Jewell's car to Manchester that night. She also said something about leaving them alone so they could make out all they wanted. With relief that Benjamin couldn't hear Ruby's comments, Jewell told her sister to wear a warm jacket and let her go.

"Yes, Mother," Ruby said with a warm smile as she headed for the door. Jewell grinned and blew her little sister a kiss before she disappeared.

Benjamin followed her into the kitchen and Jewell tossed a bag of mini marshmallows at him, which he caught against his chest as she opened the refrigerator to retrieve a container of whipped topping. Setting the tub beside the marshmallows where he'd set them, she bounced up on the counter, crossing her ankles. From her perch, she took a large glass bowl from a cabinet and added it to the growing pile of ingredients. Without getting down, she opened a cabinet door and retrieved canned pineapple, walnuts, maraschino cherries, and pistachio pudding mix. Under her instruction, Benjamin strained, dumped, and poured the individual items into the bowl.

Jewell found it surprisingly amusing to watch him make such a mundane dessert as Watergate Salad. She'd watched him work in the kitchen, but that was creating succulent meals with elaborate preparations. There was nothing fancy or posh about the simple dish, but it was a staple at every holiday meal in the Kincaid house. There he stood, in his Giorgio Armani suit pants and Calvin Klein dress shirt, plopping non-dairy whipped topping into a mixing bowl. Never had a man looked so sexy. Benjamin Prescott Roth was the white-collar version of small apartment domestication.

She snatched a cherry from the jar before he had a chance to empty it into the bowl. Benjamin tapped her hand in mock punishment. "You're as bad as Victoria," he teased and scooped the pale green mixture on his finger and smeared it on the end of her nose.

"*Don't be fresh,*" she ordered and snagged a dish towel to clean her face.

Jewell fully enjoyed her position of power. With her ankles crossed and her feet swinging in the air, she pointed to the drawer where she kept the plastic wrap. Benjamin obediently tore off a sheet and smoothed it over the bowl. She laughed when it took three attempts to get the clingy cover in place properly. Benjamin and plastic cling wrap were not well acquainted. He opened the refrigerator and set the salad on an empty shelf.

"You just made Watergate Salad. Aren't you proud of yourself?"

Benjamin smiled widely and genuinely. "Exceptionally proud. Do I get the credit with your mother for making it?"

"Oh, no, I think this was a team effort."

"Yes, you gave orders and I followed them."

Jewell snapped the corner of the towel at him. "Precisely."

He grabbed the dishtowel out of her hand. Before he could return the favor, Jewell grabbed his open collar and pulled him to her. He didn't argue but tossed the towel aside, his gaze never leaving her face. With a sexy leer, he nudged her ankles apart and stepped between her knees so they bracketed his hips. He set his hands at her knees and slid his palms up her thighs, nudging her skirt hem a little higher. Jewell slid her hand inside his open collar to the back of his neck, teasing the edges of his soft hair at the nape of his neck.

Benjamin drew in a long breath and gripped her hips, shifting her a little closer, before skimming his fingertips up her side, eliciting a shiver from her at the touch. "How did I get here?" he asked, holding her jaw in his warm hands.

Jewell smiled and hooked her feet behind his legs. "Define here. I'm pretty sure you drove across town…"

He chuckled, stroking her lower lip with his thumb as she spoke. "I mean…here." He kissed her. "How did I earn you?"

Jewell didn't make the actual decision to release the buttons of his shirt and didn't realize she was doing it until she'd opened four of them and ran her hands over his chest. His heart pounded hard against her palm. "I'm pretty sure you stole me out from under the nose of Kevin Burke. A fact for which I've never properly thanked you."

Benjamin used the edge of his thumbs to urge her lips apart before he covered her mouth in an open kiss, his tongue sliding past her teeth to steal her breath. The pitch of the kiss went from sensual to intense in one breath, and Jewell let herself fall into it. He held her head captive, kissing her with such need it made her ache.

When she thought she might either faint from the lightheadedness his deep kisses caused, or spontaneously combust from the simmering heat beneath her skin, he moved from her lips to her jaw and further to her throat. Strong, long fingers curled into the bunched fabric of her skirt at her hip and he yanked her toward him, holding her hard against his waist. She ached, needed, and wanted all at the same time. So much so that she couldn't think beyond his touch and kiss.

Benjamin pulled back, his rapid breath bathing her face. "Jewell…" He punctuated her name with another brief but firm kiss. "I want to be with you."

A cold flush hit her in the center of her body, and flashed outward, making her breath catch. She set her hands at the edge of the counter, curling her fingers underneath to balance herself, and leveraged herself off the edge, her body pressing against his as she slid down to her feet. He pressed his lips together, heavy eyelids sliding over his brown eyes as a low rumble shifted through his chest. Waiting until he opened his eyes again and looked down at her, Jewell slid her hands into his, lacing her fingers between his, and stepped out of the space between them toward the kitchen door.

CHAPTER EIGHTEEN

"*W*ould you care for some more turkey, Benjamin?"

He raised his hands, waving them in surrender before answering Jewell's mother. "*Honestly, I couldn't eat another bite.*"

She smiled, the sweetest and most honest smile Benjamin had ever seen on a woman other than her daughter, and stood to stack dishes and take them away. Immediately, Benjamin and all the Kincaid children jumped to their feet, gathering plates and serving dishes still teeming with some of the most delicious food Benjamin had ever eaten. The house was filled with activity and aromas and life that nearly vibrated through him. Garnett had brought Jackie, whom Jewell described as Garnett's perpetual girlfriend. This was her third Thanksgiving with the family, and their mother was gently putting pressure on Garnett to finally propose.

Cecil's brother and wife were there, with their two grown children and spouses and four grandchildren. Another brother came alone, and Jewell had explained he had never married. Opal's sister, who was a widow, came alone. Her children had left New Hampshire when they married and now lived too far to come home for the holiday.

There were also some cousins, but after the tenth introduction, Benjamin had lost complete track of any names. Only a few knew sign language with a limited vocabulary, and Benjamin noted how the Kincaid children always made sure someone was near their mother to provide interpretation when needed. The home was warm, and not just from the fire burning in the parlor fireplace. He had felt just a fraction of the sensation when he'd come to peel apples and meet her family, now it was almost overwhelming.

"Do you do this every Thanksgiving?" he asked when the table had been cleared and the crowd had disbursed to various rooms throughout the first floor. Two of the cousins had stepped into the backyard to smoke cigarettes because while Cecil was free to smoke his pipe in the house, cigarettes were sanctioned to outside.

Jewell nodded and led him through the front room to a loveseat positioned in front of a double window that looked out onto the front porch. A cool draft squeezed in through the frame of the old window, helping to balance against the intense warmth thrown off by the fireplace. He slipped his arm across the back of the settee, and Jewell shifted to sit close to his side.

"Thanksgiving. Christmas. Easter. Everyone in the family comes here if they're in the area. It's been that way as long as I can remember."

"It's amazing," he spoke, not wanting to take his arm from around her to sign. "I—we—Victoria and I never had anything like this." He looked down at her, accepting and enjoying the warmth that spread through his chest at her open smile. "I wish I hadn't asked you to leave with me this afternoon."

"Mama and Daddy understand."

Benjamin shook his head. "No. I want you to stay."

She pressed her finger to his lips and shook her head. "No, Benjamin. Today is about family, and your sister is waiting for you. And I want to be with you if you want me there."

Benjamin nodded and kissed her finger. "Okay."

"Do you want to stay for dessert? We usually wait an hour before we break out the pies."

He turned his wrist and looked at his watch near her ear. "I'd hoped to leave before then. It's a long drive, and even now we probably won't see her tonight." He focused on Jewell again, hoping his grin came across as lecherous as his thoughts. "Besides, if we leave soon, it won't be too late when we get to the hotel." He bobbed his eyebrows.

Jewell smiled slow and sexy, tilting her head to kiss him. He crooked his elbow, cradling her head to deepen the kiss, wishing as a thrust of heat hit him that they weren't in a room full of her family and friends…and impressionable young children. Garnett walked by the couch with Jackie, and kicked the leg, making the whole thing shift. Benjamin smiled and chuckled against Jewell's mouth before looking at her brother. Garnett just dismissed them with a flip of his hand and headed into the hallway, Jackie's hand in his. He was probably the smart one, finding a less crowded room in the house.

Opal stepped into the parlor from the doorway leading to the kitchen and scanned the crowd of family and friends, smiling wide when she spotted them. She wove her way around chairs and scattered children, holding up a brown bag. As soon as she reached them, she handed Jewell the bag.

"I know you two need to leave, so I packaged up some desserts. A little bit of everything. You might be able to snack on the cookies on the ride, but I included some forks for the pies that you can eat when you get there. I also made turkey sandwiches, in case you want something other than sweets."

Jewell stood, kissing her mother on the cheek. *"Thank you, Mama."*

Benjamin stood beside her and laid his hand on Opal's elbow, leaning in to kiss the other cheek. *"Yes, thank you so much for opening your home to me."*

She laid her warm hand on his cheek, and her smile wrapped around him. *"You and your sister are welcome here any time, Benjamin. We'll set a table for both of you at Christmas."*

Rapid pounding nudged Jewell from the deep, sated sleep she'd slipped into a couple of hours after they arrived at the Hartford Crowne Plaza. Benjamin had kept to his implied promise and had made love to her until they both curled up together under the blanket of heavy, sweet exhaustion. She thought at first it might be thunder, and opened one eye to look at the hotel room window, but saw nothing but darkness. Somewhere in the back of her mind, she knew that thunder in Connecticut in November was highly unlikely, but she wasn't awake enough to process the fact. She closed her eyes and snuggled back into the soft hotel bed.

The pounding came again and yanked her fully out of her sleep. As her senses came to the front, one by one, she realized the rude cadence was too fast and insistent for thunder. Jewell tried to turn over and sit up, glancing around the suite bedroom, still feeling disoriented at waking in a different place. She smiled as Benjamin's strong arm tightened around her waist and pulled her against his chest.

Sleep settled back down over her, as sure as the warm blanket Benjamin pulled closer to them. She drifted again into his comfort as Benjamin settled his chest against her back and spooned his body with hers. Jewell sighed and hummed her content.

The next thump shot her up off the mattress. For a moment, her heart pounded faster and a cold wave rushed over Jewell's heated skin. Benjamin came awake and sat up beside her. She fumbled to find the switch for the wall lights at each side of the headboard. He didn't wait for her to find the switch before he pulled on her arm for her attention. The faint moonlight coming through the window was enough to light his face.

"What's wrong?" he asked, a bleary haze in his eyes.

"*Someone is pounding on the outer suite door.*"

Benjamin swung around in a fluid motion and pulled on his boxers and jeans before he stood. Barefoot, with the top button of his jeans still undone, he headed for the bedroom door. Jewell looked furtively around the room and grabbed one of the fluffy white hotel robes from a chair near the bathroom door. By the time she slipped it on over her cotton shorts and tank top and made it to the bedroom doorway, Benjamin was already at the suite door leading into the hotel hallway.

Jewell padded in bare feet across the carpet. Benjamin stood at the door, his hand on the wood. The next round of pounding made her jump, and he yanked his hand back. Who could be pounding on Benjamin's door at three o'clock in the morning? Benjamin opened the door, and Jewell gasped, covering her mouth with her hand.

Benjamin and his father faced off through the open door. Jewell clutched together the front of her robe and pressed her other hand against the wall. She took in a quick, sharp breath.

Jon Roth turned his head slowly to bring his stony gaze down on her. A chill sank into her bones, and Jewell's eyes burned as she found herself unable to blink or look away. At least two days' worth of stubble peppered Mr. Roth's cheeks, and his dark hair spiked out in disarray about his head, some falling forward over his brow. The stench of stale alcohol and two-day body odor wafted in on the evening air and assaulted Jewell's nostrils. The stories Victoria had shared with her, about the violent combination of Jon Roth and alcohol, churned Jewell's stomach.

"What the hell are you doing here?" Benjamin snapped.

"I'm here to kick your bastard ass," Jon Roth boomed.

Benjamin's jaw was set and the muscle across his cheek bounced. "I'd like to see you try."

He tried to shut the door, but his father's palm slapped against the thick wood. Jon's other hand came up with one extended finger, which he wagged in Benjamin's face. It was quickly slapped away. The hostility was tangible and hung in the air like a veil.

"You bastard. You ungrateful son of a bitch. Who the hell do you think you are to believe that murdering punk over me?"

Jewell couldn't move, couldn't breathe.

"I believed him because I knew he couldn't hurt Victoria. He loves her. I *know* what you are capable of."

Jon Roth shoved hard against the door and pushed his way into the suite. Benjamin stepped back and put himself physically between his father and Jewell. She raised her hand and laid her hand against his back, letting him know with her touch that she was there.

"You owe me! I put you where you are today! You haven't the right to fuck with me!"

Shock and disgust registered immediately on Benjamin's face. Jewell's breath caught in her throat. She wanted to step in and stop this, but the testosterone-charged air acted like a force field and kept her from moving.

"You had nothing to do with it. And one thing has nothing to do with the other. You shot her! You could have killed her!"

She nearly choked. She saw Jon Roth's smoldering eyes dart in her direction when she involuntarily gasped.

"She's my daughter! My life!"

"Everything I wasn't."

"Damn straight."

Benjamin's body tensed. Jewell's heart ached and she wanted to scream out for him to stop. "Why the hell should I do anything for you?"

"I educated you."

"What? You want to take credit for sending me to a good school? You did it to get rid of me."

Jewell tried to breathe against the ache in the center of her chest. Her focus switched from Benjamin's incensed face to his father's furious expression.

"You all but told the police you think I'm guilty when you hired a lawyer to defend that no-good punk that shot your sister."

The argument bounced back and forth like a ball bearing in a pinball machine. One moment it was about Benjamin's childhood, the next Victoria's shooting.

"You are guilty. I didn't have to tell them. Victoria did."

Jon's fist impacted Benjamin's jaw with a smack that ricocheted through the suite. He stumbled back and took Jewell with him as they both collided with the wall behind them. Her head hit the plaster and the room momentarily spun. Benjamin was back standing instantly, his fists clenched at his side and a fine stream of blood flowing from the corner of his lips. His head snapped around and their eyes locked. Jewell nodded in his silent question, her hand pressed against the forming lump. She was fine.

"You won't say a damn thing, or so help me, I'll kill you with my own goddamn hands!"

"Stop this!" Jewell screamed. She heard her own voice but didn't know from where it came. "Stop and leave now or I'm calling the police."

"Shut up, you little bitch."

Benjamin lunged and shoved Jon Roth back, directly into the chest of Ben Prescott as he came through the door. Jewell watched in horror as Jon turned and swung at Prescott, but was immediately knocked back with a two-handed shove. He tripped over the leg of a bench and landed on his back. As Prescott stepped into the suite, Jewell saw Barbara Roth come through the door.

"What the hell?" Benjamin cursed, standing in a ready-for-battle stance, his fists pulled up near his side.

"Don't do this, Jon," Prescott said in a surprisingly calm voice.

Jon struggled to his feet, his semi-drunken state making him clumsy. "Get away from me, you backstabbing son of a bitch. Take your whore with you," he shouted, pointing at Barbara Roth.

Benjamin lunged and shoved Jon back against the wall, his forearm pressed against the man's throat.

"Shut your filthy mouth,"

"What? Don't like the truth?"

"Jon, please," Barbara called from the door.

Jewell knew Benjamin wasn't hearing most of the yelling between his father and the new arrivals. She wasn't sure it would make any difference if he did. None of it made any sense to her, and she heard every word.

"I've had it. I'm sick and tired of paying the price for your mistakes. I have been for thirty goddamn years, and I won't do it anymore," Jon yelled.

"Please. This isn't the way," Barbara called again.

Jon locked glares with Benjamin, his mouth twisting into a sinister snarl. "You want to know why I shipped you off to that school? Why I couldn't stand the sight of you?"

"Please," Jewell whispered, tears blurring her vision. She didn't know what she begged for, but she prayed someone would hear her and make it stop.

"I know why. You couldn't stand the thought of having an imperfect son. I wasn't worth your time."

"Wrong," Jon shouted, his eyes rounded wide with what seemed to be untapped fury. "I couldn't stand you. I couldn't stand the sight of you because you reminded me every single goddamn day of what your mother did to me. While I was building a life for us, she was screwing my business partner."

Benjamin's shoulders slumped and his arm slipped from Jon's throat.

"You're not my son, you little bastard."

"Oh, God," Jewell whispered and covered her mouth with her hand.

Benjamin stepped back and walked backward away from the door. His gaze darted from Jon Roth to Ben Prescott to his mother. No wonder there was such a strong resemblance between Benjamin and his godfather. They were father and son. Tears streamed down Jewell's cheeks and her lungs hurt to breathe.

Barbara Roth stepped forward, her face glistening with moisture. A small sob escaped as she crossed the space to her son. She reached out a hand, but Benjamin stepped back before she could touch him.

"Benjamin, please. Let me explain. Let us explain," she said, motioning back towards Prescott.

"No," he said through clenched teeth. "I don't want to hear it."

Echoed shouts came down the hall, and two Hartford police officers reached the suite door, followed by a security guard and the hotel manager. After another round of shouting and accusations, Jon Roth was handcuffed and escorted out of the hotel. The hotel manager explained to Benjamin, while apologizing profusely for the intrusion and that Jon had made it past the front desk, that several other hotel guests had called to report the disturbance. All Benjamin did was nod.

As the officers questioned his mother and Prescott about the events of the last half hour, Benjamin took hold of Jewell's arm and led her to the small kitchen area, his grip on her arm firm but gentle considering the tension in his body. Once there, he pulled her near a light and turned her so he could see her face. His fingers pressed gently against her scalp and felt the bump.

"Are you okay?" he asked.

Jewell nodded and gingerly touched the corner of his mouth. He flinched away, grimacing. "Let me get some ice for that," she said.

"No," he snapped and Jewell stopped. A face that was harsh and tense one second, softened slightly. "No, I'm fine."

Jewell didn't know what to say or do. Hesitantly, though she wasn't sure why, she looked up at him. The corners of his mouth were turned down slightly, and one tight muscle jumped along his jaw. Benjamin's stare shifted over her face. She took a deep, shaky breath and laid her palm over his heart. It still pounded ferociously with adrenaline. He touched his hand to her waist, and they moved together. Her arms circled his body and Jewell pressed her cheek against his chest. Neither said anything more. In his arms, holding him, Jewell felt some of the rigidity slip from his body.

"Could we have a moment, Mr. Roth? Ms. Kincaid?" said one of the officers, approaching them, and stepped into Benjamin's line of sight. His name tag indicated Sgt. Ryan.

Benjamin turned on the man, his arm still protectively around Jewell. "How the hell did he get out of jail? I was told bail wouldn't even be set until later today." His tone barely hid the shout Jewell heard just below the surface, only because she knew him.

"I'm not in a position to answer you, sir."

"Jon Roth holds a lot of power in this town," Ben Prescott said from somewhere behind the officer. "He threw his weight around until a judge heard the case late Thursday. None of us knew, not even Barbara."

Jewell relayed the information, indicating to Benjamin that it was Ben Prescott who imparted the details. Benjamin's jaw clenched when she pointed to indicate Prescott.

Ben Prescott stepped closer, but Benjamin didn't look at him, keeping his focus between Jewell and the police officer. Prescott continued.

"Barbara received a phone call from the hospital that Jon was trying to get in to see Victoria but was retained by security. He left on his own accord before they called the police. She called me, and we came here, thinking this might be his next stop."

Benjamin jerked a short nod, acknowledging what she relayed.

"Mr. Roth," interrupted Sergeant Ryan, and Jewell pointed to him to let Benjamin know he spoke. Benjamin looked up, meeting the uniformed man's eyes. "We need to confirm whether you wish to press charges against your father for assault."

Benjamin's lips pressed together so hard that a thin white line outlined his mouth. His lips twitched and he swallowed, drawing in a long breath. "I fully intend to press charges."

Sergeant Ryan spent the next twenty minutes taking statements from her and Benjamin. Exhaustion dragged at Jewell's limbs and made her eyelids heavy. She stood beside Benjamin, turned into his side, fighting the urge to rest her forehead against his chest and close her eyes.

Only when the sergeant said he was finished did Jewell manage to blink enough to focus on the officer. He shook Benjamin's hand, then tipped his hat at her, and left them alone. Benjamin wrapped his arms around her again and kissed the top of her head.

"Benjamin?" Prescott's voice came from near the door. She hadn't realized the two of them were still in the suite.

Reluctantly, Jewell pulled back and pointed in Prescott's direction. Benjamin turned, and his arms tightened a fraction around her. He still held her close against his side. Behind Prescott stood Barbara Roth, a pained and sorrowful look on her face.

"You need to leave," Benjamin ordered.

"Benjamin, just listen to us," Prescott asked.

He pulled her tighter against his side. His hold was so intense, Jewell found it hard to breathe. She wished Barbara and Prescott would leave to give him time to digest everything. How much more did he have to go through? What else could he be expected to accept?

Benjamin's ribcage expanded beneath her hands as he took a deep breath. His head dropped forward and he nodded slowly.

"Fine."

He laced his fingers through Jewell's and they led the way to the small sitting area across from the kitchenette. She and Benjamin sat on the couch, while Barbara Roth and Ben Prescott sat in the chairs facing them. Jewell had a hard time wrapping her mind around the idea that these two were his true parents. How hard was it for Benjamin?

Jewell laid her hand on his thigh to bring his attention to her. "*I'm going to go in the bedroom. Let the three of you talk,*" she signed.

Benjamin shook his head. "*No. Stay right here.*"

"*Benjamin, I don't belong.*"

His hand covered hers. "Stay."

"If my son wants you here, Jewell, so do I," Barbara Roth said in a small voice, drawing Jewell's attention.

She looked from Barbara to Prescott and finally Benjamin. His dark eyes were all she needed to see. Jewell nodded and turned her hand to squeeze his.

"Okay. I'll stay."

Benjamin slumped back on the couch, looking at Ben Prescott. "So, it's true."

Prescott nodded and looked to the woman at his side. He took her hand and Barbara tried to smile. "Yes. And you have no idea how much we've wanted to tell you."

Benjamin sat forward again, his body a bundle of nervous energy beside her, and pushed his fingers through mussed hair. "You had no right," he said in a low, half-muted voice. He lifted his head and Jewell nearly flinched at the angry twist to his lips. "To keep this from me."

"We know that now," Prescott tried to say, but Benjamin's words overrode everything else.

Benjamin pointed a finger at them. "You let him hate me. Let him beat the crap out of me. Let him hide me away and tell me how worthless I was, knowing the whole time he wasn't even my father."

"Benjamin, you don't know how many times I wanted to step in," Prescott said.

"Not enough to stop it." Benjamin's voice was cold and flat.

Jewell's heart ached in her chest. She pulled the robe tighter around her body and kept her gaze on Benjamin's face. The storm brewing behind his eyes was almost frightening.

"Did you know from the beginning?" Benjamin asked.

Barbara shook her head. "I suppose part of me suspected when I was pregnant with you. But Prescott and I had only been together once, and we both decided that could never happen again."

"Jon was ecstatic when he was told he had a son, Benjamin. I've never seen a man so proud," Prescott explained, his voice tight and tired.

"When did he find out the truth?"

Barbara took a deep breath and let it out in a long sigh. "Shortly after the doctors told us your condition was complete, irreversible… and genetic. You were almost three years old."

"I told you, Benjamin, Jon's hostility with you had nothing to do with your deafness," Prescott added.

Benjamin's eyes squinted together as he glared at his father, the man that had always been his godfather and namesake. "I guess you knew better than anyone."

"From the time doctors told Jon and I you were deaf, he was more than ready to help you in any way he could. He wanted to learn sign language and started to look into doctors who could help you speak. We even began seeing specialists, hoping that if we could discover the reason you were deaf, there might have been a way to reverse it."

"Did Gladys know?"

Benjamin's question pulled Jewell back to the traumatic circle.

Prescott hung his head, his shoulders slumping. When he looked up again, his eyes were red-rimmed and his lower lip pulled tight across his teeth. "I never told her, and she never spoke of it. Whether she suspected, or not, I don't know. As much as I miss her, I'm glad she's not here now to see the mess I've made of things."

"Do Logan and Abigail know?"

The older man sighed. "No. I intend to tell them today."

Prescott rubbed the side of his finger along his upper lip, then raked his hand over his hair. A familiar action that squeezed at Jewell's chest. She had to blink and look away, focusing on the moonlight streaming in through the suite sitting area windows.

Benjamin lunged to his feet, marching across the room to the kitchen area with his back to all of them. He stopped at the counter bar and braced his hands on the edge, hunched over with such tension ratcheting his body that his back muscles visibly bunched. All any of them could do was wait for him to rein in the tumult and turn back to them. Jewell brushed at the hot tears on her cheeks, purposefully refusing to look in the direction of his 'parents.' This was unconscionable and cruel.

When he turned around, the unmitigated rage in his eyes made Jewell gasp. He clenched his fists at his side so hard his hands and arms shook with the tension. When he spoke, his voice was so tight with his anger it barely carried across the room to them.

"Do you have any idea what you've done? Do you know what I've done because of who and what I thought I was?"

The two people who had given him life behind a veil of lies and deceit exchanged looks.

Benjamin took two long strides toward them, stopping short just feet away. He closed his eyes and rolled his head to the side, his lips pressed together in a thin, white line. When he opened his eyes again, he looked down at Jewell, and the rage was now mirrored with a deep, painful-to-see regret.

"I had a vasectomy when I was twenty-one," he confessed, his voice so low she barely heard him. An instant and intense tightening in her chest made it hard to breathe. Benjamin swallowed and focused on his mother and father. "I was so filled with hatred and rage I didn't want to pass on to a child the defective gene pool that had spawned me."

Prescott stood, shaking his head, looking Benjamin in the eye. "But, that doesn't change anything, Ben. The deafness is still hereditary, so whether it was Jon or I—"

"No!" Benjamin shouted, making all three of them jump. "It changes everything. I didn't exclude the possibility of ever having children because I didn't want them to be deaf. I wouldn't have cared." He spoke through teeth clenched so tight his school speech patterns were difficult to understand. "I didn't want the twisted, hate-filled genes of Jon Roth to carry through me to a child who deserved better."

Jewell couldn't hold back the tears anymore, pressing her curled fingers against her lips in a vain attempt to smother the sound.

Benjamin leaned into the marble vanity in the *en suite*, letting the faucet run in the sink until steam curled upward from it. He took a washcloth from the sideboard and soaked it in the hot water. The liquid burned his fingers as he wrung out the terrycloth, and he took a deep breath through the moist heat as he pressed it to his face.

He dropped the cloth on the countertop and pushed his fingers through his now-damp hair. Reluctantly, he raised his eyes and looked at his reflection in the mirror.

Who was he?

Benjamin always believed he was his own man. Because of the way his father—the way Jon Roth—pushed him, it made him the person he grew to be. He was the hated son of Jon Roth.

Now who was he?

He wanted to remember the fact that he was no blood relation to the bastard that almost killed Victoria. Benjamin had worried that whatever sick dementia drove his father to such a rage that he could shoot his daughter somehow dwelled in him. Someday that insanity might snap in his mind and push him into hurting someone he loved. Which had been why he had done what he'd done at twenty-one.

So, now he knew.

But what did that mean? Some part of him was a result of his child-hood. His upbringing. Yet other parts of him were a result of his parents. The genetic soup that created him. Ben Prescott was supposed to be just his godfather. His namesake. Not a man who'd spent one night with his mother.

In one night, he went from being the outcast son to an unwanted bastard. Which was worse?

With a deep breath and heaviness in his chest, Benjamin wiped a dry towel over his face and turned to walk into the bedroom. Jewell sat near the foot of the bed, still wrapped in the white hotel robe, with her arms crossed over her chest. Her eyes and cheeks still bore the evidence of her tears. She looked at him when he opened the bathroom door. A small smile bowed her lips.

She hadn't said much since Barbara and Prescott left—he couldn't yet see Ben Prescott as his 'father', and 'mother' seemed too good for Barbara Roth. Benjamin worried about what kind of effect all this insanity and garbage had on Jewell. Never had he imagined he would pull her into such a sick and twisted drama that the first time he'd kissed her in his office. Of course, he never believed then that they would come this far. That she would spend her nights in his arms and look at him with eyes that held a universe of thought and emotion in one glance.

Jewell stood as he approached the bed. He reached out his hand and she took it with both of hers. She stepped against him, pressing their joined hands between them, and her breath brushed across his chest.

"How are you?" she asked.

Benjamin brushed a wave of auburn hair behind her ear. "I wish I could answer that question."

"Is there anything I can do?" Jewell leaned forward and pressed a soft kiss to his chest.

Heat spread out from the spot, quickly warming his body and limbs. Benjamin pulled in a long, deep breath through his nostrils. He pulled his hand from hers and found the knot of the robe's belt. With a tug, he worked the tie loose, holding her gaze as he did. Jewell's delicate hands touched his sides and slid along his bare skin as he worked to open the front of the robe. She wore the same cotton shorts and stretchy tank top she'd worn that night he went to her apartment, and a silk negligee couldn't be any sexier.

"Yes, there is something," he said, feeling his throat restrict as his need for her exploded in his chest.

She stood unmoving as he pushed the robe off her shoulders, her green eyes still looking up at him through auburn-tinted lashes. He ran his fingertips along her throat and arms, catching the strap and pulling it off her shoulder. As he moved along her breasts, Benjamin felt her breath catch and her eyelids fluttered.

"Make me feel real, Jewell."

She raised her arms and laced her fingers into his hair. She didn't speak, but pulled him down for a hot and sweet kiss that sucked the air from his lungs. The need to somehow affirm himself, whatever way he could, flooded him. If Jewell could still make love to him, if she could be with him, that had to mean he was worth having. Because Jewell chose him, he was worth choosing.

He pulled her against him in an intense embrace. Benjamin was a man incensed. Her touch fed him. The taste of her, as he pulled the skin of her throat between his teeth, increased his hunger. Her hands skimmed along his waist and his breath caught when she released the button of his jeans.

Benjamin lifted her off the floor and laid her down on the mattress, her hair fanning out around her head like a flame. Her emerald eyes still held his stare, unwavering.

He hovered over her, shucking his jeans as quickly as possible. Jewell beckoned him with her eyes and with her hands. "Benjamin," she started to say, but he devoured the words from her lips.

He reached over and turned off the light, plunging them into total darkness. Tonight, he wanted to only feel.

Her hands shifted over his back and brushed his ribs. Long fingernails dug gently into his backside, forcing a groan through his chest.

He was real. *He was real.*

CHAPTER NINETEEN

Victoria's private room was already crowded by the time they arrived at the hospital half an hour into visiting hours. Jewell hung back, a step behind Benjamin holding his hand while he looked around the room.

Barbara Roth sat beside the bed, holding Victoria's hand. Ben Prescott was in the corner of the room with his arms crossed and his head down. Abigail Prescott sat in a chair beside her father, and Logan Prescott stood several feet away, his stance mirroring his father's. Logan's entire expression portrayed tension and anger, and Abigail's eyes were red and puffy.

Prescott must have stayed true to his word and told his children.

Victoria was still pale, and pinched around the eyes. Her eyes were closed until Benjamin pushed her door completely open, then the attention of everyone in the room shifted to them.

"Benjamin!" Victoria cried and held her hand out to him. Her voice was weak, rough, but her smile lit up her face at the sight of her brother.

Benjamin released Jewell's hand and rounded the end of the bed, ignoring everyone else in the room to lean over the bed and carefully embrace his sister. His mother rose from her chair and stepped back, moving closer to Prescott without moving past his children. Feeling like an outsider still, Jewell crossed her wrists and linked her fingers, holding her hands in front of her body as she tucked herself against the wall furthest from everyone else.

The communication between Victoria and Benjamin was silent, limited to the near frantic signing in the space between them. Knowing that no one else in the room signed fluently, the conversation remained private but their faces said it all. Tears streamed down Victoria's cheeks, and soft sounds of restrained weeps carried across the room. Benjamin stroked her cheek to dry the tears, and followed the path of his thumb with a kiss. Jewell made sure to keep her eyes averted so she didn't inadvertently pick up too much of their conversation.

She looked away, and found Logan watching her, his jaw set firm and his eyes angry. He pushed away from the wall and crossed to her, keeping his back to his father. Logan was tall, like Benjamin, and Jewell noted for the first time the way his hair waved away from his forehead, not quite curly but not straight, just like Benjamin's. Logan's hair was brown, like Abigail's, and Jewell wondered if their mother had been a brunette. There were similarities between them, now that Jewell knew to look. Now that she knew they were half-brothers.

"Hi," he said when he reached her, and the simplicity of the greeting surprised her.

"Hi, Logan."

He still had his arms crossed over his chest, and pivoted at the hips to look over his shoulder to where Benjamin sat with Victoria. When he turned back to her, some of the anger had faded from his face. "How is Ben doing?"

Jewell sighed and shifted to tuck her hands behind her, leaning against the edge of the large window that looked out into the hall. "I'm not sure he's processed everything yet. He's trying, but it's a lot to take." She looked up at Logan. "How are you doing? I'm assuming—"

He nodded; a sharp jerk of his chin toward his chest. "He told us this morning."

"Abigail looks upset," Jewell said softly, looking past him to his younger sister, who dabbed at her cheeks with a crumpled tissue.

"We both are." Logan chuckled, but it was a humorless laugh. "I don't know what's the worst part of it all. That our father betrayed our mother the night before their wedding—"

Jewell gasped. Logan nodded, his smile barely a curl of his lips.

"Didn't tell you that part, did he? Benjamin is four months older than me, which means Barbara and my mother were pregnant at the same time." Jewell closed her eyes, fighting the choking tightness in her throat as he continued. "So, what's worse...the initial betrayal or the fact that my father let Benjamin live with that tyrant of a man, knowing his own son was the object of Jon Roth's rage? I don't know..." He paused, his voice cracking and he looked down, sucking in a sharp breath before he looked up again. "I don't know if I can forgive him, at least not for a long time."

Jewell's initial reaction was to tell Logan that his father had done what he thought best, but she didn't believe it. Not for a moment. As far as she was concerned, Jon Roth was an abuser but Ben Prescott was a coward.

Benjamin kissed his sister's forehead and stood off the edge of the bed where he'd perched, squeezed her hand, and signed that he'd be right back. Jewell held her breath as he walked to where Abigail sat, never even glancing at either his mother or his...his father. He crouched down beside his sister and squeezed Abigail's hand. Abigail raised her head, her hair sliding back to reveal a tear-streaked face, and she smiled weakly. Benjamin leaned up and kissed her cheek before standing. Again, he didn't give his father the smallest glance before turning toward Jewell and Logan.

Some of the tension and strain had eased from his face when he reached them, and Jewell believed just seeing his sister—awake and alive—had relieved more of the pressure on him than anything else could have. Benjamin kissed her just in front of her left ear and tugged her hand from behind her to lace their fingers together before turning with slow deliberation to look Logan in the eyes. They were almost the same height, with Benjamin having no more than an inch on Logan.

Jewell held her breath again, waiting. Then Logan unfolded his arms and extended his hand to Benjamin. "Just so you know, I'm moving you to the top of my organ donor list." As he spoke, he made the sign for "brother", drawing the thumb of his "L" sign from his forehead, then bringing his hand down to the "L" sign of his other hand.

Benjamin chuckled and smiled. He gripped Logan's hand and hauled them together, their joined hands between their chests as they slapped each other's backs in a testosterone-driven show of affection that was about as close as either of them would get to an embrace.

Hours later, when everyone else had left, Benjamin sat beside his sister's bed watching her sleep. This felt so different from the last time, from every time, he'd sat beside her bed in the last few weeks. Today, he held hope that she might open her eyes at any moment...a reality that had just been a distant hope until now.

He dragged his chair closer to the edge of the bed, resting his arm on the mattress beside her to hold her hand. An IV needle bruised the back of her hand, taped to skin that had been left raw by the adding and removal of the adhesive too many times. Her nails had grown, her pink nail polish chipped and grown away from the cuticles. Benjamin stroked his fingertips over her knuckles and thin wrist. Her skin was warmer than when she'd been in the coma, with a comforting pink blush where she had once been ashen and pale.

Her hand turned in his touch, and she clasped his fingers in hers. Benjamin looked up and smiled when he saw her eyes open and the tired smile on her lips. "Hey," she said, her mouth barely moving with the word.

She was tired. The last day and a half had taken too much out of her. The police had been in and out three times that day, taking more details and an official statement from her. They'd informed the family that Jon Roth would be held with no bail until his trial because of the assault on Benjamin and Jewell during the night. The fact that Jon Roth wouldn't have a chance to get near Victoria eased some of the worries that had eaten at Benjamin from the time he found out his sister had woken up and named Jon the shooter.

"Hey," Benjamin parroted, lifting her hand to kiss her knuckles. "How are you feeling?"

She blinked slowly. "Heavy. Like a sloth."

"Are you in any pain?"

She rolled her head on her pillow. "No. They've got me pretty well drugged up," she said with a feeble smile. "I don't feel much of anything."

He didn't sign, knowing that if he did, she'd probably try and she looked too tired to lift her arms. "You should go back to sleep. Rest and heal."

Victoria slipped her hand from his and laid her palm against his cheek. "Mom told me, Benjamin. She told me about Prescott..."

Cold dread hit his chest and he sat back, breaking the contact. In the course of a few hours, he'd gained a 'new' father, lost a tyrant, gained a brother and a sister from once just good friends...but he wondered if he'd lost a sister in the process. She tried to roll onto her side, reaching for his hand with both hers, and when he saw the pinch of pain on her face he immediately returned to his original position so she wouldn't have to reach. She touched his face again, stroking his cheek, and smiled with a shine of tears in her eyes.

"Don't you pull away from me, Benjamin. You have always been, are now, and forever will be my brother. Do you understand?" Tears ran from the corners of her eyes across her temples to her hairline. Benjamin swallowed, the sight of his sister's tears tearing at him. He brushed away the line of moisture and ignored the choking lump in his throat. "Half brother, whole brother, whatever you want to call it...it's all the same. You're my *brother*," she stressed, pressing her hand over her heart. "Please, please..." Her mouth twisted as she fought not to cry.

"Stop, Victoria. Don't cry."

She gave up on talking, raising her frail hands—IV and all—to sign with shaking fingers. *"Please tell me I'm still your sister, not just half, but your sister—"*

He stopped her by folding her hands between his. "You have always been, and always will be my baby sister."

She pressed her lips together, her mouth twisting into a feeble smile, and nodded, tears running freely down her face. Benjamin kissed her knuckles, then rose off his chair to lean over her and kiss her cheeks and forehead. The salt of her tears was tangy on his lips.

It took her several more minutes, and several soaked tissues, to stop crying and calm down enough to relax back on the pillows and take a deep breath. With a heavy sigh that shuddered through her whole body, Victoria smiled genuinely and made one final swipe of her tissue across her cheek.

"Where's Jewell?"

"She went to make a phone call," he answered, then decided to switch to sign. *"Her father called earlier, wanting to make sure you were okay. I'm sure she's filling them in on all the sordid details now."*

"Does that bother you? That she's telling them?"

He knew it probably should, and at a time it probably would have, but it didn't. He knew asking Jewell not to share with her family would be to ask her to go against her very nature. As much as it was the way of the Roth—and, apparently, Prescott—family to deny and ignore, it was the way of the Kincaid family to share and support.

He shook his head and leaned forward to set his elbows on the mattress beside her. "In fact, Opal has invited both of us to Christmas. So, you'd better get out of here soon."

Victoria touched his face again, apparently needing the contact. "Do you love her?"

Benjamin drew in a slow, deep breath and swallowed before he answered. "I will adore her as long as she can stand to be with me, and when she can't, I'll let her go. I consider that love."

CHAPTER TWENTY

Benjamin stood at the window of the suite that had become his second home in the last several weeks, watching the snow come down so fast that the Hartford DPW trucks couldn't keep up with the accumulation. He'd spent so much time at the Crowne Plaza since the shooting, he'd permanently reserved the room so he could come and go as he pleased.

Despite the warmth in the room, a raw cold sat in the center of his chest. It had started as a nugget of ice lodged beside his heart, and had grown steadily for three days.

He'd taken some of the four months of vacation time he'd accrued and never used to be in Hartford during Jon Roth's criminal trial. The same influence Jon Roth had used to get a bail hearing rushed through pushed his trial for attempted murder on the fast track, and now on day three of the trial he could be sentenced and imprisoned by Christmas.

For three days, Benjamin had sat in the courtroom and learned the sordid, dark details of a life both foreign and all too real to him. The prosecution did their job without restraint, pulling out of the deepest, darkest corners of the model of dysfunction that was the Roth household. They painted a picture of a drunk, a man losing his business, a man pushed to his limits who finally snapped and lashed out. While they conceded that Victoria had not been the object of his rage, or the intended target for his bullet, she was the ultimate victim. They argued that a man who would pull a weapon with his child in the line of fire was a man who couldn't be trusted to exist in society, a man who wouldn't hesitate to take out his vengeance on anyone who stood in his way.

The defense took another approach, and as would be expected by the legal team defending Jon Roth, they painted a picture of a victim. A man pushed to his limits, a man who could not be expected to bend and finally break under the strain of a crumbling life.

Forever to be documented in the tomes of judicial history, they told the story of a young man who worked hard to create a life for his wife. A man who built a business with a partner and friend he trusted, only to be betrayed by that same friend. They portrayed Ben Prescott as a user, a backstabber, and a heartless bastard who seduced his best friend's wife the night before his own wedding. A man who never claimed responsibility for his transgressions.

Jon Roth was an honorable man if his legal council was to be believed. He hadn't wavered in his love when he learned his son, his first child, was Deaf. He'd given his whole heart to helping his son. When he learned his firstborn child was not his child at all, he reacted with more restraint than any man could be expected to have. He had decided to save his family from disgrace by raising the boy as his own.

Throughout the entire testimony, Benjamin was never identified by name. The defense attorney told Benjamin it was to prevent the jury from connecting Benjamin with his natural father in any positive light. During cross testimony, the prosecuting attorney did just the opposite, continuously naming Benjamin and pointing out the wrath he had suffered at the hands of his 'honorable' and 'respectable' father.

By the end of the three days, Benjamin's head pounded from grinding his teeth and his hands ached from clenching his fists.

No matter how he looked at it, he was the source of everything. It didn't matter that he hadn't asked to be conceived, he didn't ask to be the product of his mother's infidelity, and he didn't ask to be a constant reminder to the man who 'claimed' him.

To the prosecution, Benjamin's existence was just an excuse for Jon Roth's abhorrent behavior. To the defense, Benjamin was a burden that finally pushed Jon Roth past his breaking point, and Victoria was the innocent victim of years of strain and stress on her father.

Benjamin hung his head and closed his eyes, resting his forehead against the cold window. A tight headache pulled from his temples along the back of his head and down to the tense knots that twisted his shoulders.

His phone vibrated in his pocket, but he didn't reach for it. He knew who it was. The same person who had texted him several times in the last day and a half. The same person he couldn't bring himself to answer.

Jewell.

He couldn't bring himself to answer her. Couldn't put on a convincing enough façade to make her believe everything was going fine, that he could look himself in the mirror without feeling…disgust? Anger? He didn't even know, so he hadn't looked in two days.

Benjamin figured a therapist would have a field day with him.

Not willing to risk a trip on the road, and knowing he had to eat something more than the bagel he'd grabbed that morning with his coffee, he decided to head down to the lobby for a late dinner. He wasn't a fan of 'fusion' cuisine, but they had a full bar.

He was on his second scotch when he looked up and saw Ben Prescott weaving his way through the restaurant to the back table Benjamin had chosen. Catching his waiter's eye, Benjamin held up his glass and tapped it with his finger. The waiter nodded and moved off to bring him another. He'd probably need a double after this conversation.

Prescott sat across from him without invitation. When the waiter returned with Benjamin's scotch, Prescott ordered the same. Except he ordered the double Benjamin wished he had. Done with the walnut salmon he'd ordered, with barely a third of it gone, he pushed the plate away and wiped his lips, tossing the napkin on the table. Prescott didn't say anything until his drink arrived. Even then, he swallowed half and set the glass down with enough force to vibrate through the table.

As far back as he could remember, Benjamin wished he had no father. He never went so far as to admit—even to himself—that he wished Jon Roth dead, but he would have willingly accepted just about any scenario that freed him from the hatred and abuse for which he was the main target. Now, Jon Roth was only the name on his birth certificate and Ben Prescott was the father who walked away. Neither of them wanted him, and he wanted neither one of them.

Prescott finally lifted his head, the red rims around his eyes obvious under the restaurant lights. He picked up the scotch glass again, swirling the amber liquid in the bottom of the glass. "I'm sorry you've had to hear—"

Benjamin raised his hand, cutting off whatever apology or explanation Prescott might offer. "Did you come here for a reason, Prescott?"

Prescott shrugged and downed the last of the scotch. "I don't know. I just...I told Barbara I'd come check on you."

"Why?"

Prescott finally looked straight at him, but only held the stare for a few seconds before he looked away. "We—your mother and I—we didn't want things to happen this way. We didn't want—"

"You didn't want everyone to know your dirty little secret, including your dirty little secret."

"It's not like that, Benjamin."

"Just exactly what is it like?" Before Prescott could speak, Benjamin stood and took his wallet from his pocket, tossing four twenties on the table, then added another ten to make sure Prescott's drink was covered. "You know what, Prescott? I don't care enough to hear whatever excuse or reason or justification you may have convinced yourself made this okay somehow."

His 'father' didn't follow him into the lobby. Instead of walking to the bank of elevators leading to his room, Benjamin strode across the marble tile lobby and straight into the storm. Left or right, it didn't matter. He just started walking.

Jewell unlocked the suite door and pocketed the extra keycard, dragging her small suitcase in behind her. The drive from Boston had been challenging, to say the least, especially once she hit the Connecticut border. Travis Traynor had decided around noon to let everyone leave early, and give everyone but essential personnel the next day off—extending the already extended Christmas holiday. Jewell wasn't sure she'd ever packed so fast, thinking only one thing. Get to Hartford and be with Benjamin for what would hopefully be the last day of Jon Roth's trial.

She'd tried to reach him since leaving Bulwark, but just like the last two days, Benjamin didn't answer any of her texts. She only hoped the worst of scenarios running through her head weren't reality.

Leaving her suitcase in the main sitting area, she shrugged off her heavy coat and glanced around, searching for him in the large room. When she didn't find him there, she moved into the bedroom, even glancing into the bathroom. With no sign of him, Jewell sighed and sat on the edge of the bed, running her hand over her hair. Enough snow had accumulated in her hair just coming from the car to dampen her curls and make them twist into tight ringlets around her face.

Fighting the nervous energy that had been building just beneath her skin for two days, Jewell stood and went to the window. The snow was really coming down, and now that she saw the storm from this perspective, she was amazed she'd made it without going off the road. The daughter of a friend of her mother's had been in an awful accident the year before in the middle of a Nor'easter, and had nearly died. Since then, Jewell's mother had begged her not to drive in weather like this.

With a deep sigh, Jewell turned away from the window. She gasped and jumped back when she saw Benjamin standing just inside the suite door, watching her. His hair was wet and smattered with snowflakes, and the shoulders of his shirt were soaked through as though he'd been in the storm without a coat. Jewell pressed her hand over her heart.

"Benjamin, you frightened me," she signed as she crossed to him, a smile spreading her lips as relief washed over her like a cool wave. "Where were you?"

He stared hard at her, his eyes never leaving her face as she walked to him. It wasn't the cold stare of anger, or the tense stare of thought, but something she didn't know or understand. Suddenly, Jewell was afraid. The worst part was that she didn't know what she was afraid of.

She stopped and touched her palm to his chest. Cold emanated from him. His heart pounded hard and fast beneath her hand. "Benjamin? What is it? What's wrong?"

He covered her hand with his own and wrapped his arm around her body, pulling her close. As his eyes skimmed over her face, gooseflesh spread out over her arms and body. His fingertips curled and pressed into her spine. She didn't know why, but tears burned behind her eyes.

"Benjamin, please."

He snatched the words from her lips with a devouring kiss desperate in its intensity. Jewell had to wrap her hands behind his neck just to hold on. His tongue delved into her mouth and his arms held her so tight it stole her breath. Just as suddenly as the kiss began, he broke away and buried his shocking cold face into her hair and against the curve of her neck.

Jewell pushed her fingers into his damp hair and held him, her own heart now pounding at a ferocious pace. What happened? What had him acting this way?

Benjamin mumbled against her throat, and Jewell strained to hear him. When she did, her thundering pulse nearly stopped.

"I love you," he whispered again and again.

Jewell swallowed, her throat suddenly parched, and reluctantly pulled back, urging him to raise his head with her touch. His smoldering brown eyes met hers, and what she saw was pain. As much pain as when Victoria was shot.

"Benjamin, please," she forced out, thankful he didn't need to hear the weak quiver in her voice. "Tell me what is going on."

"I love you, Jewell."

Tears momentarily blurred his face, but she blinked them away. "I love you, too."

He shook his head, a sad, slow action. "Soon, I think you'll hate me."

So many thoughts rushed her mind, Jewell couldn't begin to decipher them or pull them apart to make sense of any of them. She held his face in her hands, his skin still cold from the winter wind.

"Benjamin, *nothing* could ever make me hate you."

His arms dropped and he stepped away to stand behind the same chair his mother had sat in the night when she and Ben Prescott told him the truth. He clutched the back until his knuckles whitened and his head dropped, golden brown waves of hair falling forward. Benjamin spoke, his head still down, and Jewell knew it was to avoid any interruptions. If he couldn't read her lips or see her signs, she couldn't speak.

"You have changed me," he said in a strained voice, even the soft quality of his speech sounding hard. "I wasn't looking to fall in love. Didn't want to fall in love. Never considered falling in love. But I have, and it happened so easily."

Tears fell from Jewell's eyes, but she made no effort to wipe them away. She crossed her arms over her body and waited. Waited for whatever bomb he was going to drop. There was one coming. Jewell knew it just as surely as she knew her own name.

He slammed the heel of his hand against the chair's back and Jewell could see a tense muscle jump along his jaw. Jewell took a step toward him but his hand shot up in an indisputable sign for her to stop. She held her breath, waiting.

"I can't ask you to be a part of my life. It is too twisted and too hard."

Jewell shook her head back and forth, slowly. Words formed on her lips as realization sank in. Her stomach flipped. "No," she whispered pointlessly.

"I don't know who I am anymore. I don't know what I am. Everything I ever thought has been thrown in a blender and shredded. How can I expect you to love me? How can you even know who I am when I don't know who I am?"

Jewell ignored his silent request to stay away. She moved to him and pushed his shoulder to make him stand and face her. The anguish in his expression was excruciating to her.

"Stop it," she demanded.

"I can't. This is…this is what I have to do."

"Benjamin, this is crazy. You just told me you love me, and now you're saying you want to end it?"

"I don't want to."

"Then don't." It was all Jewell could do to keep herself from screaming.

Benjamin grasped her face with his hands, his fingers pushing into her hair and his palms cold and damp against her cheeks.

"Tell me who I am, Jewell. Am I Benjamin Prescott Roth or am I Ben Prescott Junior?"

"I love you, not your name."

"But isn't that who I am?"

Jewell pushed back, anger flashing in to mix with the tumult of emotions raging through her. "Who do you love, Benjamin?"

He stared at her, furrows creasing his brow, and he shook his head slowly.

"Are you in love with Frances Louise Shackley?"

The furrows deepened and his eyes squinted. "Who the hell is Frances Louise Shackley?"

"I am."

"What the hell are you—" he began but stopped as understanding crossed his expression.

"Yeah," she shot back. "Tell me again how much a name means. Do you love me—Jewell Kincaid? Or do you love Frances Shackley? Would you love me if you knew me as Frances?"

He nodded slowly. "Of course, I would."

"Then why don't you believe I can love you?"

Benjamin pressed his fists against his eyes and sank into a chair. "I don't know. I don't know," he mumbled over and over again.

Jewell dropped to her knees and knelt before him, pulling his hands from his face. "Benjamin, don't worry about me. Don't worry about my ability to love you. I love you, that is all you need to know. I can handle whatever happens because I know we are doing it together."

"You shouldn't have to handle it."

"Neither should you. But you are. And so am I."

"Jewell, I don't know if I can get beyond the things that happened when I was a kid. They made me who I am—"

She covered his lips with a finger. "Yes, they did. And I love the man you are."

"But I might have been a different man if they hadn't."

Jewell nodded. "You might have, that's true. You might have been a worse man. A man I would have never known. Benjamin, we can't live around what-ifs. What if my mother hadn't been an addict? What if she hadn't given me up? What if I grew up in a home of drugs and abuse? What if Cecil and Opal Kincaid weren't the ones who adopted me? Don't you see? Everything that happens can go another way. Every choice we make affects the rest of our lives. Everything, *everything* has brought us here. Brought us together."

He touched her cheek with his fingers. Jewell clutched his fingers to turn into his hand and kiss his palm. Benjamin leaned forward and gently touched his lips to hers. Relief burst in her chest and spread out through her limbs. She closed her eyes and relished the kiss.

Then it was over. Benjamin stood, pulling her to her feet. The loss of his touch and sudden position change made her dizzy. He held her hand for a moment, squeezed her fingers, then released her and walked to the door leading out of the suite. He pressed his hand high up on the doorjamb and leaned into his arm. Jewell watched him, waiting for him to turn and gift her with the smile that always made her knees weak.

He did turn, but there was no smile. Benjamin took in a long, slow breath that pushed up his shoulders and expanded his chest.

"I contacted Travis at home. I tried to give my notice, but he refused to accept it. So, I'm taking a leave of absence. I don't know how long."

"Where are you going?" she whispered, her throat so tight the sound barely escaped.

"Nowhere. I'm staying here in Hartford for the trial. I'm going to bring Victoria back to Boston when the trial is over. If she'll come me now that—"

"Benjamin, please don't do this."

"I have to. I don't know how else to say it."

She took a step toward him, but he stepped back and opened the door. Benjamin held her stare for several seconds, and the tears flowed down Jewell's cheeks. He pressed his eyes closed and placed his hand over his heart, then brought his other arm across in a far more intimate sign for love, signed "forever," and then he was gone, closing the door behind him.

A harsh burst of air ripped into Jewell's lungs and she stumbled back to fall into the chair behind her. She sucked in her breath, trying to stop the dizzy whirl of the room around her as a sob racked her body. Jewell buried her face in her hands and cried.

When she'd cried herself dry, she drew in a shaky breath and rose to her feet. She'd come to Hartford for a reason, and she'd be damned if she'd do anything less. With her heart aching in her chest, she retrieved her coat and suitcase and left the suite. Hopefully, the hotel had an empty room that wouldn't cost her a week's salary.

CHAPTER TWENTY-ONE

Despite the nasty storm that had half buried Hartford the night before, local media had camped out on the front steps of the Hartford appellate courthouse. Beyond Hartford, the attempted murder trial of local attorney Jon Roth was nothing more than a blip on the news radar. But, in Hartford, he was big news. Local television and newspaper reporters swarmed around both defense and prosecution legal teams as they climbed the stairs, the defense attorneys flanking Jon Roth on all sides.

Jewell stood at the top of the steps, off to the side watching the circus unfold. Since she hadn't been present at the trial before now, and no one knew her as having any connection to the case, no one blinked twice when she walked past the media horde. She stood now, watching, her heart in her throat.

Jon Roth entered the courthouse with his team, neither him nor his lawyers making any comment to the shouted questions and accusations. As they cleared the courthouse doors, the prosecution started up the stairs. Barbara Roth and Ben Prescott walked a step behind the prosecution for the State, holding hands.

Benjamin arrived minutes later, once everyone else had disappeared outside. It didn't matter that he hadn't arrived with Barbara and Prescott, the media still swarmed on him. Jewell had to force herself to stay in the shadows watching him wave off the persistent horde. Some clearly understood his need to see a face to read lips, because they purposefully stepped in his path and shoved themselves into his direct line of vision. He never spoke, never responded, and just stepped around them to the main door.

Finally, he broke away and went inside.

Jewell waited until the chaos on the steps subsided, and the media that wasn't allowed inside the courthouse disbursed, heading back to cars and various news vans parked along the curb. Drawing in a final, cold breath she stepped out of the shade from the massive pillars bracketing the stairs and headed for the door. She slipped into the courtroom with two other people she recognized as reporters from the steps, and found a seat on the prosecution side near the back. Benjamin sat two rows in front of her and slightly to her left so she could see his profile but he would probably have to turn in his seat before he noticed she was there.

He sat hunched forward, his head down and his hands laced together in front of him. Exhaustion sat on his shoulders as palpable and visible as a stone wedged between his shoulder blades. Jewell swallowed hard, fighting the lump in her throat. Moments later, all in attendance were called to order and day three of the trial began. A young girl, probably a college student working toward her practical credits, took her position to the side of the judge's podium within Benjamin's line of sight. As the room was called to order, the girl signed each word. Her motions were jaunty and she lacked finesse, probably having never communicated an entire conversation in Ameslan, let alone an entire trial.

District Attorney Audrey Whitman for the prosecution stood to address the judge, a staunch, late middle-aged man with more hair on his chin than on his head. Jewell gasped softly when D.A. Whitman called Benjamin to the stand as the final witness for the prosecution.

He stood, but an apparent stiffness made his motions slow. With a sharp tug at the leg of his trousers, he straightened his tie and side-stepped out of the row of seats, heading to the stand. The translator shifted her stance so her back was more to the courtroom, but within view of both Benjamin and the D.A. The short, stocky woman dressed in a navy skirt suit in charge of prosecuting Jon Roth walked toward Benjamin, stopping a few feet from the witness stand.

"Could you please state your name for the records?" she asked.

His features twisted before he even spoke, and he said the words as if they tasted foul in his mouth. "Benjamin Prescott Roth."

"Mr. Roth, could you please explain your relationship to the defendant?"

Jewell clenched her hands in her lap to keep from twisting them together.

"Until recently, I believed him to be my father."

The defense attorney, a pathetically thin man with a glistening pate she'd heard introduced as Attorney Pattinson, shot to his feet. "Objection, Your Honor, as to relevance."

"Your Honor, Benjamin Roth has been mentioned frequently in the course of this trial, though the defense has been very careful not to use his actual name, as if that might somehow allow the jury to harbor the opinion that he is somehow the helpless, useless burden to which Jon Roth has acted as benefactor. If the defense feels he is relevant enough to mention prior to now, he certainly should be given the chance to speak for himself."

"Benjamin Roth was not present at the incident and cannot speak—"

"And yet, you keep bringing him up in your own defense. He can speak to the character of the defendant, Your Honor," the D.A. finished.

Benjamin's attention shifted rapidly between the two attorneys and the translator. With each word, each jaunty sign, his features pinched harder.

"I'll allow it," the judge declared.

D.A. Whitman nodded and turned back to Benjamin. "Mr. Roth, the defense has spoken frequently to the level of strain and stress Jon Roth accepted when he agreed to accept a child he didn't father, especially considering the fact that this child was handicapped. I realize this may seem like a crass question, Mr. Roth, but are you the child the defense has referenced throughout this trial?"

"I am," he answered, snapping an angry glare in his father's direction.

Whitman turned her back on Benjamin, addressing the jury and his attention shifted fully to the translator. "Mr. Roth, the defense has tried to convince this jury that Jon Roth was practically a saint for taking on a handicapped child who could never be anything more than a burden and a challenge. A child who would have to be taken care of, unable to function on his own in society."

Jewell never looked away from Benjamin, watched as each word made him grind his teeth and press his lips together until they were practically white. He looked away from the translator to answer, and she felt the tug in her chest the second he saw her. His dark eyes widened for a moment, staring at her. Then he closed them, visibly swallowing. When he looked at her again, Jewell nodded, just a dip of her chin.

"I would argue to this jury that you seem far from incompetent, Mr. Roth. Could you please tell this court what you do?"

"I am a fund manager in the aggressive growth capital management division of Bulwark Mutual Funds," he stated, his voice flat.

The D.A. scoffed, turning back to him. "You are modest as well, Mr. Roth. Aren't you, in fact, hailed as one of the top ten fund managers in the country, and one of the top five fund managers for international and global funds?"

"Yes, I am."

"Objection, Your Honor. What is the relevance to this line of questioning?"

"Your Honor, the defense would like us to believe that Jon Roth is an honorable man who finally snapped under the burden of responsibility. I'm merely establishing that he holds no responsibility for Benjamin Prescott Roth."

The prosecution asked a handful more questions, and Benjamin provided short, succinct answers. It was obvious to Jewell that he didn't want to be there. She had no doubt that he would do nearly anything to insure his father was found guilty, even if it meant putting himself on the stand. The prosecution focused on Benjamin and his accomplishments, continuously repeating his name whenever she could. It was clearly a ploy, but having not been in the trail before then, Jewell didn't understand what the ploy hoped to accomplish. Eventually, Whitman ended her line of questioning, and opened Benjamin up to the defense.

Jewell sat up straighter, a steel coil of tension wrapping around her, as Attorney Pattinson for the defense stood and stepped toward Benjamin. "The prosecution has painted a very disturbing picture of Jon Roth as a man who lashed out against the boy he raised as his son, a boy who was conceived in betrayal but still benefitted from the wealth and status a man who was not his father could give him."

Benjamin's only response was a twist of his lips into a mocking smirk.

Pattinson didn't seem to notice, turning his focus to the jury. "If we're going to paint pictures, let's make sure it's authentic. In truth, Jon Roth is responsible for the success you are today. Isn't that true?"

Benjamin stared across the courtroom to Jewell. He drew in a long breath through his nose, pulling his shoulders back as he straightened in his chair. With slow, deliberate movements he raised his right leg and rested his ankle on his left knee, adopting a casual stance.

"Absolutely," he said with feigned sincerity.

The defense attorney twisted away from the jury, his momentary shock making his eyes pop. But he quickly regained his composure, shifting to lean on the edge of the defense table. "Based on the other line of evidence the prosecution has presented, your agreement surprised me, Mr. Roth."

"I am absolutely the man I am today because of Jon Roth."

"It's refreshing to hear your appreciation."

"Don't misunderstand me, Counselor." Benjamin's voice held the cold authority Jewell had recognized the first time she met him. "It's not appreciation you're hearing."

Before Pattinson could rebuff Benjamin's statement, he leaned forward in his chair and continued. "I don't know what it sounds like to be called names. I don't know what screaming sounds like. I don't know what hatred sounds like, Counselor, but I know what it looks like. That's what Jon Roth gave me."

The lawyer turned away and lowered his head, rubbing his hand across his mouth as he walked in front of the defense and prosecution tables, apparently engrossed with the wood grain of the floor. Jewell figured it was a ploy to set Benjamin on edge, to put him off balance, but this lawyer didn't know him. Not like Jewell did. Not like the business world did. Benjamin was unshakable, determined, and had stood unwavering against more intimidating men than this schmuck.

"Your father—" Pattinson began.

"Jon Roth isn't my father," Benjamin snapped before the translator managed to bring her hand down from her brow in the sign of 'father' and point toward the defense table.

Pattinson held up his hand in concession. "I understand you only recently discovered your actual paternity, Mr. Roth, so I'm sure the court will forgive any harsh words on your part in regards to the man you've known as your father your entire life. So, I'll reword. The defendant made sure you attended one of the best schools on the East Coast. You received a stellar education. Do you wish the jury to believe that this was an act of hatred toward you?"

"An act of revulsion, resentment, punishment…whatever you want to call it."

Pattinson chuckled and held his arms out away from his body, facing the jury. He consistently addressed the panel of men and women, and not Benjamin. "If that's punishment, what do you think he would have done as a reward?"

D.A. Whitman stood. "Your Honor, I object. Counsel is grandstanding."

"I agree. Counsel, please keep your statements relevant and to the facts."

Pattinson smoothed the front of his jacket. "Fine. Facts. Your fa— Excuse me. Jon Roth made sure you saw a variety of specialists in the hopes of curing your handicap. He sent you to one of the best schools in the region. He encouraged you to greatness, which you apparently have achieved. He left you wanting for nothing. And now, you would like this jury to believe him to be what—Abusive? Violent? Capable of harming his children?"

"He left me with barely any means to communicate until I was five years old, when he sent me to Bridlethorpe because it was the only school willing to take a pupil so young in exchange for his sizable contribution. I was left there except for the vacation breaks when he was required to allow me to come home. He encouraged me by telling me I would be a constant burden and a useless drain on society. And the back of his hand encouraged me to take what I had to from him only as long as I had to."

Pattinson sighed and returned to his table, tossing a pen down on his legal pad. "Your Honor, I have no further questions for this witness. I have not yet heard anything relevant, and nothing more than the angry diatribes of a disgruntled son."

The judge turned his focus to D.A. Whitman. "Do you have any further questions, Counsel?"

"Just a couple, Your Honor." She walked around the table and approached Benjamin again. "Benjamin, I'm not going to ask you to rehash a difficult childhood, but I do have some questions for you."

Benjamin nodded, his gaze shifting past D.A. Whitman to connect briefly with Jewell's.

"Benjamin, how old were you when you graduated high school?"

"Sixteen."

"So, you skipped a few grades."

He shifted, smoothing his tie. "I took a very heavy class workload, essentially completing four grades in two years."

"What was your GPA when you graduated?"

"3.96."

"Impressive. So, after graduating at sixteen, you went on to college."

"Yes, Harvard."

"How did you pay for your education?"

"Full scholarship to Harvard School of Business."

Whitman turned and walked to the jury as he answered her questions, confirming the lengthy list of accomplishments he achieved before the age of twenty-four. Some members of the jury shifted in their chairs, some looking surprised and others impressed. Jewell hadn't thought to look at the panel of individuals when Benjamin spoke of his childhood. The difference in reactions might have been an interesting gauge for their response.

"Final question for you, Benjamin," she said, turning back to him. "I apologize if these questions seem crass. Could you please confirm for the court…are you completely deaf?"

"Yes."

"You have been since birth." He confirmed with a nod. "How did you communicate with your family when you were a child?"

"I don't recall the earliest years, but I had a rudimentary ASL vocabulary until I was three or four years old. My nanny knew sign language, though not strictly ASL, and through her, my vocabulary expanded. I didn't communicate with anyone but her until I was able to read lips and speak."

"Learning to speak with total hearing loss is a massive challenge, and one not all hearing impaired persons choose to tackle. Why did you, Mr. Roth?"

"A dyslexic learns to read and goes on to become a teacher. A paraplegic uses a wheelchair and wins a marathon. A blind man learns to program computers. My deafness is an element of my life, but it is not the definition of my life. I wanted to succeed in business. To do that, I learned the nature of global markets, I studied trends and predictions, and I learned to communicate with my peers."

"Part of learning to speak is learning to read lips, is that correct?" He nodded again in answer to her question. "At what age did Jon Roth enroll you in speech therapy?"

"He didn't," Benjamin answered, his gaze shifting back to her. "Bridlethorpe Academy offered the option to me. Once I hit junior high level, I began to seek speech therapy options outside the school. By the time I graduated, I communicated in the classroom almost completely through lip reading and speech."

"You did this. Not Jon Roth. Why do you think that is?"

"The only thing worse than hatred is indifference."

Finally, the questions were over and Benjamin was dismissed from the stand. He stood, smoothed his shirt and tie, and stepped down, crossing the space in front of the judge's bench to the rows of seating behind the counsel tables. His stone face was a mask of control, nothing but the pinch beside his eyes giving anything away to anyone who might look. Except for Jewell. She watched him every step, clenching her hands in her lap. Her heart hurt and her chest ached. He raised his head and his gaze connected with her as he walked down the aisle. He stopped at the end of the row he had sat in before the trial began, and Jewell held her breath.

Then he took the two final steps needed to bring him to her row, never breaking their eye contact. Jewell had to lean back and tip her chin to look up at him. He stood there for what felt like an eternity before turning and taking the seat beside her. Jewell reached for his hand, and he laced his fingers through hers, pulling their joined hands into his lap so he could enfold her hand between both of his. He dropped his head forward, his eyes closed tight and his jaw clenched so tightly that small muscles jerked in front of his ear. One hand held hers while the palm of the other caressed a constant rhythm across the back of her fingers and knuckles, an assurance perhaps that she was there.

The prosecution rested and both offered their final arguments, which continued for another three hours. The prosecution rehashed every piece of evidence, including Victoria's testimony taken minutes after she woke and before she spoke to anyone in the family. Or with Dillon. They pointed out how every detail of her testimony matched the details provided by Dillon throughout his entire interrogation. Character witnesses. Expert testimonies. Forensic evidence that stood in direct conflict with Jon Roth's statements. They droned on for nearly two hours. Then the defense did the same, shooting down every piece of evidence brought up by the prosecution. They treated every element as a waste of time, playing the confidence card, attempting to convince the jury that to even consider Jon Roth guilty of such a crime would be ridiculous. They placed incompetence on the police force who released Dillon once their suspicion switched to Jon Roth—who was *clearly* innocent.

It was nearly three in the afternoon before all closing arguments had been presented and the jury was prepped on their responsibilities.

The judge released the jury to deliberate and released everyone in attendance until the jury returned. That could mean they would have enough time to get a coffee before being called back should the jury be convinced without a doubt one way or another, or it could mean several more days of waiting—even past the holiday—if the jury couldn't come to a unanimous decision.

Everyone stood, and rows emptied as people shuffled out of the courtroom. Benjamin held her hand at his side but didn't look down. She tried to steal a glance at his face, but his body was rigid and his profile stoic. Once in the hall, he led her away from the hustle of people dispersing out the front door into a quieter, less crowded corner. Her heart pounded viciously in her chest. After last night, what would he have to say to her?

He led her around a massive pillar leading down a side hallway, and turned into her, pulling her into his arms. Jewell's knees gave and she leaned into him, pressing her cheek against his chest. She inhaled the mingled scent of his laundry detergent, his cologne, and the mix of everything that made him Benjamin. His heart thumped hard against his ribs and he held her so tight she couldn't move.

She didn't want to.

"I'm sorry," he said against her hair, muffling the sound. "I'm so sorry."

She shook her head against him but didn't pull back. Benjamin stepped behind the pillar, hiding them completely from curious eyes, and held her tighter until he could bury his face against the side of her throat. Jewell wrapped her arms around his shoulders, holding tight as his body shook. Tears burned her eyes and she pressed her eyelids together so tight they hurt.

He broke away and slumped back against the pillar, his knees bent so he was closer to her eye level. His eyes shined, but he restrained whatever raging emotions tore at him. Jewell stroked his cheeks and took his face in her hands, kissing his lips.

He raised his hands to sign in the small space between them. "*I knew when I left the suite last night I'd made a mistake. I just couldn't—*" He fisted his hands and pressed his eyes shut, shaking his head in her hold. Without opening his eyes, he continued. "*In three days I heard everything he ever thought of me, everything he ever said to me, and I couldn't...*" His hands shook and he opened his eyes, looking at her. "*I couldn't believe you could love me.*"

Jewell cried the tears she knew he held back. "But, I *do* love you, Benjamin," she emphasized with a nod. "Don't ever doubt that."

He nodded. "*I know. Now. I know you told me last night, but I didn't accept it—I didn't 'hear' it,*" he signed, making a combined sign between actual hearing and comprehension, "*until I left you. And when I realized it...you were gone. I thought I'd lost you.*"

She didn't want to take her hands from him, so she leaned closer and whispered. "I couldn't leave you to do this alone when I could be here. I just got a room at the hotel."

Benjamin came forward off the pillar and wrapped his arms around her, lifting her off her heels with the intensity of the embrace. He hid his face in her hair, against her throat, and she cupped the back of his head, holding him there. His fingers curled into her jacket, his entire body tense with whatever demons had raged against him in the last few days. This was what she'd wanted to be for him last night, but he hadn't been ready to let it happen. It didn't matter, he knew now. And she wouldn't let him ever doubt how much she loved him.

He turned into her neck, his lips kissing softly. Immediately, every part of her zinged with awareness. Benjamin kissed her throat, her jaw, her cheek—tiny, quick touches—until he reached her lips. Jewell opened to him, accepting the—panic?—that drove him, and kissed him so he knew, without any doubt, that she was there for him.

All too soon, Benjamin eased the intensity of the kiss to just a contact of mouth-to-mouth and finally broke away, his fingertips immediately coming to rest on her cheeks and slick lips. Her breath reflected back to her from the touch, and his own rapid breathing filled the space between them.

"Why don't you get angry with me?" he asked, his gaze skimming her face to try and take in both her eyes and her mouth at the same time.

Jewell blinked, trying to process the rapid switch in topic. "Why don't I get angry with you?" she repeated.

He nodded. "I've been an ass. I've taken it out on you. I've screwed up. Why don't you get angry with me when I do?"

Jewell shook her head, the motion making his fingers skim her skin. He smoothed her hair back from her cheek, hooking it behind her ear. "You didn't need my anger, and it wouldn't have helped anything."

Benjamin smiled, and the light that reached his eyes made her smile back. "You are amazing, Jewell Kincaid. And I love you."

CHAPTER TWENTY-TWO

The heady aromas of evergreen, cinnamon and peppermint mixed together with burning wood and more baked goods than Benjamin could categorize, every scent soaking into his memories as much as they permeated his clothing. He stood in the parlor in front of the Kincaid Christmas tree, its lights blinking and reflecting off the frosted windows facing the porch. Christmas had been a week before, but one of the many traditions of the Kincaid family was to leave the Christmas tree up until after the new year.

He'd missed Christmas, caught up in the final stages of Jon Roth's trial and dealing with his mother as she worked out the details of having her husband incarcerated for the next five years for assault with a deadly weapon and attempted murder. He was sentenced to five years for each crime—which Benjamin felt was pathetic for the pain he caused—to be served consecutively, and an additional fine equaling $55,000. Benjamin was still angry with his mother and Ben Prescott for their deception, but in the end, he couldn't leave her alone to deal with the mess Jon Roth left behind. As soon as things were wrapped up as much as they could be, he'd bundled up his sister and left Hartford for Boston. Both he and Victoria needed space between them and Hartford to sort through everything.

Tonight, he would bring in the new year with the Kincaids while Victoria and Dillon celebrated together at the townhouse. She was improving, but she wasn't ready to spend too much time out, and she'd ordered Benjamin to get out of the house before he smothered her—or she killed him.

He chuckled and smiled at his little sister's demands.

Motion past the window caught his attention, and he squinted to see through the frost and light reflection. Benjamin didn't even attempt to hold back the smile when he saw Jewell and Garnett climb out of Garnett's SUV, both carrying large paper takeout bags. Another tradition of the Kincaid family was a massive feast of Chinese takeout on New Year's Eve, and Cecil Kincaid had told Benjamin when he arrived that Jewell had gone with her brother to pick up the food. She came up the porch stairs beside her brother, and a gust of cold air curled into the parlor from the foyer when they entered. Benjamin stayed in his spot but turned to face the room so he could see her when she entered.

A few minutes later, the aromas of various Chinese dishes mingled with every other smell in the house, she came through the doorway from the kitchen and smiled when she saw him. She was so beautiful it stole his breath. Her thick waves of auburn hair hung unhindered around her shoulders, parted on the side so the waves slanted across her forehead to brush her cheeks. A soft yellow sweater over perfect-fitting jeans showed off her amazing figure and the blush in her cheeks from the cold made her glow. She crossed the room, pausing to fluff Pearl's hair where she sat in front of the fireplace coloring, and stepped into his arms when she reached him. Benjamin only considered for about half a second that her parents were in the next room and her little sister was a few feet away before he pushed his fingers into her hair and tipped her head for a deep kiss, one he'd wanted since he'd seen her three days earlier.

Jewell lifted her arms slowly, wrapping them around his neck as she leaned into the kiss, her hum vibrating against his lips. When he felt her smile, he pulled back and wrapped his arms around her, his palms against her back.

"I've missed you," she said before kissing him again.

"I've missed you, too. Your nose is cold."

She laughed, the rumble shifting through her body against his hands and chest. A tug on his sleeve forced him to look away from her and down to Pearl. She beamed up at him, her pale blonde hair escaping from her loose ponytail to frame her face like a halo. She held out a construction paper circle in green, with glitter and glue stripe decorations and a marker drawing in the middle of what might have passed as Benjamin. A red gift ribbon was tied through a punched hole at the top, and across the bottom was his name: BenJaMIN.

Benjamin crouched down to be eye level with her and took the ornament. "*Is this for me?*" he asked, and she nodded. "*Thank you, Pearl.*"

"*It's for our precious tree,*" she signed and pointed at the Christmas tree beside him.

Benjamin looked up at Jewell, curious about Pearl's description of their tree, and wondered at the glisten in her eyes. Jewell smiled and smoothed Pearl's hair before signing, "*Why don't you explain our precious tree to Benjamin, sweetheart.*"

Pearl nodded and took Benjamin's hand, tugging on him to turn so he had to stand and follow or fall over. She pointed at several other handcrafted ornaments that hung from the evergreen branches. Some were made of construction paper like the one she'd given him. Some were made from felt. Some were glued together wooden tongue depressors. Each one had a word or a name written on it: Jewell, Garnett, Red Sox, Ruby, pumpkin chocolate chip cookies, Pearl, Mama, Love, God, My New Family, Snow, Daddy.

"*These are all our precious things,*" Pearl signed, her gaping smile enough to make him smile just as wide. "*Precious means something very valuable, or one who is dear or beloved.*" As she signed, she had an expression of deep concentration, like she wanted to make sure she got every word correct. "*See? I said Mama and Daddy, those are mine. And I said pumpkin chocolate chip cookies because they're my favorite. And now you.*" She touched the end of his nose.

The lump in his throat surprised him, and he didn't quite understand it. Drawing in a slow breath through his nose, he touched his fingertips to his lips and brought his hand down, palm up. "*Thank you.*"

She smiled and threw her arms around his neck, pressing a sloppy kiss to his cheek before she ran out of the room. Benjamin rose from his crouch, watching her disappear around the corner into the hallway like a streak of white lightning. Cecil Kincaid deftly stepped sideways to avoid her and waved to them.

"Dinner is on the table. Come eat."

He looked down at the ornament, running his finger across the smooth wax crayon lines. Turning to the tree, he reached above his head and hung the construction paper decoration. Jewell's fingers laced through his and he looked down at her. She smiled, but a single tear slipped from her eye. Benjamin smoothed the trail away with his thumb. "Why are you crying?"

"It's official."

He led her toward the dining room, maneuvering around the couch without looking away from her face. "What's official?"

"You're on the precious tree. You're part of the family."

He stopped, cupped her cheek, and kissed her. She had no idea how much courage little Pearl's ornament had given him. He only hoped he could hang on to that courage a little longer.

Jewell stacked the various containers of eggs foo yung, pork chow mein, fried rice, and teriyaki steak before setting them on a refrigerator shelf beside the rest of the leftovers from dinner. She was so full she felt like she'd burst, but knew in an hour she'd probably be in here to steal an egg roll.

With the counter wiped down and the last dish in the dishwasher, she sighed and headed for the parlor. Her mother and father sat together on the couch, his arm behind her while he smoked his pipe. The soothing, comforting smell mingled with all the holiday aromas that she forever connected with home. Pearl was asleep on the floor beside the Christmas tree, her hands folded under her cheek. She had fallen asleep an hour short of making it to midnight, but not for lack of trying. The little girl had consumed enough hot chocolate and cookies she should have been on a sugar high for a week.

"Have you seen Benjamin?" she asked her father.

He looked away from the fire, taking the pipe from his lips. "No,

Pipsqueak. Last I saw him, he was headed for the kitchen. I thought he was with you."

"Humph. Okay."

She wandered the house, and only managed to find Garnett and Ruby playing chess in the living room. They hadn't seen Benjamin either. Since her father had last seen him heading for the kitchen, she doubled back through the hall. She scanned the empty room and nearly left again when she saw him outside on the back porch, his hands shoved in the front pockets of his long wool coat, his head down. A light snow had begun to fall, and drifted down in the soft glow of the Christmas lights over his head. Jewell grabbed one of her father's sweaters from the hook near the door and slipped it on, opening the door to step out onto the porch.

He didn't look up until she touched his arm, and smiled when he saw her. Without taking his hands out of his pockets he leaned over to kiss her. His lips were chilled and his cold nose rubbed against hers.

"Why are you out here?" she signed.

He shrugged and looked out across the large backyard. A snowman stood in the corner, wearing an orange and yellow striped scarf and hunter's cap. His face was painted on with food coloring. Ruby's flying saucer sled sat against the side of the porch, along with an assortment of snow toys. The A-frame swing was nearly buried to the back of the seat.

She touched his arm again so he'd turn back to her. *"Is something wrong?"*

Benjamin smiled and shook his head. "No. As insane as the last few weeks have been, I think I'm as far away from wrong as I've ever been."

Jewell tipped her head, studying his profile in the flickering, multi-colored light. Instead of trying to pull out of him whatever was on his mind, she turned to lean back against the porch railing, wrapping her father's sweater around her body. The wind had a bite, stinging her cheeks and whipping her hair around her face. Benjamin watched her for a few moments before looking out across the yard again. He squinted against the wind that hit him in the face.

"I talked to Travis this morning," he said after several minutes of silence between them.

She pulled her hair back from her face, curling it behind her ears. "*About what?*"

"I'm coming back to Bulwark mid-January." He chuckled softly. "If I stay home much longer, I think Victoria might try to kill me in my sleep. She says I'm driving her crazy."

Jewell smiled, happy at the idea of having him in the office again. He had been out of the office since the trial began, and Jewel had been working with Alexi Rouan on Benjamin's funds, with the intent that Benjamin would step back in when he returned from his leave. Alexi was a good manager, but he wasn't Benjamin. In more ways than one.

She scooted closer to him and laid her hand on his lower arm, but he still didn't take his hands out of his pockets. Jewell waited until he shifted his attention to her. "I'm glad. I've missed you."

His gaze lingered on her lips before coming back to her eyes. "I've missed you, too." He smiled, a tip of one corner of his lips. Then he cleared his throat and looked down, shuffling his feet on the icy porch floor. "I've been thinking about that, actually. A lot."

She waited for him to look up. "About how much you've missed me?"

He nodded. "I think I have a solution."

She couldn't quite follow his line of conversation. "What's your solution?"

Benjamin cleared his throat and shifted his weight on the balls of his feet. She just waited. He shifted more, jabbing his hands in his pockets. After another few minutes of strange silence, he laughed more to himself than to any joke she wasn't privy to. "I can't remember the last time I had a problem saying what was on my mind."

Jewell swallowed and took a deep breath, unsure whether she wanted to hear what he had to say, or not. If he hadn't tried to end them—whatever they were—just over a week before she probably wouldn't feel any apprehension at all. But, considering that painful conversation, she couldn't help the niggling apprehension in her stomach.

Benjamin huffed a breath and raised his head, turning his whole attention on her. "Jewell, I want to wake up with you beside me every morning, not just on weekends or when we can get away. I want to work beside you, with you. I want to take you home at night and cook you dinner." He said everything rapidly, like he needed to get it out, then stopped. The twinkle lights reflected in his eyes. "I want to make love to you, and I want to fall asleep with you beside me. Every night. I love you, Jewell."

Jewell knew her mouth hung open, but she couldn't seem to get her tongue to work. A minute ago, he couldn't get out what he wanted to say, and now she couldn't form a complete thought to respond. He finally took his hand from his pocket, a key held between his thumb and index finger when he held up his hand, his other fingers curled into his palm.

"I have four bedrooms," he continued. "Victoria is going to stay with me for a while, but she and Dillon intend to get married this summer. Ruby can have her own room, so you don't have to worry about where she'll stay. I'd love to have her there." He stopped and looked back to the house, maybe seeing there whatever it was that would help him get everything out. "I've discovered I like a house full of people."

Jewell looked at the key in his hand. Her hands shook with cold, or maybe nerves when she uncrossed her arms to sign. *"Benjamin, are you asking me to move in with you? Me and Ruby?"*

He smiled, one corner of his mouth tipping up, followed by the other. "I am."

"I..." She shook her head, staring again at the key held between his fingers.

"Take the key, Jewell." He held the key out to her. "Just because you take the key doesn't mean you're agreeing. You should think about it."

Staring at him, Jewell wrapped her fingers around his hand, the cold of hers a sharp contrast to the warmth of his from being in his pocket. As she took the key, he opened his hand and a ribbon dropped from the key, a diamond ring on a simple silver band dangling from the other end of the ribbon.

Jewell gasped, staring at the ring. Red and green twinkling lights reflected off the facets of the diamond. She grasped the ring between her fingertips and held it in front of her face, then looked at him again. He smiled, but his grin was hesitant, nervous. Benjamin lifted her left hand and took the diamond from between her fingers. She wasn't sure, but she thought his own hands shook as he slipped the diamond on her finger and lifted her hand to his mouth, kissing her knuckles.

He stepped in front of her, bracketing her feet on both sides with his own, and kissed her. She realized when his mouth brushed hers that her lips were slick with tears. With a smile, he blew on his fingers before signing in the space between them.

"I'm sorry if my attempt at a proposal was lame, but..." His hands stilled, and he paused long enough to touch her cheek with cold fingertips. *"I've never asked a woman to marry me. I've never even considered it before you. I've been trying to figure out how to do it and had the key idea, but until you came out I didn't know what I would do. I didn't even know if I'd have the courage to ask you at all. I was afraid you'd say no. I'm still afraid you'll say no."*

Jewell swallowed, trying to calm the rapid beating of her heart. Her breath billowed in front of her face. Tears blurred her vision, but she smiled and laughed and knew she probably was a confusing picture. She laid her palms on his cheeks and stroked her thumbs across his lips.

"I know you need time to think about this," he continued. *"Jewell, I can't..."* He paused, huffing a cloud of steam in front of his face. He sniffed and clenched his fingers before opening his hands again. *"I made a choice when I was young, and I never regretted it until I fell in love with you. Even before I knew about Prescott. I can't give you a family, Jewell."*

"Of course you can."

He shook his head. *"You know what I said in Hartford. I can't father children."*

She wrapped her fingers around his and urged him to turn toward the house, drawing him to the kitchen window. If they stood at just the right angle, they could see through the kitchen window into the parlor beyond where her parents sat, and the tree twinkled behind them. Looking through, she saw Garnett come into the parlor and scoop a sleeping Pearl off the floor. She flopped in his arms like a rag doll, her little heart harboring no fear for who might be carrying her off to bed.

Ruby passed him, kissing Pearl's forehead, and flopped down on the couch on the other side of her mother so the three of them—Mama, Daddy, and Ruby—sat side by side.

Jewell looked to Benjamin. "You see," she said, not wanting to let go of his hand. "Biology is nothing. You can *be* a father, Benjamin. If you want…"

He gripped her wrists and brought them together, turning his head within her hold to kiss her palms. With a deep huff, he stepped back, putting some space between them, and dropped to his knee. Jewell covered her mouth, trying to hold back the small sob in her throat. She had to blink to clear the tears that ran icy cold down her cheeks.

Looking up at her, Benjamin pressed his palm to his heart before he signed, "*Jewell, please marry—* "

"Yes," she said before he could finish. She grabbed his hands and tugged him to his feet. She was kissing him before he was fully standing. Their lips were cold, and she was pretty sure she'd lost some feeling in them, but no kiss had ever been so sweet.

The back door opened, and her father cleared his throat. "Would the two of you like to come in? It's nearly midnight. Or are you staying out here?"

Jewell laughed, a wellspring of just plain happiness bubbling up from her chest. She pointed at her father and signed his question to Benjamin. He turned, his smile wide, and extended his hand to her father.

"Sir, she said yes."

Jewell's mouth fell open and she thumped Benjamin on the chest. "*You told my father you were going to propose?*"

"No," her father answered. "Benjamin *asked* me if it was acceptable to your mother and me if he asked you to marry him." He smiled at Benjamin and took his hand in a firm shake. "It is more than acceptable. Now, you two get in here before you freeze to death."

Benjamin took her hand and led her into the house. Once inside, he took off his coat and helped her with her sweater, hanging them at the door. They joined the family in the parlor where everyone gathered around the flaring fireplace. Jewell's mother met her with an embrace, immediately moving to Benjamin and kissing his cheeks before she hugged him. As soon as he was free, Benjamin stepped behind her and wrapped his arms around her, linking them at her waist. She leaned back against his chest and released a long sigh.

Benjamin let her go just long to sign in front of her, "*Happy New Year.*"

She tilted her head and looked up at him, meeting his lips for a kiss.

The End

ABOUT THE AUTHOR

 Gail R. Delaney is a multi-published, award-winning author of romance in multiple sub-genres, including contemporary romance, romantic suspense, and epic science fiction romance. She always wrote stories as a kid through her teens, but didn't decide to write 'for publication' until her early twenties after the death of her mother. While helping her father go through her mother's papers, she found a box her mother kept with everything Gail had ever written—from book reports to short stories. It was then she realized her mother saw her as a writer, and it was time to live up to her mother's vision.

While her father will attest to the fact that Jewell Kincaid is nothing like her mother, she stands as Jewell Maxine Hughes' namesake. In many ways, Gail's mother influenced this book even though she never saw the book published, never saw Gail write it. Growing up with a mother who was very hard of hearing helped Gail portray the life of a severely hearing impaired person with some reality, as well as how those people close to that person might interact. Gail's mother taught her that love can happen quickly, and the road can be rough, but when love is love it will last.

You can find out more about Gail R. Delaney's body of work at: http://www.GailDelaney.com

ALSO BY GAIL R. DELANEY

Contemporary Romance

Something Better

Feel My Love

Fools Rush In

Baker Street Legacy

Book One: My Dear Branson

Book Two: The Empty Chair

Book Three: Indefinite Doubt

Coming Soon

THE FUTURE POSSIBLE SAGA

PART ONE: THE PHOENIX REBELLION

BOOK ONE: REVOLUTION

BOOK TWO: OUTCASTS

BOOK THREE: GAINING GROUND

BOOK FOUR: END GAME

PART TWO: PHOENIX RISING

BOOK ONE: JANUS

BOOK TWO: TRIAD

BOOK THREE: STASIS

BOOK FOUR: LIBER